The Fortunes of Texas: Welcome to Horseback Hollow

A branch of the powerful Fortunes family is discovered in a small Texas cattle town.

Look for all the books in this bestselling classic miniseries!

Happy New Year, Baby Fortune! &
A Sweetheart for Jude Fortune
New York Times Bestselling Author Leanne Banks
and Cindy Kirk

Lassoed by Fortune & *A House Full of Fortunes!*
USA TODAY Bestselling Authors Marie Ferrarella
and Judy Duarte

Falling for Fortune & *Fortune's Prince*
Nancy Robards Thompson and
New York Times Bestselling Author Allison Leigh

THE FORTUNE CONNECTION

Nancy Robards Thompson

NEW YORK TIMES BESTSELLING AUTHOR
Allison Leigh

Previously published as
Falling for Fortune & Fortune's Prince

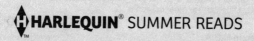

HARLEQUIN® SUMMER READS

Special thanks and acknowledgment are given to Nancy Robards Thompson and Allison Leigh for their contribution to The Fortunes of Texas: Welcome to Horseback Hollow continuity.

ISBN-13: 978-1-335-00525-0

The Fortune Connection
Copyright © 2018 by Harlequin Books S.A.

Previously published as Falling for Fortune & Fortune's Prince
Copyright © 2016 by Harlequin Books S.A.

The publisher acknowledges the copyright holder of the individual works as follows:

Falling for Fortune
Copyright © 2014 by Harlequin Books S.A.

Fortune's Prince
Copyright © 2014 by Harlequin Books S.A.

Recycling programs for this product may not exist in your area.

Printed in U.S.A.

HARLEQUIN®
www.Harlequin.com

CONTENTS

National bestselling author **Nancy Robards Thompson** holds a degree in journalism. She worked as a newspaper reporter until she realized reporting "just the facts" bored her silly. Much more content to report to her muse, Nancy loves writing women's fiction and romance full-time. Critics have deemed her work "funny, smart and observant." She resides in Florida with her husband and daughter. You can reach her at nancyrobardsthompson.com and facebook.com/nancyrobardsthompsonbooks.

Books by Nancy Robards Thompson

Harlequin Special Edition

Celebrations, Inc.

How to Marry a Doctor
A Celebration Christmas
Celebration's Baby
Celebration's Family
Celebration's Bride

The Fortunes of Texas: Cowboy Country

My Fair Fortune

The Fortunes of Texas: Welcome to Horseback Hollow

Falling for Fortune

The Fortunes of Texas: Whirlwind Romance

Fortune's Unexpected Groom

Visit the Author Profile page at Harlequin.com for more titles.

FALLING FOR FORTUNE

Nancy Robards Thompson

This book is dedicated to the memory of my sweet mother-in-law, Juanita Eitreim. I miss you every day.

Chapter One

"I'm sorry, sir, I've checked the directory three times. There's nobody by that name listed."

Strains of the new receptionist's voice carried in through Christopher Fortune's partially open door. He looked up from his in-office putting green.

What was her name again? He couldn't remember. It was only the start of her second week. Jeez, but she was shrill. He'd have to talk to her about her tone. Not good for community relations. But first…

He realigned his stance as the golf pro had taught him, making sure that his toes were parallel to the pin at the end of the fourteen-foot portable green. He set the putter in the hollow part of his left hand and placed the right hand so that his right thumb rested on the left side of the shaft. He pulled back to take his shot—

"Sir, I don't know what else to tell you." Now her voice

was teetering on exasperation. He couldn't hear what the other person was saying, but she was giving him a headache. "We have a Christopher Fortune, but nobody by the name of *Chris Jones* works here. Could he be the one you're looking for?"

The words made Christopher hit the ball a little too hard. It rolled off the end of the green and under the coffee table that was part of the furniture grouping at the end of the room.

Who was asking for Chris Jones?

Two months ago, Chris Jones had adopted his mother's Fortune family name and moved to Red Rock from Horseback Hollow, Texas. He'd dropped the Jones portion of his name when he'd accepted the new job. Now, he was Christopher Fortune, vice president in charge of community relations for the Fortune Foundation.

Christopher set down his putter, walked over and fully opened his office door to see what the ruckus was about.

What the hell—

"Toby?" Christopher said flatly when he saw his brother and his new sister-in-law, Angie, standing there. "What are you doing here, man?"

The receptionist, a slight woman with close-cropped black hair, looked so young that she could've easily been mistaken for a sixteen-year-old. She turned and froze, all wide dark eyes and pale skin, when she saw Christopher.

"Oh! I'm sorry, Mr. Fortune. I didn't understand that they were looking for you. They asked for Chris Jones."

Now she was blushing.

Christopher glanced at the name plate that was front and center on the reception desk.

"Don't worry about it, Beverly. It's fine."

"Hey, little brother," Toby said, extending a hand. "Good to see you."

Christopher shook Toby's hand. His brother immediately pulled him into an awkward hold that their sister, Stacey, was fond of calling a *man hug:* a greeting that started as a handshake and ended with the guys leaning in and stiffly slapping each other on the back a couple of times.

When they broke apart, Christopher stepped back, reclaiming his dignity just in time to see both elevator doors open and Kinsley Aaron, the Foundation's outreach coordinator, step into the reception area.

Her long, straight blond hair hung loose around her shoulders, framing her pretty face. God, she was gorgeous, even if she was a little too uptight for his taste. He straightened his tie and raked his fingers through his hair, trying to right what Toby's enthusiastic bear hug had mussed.

Kinsley had the bluest eyes he'd ever seen. Those eyes were two of the reasons he always remembered her name. Although, the dowdy way she dressed wasn't much of an enticement. He couldn't figure out why such a beauty chose to dress like a schoolmarm. She always covered up as much of herself as possible. Didn't she know her modesty only made him daydream about the gifts that were undoubtedly hidden beneath all that wrapping?

As Kinsley approached Beverly's desk, she arched a brow at him. For a split second he could've sworn she'd read his mind. But he knew it was a ridiculous thought. She was probably just curious about Toby and Angie, since she tended to take her job so seriously. After all, this was an office where visitors generally came seeking help, something that typically fell into her community outreach division.

Before Kinsley could start asking questions, Christopher turned to his brother and sister-in-law. "Why don't we go into my office? We can talk in there."

He made quick work of ushering them out of the reception area. This sure as hell wasn't the most ideal time or place for a family reunion. Especially when he was determined to keep his life in Horseback Hollow worlds apart from the new life he'd created for himself in Red Rock.

Before he shut the door, he cast one last glance back at Kinsley, who was still lingering by Bev's desk. They locked gazes, and Christopher felt that old familiar *zing* that always happened when he looked into those eyes. The virtual vibration lasted even after she looked away.

And she was always the first one to look away.

He was pondering that when Toby said, "Since you were too darned busy to come home for the wedding, I decided I'd bring my beautiful bride to see you. Angie, you've met Chris before. Chris, this is my wife. Can you believe it?" he said, grinning. "I have a wife."

"Good to see you again, Angie," Christopher said, keeping his tone all business and shaking Angie's hand.

"So, they call you *Mr. Fortune* around here?" Toby asked, a note of good-natured ribbing in his voice. But before Christopher could answer, Toby let loose a low whistle as he glanced around Christopher's new digs. "Would you look at this fancy place? I guess you're doing all right for yourself, little brother."

"It's a pretty sweet gig," Christopher said. "Actually, I wanted to work directly for Uncle James at JMF Financial, but how could I argue after I found out that he'd created a position just for me? I'm sure he could do something for you if you want. All you have to do is ask."

What Christopher didn't say was that the work was a little boring and "do-gooder" for his taste. But the salary they were paying him, which was commensurate with the Fortune name rather than his experience, more than made up for the lack of excitement.

If Christopher had learned one thing over the past two months it was that he had to create his own excitement, ensure his own future. It wasn't as if he'd been blazing trails in Horseback Hollow. Nope, back home, he'd been bored and broke.

And a nobody.

Now he had a job that people respected and the bank account to go with it. So he figured why not go for the trifecta and take on the Fortune name? It was his birthright, after all, even if his old man would be mad as hell when he found out.

But those were the breaks, weren't they? His father Deke's attitude was one of the things that had driven Christopher to Red Rock in the first place. Once he was settled, he'd gone to court and filed a petition to change his name. Once the judge had signed the order, Christopher Fortune said *Hasta la vista, baby* to Chris Jones and Horseback Hollow and claimed what was rightfully his.

Christopher glanced around his office, trying to see it through Toby's eyes. The Fortune Foundation had been founded in memory of Lily Cassidy Fortune's late husband, Ryan Fortune, who had died of a brain tumor nine years ago. The Foundation had started out in a small storefront on Main Street in downtown Red Rock but had since expanded and was now located in a stately three-story brick building just outside of town. Christopher had

one of the corner offices with rich polished mahogany
architectural wall paneling on the walls—or at least the
ones that didn't have floor-to-ceiling windows with a to-
die-for view of the local landscape. His traditional executive's desk and credenza still left enough room for the
putting green, two chairs and a couch that were grouped
conversation-style around a coffee table.

Hell, his office was bigger than his old studio apartment back in Horseback Hollow.

He directed Toby and Angie over to the couch. Until
now, he hadn't even tried out the office's living room
furniture.

"I just can't get over the change in you," Toby said.

Christopher turned to Angie, who was still as pretty
as she had been in high school with her light brown hair,
blue eyes and delicate features. His brother had done well
catching her. He'd tell him so later if they had a private
moment. But just as the thought crossed his mind, it was
overshadowed by the hope that the newlyweds weren't
planning an extended visit in Red Rock. Christopher had
work to do.

He hoped this visit wasn't because Deke had sent Toby
to do his dirty work. If any of his family got him it was
Toby. But it would be just like Deke to send one of Christopher's brothers to hassle him.

But right now, Toby was talking to Angie. "The Chris
I knew never wore anything but jeans and boots. I don't
know who this suit is standing in front of me with those
shiny pointy-toed shoes. How many crocodiles had to
die to make those shoes?"

Christopher laughed, but it was a dry, humorless
sound. "They're not made out of crocodile," Christopher said.

"It was a joke, Chris." Toby frowned. "No offense, but you're even acting differently. Just remember, I know where you came from."

Awkward silence the likes of which he had never known with Toby hung in the air. He didn't want to fight with him, and it seemed every time he opened his mouth he said the wrong thing.

That was the story of his life when it came to family. But Christopher wasn't about to sit here in his own office and let family drag him down to feeling bad.

"How was the wedding?" Christopher asked, hoping for neutral ground. He directed the question to Angie, who had been remarkably quiet.

"I would say it was the happiest day of my life, but each day I wake up seems to take that title," she said. "We wish you could've been there."

"Yeah, well, it's better that I didn't come. That way the focus was on the two of you. All sunshine and happiness. No dark clouds, you know?"

Angie looked at him with big blue eyes.

"Well, we certainly did appreciate your generous gift. A thousand dollars was…" Angie shook her head as if at a loss for words.

"It was too much," said Toby as he leaned forward and plucked a business card out of a brass holder sitting on the coffee table. "Ten crisp $100 bills. Leave it to my little brother not to miss an opportunity to show off— Wait. Christopher *Fortune?*" he read aloud from the business card. "Did they forget to print your entire last name on here?"

"No," said Christopher.

Toby held up the card. "Where's the *Jones?*"

Christopher shrugged, but didn't feel the need to explain himself.

"So, that's why the receptionist was having a hard time helping us." Toby gestured with his thumb toward the reception area. "It's true, then? They don't even know who Chris Jones is?"

"Don't take it personally, Toby," Christopher said. "I just needed to make a fresh start."

"How can I not take it personally? I mean, I get that you and Dad don't see eye to eye on your moving to Red Rock and working here at the Foundation, but come on, Chris. What the hell? Aren't you taking this a little too far?"

"Is that a question or an accusation?" Christopher challenged, holding his brother's gaze until Toby leaned forward again and put the card back where he'd found it.

This life was exactly what he wanted.

He wanted what the Fortunes had: money, power, respect. He had gotten none of that back in Horseback Hollow. What was wrong with claiming it now?

"I figure the family can't be any more disappointed in me now than they've always been. I never was any good to anyone around the ranch, anyway. Don't you think they'd consider the new and improved Christopher Fortune a vast improvement over Chris Jones, the son who couldn't do anything right?"

Toby looked down at his hands, then back up at Christopher. A somber expression crept into his eyes. "I don't even know what to say to that, except that Mom asked me to tell you she loves you."

Touché.

That was just about the only thing that Toby could've said to hit Christopher where he'd feel it.

The thing was, he didn't even sound mad. Just…disappointed. A look that said, *remember where you came from and don't let the Fortunes change you into something you're not.*

He hadn't forgotten and the Fortunes hadn't changed him. He would be the first to admit that embracing the Fortunes' world and starting on a desk job had taken some getting used to. He was surprised by how he sometimes missed not getting outside between the hours of nine and five. This indoor, sedentary job had been a challenge, but every time he looked at the view outside the windows of his executive's office or at his bank account balance, it got easier and easier.

"Y'all must be hungry," Christopher said. "Come on, let's go get a bite to eat. I'll treat you to lunch."

"Excuse me, darlin'." Kinsley Aaron frowned as she looked up from the notes she was taking while manning the third-floor reception desk for Bev. Christopher Fortune stood outside his office door, smiling broadly, no doubt thinking he was God's gift to women.

Darlin'? Excuse me?

Had they somehow time traveled back to the 1960s?

"My name is Kinsley," she said, doing her best to keep the bristle out of her voice. He may have been young and good-looking and a Fortune, but how dare he call her that?

"I know what your name is," Christopher said.

"Then why did you call me *darlin'?*" She didn't smile.

The man and woman who were with him looked a bit sheepish, perhaps a little embarrassed for him, before they ducked back inside his office. Actually, Christopher should've been embarrassed for himself. But did the guy do anything for himself?

The only reason he worked at the Foundation was because his uncle was James Marshall Fortune.

"Where is Betsy?" he asked

"Who is Betsy?" she returned.

"The new receptionist?" he answered with a tone better suited for talking to a small child.

Well, Mr. Man, two could play that game. "Nobody by the name of *Betsy* works here. Do you mean *Beverly?*"

Christopher shrugged. "Yes, the one who was here earlier." He motioned to the desk where Kinsley was sitting. "Where is she?"

If Bev was smart, she'd handed in her resignation and left.

Kinsley blinked away the snotty thought. She hadn't meant it. The Fortune Foundation was a fabulous place to work. Even though Christopher Fortune was full of himself, other members of the Fortune family had been very good to her. Not only did they pay her a decent salary to work as an outreach coordinator, a position she considered her life's work, but also she would be forever grateful that they had taken a chance on her.

She'd come to them with little experience, having not yet earned her degree. She was working on it, but with a full-time job and going to school part-time at night, it was going to take her a while before she completed her coursework.

"I'm covering for Beverly while she's on her break," Kinsley said. "She should be back in about fifteen minutes. In the meantime, is there something I can help you with?"

Christopher smiled and looked at her in that wolfish

way he had that made her want to squirm. But she didn't. No way. She wouldn't give him the satisfaction.

What was with this guy? Better question, what was with her? Kinsley had always subscribed to the Eleanor Roosevelt philosophy: nobody could make you feel *anything* unless you gave them permission. Actually, the quote was nobody could make you feel inferior, but this adaptation felt just as authentic.

"Yes, will you please call and make a lunch reservation for three at Red for 1:15?"

At first Kinsley thought he was kidding. But as she squinted at him, it became quite clear that he was indeed serious.

News flash! She had not been hired as Christopher Fortune's personal secretary! And why did he want to eat at Red, of all places, today? She rarely went out to lunch, but today she had a 12:45 business lunch at the restaurant. She was meeting Meg Tyler, the Red Rock High School PTA president, to discuss the school's Cornerstone Club, an extracurricular student leadership organization, and to talk about the role the kids could play in implementing an anti-bullying program.

For a split second, Kinsley thought about calling Meg and asking if they could change restaurants, but then quickly decided against it. She'd been looking forward to lunch at Red. Why should she deny herself her favorite Mexican place just because he was going to be there?

Yeah, what was up with that? Why was she still feeling so shy around him? He'd started working with the Foundation about two months ago. They hadn't had much contact until recently, when Emmett Jamison had asked them to work together to establish a stronger online presence for the Foundation's community outreach program.

Why did she allow him to make her feel twelve years old? Worse yet, why did she shrink every time Christopher walked into the room? She didn't need his approval. So what if he was charismatic and good-looking? He skated through life on his looks and charm, much like her father had done when he was sober. At least she did her job better than he did.

Fighting the riptide of emotions that threatened to sweep her under, Kinsley stared unseeing at the notes she'd been writing before Christopher had come out of his office. She wasn't going to allow herself to be drowned by the past. Her father had been dead for six years, and she certainly wasn't twelve anymore. In all fairness, despite Christopher's bravado, he really didn't have the mean streak that had possessed her father when he had been drunk. That was when her dad had drummed it into her soul that she would never amount to anything. That she wouldn't be good enough, strong enough, smart enough, pretty enough. No man in his right mind would ever want her.

But that was then and this was now. She was well on her way to proving him wrong. She had a good job, and she was making her own way in the world. No matter how the scarred memories of her bastard of a father tried to convince her that she would never be enough, she needed to muster the strength to exorcise his ghost and set herself free. She needed to quit projecting her father and his twisted ways onto Christopher, who, like so many other men, had a way of making her feel overlooked, dismissed.

She knew her value and what she was capable of. That was all that mattered.

Because she was sitting at the reception desk filling

in for Bev, she swallowed her pride and placed the call to Red. A few minutes later, Christopher and his posse emerged from his office and made their way to the elevator. But Christopher hung back. "Thanks for taking care of my family and me, Kinsley."

He looked her square in the eyes in that brazen way of his and flashed a smile. For a short, stupid moment part of her went soft and breathless.

"Mmm" was all she managed to say before she tore her gaze from his and he walked away to join his party.

Mmm. Not even a real word. Just an embarrassing monosyllabic grunt.

Kinsley sat at the reception desk waiting for Bev to return, pondering the shyness that always seemed to get the better of her whenever he was around.

Why?

Why did he have this effect on her?

It was because this job meant so much to her.

And maybe she found his good looks a little intimidating. But good grief.

So the guy was attractive with his perfectly chiseled features and those mile-wide broad shoulders. He had probably played football in college. One of those cocky jock types who had a harem clamoring to serve him. Not that Christopher Fortune's personal life—past or present—was any of her business.

Kinsley blinked and mentally backed away from thoughts of her coworker. Instead, she reminded herself that she had done the right thing by taking the high road and making his darned lunch reservation rather than trying to make a point.

Looks didn't matter. Not in her world, anyway. She had Christopher Fortune's number. He was a handsome opportunist who was riding his family's coattails. In the two months he'd been in the office he hadn't done much to prove that he had high regard for the actual work they were trying to do at the Foundation.

Obviously, he didn't *get it.* Guys like him never did.

But one thing she was going to make sure he understood in no uncertain terms—he'd better never call her *darlin'* again or there would be hell to pay.

Chapter Two

"Oh, look at the flowers." Angie sighed as Christopher guided her and Toby up the bougainvillea-lined path to Red.

"Just wait until you see the courtyard inside," Christopher said with as much pride as if he were showing off his own home. "Red is built around it. There's a fountain I think you'll love."

Angie stopped. "Red?"

"Yes, that's the name of the restaurant." Christopher gestured to the tile nameplate attached to the wall just outside the door, which he held open as he tried to usher them inside, but Angie stopped.

"Is this the same Red that's owned by the Mendozas?" Angie asked.

"One and the same," Christopher said.

"Wendy and Marcos Mendoza catered our wedding

reception." Angie sighed again as she looked around, taking it all in. "They have to be two of the nicest people I've ever met." She turned to Toby. "I can't believe we're here. Chris, did you plan this?"

He wished he could take credit for it, but until now, he'd had no idea what had taken place at their wedding. He'd been so intent on staying away to avoid clouding their day with bad vibes that he hadn't realized he didn't know the first thing about the event other than the fact that his brother had taken himself a bride.

Regret knotted in his gut.

"The Mendozas catered your wedding?" Christopher asked.

"Yes, they did a beautiful job," Angie said. "Everything was delicious. Oh, I hope that chicken mole they served at the reception is on the menu. I've been dreaming of it ever since."

A twinge of disappointment wove itself around the regret. Christopher knew it was totally irrational, but he had brought them here because he'd wanted to introduce them to something new, something from his world that he had discovered. Yet by a strange twist of small-world fate, Red was old news to them.

"This place is so beautiful," Angie cooed. "I could live here quite comfortably."

"I'll bet we could." Toby beamed at his wife. His love for her was written all over his face. Watching the two of them so deeply in love blunted the edges of Christopher's disappointment. He wasn't surprised that Toby had settled down. Of all of his siblings, Toby had been the one who was the most family oriented, especially after taking in the three Hemings kids. He was happy for his brother and Angie. He hoped things worked out and that they would be able to adopt the kids. But although Christopher looked forward to being an uncle, he couldn't imagine any other kind of life than the one he was living now.

On their way to lunch Christopher had seized the opportunity to show off his new town and lifestyle. He'd loaded the newlyweds into his spankin' new BMW and given them the fifty cent tour of downtown Red Rock.

Although there were certainly fancier restaurants in town, none spoke to Christopher quite the way Red did. Obviously the Mendoza appeal wasn't restricted to Red Rock, since Toby and Angie seemed to love their food as much as he did.

Christopher held open the door as Angie and Toby stepped inside. He breathed in deeply as he followed them. It smelled damn good…of fresh corn tortillas, chilies and spices. There was something about the mix of old and new that appealed to him. The restaurant was housed in a converted hacienda that had once been owned by a Spanish family rumored to have been related to Mexican dignitary Antonio López de Santa Ana. Santa Ana was known as the Napoleon of the West. Christopher had recently learned that the current owners of the property, Jose and Maria Mendoza, had been fortunate to purchase the house and land at an affordable price before anyone realized its historical significance. The place couldn't have been in better hands because the Mendozas had given the place its due reverence. That was especially true after the restaurant had been largely destroyed by an arson fire in 2009. Luckily, the family rebuilt and reopened after several months and had been going strong ever since.

Inside, the restaurant was decorated with antiques,

paintings and memorabilia that dated all the way back to 1845 when President James Polk named Texas the twenty-eighth state of the Union.

In college, Christopher had complemented his business major with a history minor. So it was only natural that he liked the place for its history.

But the food...he *loved* the place for its food.

Red offered a mouthwatering selection of nouveau Mexican cuisine. The chef had a talent for taking traditional dishes such as huevos rancheros, the chicken mole that Angie was so crazy about and tamales, and sending them to new heights using fresh twists on old classics. The menu was bright and vibrant, familiar yet new and exciting.

Christopher had experienced nothing like it in Horseback Hollow. His mother, Jeanne Marie, was a great cook, but her repertoire was more of the meat and potatoes/comfort food variety. The food at Red was an exotic and surprising twist on traditional Mexican.

The chef was always coming up with new specials of the day and anytime Christopher was in, he asked him to taste test and share his opinion. Christopher loved being able to offer his input.

"Good afternoon, Mr. Fortune," said the hostess. "We're so glad you chose to join us for lunch today. Come right this way. Your favorite table is ready."

The shapely brunette shot Christopher a sexy smile before she turned, hips swaying, as she led the three of them to an aged pine table next to a large window where they could enjoy the comfort of the air-conditioning, but still look out at the well-landscaped courtyard. As far as Christopher was concerned, it was the best seat in the house.

After they were settled, the hostess handed each of them a menu. "Enjoy your lunch, and please let me know if you need *anything*."

She winked at Christopher before she turned to make her way back to the hostess station.

That was quite obvious of her, Christopher thought as he watched her walk away on her high-high heels with the grace and assurance of a tightrope walker. Her skirt was just short enough to draw the eye down to her firm, tanned calves. Now, that was a woman who knew how to dress. Unlike Kinsley, who hid herself under all that heavy tweed fabric that left her looking buttoned-up and shapeless. What a shame.

Suddenly, seeing Kinsley in a skirt and heels like that became his new fantasy.

"I see you come here for the good service," Toby said, a knowing glint in his eye.

"Of course." As Christopher turned back to his brother and Angie, a blonde caught his eye. She was was seated at a table to their left—and he couldn't help noticing that she resembled Kinsley—

Wait, that is *Kinsley.*

She was dining with a woman he didn't recognize. He had a view of Kinsley's profile. If she just turned her head ever so slightly to the right she would see him, but she seemed engrossed in her conversation. Just as he was contemplating getting up and going over to say hello, her server brought their food.

She must have gotten here before him and ordered already. Besides, he, Toby and Angie had just sat down. They hadn't even placed their drink order. He would wait.

When she'd made his reservation she hadn't mentioned that she'd be dining here herself, even though she knew he was going to be here right around the same time. Maybe she was afraid that he would think she was angling for an invite to join them. Most of the women he knew wouldn't have been shy about doing that. But Kinsley was different. Quiet, understated, more conservative.

She was a refreshing change from all the other women he'd met since he'd been in Red Rock. And there had been more than a few. Most of them were sassy and assertive, not at all afraid to reach out and let him know exactly what they wanted and how they wanted it. None of them was a keeper, either. They were all nice and fun, of course, but they left him wanting.

Kinsley, on the other hand, was a puzzle, and most definitely, he realized as he was sitting there, one he was interested in trying to solve.

Hmm. Why had he never thought about her like that before? He'd always thought she was pretty, and on occasion he'd tried to flirt with her, but until right now, he'd never really thought about what made her tick.

As if she felt him watching her, she glanced his way, and their gazes snared. He waved and she lifted a finger before turning her attention back to her lunch companion.

Despite this strange new Kinsley-awareness coursing through him, Christopher decided he should do the same and turned his focus to his brother and Angie. But pushing her from his mind was harder than he had expected.

The view of the courtyard helped. It was spectacular, with colorful Talavera tiles scattered here and there on the stucco walls, Mexican fan trees and more thriving bougainvillea that seemed to be blooming overtime today in a riot of hot pink, purple and gold. But even the crowning glory of the stately, large fountain in the center of the courtyard couldn't keep Christopher's gaze from wandering over Kinsley's way.

"Too bad we couldn't sit outside," Toby said.

If the temperature wasn't pushing ninety, Christopher would've insisted that they sit out by the fountain. Even though the outside tables were shaded by colorful umbrellas, the humidity was a killer. He didn't want to sweat through his suit and then go back to work.

Not the image he wanted to portray, he thought, glancing at Kinsley.

"Is this okay?" he asked Toby and Angie. "We could move, but it's a killer out there."

"No, this is so lovely," said Angie. "I want to stay right here."

Before she could say more, Marcos Mendoza, the manager of Red, appeared at their table.

"Christopher Fortune, my man." Marcos and Christopher shook hands. "It's great to see you."

"You, too," said Christopher. "My brother Toby and his wife, Angie, are visiting. I couldn't let them leave Red Rock without dining at Red."

"Well, if it isn't the newlyweds." Marcos leaned in and kissed Angie on the cheek then shook Toby's hand. He hooked a thumb in Christopher's direction. "This guy is your brother?"

"Yep, I'll claim him," Toby said without a second's hesitation. His brother's conviction caused Christopher's heart to squeeze ever so slightly, but he did a mental two-step away from the emotion and everything else it implied: the problems between him and Deke; the way he'd left home; the fact that he'd allowed all the ugliness to cause him to miss his own brother's wedding.

"Christopher here is one of our best customers," Marcos said. "I can't believe I didn't put two and two together and figure out that the two of you were related. But different last names?"

"I go by Fortune. Toby goes by Fortune Jones." Angie flinched. Christopher hadn't meant to bite out the words. There was a beat of awkward silence before Toby changed the subject.

"Did you know that Marcos and Wendy are opening a new restaurant in Horseback Hollow?" he asked Christopher.

"Seriously?" Christopher said. He'd only been away a couple of months and he felt like a stranger.

"We're opening The Hollows Cantina next month. In fact, my wife, Wendy, and I are in the process of packing up and moving there with our daughter, MaryAnne." Marcos paused, a thoughtful look washing over his face. He turned to Christopher. "So if you and Toby are brothers, that means Liam Fortune Jones is your brother, too?"

Christopher nodded.

Marcos smiled. "I've hired his fiancée, Julia Tierney, to be the assistant manager at the restaurant."

Christopher forced a smile.

"I had no idea that you were leaving Red Rock, or that Julia would be working for you," Christopher said.

"I kept it on the down low until I was sure that everything would pan out," said Marcos. "This is a great opportunity for my family, and having my own restaurant will be a dream come true. Really, we owe this happy decision to Julia. She is the one who talked us into opening a place in Horseback Hollow. Your future sister-in-law should work for the Horseback Hollow Chamber of Commerce—she can't say enough good about the place."

"Congratulations," said Angie. "We will be sure to come in after the Cantina opens."

"I have your contact information," said Marcos, "and I will make sure that the two of you are invited to the grand opening. The Fortunes are like family, and family always sticks together."

Toby shot Christopher a knowing look. "Yes, they do."

"In fact, Fortune," Marcos said to Christopher, "I'd better see you at the grand opening celebration, too. Especially now that I know that you're a native son of Horseback Hollow."

Christopher gave a wry smile. "Yeah, well, don't go spreading that around."

Everybody laughed, unaware or ignoring the fact that Christopher wasn't kidding.

"I need to get back to work," Marcos said. "So please excuse me and enjoy your lunch."

The men shook hands again and Marcos planted another kiss on Angie's cheek before he moved on to greet the next table of guests.

"When are Julia and Liam getting married?" asked Christopher.

"That remains to be seen," said Toby. "It's a big step that he's committed to one woman. Julia is good for him. She gets him, but doesn't let him get away with squat. I think she's about the only woman who could make an honest man out of him."

Nodding, Christopher gave the menu a cursory glance. He wanted to hear the day's specials, but it would take something extra appealing to sway him away from his favorite beef brisket enchiladas.

Toby looked up from his menu. "It looks like the marriage bug is infesting our family. I just heard that our cousin Amelia Chesterfield Fortune has gotten engaged to some British aristocrat."

"That just seems so odd," mused Angie. "She was dancing with Quinn Drummond at our wedding. It was the way they were looking at each other... The two of them seemed so happy. In fact, I would've wagered that something was blossoming between them. I just can't imagine that there's another man in the picture."

"Yeah, but I heard the news from Mama and she usually gets things right." Toby shook his head as if trying to reconcile the idea.

Their server was a woman named DeeDee. Christopher had seen her socially one time, but he hadn't called her again. He hadn't realized that she worked at Red. Within the first hour of their date, he'd realized DeeDee was after a whole lot more relationship than he was able to give. No sense in stringing her along, even if she was nice. The world was full of nice women and he needed to get to know a lot more of them before he settled down. He found his gaze sliding over to Kinsley's table yet again. It looked as if they were finishing up with their meals. "Well, if it isn't Christopher Fortune as I live and breathe," DeeDee said, a teasing note in her voice. She twisted a strand of her long red hair around her finger as she talked. "It's been so long since I heard from you, I thought maybe you'd fallen off the face of the earth or maybe you moved to some exotic, faraway land."

Christopher laughed, keeping things light. "It's good to see you, DeeDee. How long have you been working here?"

"It's only my second day."

"Which explains why I've never seen you here," said Christopher.

After a little more playful banter, DeeDee flipped her hair off her shoulder with a swift swipe of her hand and took their drink orders. Next, she described the day's specials, which didn't tempt Christopher's taste buds away from his usual order. After she left to get their drinks, Christopher recommended some of his favorites from the menu to Toby and Angie.

A few minutes later DeeDee returned with a bottle of champagne and three flutes. "This is for the newlyweds, compliments of Mr. Mendoza and the staff at Red."

"Oh, my goodness," said Angie. "Champagne in the middle of the day. How decadent. And how absolutely lovely. Thank you."

"Well, the way I see it," said Toby, "I'm only getting married once, and it's an occasion to celebrate. Right, little brother?"

Toby didn't wait for Christopher to answer. He put his arm around his bride and leaned in, placing a sound kiss on Angie's lips. If DeeDee hadn't been standing there, Christopher might have joked and told them to get a room. But really, it was nice to see Toby and Angie so happy.

"So this is your brother and sister-in-law?" asked DeeDee after she popped the cork and filled the glasses with the bubbly.

Christopher didn't want to be rude, but he didn't want to get too personal. "Yes," he said. "They're visiting, but I'm on my lunch hour so we should place our orders now."

"Of course," said DeeDee, snapping into professional mode. She wrote down their selections and headed toward the kitchen.

After she left, Christopher said, "I just can't get over

the fact that you're *married*. But it suits you. It really does."

Toby gave Angie a little squeeze.

"Where do the adoption proceedings stand?" Christopher asked. Seven months ago, Toby had taken in the Hemings children: eleven-year-old Brian, eight-year-old Justin and seven-year-old Kylie. The kids had had nowhere to turn and faced possible separation when their aunt was ordered into rehab for a drinking problem and child neglect. Both Christopher and Toby had known the kids from the Vicker's Corners YMCA where they had worked as coaches. Most people would've run from that kind of responsibility—Christopher knew he certainly couldn't have handled it—but Toby hadn't thought twice before agreeing to take them in.

Unfortunately, the kids' aunt, who obviously didn't have the children's best interests at heart, had decided to try and take the kids from Toby and send them into another unstable situation in California. Her reasoning was the kids should be with relatives. Never mind that the relative she'd chosen was out of work and on parole.

That's all it took for Toby to decide he needed to legally adopt the children.

"Everything is still pending," said Toby. "Frankly, it's taking so long I'm starting to get worried."

"I just don't understand what the holdup is," said Angie. "They not only have a loving home with us, but they also have become part of the family. They call Jeanne Marie and Deke Grandma and Grandpa. They're calling your sisters and brothers Aunt and Uncle. How anyone could think that uprooting these poor kids is what's best for them is beyond me. It breaks my heart."

Toby caressed Angie's shoulder. "We are going to do everything in our power to make sure they stay with us."

"What can I do to help?" asked Christopher.

Toby shrugged. "At this point I don't know what else anyone could do."

"The Fortune name carries a lot of clout," said Christopher. "Maybe we can use its influence to get things going in the right direction."

Toby peered at him. "What exactly are you suggesting?"

Christopher gave a one-shoulder shrug as he rubbed the fingers of his left hand together in the international gesture for *money*. "Money talks, bro."

Toby frowned and shook his head. "Please don't even suggest anything like that. I don't want to be accused of doing anything unethical. That might hurt the situation more than it helps."

"Nonsense," said Christopher. "I think you're being very shortsighted if you don't take full advantage of your birthright."

Christopher saw Toby take in a slow deep breath, as he always did when faced with conflict. It was as if he were framing his response so that he didn't lose his cool.

"I appreciate your concern, Chris," said Toby evenly. "But the caseworker told me she's worried that the Fortunes themselves may be part of the problem. Since the Fortunes invaded Horseback Hollow so many strange things have happened. The authorities still think Orlando Mendoza's accident might have been directed at the family."

"Don't be ridiculous," said Christopher. "Why would anyone want to hurt the Fortunes? I mean, look at me.

I'm living proof. Since I changed my name nothing bad has happened to me."

Christopher turned his palms up to punctuate his point.

"That is, if you don't count your running away from home and shunning your entire family as something bad."

Toby cocked an eyebrow at Christopher.

Christopher locked gazes with his brother and crossed his arms.

"Look, I know this Fortune Foundation gig is still new and exciting to you," said Toby, "so don't take this wrong. But someday you're going to learn that some things are more important than money."

Christopher glanced over at Kinsley, but she and her friend were gone. His gaze swept the restaurant, but she was nowhere to be seen. How had he not seen her leave?

He picked up his champagne glass and knocked back the contents.

"Come on, Chris," said Toby. "When are you coming home? No one has seen you in months. They certainly have no idea that you've completely disowned Daddy's name."

Toby was usually the only one who could see Christopher's side in times when he and Deke disagreed, which was more often than not. Awkward silence hung in the air and, for once, Christopher didn't know how to fill it. He didn't want to fight with Toby, but he wasn't going back to Horseback Hollow. His life was here now, and he would prefer to keep his old and new lives separate. The contrast between the Joneses and the Fortunes was stark. Christopher couldn't take the chance of losing the respect he'd earned at the Foundation.

"Man up, Chris," Toby urged. "Take the high road and be the one who extends the olive branch to Deke."

"Yeah, well that high road has two lanes. Deke can bring that olive branch to me easier than I can bring it to him. I'm a little too busy right now to coddle a grown man."

Toby made a *tsk* sound. "An *old* man. Don't wait too long. You may be sorry if you do."

"Don't pull that guilt trip crap on me," said Christopher. "Just don't. But please do tell me why it's okay for Deke to resent me for making an honest living in a career I love. For making my own way. For not having dirt under my fingernails. No offense to you, but why should I have to grovel to him because the ranch life is not the kind of life I want? Until Deke understands that, I don't think we're going to meet anywhere, much less with an olive branch."

Truth be told, he would rather be known as James Marshall Fortune's nephew than as the son of Deke Jones, crusty old cattle rancher. Christopher hoped that Toby wouldn't make him come out and say that.

Toby stared at Christopher, looking thin-lipped and angry.

"So you've got the fancy suits, the brand-new car and a parade of women who think you're a big shot," said Toby, virtually rolling his eyes at what he obviously perceived as self-importance. "Looks like you've finally achieved your dream, haven't you?"

"You shouldn't knock it since you've never tried it," said Christopher. "No offense to you, Angie. I'm just saying."

Toby took his wife's hand and laced his fingers through hers. "No loss. Believe me, I wouldn't trade my life for yours. I couldn't possibly be any happier than I am with Angie and the kids. On that note, I think we'd better start heading toward home."

Toby pulled out his wallet and tossed a crisp $100 bill onto the table in payment for the food they hadn't managed to stay long enough to have delivered to their table. It was probably one of the ten that Christopher had given him as a wedding gift.

Christopher slid the bill back toward his brother. "Here, Toby. I've got this."

Toby stood. "No, you don't. If you *got this,* you would stop acting like such a pretentious jackass and come home and make amends with Dad. You may have given up on us, Chris, but we'll never give up on you. Take care of yourself and call me when you're ready to talk."

Chapter Three

With his long lunches and daily putting practice, was it any wonder Christopher Fortune didn't get much done? Kinsley mused after fielding a call from Emmett Jamison, the head of the Foundation. Even so, she'd covered for Christopher when Mr. Jamison had asked if she'd seen him. She'd explained that he'd taken a late lunch with family visiting from out of town. She didn't mention that he'd been gone nearly two-and-a-half hours.

She may not have agreed with the way Christopher conducted himself, but she wasn't about to throw him under the bus. That would just make her look bad in the eyes of Mr. Jamison.

She wanted him to see her as a problem solver, not the type of person who pointed fingers and ratted people out. Besides, with the Fortunes, blood was definitely thicker than water. If she wasn't careful the situation might get turned around and come back to bite her. She was sure if it came down to her or Christopher Fortune, Emmett Jamison would side with the man whose last name was on his paycheck.

Kinsley drummed her fingers on the desk. The Fortunes were all about family. She knew Mr. Jamison would excuse him for that. She couldn't deny that she envied Christopher and his huge support system. What was it like to come from such a large, protective family that would circle the wagons at a moment's notice?

Kinsley had no idea. Growing up the only child of an alcoholic father and a mother who couldn't stand up for herself didn't give her much experience to draw from.

She and her mother only had each other to intervene when her father was on a drunken bender. When they did stand up to him, there was always hell to pay.

Her grandmother—her mom's mom—had passed away when Kinsley was about eight, but Grandma hadn't had the wherewithal to extract her daughter from what Kinsley would later look back on and realize was a situation that had robbed her mother of her life.

But wasn't hindsight always perfect?

From the moment Kinsley was old enough to realize she could take care of herself, she vowed she would never personally depend on a man. For that matter, she preferred to not depend on anyone, because didn't people always let you down?

She'd only had two boyfriends, and both of them had proven that to be true. They were hard lessons, but she'd learned. And she prided herself on not repeating the same mistakes.

Family ranks or not, Emmett had said he was concerned because he had received a call from a woman named Judy Davis who was perplexed because she'd emailed the community relations office three times about a donation she wanted to make and still hadn't heard back. She was beginning to think the Foundation didn't want her money.

Kinsley made an excuse that there had been technical difficulties with the email account and had assured Mr. Jamison that she and Christopher would make sure everything was working as it should as soon as he got back...which should be any minute.

Technically, Christopher was being *difficult.* Right? Did that count as technical difficulties? She hoped so. Because it was all she had.

She would cover for Christopher this time, but they were definitely going to have a little heart to heart.

She wrote down Judy Davis's information and assured Mr. Jamison that they would follow up with her today and make sure she knew how much her donation was needed and appreciated.

Kinsley's cheeks burned.

She didn't appreciate being left holding the bag for matters like this, especially when it was something Christopher had insisted on handling. The new Foundation Community Relations email address had been her idea, but they had decided to split the work: as she went out into the community, Kinsley would get the word out about the new way to contact the Foundation; as vice president of community relations, Christopher had insisted on being the one to respond to the emails.

Thank goodness Kinsley had insisted on knowing the password. Christopher had agreed that it was a good idea for more than one person to have access to the account, but he had assured her that he would check it regularly.

She had taken him at his word. Kinsley mentally kicked herself for trusting so blindly. People might have been reaching out for help or there could be more potential funding for the Foundation in these unread messages. Yet Christopher was too busy perfecting his putt…and she'd covered for him.

Feeling like a fool, Kinsley gritted her teeth as she typed in the URL to bring up the login page so she could sign into the account.

As a Fortune, Christopher was set for life. Unlike the other family members who worked at the Foundation, he didn't seem grounded in the realities of what mere mortals had to face in the world.

No, Christopher Fortune was fat, spoiled and smug—

Well, maybe not fat. Kinsley hated herself for it, but somehow her gaze always managed to find its way to Christopher's abs. The way his expensive, tailored dress shirts tapered in at his trim waist, she could plainly see that the guy didn't have an ounce of fat on his body.

No, he was all broad shoulders and six-pack abs—or at least she imagined he was sporting a six-pack under his buttoned up exterior. Who wouldn't be if they had time to work out daily? Actually, it didn't matter what Christopher Fortune was packing under his crisp cotton shirt. Mr. Vice President was still spoiled and smug. And completely irresponsible when it came to doing his job.

When the login page came up, she was relieved to see that it hadn't been that long since Christopher had checked the account. In fact, it had only been two days. She scrolled through the ten emails in search of Judy Davis's three messages. When she found them, she realized the three emails had arrived within a span of 36 hours.

Mr. Jamison had been under the impression that she'd

been waiting a long time to hear back. Though it really hadn't been an excessively long time since Christopher had checked the account, it did need to be monitored regularly. Several times a day, in fact, to keep something like this from happening.

If that was too much for Christopher to handle, he needed to hand it over to someone who could keep a closer eye on it, Kinsley thought as she started to click on one of the unopened message.

But then she stopped. Instead, she had a better idea.

She took a screenshot of the emails that still needed attention and printed it out. Then she took a fluorescent yellow highlighter and marked each one that he needed to check.

She'd already covered for him. If she did his work for him, too, she would simply be fostering his habit of letting someone else pick up the pieces.

The thought took her back to another place and time that made her unspeakably sad. Maybe if she'd intervened a little more on behalf of her mother things would've turned out differently. She stared at the computer screen as the memory threatened to cut into her heart. But she shrugged off the feelings before they could take root. What had happened to her mother was entirely different from what was happening now. No amount of wishing or dwelling would change the way things had played out. That's why Kinsley's job at the Foundation was so important. She couldn't change the past, but maybe, if she did her job well, she could make a difference for someone else.

Christopher Fortune didn't need saving. He needed a good swift kick in the rear.

Kinsley had her own workload to worry about. The

last thing she needed was to try and reform Mr. Silver Spoon. He was a big boy; he could take care of himself. He needed to start pulling his load. She fully intended to tell him as much when he got back.

Well…in so many words.

She wasn't going to do anything to jeopardize her job. But she could still stand up for herself.

This would be a good time to make sure Christopher knew that, although she didn't mind helping him out with things like checking the Foundation's Community Relations email account and making his lunch reservations, she wasn't his secretary. She didn't intend to mince words about that.

She paper clipped Judy Davis's contact information on top of the highlighted list of unanswered emails and set the papers on the corner of her desk.

She knew it wasn't her place to call him out; she intended to do it tactfully. She'd make him think it was all his idea. But yes. They were going to have a little reality check when he got back. She glanced at the clock on her cell phone—was he even coming back to the office today?

She picked up the phone and dialed. "Hi, Bev, would you please let me know when Mr. Fortune gets back into the office? I want to schedule a meeting with him."

"Speak of the devil," Bev whispered. "He just walked in from lunch. Want me to see if he's available?"

"No, that's okay," Kinsley said. "I'll just walk down the hall and stick my head in his office."

Christopher swiveled his office chair so that it faced the window. He leaned back, stretching his legs out in front of him and resting his hands on his middle.

The more he thought about what had happened at lunch, the more he was sure Deke had sent Toby to do his bidding. It made him so angry he wanted to wrap his putter around the trunk of the magnolia tree out in front of the building.

It could've been a good visit with his brother. A chance to get to know his new sister-in-law a little better. But Deke had to insert himself, even if it was virtually, and mess things up.

His father was so good at messing things up.

But then Christopher had to wonder if his brother would've come to Red Rock if it hadn't been to prod him to go home. Well, it hadn't done any good. If anything it had given him more incentive to stay away. The Joneses couldn't stand anything that varied from their idea of normal. But Christopher had news for them all—this was his new normal.

He looked up at the sound of a knock on his door. He straightened up in his chair and turned back to his desk, moving the mouse to wake up his computer screen.

"Come in," he said.

He was delighted when he saw Kinsley standing in the threshold. Suddenly the afternoon was looking a lot brighter.

"Do you have a moment?" she asked.

"For you, I would clear my schedule."

She rolled her eyes. Not exactly the response he was hoping for, but he would've been surprised if he'd gotten a more enthused reaction.

"I'm just kidding," he said. Actually, he wasn't. "Come in. I'm not the big bad wolf. How was your lunch?"

She shut the door and walked over to stand in front of his desk. "It was fine."

"I saw you at Red," he said. "I was going to come over and say hello, but by the time we ordered you were gone."

"I only had an hour for lunch. I had to get back."

Since he'd seen her at the restaurant she'd pulled her hair back away from her face. And what a face it was; she had a perfect complexion that didn't require much makeup. In fact, he wasn't even sure if she was wearing any makeup. His mind wandered for a moment, imagining the curves that hid beneath the conservative clothes she wore. He smiled at the thought. But then he realized she wasn't smiling at him.

God, if he didn't know better, he might be afraid she'd read his mind.

"Is something wrong?" he asked.

"Since you asked," she said, "actually, yes, there is something wrong."

She held out a piece of paper. He reached across the desk and took it from her.

"What's this?"

She was standing there with her arms crossed—defensive body language. Her sensible blue blouse was buttoned all the way up to the top and was tucked into a plain lighter blue skirt that didn't show nearly enough leg. Legs, he thought, that would look killer in a pair of shiny black stilettos, ones like the hostess at Red had worn, rather than those low-heeled church lady shoes that looked like something out of his mama's closet.

"It's a message from a woman who has been trying to get a hold of you to make a donation to the Foundation," she said.

Christopher read the name and number scrawled on the paper. Judy Davis? He didn't know a Judy Davis.

"Who is she and when did she call?"

Kinsley crossed one ankle over the other, keeping her arms firmly across her middle. Good grief. If she twisted herself any tighter she was going to turn herself inside out.

"After she emailed you three times, unsuccessfully, she called Mr. Jamison to voice her displeasure. He called me while you were at lunch, none too pleased."

What the hell?

Christopher lifted up the paper with the message and saw a photocopy of what looked like a list of emails. Someone had taken a highlighter to it.

"Did Emmett do this?" he asked, gesturing at her with the paper.

Her cheeks flushed the slightest hue of pink, which made her look even prettier, if that was possible.

She cleared her throat. "No, I did. Christopher, you haven't checked the community relations email account in two days. She emailed us three times—"

"Three times over the course of what, 48 hours?" he asked looking at the paper to check the time the emails came through.

"Actually, it's closer to 36 hours," she said. "I know she was a little impatient, but she wants to give us money and nobody contacted her in a reasonable amount of time. I can understand why she was a little upset."

Christopher watched Kinsley as she stood there, obviously irritated with him. The funny thing was, usually when people nagged him it made him mad, but he found her completely disarming. His gaze dropped to her full bottom lip.

He'd be willing to wager that those lips would taste better than that expensive champagne that Marcos had given them at lunch, and he was getting a little hot and bothered at the realization that he hadn't yet had a taste of Kinsley's lips.

He smiled as he added that task to his mental to-do list.

"I'll be happy to call her now," Christopher said, offering his best smile.

"That's a good idea. The sooner the better. I don't mean to tell you what to do, but you really should check that email account several times a day."

"I checked it three days in a row and there was absolutely no email," he said. "I've been busy. I know this is your brainchild, but people aren't exactly lining up to leave us messages."

Her brows knit. "Christopher, do you see that piece of paper I gave you? There are ten unanswered messages on there. Well, seven if you don't count the three from Judy Davis."

Her face was so expressive. Those lips were so full. It was mesmerizing to watch her mouth as she talked. He realized he was sitting there grinning stupidly as she reprimanded him. Still, he wanted to laugh. Not at her, but at the situation—at the way the woman had somehow gotten under his skin, but in a good way. A sexy way. A way that made him want to walk over and unbutton the top button of her blouse to loosen her up a bit. Hell, he didn't want to stop there—

"Are you listening to me?" she asked.

"Every single word." He pursed his lips to remove the grin from his face.

Now her hands were on her hips. The stance drew her blouse tight across her breasts. The fabric between the middle buttons gaped a little bit. He forced his eyes back to her face. And she wasn't smiling.

Uh-oh. Busted.

"Then would you please tell me what I just said to you?" she said.

"You were talking about the messages from Susan Davis."

"Judy," she enunciated. "It's *Judy* Davis. For goodness' sake don't make matters worse by calling her the wrong name."

He looked down at the papers he was still holding in his hand. He shuffled the two sheets and saw that yes, indeed, the message said *Judy* Davis.

He smiled to mask his embarrassment. He never had been good with names. "I know her name is Judy. Says so right here." He waved the paper at her. "I was just seeing if you were paying attention."

She rolled her eyes again.

"You don't like me very much, do you?" he asked, eager to hear what she would say. Of course, he was daring her, and he got exactly the reaction he was hoping for.

She blanched. Her eyes flew open wide, and a look of innocence overtook her formerly contemptuous expression.

"I have no idea why you would say that," she said. "You're my coworker and I respect you."

Respect, huh?

But then she surprised him.

"And while we're on the topic of respect," she said, "I need to make sure that we understand each other in a couple of areas."

"Of course," he said. He gestured toward the chair in front of his desk. "Kinsley, please sit down."

She shook her head. "No, I'd rather stand, thank you."

Christopher shrugged. "Okay, suit yourself, but if you're going to stand I guess that means I will, too."

He stood and the slightly panicked and perplexed look clouded her face again. "You don't have to do that. Really, you don't."

"Of course I do. It makes me uncomfortable to have you towering over me."

"What? You're not going to tell me that you're one of those people who believes his head should always be higher than the heads of his subordinates?"

What was this? A dry sense of humor?

He walked around to the other side of the desk, careful to respect her personal space.

"No, but that's not a bad theory."

This time she looked at him as if he had just grown another head on his shoulder.

"You do know I'm kidding, right?"

"I wasn't sure."

"Kinsley. We've been working together for what—two months now? I would *hope* that you would know me better than that by now. You're great at what you do. But you need to loosen up just a little bit. This isn't brain surgery."

"It may not be brain surgery, but I take what I do seriously and I would like for you to take *me* seriously."

What?

Was that what she thought? That he didn't take her seriously? She was one of the most competent, capable people he'd ever worked with. He liked her poise, he liked the way she related to their clients and of course, he loved the way she looked. But maybe that was the problem....

The Fortune mystique didn't seem to work on this woman who was all business, all the time.

Why not?

Why was she immune when most of the women in Red Rock practically bowed down when a Fortune entered the room?

He liked that about her.

All she wanted was to be taken seriously. He understood. That's all he'd wanted from Deke. To be respected for what he did and how he did it.

"Point taken," he said.

She took a deep breath, held it for a moment and then silently released it. He saw her shoulders rise and fall as she did so.

"There's one more thing," she said.

Christopher gestured with both hands. "Please. Anything. You can talk to me."

"First—"

"I thought you said there was only *one* more thing?"

She gave him that look again, as if she were saying *really?*

"I'm sorry," he said. "I do respect you, Kinsley. But could you please unfurrow your brow for just a moment? Unfurrow your brow and smile. Will you do that for me?"

She stood there for a moment looking at him as if she still wasn't sure whether or not he was joking. He held his ground, looking at her expectantly. Finally, she forced a smile. It was the most pathetic and amusing attempt at one he'd ever seen.

"I mean a real smile."

She put her palms in the air, finally uncrossing her arms. "I don't understand what you want from me. But I'm going to tell you what I expect from you—I'm not your Girl Friday. I don't mind helping you, but I'm not your secretary. Secretaries make lunch reservations. Outreach coordinators, which is what I was hired to do for the

Foundation, will check the email account if it's something
you don't want to do. But you have to communicate with
me, Christopher. I'm the one who had to deal with Mr.
Jamison when he called wondering why we had dropped
the ball. I told him we were experiencing technical difficulties with the new email account. But I don't want to
lie, and I can't continue to cover for you."

Her voice was serious but surprisingly not accusatory.
What amazed him even more was his reaction to what she
was saying. He simply nodded and said, "You're right.
We do need to communicate better. If you have suggestions on how we could do that, I'm happy to listen to
what you have to say."

"Maybe we could have regular meetings and discuss
where we're going with the new venture…er, the Foundation's community relations and community outreach
efforts?"

"I think that sounds like a wonderful idea," he said,
trying not to acknowledge the voice inside his head de-
tailing exactly how he would like to *communicate* with
Kinsley.

The woman had asked for respect. He understood that
and revered her even more for telling him that was important to her.

"I'm sorry if I gave you the wrong impression. Because you're a very important part of this team and I don't
want you to ever feel uncomfortable."

There it was. An almost imperceptible shift in her de-
meanor, but he saw it. She had re-crossed her arms and
was still standing there with her closed-off posture, but
her brow was slightly less furrowed and her shoulders
were somewhat more relaxed.

"I appreciate that," she said.

He resisted the urge to tell her that he knew there was a lot more to Kinsley Aaron than a pretty face and a potentially great pair of legs. There was something guarded and a little troubled about her and he wanted to know who or what had made her that way because she was way too young and pretty to be that uptight.

He silently vowed that he was going to find out. He was going to be the one to teach Kinsley Aaron how to loosen up.

Chapter Four

Two days later, Kinsley got a call from Emmett Jamison's assistant, Valerie, asking her to meet with Mr. Jamison at two o'clock. Apprehension knotted in her stomach.

Christopher had called Judy Davis right after their discussion. Kinsley had followed up and made sure that Christopher had placed the call. Christopher could be all wit and charm, so Kinsley had been certain that he would win the woman over. She hadn't given it a second thought.

Until now.

Now, Kinsley was nervous that maybe Judy Davis had called back with more complaints and, once again, she would take the fall. Well, she wasn't going to lie and she wouldn't go down without a fight. As she made her way to Mr. Jamison's office, she racked her brain for the words to defend herself if he was calling her in to level the boom.

She loved this job. She was good at it. She'd made great strides with the community outreach program. Really, her work should speak for itself.

When her heartbeat kicked into an irrational staccato, she took a deep breath and reminded herself not to jump to conclusions. Just because Mr. Jamison had never called her to his office before in the year and a half she'd worked there didn't mean the first visit spelled doom.

Valerie looked up and smiled at Kinsley as she approached.

"Hi, Kinsley," she said. "Have a seat. I'll let Mr. Jamison know you're here."

Kinsley had no more than settled herself on the edge of the maroon wingback chair when Valerie hung up the phone and said, "He said to come right in. He's ready to see you."

Kinsley dug deep to offer her most self-assured smile. "Thank you."

When she opened the door, Christopher was the first person she saw. What was he doing here?

He wasn't her boss. Yet he was her superior if you went strictly by job title. When he had started at the Foundation, his place in the chain of command hadn't been officially defined.

But here he was, sitting on the sofa in Emmett Jamison's office. Mr. Jamison occupied the chair across from Christopher. Notes of their laughter still hung in the air. They stood up and smiled at Kinsley as she walked in.

She hoped the convivial air was a good sign. Usually, people didn't sit and joke when they were planning on letting an employee go. She was eager to know what this was all about.

"Hello, Kinsley," said Mr. Jamison. "Thanks for taking time out of your day to meet with us."

That was a good sign.

"No problem at all," she said.

He gestured to the empty space on the couch next to Christopher. For a moment Kinsley silently debated whether she should sit in the chair next to her boss, but she walked over and took the seat he'd indicated.

After their talk the other day, Kinsley had forgiven the flirtation. Maybe it was because despite how incredibly maddening—and flirty—the guy could be, he seemed to have taken seriously her requests to be treated professionally. She couldn't ask for more than that.

She felt him watching her as she settled herself next to him. Okay, so maybe the old dog hadn't completely changed his ways. Or maybe she just needed to relax and own up to the fact that maybe she was the one with the problem. That maybe she found Christopher just a little bit more attractive than she would like to admit. *There.* She'd said it. And immediately blinked away the thought, wondering where it had come from.

"I want to thank both of you for the way you handled Judy Davis," said Emmett. "She called back to say she was delighted with the response she received. I think you charmed her, Christopher."

No doubt.

"But, Kinsley," said Emmett, "Christopher tells me you're the one who alerted him to the fact that there was a problem, allowing him to correct the situation. That's great teamwork. It started me thinking that the two of you should collaborate on another community relations project."

Christopher had admitted that there had been a problem?

Kinsley checked herself to ensure that her expression didn't expose her surprise.

So he'd fessed up... Hmm... Maybe I need to give him more credit.

"Do you have something in mind?" Christopher asked.

"As a matter of fact I do," said Emmett. "Jed Cramer, principal over at Red Rock High School, told me that you, Kinsley, had lunch with his Cornerstone Club president the other day. He was telling me that there has been an increase in bullying among the students, and he's very concerned. He believes the Foundation can help since we've been successful in reaching teens through our community outreach program. Kinsley, you're really doing a wonderful job with that. I think this is a project that the two of you could really sink your teeth into. Together you could do some real good and put a stop to this bullying problem."

Emmett's eyes darted back and forth between Christopher and Kinsley. "Does this sound like something you would like to handle?"

Kinsley and Christopher both looked at each other and started to speak at the same time. Then they stopped talking and started again at the exact same time.

Finally, Christopher smiled and gestured to Kinsley. "You go first."

She felt her stomach flutter a little, but she ignored it and simply said, "Thank you. Meg was telling me this is an unfortunate reality that's happening more and more these days. The challenge is getting the kids to speak up—not only the ones who are being bullied, but the ones who witness the bullying. A lot is going on here—self-esteem issues, cliques and a general feeling of wanting—no, needing—to be accepted."

Christopher was nodding his head. Kinsley paused to let him put in his two cents, but he remained quiet. So she continued.

"To reach the kids, we have to not only go where they are, but we also have to reach them on a more personal level. What would you think about the Foundation having a booth at the annual Red Rock Spring Fling?"

"I think it's a wonderful idea," said Emmett.

"I agree," said Christopher. "But we will have to move fast because it's happening toward the end of the month. How about if I check into the logistics of securing the booth?"

"That sounds like a plan," said Emmett. "The two of you can work together to plan the approach you'll take and the material you'll use. Here's more good news. We have about $20,000 in the unspecified reserve account. We had a board meeting yesterday and the board of directors approved your using some of that money to implement an anti-bullying program. How about if we make the Spring Fling our target launch date? Does that sound doable?"

Again, Christopher and Kinsley's gazes met. Maybe it was her imagination, but Kinsley could've sworn that something vaguely electric passed between them. For some reason, despite everything that had already happened, it didn't bother her like it would've before she and Christopher had talked. And that felt a little reckless. She refocused her attention on Emmett.

It was probably just the residual adrenaline rush she'd

felt at Mr. Jamison's praise. He'd noticed her hard work. She was having a hard time keeping herself from smiling.

"It sounds doable to me," she said. "We will have our work cut out for us, though, with this timeline. But we can do it."

"Sounds like a very worthy project," said Christopher. "I'm definitely up for the challenge."

His words made Kinsley's breath catch in her throat, which was ridiculous. She needed to stop this nonsense. After her big declaration the other day, if she knew what was good for her she would just keep her mind on the job and stop thinking about how blue Christopher Fortune's eyes were and relishing the times when those eyes lingered and seemed to only see her.

What was wrong with her? Two days ago she had all but read him the riot act about treating her with respect, and here she was in her boss's office contemplating Christopher Fortune's eyes. She needed to get her head on straight. She would do this project and do it right without allowing inappropriate thoughts to get in the way. The last thing she wanted was to let a fickle man come between her and the only stability she'd ever really known.

If her mom had been strong enough to do the same, things would be so different today for both of them.

Well, she would just have to be strong...in memory of her mother.

"Fantastic," said Emmett. "I know the two of you will make a fabulous team. You complement each other. Christopher, you bring the charm, and Kinsley, I know you will keep Christopher on task. I have a very strong feeling I will be calling the two of you my dream team."

Dream team, Kinsley mused.

Why did that seem to work on so many different levels?

* * *

Over the next few days, Christopher realized just how many members of the Fortune family worked at the Foundation. The organization was run by Emmett and his wife, Linda Faraday, but working here had given him so many opportunities to meet his cousins: Susan Fortune Eldridge and Julie Osterman Fortune, who were doing great work with troubled teens; Nicholas Fortune, a financial analyst who monitored the Foundation's investments; and Jeremy Fortune, who was a doctor for the Foundation's medical clinic. Yet they always seem to have room for one more. He didn't want to be the slacker amid the bunch. He wanted to make sure that Emmett and Linda didn't regret hiring him. He vowed to be his most professional self.

Christopher had taken to heart Kinsley's request for him to treat her with respect. The anti-bullying project Emmett had assigned was the opportunity for him to prove himself—to Emmett, to his family and, of course, to Kinsley.

If he wasn't able to woo her with the Fortune name and charm that seemed to work on every other woman in Red Rock, he would win her over with his new-and-improved work ethic. She was an inspiration. She made him want to be a better man.

He would show her that he wasn't just hired because he was a Fortune. Though she hadn't come right out and said it, he knew she must be thinking it.

The anti-bullying project was a worthwhile venture. It was an opportunity to do some good for the community. After two months of feeling as if he was spinning his wheels, he finally felt as if he had a foothold. Plus, it offered the bonus of extra time with Kinsley. It would be a chance for him to get closer to her, a chance for him to woo her and win her over.

Because they didn't have much time to put the display together, the two of them had been spending a lot of time together. They had agreed to a standing hour and a half meeting every afternoon so they could plan their approach.

He should've known by now that Kinsley would throw herself wholeheartedly into anything she committed to. Even so, he hadn't planned on her practically transporting her office to his. But for their first meeting, there she'd been with reams of files and at least a dozen three-ring binders that detailed the different branches of the Foundation's outreach program.

She'd brought so much stuff it required several trips to transport it all. Christopher had helped her carry the bulk of it. Now, the two of them sat across from each other in his office—since it was the larger space—with the information spread out across the coffee table.

"First, I think we should figure out what sort of printed material we need," Kinsley suggested. "I was thinking we could put together a brochure that offers tips about bullying prevention. Like what to do if you find yourself the victim of a bully, and what to do if you see someone else being bullied. We'll need to have these finished first because we'll need some lead time for the printing. What do you think?"

What did he think?

He thought she was one of the most beautiful women he had ever laid eyes on. With her long blond hair and complicated blue eyes, the saying *still waters run deep* came to mind. Kinsley might seem quiet and unassuming, but from what Christopher had experienced, there was a whole lot more going on beneath the surface.

"I think that sounds great," he said. "Do you want to write the copy for that? Somehow I have a feeling you would be a lot better at it than I would."

She had gorgeous skin. He just knew it would feel like silk... He balled his fists to keep from reaching across the table and running a finger along her jawline. She was a natural beauty, and he was willing to bet she didn't even know it.

"I'm happy to do it," she said. "In fact, I already have a couple of ideas for themes. Would you like to hear them?"

Smart. Beautiful. She just needed to know that she didn't have to be all business, all the time. He could help her with that. He felt himself smiling.

"I would love to hear them."

She surprised him by smiling back at him. "Well, the first one I thought of was *Take a stand. Lend a hand.*"

She paused and watched him. Though he knew she would never admit it, he could see in her eyes that she was looking for approval.

"That's great. It's catchy and concise."

Her blue eyes shone. "I'm glad you like it. I thought it served two good purposes. We're encouraging people to take a stand—that could mean standing up for yourself or stepping in when someone else is being bullied. And of course, the *lend a hand* part is all about helping those who are in distress. My research shows that one of the reasons people bully is because they're allowed to get away with it. When people speak up and then get together the bully loses his or her power."

He nodded. "That makes a lot of sense. It's important that we let people know it's okay to intervene."

"Exactly." Her eyes sparkled, and she spoke with such conviction he wondered if she was speaking from personal experience.

"I'm blown away by how much you know about this subject. Did you research it, or is this personal?"

In the seconds it had taken him to ask the question, the glint had disappeared from her eyes and her arms were crossed over her chest like body armor.

"It's just…" She shrugged. "It's really just common sense. But, hey, I have another idea. Are you familiar with the quote, 'Be the change you wish to see in the world'?"

"I am," he said.

"I thought it would be appropriate for something like this."

Christopher cocked his head to the side. "Why does that sound like something that would be your life's motto?"

Kinsley blushed a pretty shade of pink. "Oh, no, I can't take credit for that. It's a famous saying…."

As her voice trailed off, she looked down at her hands, which were tightly clasped in her lap now.

"I know you didn't invent it," Christopher said. "I was just saying it sounds like a good theory to subscribe to. I didn't mean to embarrass you."

Her head snapped up, and she looked at him with intense eyes. "I'm not embarrassed."

He was tempted to razz her about blushing, but he held back. "Kinsley, you've got to loosen up."

She stiffened. Her back was ramrod straight. Suddenly he wished he would've taken the teasing route.

"I don't know what you mean," she said.

She was fidgeting with the top button on her blouse. It wasn't the first time that Christopher had thought about reaching out and unbuttoning it. But that was a surefire way to get himself into a heap of trouble. He finally decided it was best just to move on.

"Either of those slogans would be good," he said. "Frankly, I'm partial to the first one. I think the kids might relate to it better."

She nodded, obviously just as relieved as he was to move away from his thoughtless comment about her needing to loosen up.

"I saw some rubber bracelets and pencils that we could have personalized with the slogan and the Foundation's phone number. We could have them sign an anti-bullying pledge card. And each kid who signs gets a bracelet and pencil as a sign of his or her commitment."

Christopher nodded.

"That's a great idea," he said. "I was doing some homework, too. How do you feel about some pricier giveaways?"

"What did you have in mind?"

"I was searching online and found a place that offers T-shirts, water bottles and dog tag necklaces. We could put the slogan on them and offer them to kids who stop by the booth."

Her brow was knitted again.

"What are you thinking?" he asked.

"That's a great idea, but it might get a little expensive if we gave something like that to everyone who stops by."

Christopher laughed. "I hope we get that much traffic at our booth. That would show a lot of community interest. But I do see what you mean. Plus, I don't want to giveaway throw-away swag."

"What is throw-away swag?" she asked.

"If it's free, the kids will grab it, but once they get

home it won't have any value to them. We want the free-bies we're offering to be worth something. So if we invest in higher-quality giveaways, purchase fewer of them and offer them as prizes, they will have more sticking power. See what I mean?"

"I do," she said. He followed her gaze and saw she was staring at his putting green. "Maybe we can use that as the game. Anyone who gets a hole in one wins one of the big-ticket items. We could offer less expensive prizes to those who take longer to putt the golf balls into the holes."

His putting green? Did she know how much that cost? Obviously not if she was expecting him to take it to the Spring Fling.

She laughed. "Now I have to ask you what you're thinking."

"I was contemplating one hundred teenagers with muddy sneakers running up and down my putting green."

"And judging from your expression, am I right in guessing you didn't like the idea?"

He shook his head. "No, not really."

"Oh, right. Anything for the kids, huh?"

"Well, within reason. I was thinking we could have a price. You know, one of those things that they spin, like on Wheel of Fortune. Have different sections with prizes written in each. The kids can spin the wheel and wher-ever it lands, that's what they get."

"Or they could putt for a prize."

He laughed. "I see what you're doing there. What is it that you have against my putting green?"

"Me? I don't have a thing against your putting green. I just think you should share it."

"Do you golf?" he asked.

"No. I work."

His jaw dropped. *Touché.* The woman had a quick wit.

"Hey, my putting green helps me think."

She shrugged, but the mischievous gleam was back in her eyes. "Lounging by the pool helps me think. But you don't see me doing that during work hours."

"Are you suggesting that I'm a slacker?"

"I didn't say anything of the kind."

"No, but you insinuated it. My putting green and I, you see, we're really close. It's not the kind of thing I just indiscriminately lend out. I'm kind of monogamous when it comes to my green."

"Christopher Fortune monogamous? I'm not buying it. I'll bet I could make a hole in one before you could be monogamous."

"Is that a challenge?"

She looked at him, the amusement apparent on her face.

"I'd love to say yes, but I have no idea how to quantify that challenge. Besides, out of all the women you date, who would you choose? On second thought, don't answer that. I'm changing the subject into safer territory. I don't completely understand the fascination with golf. Can you enlighten me?"

"Come on." He stood and grabbed her hand, pulling her to her feet. "I'll show you."

"Christopher, I was just joking."

As he picked up the putter, he gave her his most wicked smile. He took her hand and led her to the putting green.

"Have you ever putted before?"

"When would I have time to do that?"

Their gazes snared, held. "Don't answer my question with a question."

He handed her the putter. "Go on. Let me see what you've got."

She laughed. "I'm afraid I might put someone's eye out."

His mouth twitched a bit, but he took care not to laugh outright. He was trying to be careful, going with the flow of the chemistry, afraid he might scare her off if he moved too fast or made the wrong move.

He positioned the golf ball on the tee. "Come here." He motioned to her, and she stood where he indicated. He stood behind her and hesitated for a moment, wanting to wrap his arms around her but instead he explained how she should position herself and hold the club.

When she was in place, she looked over her shoulder at him. "Like this?"

"Not exactly."

"Will you show me?"

Her gaze held his and he was sure she knew what she was asking. So he moved in closer, put his arms around her and positioned his hands over hers, holding very loosely and hesitating a moment to give her a chance to pull away. They were so close he could smell her shampoo…or maybe it was her perfume. Whatever it was, it smelled clean and fresh and edible…fruity with a hint of floral.

He breathed in as he drew her arms and the club back. His body completely engulfed her slender frame, making him feel big and broad as he leaned into her with his chest pressing into her back. He liked holding her so close, feeling her body next to his. For a moment, he pushed aside work and the Fortunes and proper decorum and allowed himself to imagine what it would be like to be Kinsley's lover.

Only for a moment. Then he had intended to dial it back to a safe emotional distance that added up to the respect and decency that she deserved. But after she let him pull back her arm and push it forward in a quick flick of motion, he felt her relax.

He didn't move. Neither did she. They stood there together, him engulfing her and her allowing herself to be engulfed, and the ball sank into the cup at the end of the green.

"Look at that." His voice was low and raspy in her ear.

She turned her head ever so slightly to the left. Her cheek brushed his. He turned to meet her, his lips brushing hers. It was a whisper of a kiss that made his blood surge and his need for her spike. Her lips tasted like peppermint and something indefinable—sweet and female. He didn't stop, despite good sense warning him that he should even if she wasn't showing any signs of objection.

It was a leisurely, slow kiss that started with lips and hints of tongue. Until he turned her around to face him so that he could deepen the kiss. She slid her arms around his neck and opened her mouth, fisting her hands into his hair.

Christopher responded by pulling her in closer. He couldn't remember the last time he'd felt so alive, felt so much need, so much want.

When they finally pulled away, they stood there blinking, both a little dazed and disoriented. Christopher was searching for his words. But Kinsley found her voice first.

"That was unexpected," she said. "Now that we've gotten it out of our systems, let's pretend like it never happened and get back to work."

Chapter Five

That kiss.

She couldn't forget that kiss. Even if she had insisted that they put it behind them and pretend like it had never happened.

She could still taste him. Still feel his lips on hers.

What was she supposed to do now?

Focus on the bullying prevention project that Mr. Jamison had assigned her to do, that's what.

Christopher had been out of town for the past two days. They had managed to maintain their cool and continue with their last planning meeting as if nothing had happened. It was both weird and a relief. They'd kissed. And then they'd acted as if nothing had happened. But that's how Kinsley had wanted it.

Or at least, she'd thought it was what she wanted.

After the emotional dust had settled, she was no longer

sure. If she didn't know herself better, she might let herself believe that she was hoping this chemistry brewing between them could morph into a good thing.

Right now, it was a dangerous thing.

Dangerous, seductive and reckless.

Growing up, Kinsley had witnessed firsthand the havoc a dangerous, reckless man could wreak on the life of a vulnerable woman.

If she knew what was best for her, she would get her mind off Christopher Fortune and get her head back into work.

Especially because he was back and they were meeting this morning at Red Rock High School to talk to the kids the principal had identified as leaders and potential candidates for an anti-bullying advisory board. Kinsley had thought it would be a good idea to ask some students to join forces with the Foundation's initiative to help kickstart the program.

Focus on the kids.

That's what she needed to do. If she did that, she would be just fine.

All that positive self-help talk went right out the window when Kinsley pulled into the parking lot and saw Christopher's car. Her stomach flip-flopped like crazy.

Glancing around the lot, she realized the only available spot was the one next to his car. She steeled herself and steered her old Toyota Camry into place.

For a split second, she grappled with the idea of parking across the street or driving around back to see if there was anything back there—away from Christopher's pristine new car.

But she let go of that thought as fast as it had floated into her mind.

She was who she was.

She had worked hard for everything she owned, including this seventeen-year-old sedan. It wasn't flashy, but it was clean and it ran well. As she eyed Christopher's shiny red BMW, she reminded herself that she had never been embarrassed of her station in life. No one had ever handed her anything. She'd never competed against anyone other than herself or pretended to be anyone other than who she was.

And she sure as shooting wasn't about to start now.

Killing the car's engine, she sat for a minute, thinking about the situation. She had enough on her plate with work and school. She didn't have time to worry about things that were beyond her control, such as whether she wanted to be Christopher Fortune's conquest du jour. And if the sad reality—that the only reason he was probably interested in her was because he couldn't have her— wasn't enough proof that this game was a very bad idea, then she deserved to crash and burn.

And possibly lose everything.

With that reality check firmly reframing her perspective, she got out of the car and made her way up the path toward the front doors of the old brick building that had housed Red Rock High School for more than fifty years.

A plaque next to the entrance proudly proclaimed that the building was considered a historical landmark and was registered with the Red Rock Historical Preservation Society. Over the course of the years, the building's interior had been renovated to serve modern needs, but the facade still exuded an ageless charm and held true to the history that this town celebrated so steadfastly. Ancient laurel oaks dripping with Spanish moss shaded the rolling front yard, as if they were standing sentry over the school and all the children inside. The sense of history, place and peace was one of the things that made Kinsley feel so at home in this town.

She pulled back the heavy glass-and-brass front doors and stepped into the cool air-conditioned space. Straight ahead, a long hall of polished hardwood lined by lockers on either side stretched before her. The reception desk was to her immediate right.

"Hello," said a smiling middle-aged woman. Kinsley figured she must be the receptionist, Carol. She'd spoken to her when she'd called to set up the meeting with the principal. "Are you by any chance Kinsley Aaron?"

"I am," Kinsley answered. "And you must be Carol."

"That's right." Carol offered a hand. Kinsley accepted it, appreciating the warmth she felt radiating from the woman.

"Come right this way. Principal Cramer and Mr. Fortune are in his office. They asked me to bring you back as soon as you arrived."

As Kinsley followed Carol past the desk and through a set of doors, she fished her cell out of her purse and checked the time, suddenly fearing she was late. But no, she was actually a few minutes early. That meant that Christopher had been even earlier. He might have had a lot of quirks, but habitual lateness wasn't one of them. In fact, punctuality was one of the things they had in common.

Thank goodness Carol stopped in front of a closed door and knocked before Kinsley's mind could continue too far on the journey of the other things she found attractive about Christopher.

Stop that. She silently reprimanded herself as a deep voice issued the message for them to "Come in."

As Carol pushed open the door, Kinsley realized she was frowning and quickly checked herself to make sure that she not only had her most pleasant business face on, but also that all errant, inappropriate and un-businesslike thoughts were firmly contained.

There would be no more kissing Christopher.

Not even to get what remained out of their systems.

What a ridiculous thought. How had she ever thought something like that would help? Why had she allowed it to happen?

When she stepped into the principal's office, the first person she saw was Christopher. Her tummy flip-flopped again like crazy, throwing off her equilibrium. Each of her unwavering keep-it-businesslike resolutions flew out the window.

After the meeting with Jed Cramer, Christopher admitted to himself that he wasn't making much headway with Kinsley. Not on the romantic front, anyway.

When Kinsley had walked into the meeting at the high school, she might as well have been on another planet she was so distant.

Christopher was finally admitting to himself that what had started out as a game had turned into something more. He was trying to catch something unattainable.

This wasn't just about physical attraction. It was about not being able to get her out of his head.

This woman was special. She was different from anyone else he'd met. It wasn't like him to be so preoccupied over a woman.

The kiss that they'd shared…and her subsequent parting words about them getting it out of their systems and moving on had plagued him since she'd walked out of his office that day. He'd thought about calling her while he was gone, but he wanted to give her some room. And, truth be told, he needed some space to sort out his own feelings, too.

He kept coming back to the fact that even though he couldn't explain why, he couldn't keep away from Kinsley Aaron the way he had from other women who had gotten too close. Not even after reminding himself of all the problems that could arise if they started something and things ended badly.

He was not ready to settle down. He'd worked too hard to gain his freedom from the ranch in Horseback Hollow to think of tying himself down now that things were just starting to work for him.

But even reminding himself that he and Kinsley would still have to work together if things went south didn't dull this driving need that had him careening toward her.

Since he'd come to Red Rock and started the job at the Fortune Foundation, he'd struggled to keep his professional and personal lives separate. Was he really willing to rethink his personal code for one woman who had somehow managed to get under his skin?

He scrubbed his hands over his eyes as if trying to erase the undeniable answer: yes.

They'd gone their separate ways after the meeting at the high school but had agreed to meet again in his office—the site of that amazing kiss—for their standing meeting.

Christopher glanced at the Waterford crystal clock on his desk. That meeting was set to start in ten minutes.

He had to hand it to her; Kinsley had a way with the kids. The way she'd dealt with the students Jed Cramer had gathered in his office had been amazing. She seemed to have this ability to reach teenagers, especially the girls, on their own level. By the time they left the high school, she had commitments from all seven students to serve on the Fortune Foundation Community Outreach Teen Advisory Board.

During their meeting today, he and Kinsley would work out a game plan for the teen advisory board, outlining exactly what role they wanted the kids to play.

This had come up so fast, and he had a million things to do after being out of town for two days, but he wanted to come into their meeting today with some suggestions. It seemed as if showing her that their project was a priority might be the best way to break through the wall of ice that had formed since the last time they met.... The day of the kiss seemed to have changed the way he looked at everything.

Christopher spent the next five minutes jotting down some ideas that came to mind. The next thing he knew, Kinsley was knocking on his door.

"Come in." He straightened his tie and raked his hand through his hair.

She walked in with her leather folio tucked under her arm. The knotted tangle of emotions inside him threw him a little off balance.

I'll be damned.

For the first time in his life, Christopher was a little unnerved by the presence of a beautiful woman.

How had this happened to him?

Really, it didn't matter. She was here. He was here. They were going to break through this wall of ice even if he had to turn up the heat again.

"Good afternoon, Christopher," she said.

He rolled his hand in front of his body and made a show of bowing formally. "Good afternoon, Miss Aaron."

It worked.

She knit her brows. "Miss Aaron? My, my, are we a little formal today?"

Christopher smiled at her. "I thought that was the mood that we were going for here. You with your *Good afternoon, Christopher.*"

She hugged her leather folio to her chest and frowned at him. Okay, maybe glib humor wasn't such a good choice.

"Kinsley—"

She held up her hand. "If you're going to tell me to lighten up, just save it. We have a lot of work to do and not much time to do it. We better get busy."

Her voice was neutral. At least she wasn't annoyed or didn't seem to be.

Why was it that none of his usual methods of flirtation seemed to work on her?

Since they didn't, in an effort to keep things light, he decided to quit with the clowning and get down to business.

He gestured toward the coffee table, which was still cluttered from end to end with their previous notes and samples of collateral material. "We've been so prolific, it looks like we are running out of room."

He caught her eyeing the putting green. The thing that had started it all. "Yes, why don't we go into the conference room where we will have more space?" She tore her gaze away from the green and looked him in the eyes. "Plus, maybe we can use the whiteboard in there for outlining our ideas."

Christopher wasn't about to argue with her. He just

wanted things to get back on even footing. He couldn't help but wonder if she felt safer with a conference table separating them.

"Sounds good to me," he said. "The whiteboard might come in handy."

With that she seemed to relax a little bit. He had to consciously keep his mouth shut as he forced his mind away from offering her a massage because her shoulders still looked so tense.

Instead, he held his office door for her as they exited and made their way toward the conference room. He was careful to give her enough personal space so that she didn't feel crowded or compromised.

Really, he wanted to make sure he understood the new rules they were playing by.

As he passed Bev's desk in the center of the reception area, she said, "Mr. Fortune, a package just arrived for you. Would you like me to put it on your desk?"

He paused and picked up the homespun-looking package, which was wrapped in plain brown craft paper and tied with twine, glancing first at the return address. Just as he feared, it had a Horseback Hollow postmark. The return address indicated that it was from Jeanne Marie Fortune Jones.

His mother.

A pang of guilt twisted Christopher's heart. He and his father may have had a hard time seeing eye to eye, but his mother was one of the sweetest, kindest women he'd ever known. Christopher new that his move to Red Rock had been hard on her, but he also knew in her heart of hearts she wanted what was best for him.

Unlike his father, who only valued Christopher as another set of hands to help out on the ranch. As he ran his thumb over the paper's rough-hewn surface, he knew that thought wasn't entirely true, even if it did make it easier to justify the way he left.

Christopher felt Kinsley's gaze on him. He looked up to see that she had paused in the hallway that led to the conference room. She was watching him expectantly.

"Thank you, Bev. I'll take this into my office so you don't have to get up. Kinsley, go ahead and start laying things out in the conference room. I'll meet up with you in a second."

Once he was behind closed office doors, he took a pair of scissors from the top drawer of his desk and cut the twine. He used the scissors to loosen the tape and cut away the excess paper, revealing a sturdy cardboard box. He lifted the lid and was a little disappointed when he saw that the package contained what looked like a photo album rather than the cookies he'd been so sure his mother had sent.

He opened the first page and saw a handwritten letter slid into a page protector that his mother had included at the start of the album. The letter said:

My Dear Sweet Chris,

Words can't even begin to express how much I miss you every day. Our family just isn't complete without you here. While I know it's important for you to set out and make your mark in the world, I just want you to know that you will always be welcome to come home when you're ready.

In the meantime, I wanted to send you some pictures to catch you up on ev-

*erything that has been going on since
you moved to Red Rock.
With all the love in my heart,
Mama*

Christopher paged through the album and saw photos of various family members—Stacey and her baby girl, Piper; Toby and Angie's wedding portrait. He lingered over that picture, breathing through a stab of regret for not being there to support his brother on his big day.

The next picture he came to was a snapshot of the Hemings kids hugging his father, Deke. The crusty old jackass was dressed up in a plaid shirt with a bolo tie, that damn cowboy hat that he never went anywhere without perched on the crown of his head. He smiled broadly and regarded the kids with such a look of true adoration. Christopher remembered Toby and Angie mentioning that the kids had started calling his parents Grandma and Grandpa. Sometimes a man didn't know how to be a father but by the mercy of God became an exemplary grandfather. Funny thing was, even though he resented the hell out of Deke for being such a lousy dad to him, he was glad to see the old man showing the kids some benevolence. Lord knew they had been through enough in their short lives; a little compassion would go a long way with them.

An odd feeling squeezed Christopher's chest. He tried to cough, to dislodge the emotion that was blocking his windpipe, but he couldn't manage to make a sound.

He closed the album and set it down on the corner of his desk. Kinsley was waiting for him in the conference room. He'd look at the photos later.

Much later.

* * *

Christopher's grumbling stomach was the first clue that it had gotten late. He glanced at his watch and was surprised to see that it was almost nine o'clock. He and Kinsley had been hashing out the copy for the bully prevention brochure since four-thirty that afternoon. He hadn't noticed how much time had passed until his stomach started to complain.

"I don't know about you, but I'm starving," he said. "We've made some good progress here. What do you say we take a break and go get a bite to eat?"

Kinsley swiped the hair out of her eyes and shot him a weary look. "No, thanks. I'm okay, but you go ahead. We're running up against a tight deadline here and I want to make sure this gets done."

Christopher propped his elbows on the table and watched her as she continued to jot down notes.

"Come on," he said. "You have to eat. I don't want you passing out on me."

Actually, the thought of her *on him* was more appetizing than food. But he kept his thoughts to himself. They had been working for nearly five hours and neither had said a word about what had happened between them the last time they were alone.

"I'll eat after this brochure is finished."

"Even if we get this to the printer by the end of the week we'll still be ahead of schedule. Don't you think there comes a point of diminishing returns after you've been at something so long? Especially if you're hungry."

Her lips puckered with annoyance.

"I'm not hungry. I want to finish my work."

He stood.

"Everyone around here knows how hard you work, Kinsley," he said. "You don't have to prove yourself."

She leveled him with a glare. "That's easy for you to say. But other people around here do have to work hard to get noticed. We don't have everything handed to us."

Ouch. Her words cut to the bone.

"Is that what you think?" he asked. "That just because I'm related to the Fortunes I've had everything handed to me, that life's been one big easy ride?"

She gave him a one-shoulder shrug that was more sexy than it was irritating.

"That just shows how much you don't know. You don't know me at all. So I would suggest that you not judge me until you know me better."

"Is that so?"

"Yes."

"So the guy in the expensive suit who drives the fancy car and has the $3,500 putting green in his office and a different date every night is different from the Christopher Fortune who is standing in front of me now?"

Christopher cleared his throat. "You have no idea who I am on the inside or where I've come from to get where I am now."

"All I know is what I see," she said.

"Well, you've obviously formed your own conclusions," he said. "If you want to go on thinking the way you're thinking, then that's your right to do so. But if you are really as compassionate as you seem to be when you work with those teenagers, then have dinner with me tonight and get to know the real me."

She put her pen down and stared up at him with an unreadable expression.

"So what's it going to be?" he asked. "Are you going to stick to your preconceived notions? Or will you give me a chance to redeem myself?"

Chapter Six

She should be taking her own car, Kinsley thought as Christopher held open the passenger-side door of his pristine status mobile.

Actually, she should've maintained her *no, thank you* to dinner with him and kept working. But here she was, feeling an awful lot like the Country Mouse who had been ensnared in the City Mouse's grand trappings.

Oh, well, it had been her choice to come. It wasn't as if Christopher had kidnapped her.

Before he got in, he opened the back door on the driver's side and tossed what looked like a photo album onto the backseat. After he had settled himself behind the wheel, Kinsley gestured to the album and asked, "What's that?"

He glanced over his shoulder and stiffened as he looked where she pointed. His blue eyes looked pensive.

"It's nothing. Just a photo album."

"I love photos," she said, leaving the door open for him to say *take a look.*

But he didn't answer, just put the key in the ignition, started the car and backed out.

They drove in silence to Red Brick Bistro, but the place was dark and the parking lot was empty.

"What time is it?" Christopher asked. "Are they closed?"

The clock on the dashboard glowed *nine-twenty-five.*

"It looks like it," said Kinsley. "Maybe they're not open today."

Christopher shook his head. "That's one of the things that I just can't get used to. The restaurants close in Red Rock so early on weeknights. I would expect that from Horseback Hollow, but I thought Red Rock was a little more cosmopolitan."

"Why would you expect that in Horseback Hollow?" she asked.

His left wrist was draped casually over the steering wheel and his right elbow was propped on the center console. The stance caused him to pitch toward her ever so slightly. Despite everything, she was tempted to lean in so she could smell his cologne.

A lot of challenges came with working with Christopher Fortune, but his smell was not one of them. It wasn't just the cologne he wore; it was *him.* His own personal scent that had Kinsley breathing a little deeper and leaning in a little closer—even though she desperately wanted her personal space. The dichotomy was hard to reconcile. But he smelled of leather—probably from his car—soap and something else she couldn't define. It all added up to an alluring essence that made it difficult to stop everything female inside of her from roaring to life.

"That's where I'm from," he said. "It's a sleepy little town less than half the size of Red Rock. The sidewalks roll up at sundown and there's absolutely nothing to do. Well, okay, there's The Two Moon Saloon and The Grill, but I wouldn't take you to either of those places."

She blinked. "Why not?"

"Are you kidding? Neither is known for its ambience. They're just not the type of place you take a woman."

It vaguely occurred to her to remind him this was not a date. They were two colleagues who had worked late and were in search of a quick bite. But despite her better judgment, she liked the cozy feel of sitting there with him in the car, with him leaning in slightly, the amber glow of the streetlight casting shadows on his features. Cars passed on the road that ran alongside the parking lot, but in a way it felt as if they were the only two people in the world.

Strange that she would feel so safe and contented sitting in the confines of a car with a man she'd vowed to keep at a distance.

"Where is Horseback Hollow?" she asked, angling her body toward him.

Her peripheral vision caught sight of the photo album in the backseat. It reminded her that Christopher was an anomaly. In so many ways, he was all about flash and being a Fortune, but in other ways he was extremely guarded. That was evident when his brother and sister-in-law had arrived unexpectedly and he'd whisked them out in short order.

It almost seemed as if he had something to hide.

Maybe he was embarrassed. Or maybe he was simply trying to keep the Horseback Hollow part of his life private.

"It's outside of Lubbock," he said. "It's about 400 miles from here. Believe me, it's worlds apart from what you're used to."

From what I'm used to?

What did he think her background was? She was born and raised in a small town about fifty miles away from Red Rock. It was a speck on the map. No one had heard of it and she was doing her best to forget it. She'd moved out as soon as she'd graduated high school. Growing up with a verbally abusive father who sometimes physically took his frustrations out on her mother wasn't exactly the life of royalty.

Both of her parents were gone now. A pang of regret swelled inside her that she hadn't done more to help her mother. The worst fights between her parents had always seemed to be centered around her. Sometimes her mother would put herself in between her father and her, and that's when her mother always got the worst of his wrath.

In her naïveté, Kinsley thought she was doing her mother the biggest favor by leaving since she had always seemed to be at the heart of some of her parents' worst fights. But little did she know she was actually leaving her mother even more in harm's way.

Kinsley was a levelheaded woman. She knew darn good and well that all the wishing in the world wouldn't change the past. So she did what she'd always done when the past crept up behind her and threatened to take her down—she pushed it out of her mind and looked forward.

That was her motto: look forward, not back.

But right now she was looking into Christopher's eyes, and she knew that wouldn't lead to anything good.

She shifted her weight so that she was leaning against the passenger door. As if picking up on her nonverbal cue, he shifted away, too.

The pang of regret surprised her.

"I have a feeling everything else around here is probably closed or close to closing," he said. "How about we go to Mendoza's and get a bite there?"

Kinsley didn't get out much. If she wasn't working, she was studying. If she wasn't doing either of those things, she was probably sleeping or attending classes to be a Lamaze coach for a teenage girl who she had met through the Foundation.

Work, school and volunteering didn't give her much time for frequenting places like Mendoza's nightclub. This was only the second time she'd been there. The other occasion was for the grand opening celebration nearly a year ago. Miguel Mendoza, the club's owner, had invited the entire staff of the Fortune Foundation, in addition to what seemed like the entire population of Red Rock, to the club's opening night celebration. Kinsley had considered it more of a work obligation than a night on the town. She had stayed long enough to put in a good showing but had left at the first opportunity.

She looked around, taking in the place, as she and Christopher claimed two places at the long, old-style cowboy bar.

It was hard to believe that just a year and a half ago the place had been an abandoned building. After Miguel, who was a former New York record company executive, had worked his magic, the club was all flash and neon.

A pink neon sign behind the bar that spelled out *Wet Your Whistle* in flowing cursive letters. Neon boot signs illuminated the raised wooden dance floor, where couples danced to music that was accompanied by videos playing on oversize screens located around the room.

At the back a doorway with a neon arrow pointed down over a sign that read *Play Time*. Kinsley wondered if the Play Time room still had the pool tables, dart boards, Skee-Ball and old-model video games that had gotten everyone so excited about the place at the grand opening. If she remembered correctly, there was even an old-fashioned fortune teller machine back there, too. It reminded her of one she had seen once when her grandmother had taken her to an arcade, on one of those nights when her mother had sent her out of the house because her father had been in one of his *bad places*.

That seemed like a lifetime ago. She filed the thought where she kept most of her childhood memories, in a very dark corner in the back of her mind where they wouldn't get in the way. She preferred to live in the here and now rather than dwelling on the past.

And right now, she recognized Miguel Mendoza, who was manning the bar himself tonight.

"Good evening," Miguel said over the music as he placed two cardboard coasters with beer logos in front of them. "What can I get for you?"

After they placed their orders—a glass of white wine for Kinsley and a beer for Christopher—Miguel poured the wine and set it in front of Kinsley, then pulled a frosty mug out of the small freezer and served up Christopher's beer from a tap right in front of them.

"Do I know you?" Miguel asked Christopher. "Maybe I've just seen you here, but I have a feeling we've met before. I'm Miguel Mendoza."

He set the beer in front of Christopher and offered a hand, which Christopher shook.

"Christopher Fortune," he said. "I don't know that we've ever been formally introduced, but I'm in here a lot."

Figures. Kinsley did her best not to roll her eyes, but then made herself step back and reframe her thoughts. He was a young, good-looking, wealthy, single guy. Of course he would want to blow off a little steam after hours at a place like this. That's what people with normal social lives did.

She supposed he could turn the tables on her and wonder why she never made time for fun. Sometimes she wondered that herself. But once she finished her degree and had saved a little money...

Then she would start her life.

However, at the rate she was going, she'd cross that bridge in the very distant future. The truth was she'd never been much of a barfly. That just wasn't her idea of fun. After she graduated she probably wouldn't feel the burning desire to go out and tear up the town any more than she wanted to now.

To each his or her own, she thought as she sipped her white wine. But she suddenly realized that both Christopher and Miguel were looking at her expectantly. She'd obviously missed something.

Christopher leaned in, much too close for her comfort. He placed a hand on her shoulder and whispered in her ear, "I just introduced you to the owner. You might want to say hello or something." He punctuated the suggestion with a quick raise and lower of his brows. It was one of those looks that wasn't cocky enough to be annoying. Cheeky was more apropos. In fact, it was almost endearing. She hated herself for thinking so.

"Hello," she said. "I'm Kinsley Aaron. I work with Christopher at the Fortune Foundation."

Miguel shook her hand and smiled. "That's what he tells me."

"I'm sorry," she said. "The music is a little loud. I didn't hear you the first time."

"I understand," said Miguel. "It's an occupational hazard. So since you both work at the Foundation, would you happen to know Sierra Mendoza Calloway? She's my cousin and she works there."

Kinsley and Christopher answered at the same time. She said yes; Christopher hedged as Kinsley did a double-take, but she did her best to keep her expression neutral. Inside, she was aghast. Sierra had just helped them secure some stock photos for the brochures they were putting together for the Spring Fling. He really didn't remember her? He probably did, he just didn't know her name.

Well, she wasn't about to embarrass him in front of Miguel.

"I adore Sierra," she said. "In fact, just the other day she helped me find a photograph that Christopher and I desperately needed for a brochure we're putting together for a project." She glanced at Christopher and saw a flicker of recognition register on his face.

"I'll be sure and tell her we met you," Kinsley said, turning back to Miguel.

"Please do," Miguel answered. "She's a sweetheart. It's too bad. We have so much family right here in town, yet we don't get to see each other as often as we should."

He looked to Christopher. "As a Fortune, I'll bet you understand how that is."

Christopher gave a quick shrug. "Actually, I've only been in Red Rock a couple of months, and I work with so many of my relatives we get to see each other plenty."

Miguel leaned on the bar. "Oh, yeah, where are you from?"

Kinsley saw the look of hesitation flash across Christopher's face. It was only there for a moment before he stiffened and said, "I'm from a small town outside of Lubbock. I doubt you've heard of it. I moved up here to take the job at the Foundation."

"Lubbock, huh?" said Miguel. "I'm familiar with the area. Try me."

"It's a little dot on the map called Horseback Hollow."

Miguel slapped his hand on the counter. "Get out! Are you serious? I have family there. My brother, Marcos, and his wife are getting ready to open a restaurant there, and my cousin Orlando Mendoza works at the Redmond Flight School."

"I was so sorry to hear about his accident," said Christopher. "It was good of his daughter Gabi to come and care for him."

Miguel looked a little embarrassed. "I haven't seen him since the accident. But I am glad to hear he's doing better."

"You know Gabi is engaged to my brother, Jude, right? She's going to be my sister-in-law. So, doesn't that make us related in some distant way?"

"What a small world. The Fortunes and the Mendozas have always considered each other family. So tonight, your drinks are on me."

"It is a small world," said Christopher. "It's great to meet you. Thank you for the drinks, my friend. But what we really came for was a bite to eat, which, of course, I will pay for. Could we see some menus, please?"

"Of course." Miguel pulled two menus out from behind the bar. "But just so we understand each other, your money is no good here. Money does not change hands among family."

Christopher shook his head and smiled. "I appreciate the generous offer, but really I would be happy to pay. We'll sort it out at the end of the evening."

"Please let me know when you're ready to order," said Miguel. His confident smile seemed to say that he'd already made up his mind. The bill was settled, and nothing Christopher Fortune could say would make a bit of difference.

After they placed their orders for burgers and fries, Miguel set another round of drinks in front of them and went to deliver their dinner request to the kitchen.

Christopher raked his hand through his blond hair. Kinsley was beginning to recognize that habit as a nervous tic.

"What the hell? Is everyone in this town related to someone?"

She couldn't help laughing at him a little. "Pretty much. If they're not a Fortune, they're a Mendoza and a lot of the Fortunes are married to Mendozas.

"May I give you a little bit of unsolicited advice?" Kinsley offered. The beer had loosened him up, and right about now he was longing to hear anything Kinsley had to say. He could be quite content listening to her read a dictionary out loud because it would give him license to drink her in. He could watch her lips move as she formed the words, study the graceful way her delicate jawline curved into her neck and imagine kissing her at that sweet spot where they intersected....

"Sure." Even if he was in for a Kinsley-style reprimand, he didn't mind. She had a firm but gentle way about her. She didn't grate on him the way Deke did when he spouted off with his holier-than-thou statements and rubbed Christopher's nose in I-told-you-sos.

He could tell Kinsley didn't suffer nonsense lightly, but she was also sensitive enough to temper what she said so that it didn't feel like a personal attack.

He appreciated that.

"You would do yourself a world of good to start remembering names. People around here get kind of funny about that. It's off-putting."

She wrinkled her nose and something inside him went soft...and then another part of him, farther south, felt as if it was about to go rock-hard. He held his breath for a moment to get a handle on his libido.

This wasn't college. She deserved his respect, especially after she'd made it perfectly clear where they stood.

He focused on the point she'd made. Remembering names was his weakness, and if he was going to succeed, he needed to fix that.

He still hadn't gotten used to the pop quizzes that jumped out at him just when he thought he had everything under control. All the more reason that he needed to be on the ball.

Sierra Mendoza Calloway was a perfect example. Even if they did call her Sierra Calloway around the office, he should've remembered her. He should've put two and two together. If he really wanted to make his mark in Red Rock, he knew he'd better pay attention and learn the players. He had to know everyone, by sight, right away—especially because so many of them were apparently family, or practically family.

Because wasn't that all anyone wanted—to be valued and respected?

"Thanks for covering for me with Miguel. It would've been embarrassing if he'd known that I spent a good half hour with his cousin and didn't connect the dots."

She nodded. "Well, giving you the benefit of the doubt, I guess there's no way you could've known she's a Mendoza. But don't worry, as long as you pull your weight, I've got your back. And I know that you've got mine, too."

A strangely protective feeling swept through him. "Of course I do. We're a team."

Somehow he didn't think she needed his help as much as he could benefit from hers. Beauty aside—and she didn't seem to realize how stunning she was—he was in awe of her strength and people skills. She was young to be so self-possessed, so stalwartly sure of herself, yet it was all tempered with a vulnerability that made him want to gather her in his arms and promise her the world.

They sat in amiable silence for a moment, sipping their drinks and watching the people on the dance floor.

"So, Kinsley Aaron, tell me about yourself," he said.

She shook her head. "I seem to recall that we had a deal. You promised if I would have dinner with you tonight, you would tell me *your* story. So don't try to turn the tables, Mr. Fortune."

"There you go with the formalities again." He smiled so that she knew he was kidding.

"What's wrong? Does it make you feel like your father when someone calls you Mr. Fortune?"

He almost laughed. "Absolutely not. As a matter of fact, it has pretty much the opposite effect."

"Really? Do tell."

He took a long swallow of his beer, trying to think about where to begin.

"Obviously, you have a misconception that I'm someone that I'm not."

"Are you not a Fortune, or have you been impersonating one for the past two months?"

If she only knew how close to the truth that really was....

"Not exactly."

Thank goodness Miguel chose that moment to bring the food. He set the plates and another round of drinks in front of them.

"Can I get you anything else?"

The food smelled delicious and the company was perfect.

Christopher looked at Kinsley. "I think we're all set," she said. "Thanks for everything, Miguel."

Miguel gave them a salute and hurried off to attend to other customers.

For a weeknight, the place was really rocking. It was great to see it doing such a healthy business.

As they ate their burgers, Christopher told Kinsley about growing up in Horseback Hollow with his mom and dad and six siblings. She was surprised to learn that they had little money and none of the advantages of the Fortune family she knew.

"Are you kidding?" Her wide blue eyes reflected sincere surprise.

"No, I'm not kidding. I had a very humble upbringing. When you have that many kids to feed and clothe, a rancher's income doesn't go very far."

She put down her burger and looked at him with true concern.

"Was your childhood difficult?"

"That depends on how you define *difficult,*" Christopher said. "I mean, we never went hungry or wanted for the necessities. But do you know what it's like to be lost in a crowd of strong-willed siblings, always having to fight for attention and approval, even the last piece of fried chicken?"

She shook her head. "I was an only child. So, no, I don't."

"Being an only child sounds like a little piece of heaven," he said. "But I guess the grass is always greener when you're looking over the picket fence at someone else's life."

He shrugged. "To be fair, I guess I wouldn't trade my siblings. In fact, that was my brother Toby and his new wife, Angie, who stopped by the office the other day. They were on their way back from their honeymoon and stopped in to see me before they headed back to Horseback Hollow."

And he'd screwed that up, too. He and Toby hadn't spoken since that day. His brother had left the ball in Christopher's court, and Chris hadn't moved on it. What was he supposed to do? Toby had clearly come to do Deke's bidding. His sole purpose was to talk him into coming home. It wasn't going to happen. Not anytime soon.

Christopher laughed a humorless laugh. "My siblings are great at making life more challenging."

"How?" Kinsley asked.

"Compared to them, I guess you'd say I'm the black sheep of the family. My little sisters are sweethearts, but my brothers are hard acts to follow. We're just different.

I'm the youngest of the boys. They all seem to be cut from the same cloth. They're right at home on the ranch, exactly where Deke wants us all to be."

"Deke is your father?"

Christopher nodded. "Good old Deke just can't understand how I could want more than spending my entire life in Horseback Hollow and working on the ranch. He clings to that broken-down place like it's life support. And he won't take a word of advice from me on how to make it more profitable."

Kinsley sat there with attentive wide eyes, but remained mostly silent. So, Christopher continued.

"Then my mom, who grew up thinking she was an only child—" he gave Kinsley a knowing look "—discovered not only did she have siblings, but she was one of a set of triplets who had been put up for adoption when they were very young. So then my uncle James, who is one of the triplets along with my aunt Josephine, who lives in England, felt bad that he had so much and my mom had grown up with so little, and he gifted her with a bunch of money."

Kinsley's jaw dropped.

Christopher shrugged. "It seemed like our lives would finally get a whole lot easier. But then, as fast as Uncle James had given Mom the money, she decided she couldn't accept it. She gave it back.

"Every stinking penny of it," he said.

Kinsley was leaning in, rapt. "Oh, my god, this sounds like a movie."

"I know, right?"

"Why?" Kinsley asked. "Why did she give it back if he wanted her to have it?"

"She didn't want to be the cause of any tension between Uncle James and his children. She said discovering that she had this huge family she never knew about was a big enough gift."

Christopher forced himself to leave it at that, because suddenly revealing his ill feelings over getting and then losing the money felt…selfish and narcissistic.

"But on the bright side, between my mom and her three siblings there are twenty-four cousins."

"Wait, you were just complaining about being lost in a family of nine. How could adding eighteen cousins to the mix make it better?"

"My cousins—most of whom are the Fortunes that you know, or at least resemble what you think a Fortune should be, are a bit more… How do I put this tactfully… They're a bit more worldly than my humble family."

Christopher held off telling her about the fight he'd had with Deke the night he left Horseback Hollow for good.

Equal parts shame and regret washed over him as he thought about the harsh words he'd exchanged with his father that night. But what the hell was he supposed to do? If he'd listened to Deke, he wouldn't be sitting here with this incredible woman right now. If that in itself wasn't proof that he'd made the right decision to come to Red Rock, then he didn't know what was.

Kinsley shook her head. "I can't imagine having that many relatives. That would just be… I mean it would be cool, but no wonder you have a hard time remembering names. What's your mom like?"

"She is the sweetest person you could ever imagine meeting," he said. "She's all about her family and kids. But I wish she would be stronger when it comes to standing up to Deke. He can be the worst kind of bully," Christopher snorted. "Talk about someone who could benefit from a bully prevention program."

Empathy colored Kinsley's beautiful blue eyes.

"I understand what it's like to have father conflict," Kinsley said. "I was close to my mom, too. Your mom must be a good soul if she is content to build Fortune family relations with none of its monetary perks."

Christopher shrugged. "Are you saying I'm wrong for wanting a different life than the ranch has to offer? As far as Deke is concerned, my birthright is in Horseback Hollow."

"Why don't you go visit your dad and talk things out?"

Chapter Seven

Why was she trying to give Christopher advice on family relations? Kinsley knew she was certainly in no position to do that. She'd run away from problems with her own father, and in the process had left her mother high and dry. Obviously, she was no expert on making things right.

"I'm not ready to go home yet," Christopher said, answering her question after a long pause.

"Why not?" Kinsley asked.

"It's complicated."

Kinsley shrugged. "Yeah, life gets that way sometimes."

She was speechless, listening to this man who was turning out to be nothing like the shallow, glad-handing guy who on his best days had irritated her...and on her worst days had tempted her.

She didn't want to think about that right now. In fact, she felt a little guilty about the preconceived notions she'd formed.

She wanted to know more about his life at the Horseback Hollow ranch, more about what he'd been like before he'd discovered his Fortune relatives. Even though she only knew a few things about his life before he'd moved to Red Rock, she sensed she knew his heart better now.

Everyone struggles with something, even if they hide behind a smile. Or in Christopher's case, expensive clothes and a fancy car.

Her mask was work and school.

She knew that, but she wasn't ready to do anything to change. If she wasn't willing to amend herself, why should she expect Christopher to present a different face than the one he showed?

She had to give the guy credit. At least he seemed to understand how fortunate he was to have been, given a leg up to starting his new life.

His upbringing explained a lot: his need for attention, his tendency to show off and his penchant for the ladies.

Yes, there was that, she reminded herself. If she knew what was good for her, she would keep that firmly in mind.

Christopher was charming and charismatic. Kinsley was willing to bet that this revolving door of women was as new to him as his red BMW.

Even if he'd always been popular with the ladies, if Horseback Hollow was as small as he'd made it sound, he'd probably never had the smorgasbord available to him now.

Despite that, her esteem for Christopher had risen. She could tell that he had genuine affection for his mother, brothers and sisters. She had to admit that she was just a little bit envious of his big, boisterous family. When she was little, she used to long for a big brother to watch out for her. Maybe if she'd had one, things would've been different. Maybe her mother would still be alive today.

"It sounds like Toby was trying to entice you to come home when he dropped by the other day."

He shifted in his seat and his face closed. "I wish it were that easy."

"I know it's a big trip," she said. "But maybe you could take a long weekend. I'm sure Mr. Jamison would understand."

As Christopher looked at her, she could see him choosing his words. "It's not the distance. I could fly there and back in less time than it would take to get to the airport. I'm just not in a very good place with my father right now."

"I know there's more going on between you and your father than what you've told me, and I understand if it's a private thing. You don't have to tell me. But logic does dictate that he must be a pretty good man to have raised such great kids."

Again Christopher shifted in his seat. This time he moved away from her and turned his attention to his beer.

"Christopher, nobody's perfect. But please take my advice. Sometimes it seems like the people who have taken care of us will be around forever, but the truth is life is short."

Her mother had been just forty-six years old when she'd died. Way too young. It sounded ridiculous to say— she couldn't even say the words out loud, and she could barely admit them to herself—but it never occurred to her that her mother could die. Her mother, the one who had always looked out for her, the one who had thrown herself between Kinsley and that horrible man who just happened to be related to her by genetics.

Kinsley had been far too wrapped up in her own life, in getting out of the abysmal, abusive situation she was born into and starting the life she knew she was meant to have.

What she wouldn't give to go back and do everything differently. She would've insisted that her mom come with her. The man who had abused them both and cheated on her mother could've rotted in hell for all she cared.

Surely he was burning there now.

But there were no do-overs. She could only look forward and hope that she might be able to honor her mother's memory by helping some other unlucky woman who was caught in an unfortunate situation. More immediately, maybe she could help teenage girls realize that they didn't have to settle for someone who treated them poorly. That by the virtue of being born they were princesses—even if they never had a father to tell them so.

"Hey," said Christopher. "Where'd you go?"

She blinked at him, unsure what she had missed.

"You were somewhere far, far away," he said. "Would you care to share?"

This was one instance when she was glad she had never been able to cry about her mother and the whole sorry situation. She had always worried that if she let down the floodgates she might never stop crying. At that very moment, she vowed that she would never put her theory to the test.

The way Christopher was watching her she had a feeling that because he had shared his story, he was going to expect reciprocation from her. That was something else that wasn't going to happen.

The music changed to a medium-tempo Blake Shelton tune.

"I love this song," she said. "Dance with me."

She was on her feet and headed toward the dance floor before Christopher could refuse and before she could change her own mind.

By the time she'd wedged her way into a spot on the dance floor, Christopher was right there next to her. Only then did it dawn on her that he would probably hate this song that talked about red dirt roads and doing manual labor.

Oh, well.

The dance floor was small, hot and crowded, forcing them into close proximity even though it wasn't a slow dance. But that was okay because the music was even louder over here, and it seemed to keep Christopher from asking questions. Some couples tried to do a slow two-step around the perimeter of the close confines, but Christopher kept his hands to himself and didn't try to pull her into that kind of dance.

Given the kiss they'd shared, he'd proved himself unpredictable enough that she wouldn't have been shocked if he had pulled her close, but this was fine.

Really, it was.

After three glasses of wine, she would probably melt in his arms. She wasn't drunk, just nicely loosened up. Once they had established their dance M.O., she let herself be swept away by the pounding rhythm of the music. It felt good to let her hair down and lose herself.

Christopher looked as if he was enjoying himself, too, moving unselfconsciously to the beat. Maybe it was the wine talking, but suddenly she wondered why she didn't go out more often. Christopher smiled that endearingly cheeky smile as he moved next to her. It struck her that it was a pretty darn attractive quality for a guy to be willing to dance. So many of the guys she'd known had refused to let go like this.

As she took in Christopher's subtle moves, she couldn't help but wonder what he would be like in bed. She hadn't had that much experience, and really none of it was notable, but she'd always heard that the way the guy danced gave a lot of clues as to how he would make love.

If that was the case, Christopher seemed to be proving himself *quite* capable.

Lord have mercy.

She was glad the music was so loud because she felt a giggle bubble up and escape. It must have come across as a smile because Christopher beamed at her.

The two of them got into the spirit, communicating with only their eyes and expressions.

Again, this guy, who she'd been so quick to dismiss, was showing her another side. Here he was in his white dress shirt with the sleeves pushed up past the elbows getting down as well as any of the cowboys in the place. She was tempted to tease him about his ranch upbringing coming out on the dance floor, but that was for later.

This was now.

This was fun.

This was a high she wished would last…and last… and—

An overzealous couple two-stepped right into Kinsley, knocking her into Christopher. He caught her, holding her close in his strong arms. The two of them stood breast to chest, staring into each other's eyes, vaguely swaying to the song's refrain.

Then, right there in the middle of the dance floor, he didn't ask permission; he simply lowered his head and kissed her unapologetically, ravenously. And she kissed him back shamelessly, completely taken by their mutual hunger.

The kiss bypassed slow and soft, immediately igniting into a voracious fire that had her parting her lips and deepening the kiss. Her arms found their way around his neck and her hands fisted into the cotton of his shirt. They leaned into each other as if they depended on this intimate contact for their life's breath.

The whole world disappeared—Mendoza's, the dance floor, the music. She didn't care who was there or who might be watching them. The only thing that mattered was the way he was holding her so tightly against him, staking his claim, in this wordless confession of desire.

The taste of his beer mingled with her wine and merged with hints of the truffle salt from the fries. And then there was that familiar hint of *him* that she had tasted when they'd kissed in his office. But that was then. Now, she tasted a hint of the forbidden mixed with the temptation of right now.

A moment ago she had convinced herself that this was taboo, and now he was kissing her so thoroughly that she didn't want to stop. Feelings inside her that had awakened when he'd kissed her the first time were now laced with a passion that threatened to consume her.

She'd forgotten the once logical rationale for protecting her heart. Or maybe she no longer cared. The reasons had shifted and transformed *why not* into *oh, yes* were promising to be so worth the risk.

Kinsley had no idea how much time had passed as they held each other and kissed as people whirled around them on the dance floor.

As they slowly came up for air, Christopher held her face in his palms, his forehead resting on hers. Maybe it was the liquid courage talking, but this kiss felt right, and the way he was holding her seemed to say he felt it, too.

"Oh, my God, Christopher, what are we going to do now?"

No matter what Kinsley said today, he wasn't going to let this go. They couldn't go back to being purely platonic, not after last night's kiss. They were definitely in a different place now. And he liked it.

Christopher smiled to himself as he picked up the phone.

His gut told him that after he'd dropped her off at her apartment last night she'd probably overthought everything.

He dialed Red and made a lunch reservation for two at his favorite table, then sat back in his leather chair, glancing at the putting green. One kiss might have been a mistake. But two? There was no denying the fire that blazed between them last night.

Even if she resisted, he was going to prove to her that there was something special between them. Something worth fighting for.

He hadn't seen Kinsley yet today, but when he did, he wanted her to know beyond a doubt that last night meant something to him. What better way than to go back to when everything seemed to start—that day that Toby and Angie had arrived and he'd asked Kinsley to make a lunch reservation at Red. He hoped she'd see the meaning behind this lunch date.

He started to pick up the phone again to call her and ask her to lunch, but then he thought better of it. He got up and walked to her office.

The door was open, so he rapped lightly on the door frame.

"Good morning," he said when she looked up from her computer.

"Good morning." Her tone was neutral. She finished typing whatever it was he had interrupted before she said, "Come in."

He walked in and sat down in the chair across from her desk.

"I'm glad you're here," she said.

He smiled and quirked a brow, but she carried on business as usual.

"I realized this morning that we need to come up with a calendar of deadlines so that we make sure we get everything done in time for the Spring Fling. Do you realize it's less than two weeks away?"

What?

"That's not what I came in here to talk to you about, but sure. We can do that."

Her expression remained neutral, but her voice held the faintest notes of exasperation. "Would you please close the door?"

Christopher complied. When they were safe behind closed doors, he said, "I enjoyed last night."

She tensed and closed her eyes a blink that was a few beats too long before she opened them again. "About that…. Listen, I appreciate you being so nice about it, but I think we both had a little bit to drink last night."

"We did and it was a great time. I hope we can do it again. In fact, I made reservations for us to have lunch at Red today at twelve-thirty. Of course, it might not be a good idea for us to drink as much as we did last night, since we have to come back and work on these things that you're putting on the calendar." She was sitting there staring at him blankly. "And I had hoped you might catch the meaning in me making the lunch reservation instead of asking you, but…"

He thought he saw her wince ever so slightly as she continued to regard him with that neutral expression. He reminded himself that he had expected her to react this way. *See, he knew her.* And he had also been prepared for the possibility of having to take things slowly as she came to terms with the fact that this was right—and good.

And very real.

"Okay, so why don't we discuss this calendar and everything we need to put on it at lunch today? At Red."

He winked at her. Then promptly realized that was probably not a good move.

"Or if you have a few minutes now," she said, "we can talk about it and get everything all squared away."

He saw what she was doing.

He stood. "Sorry, I don't have time right now. I'll pick you up at 12:15 and we can discuss everything over lunch."

He flashed his most charismatic smile and was pleased to note that some of her bravado seemed to wither away in front of him.

"Okay. Fine. We can have a working lunch."

He opened the door. "See you soon." He left it open, exactly the way he had found it.

As he walked back to his office, he was more determined than ever to make Kinsley see just how good they could be together.

"Hello, Mr. Fortune. It's nice to see you," said the tall, thin, pretty hostess at Red. "A table for two for you and…your girlfriend?"

"Oh, no. I'm not his girlfriend. We're not… We just work together."

The hostess regarded Kinsley with a subtle air that suggested she was just being polite and hadn't been convinced they were even a couple to begin with.

"Well, that's very good to know." The hostess smiled and boldly looked Christopher up and down.

Kinsley's cheeks burned.

How rude and unprofessional.

A little voice in the back of Kinsley's mind reminded her that it was a lot more professional than she had been when she'd made out with Christopher on the dance floor at Mendoza's. Anybody in town could have seen them acting like a couple of hormone-driven teenagers who couldn't keep their hands off each other.

Even though common sense told her that nobody was looking at them as she and Christopher followed the hostess to their table, it felt as if every eye in the place was watching them.

Once they were settled and the hostess had managed to tear herself away, Christopher looked her squarely in the eyes and said, "Kinsley, we make such a good team, in and out of the office—"

"That's why we need to pretend like nothing happened last night," she said.

"That's what we said after our first kiss," he countered. "And we see where that got us. Why are we fighting this? I think we could be very good together if you would just give us a chance."

Kinsley's heart pounded an insistent staccato in her chest. It was almost like a finger tapping her chest urging her to do the right thing—to set the record straight with Christopher, to make sure he understood exactly where they stood.

As long as they both worked at the Foundation, all they would be were platonic coworkers. Since she didn't plan on leaving her job anytime soon, apparently that was all that fate had in store for them.

Christopher would be free to fully enjoy all the perks of being a young, good-looking guy with too much money and a tendency to flash it to get whatever and whomever he wanted—like the hostess who had given Kinsley the stink eye when they'd arrived.

Women like that might throw themselves at him, but Kinsley would not be his conquest, and that was at the heart of why they would never work. The two of them came from different worlds. He might think he'd had it bad off being lost in the chaos of a large family where money had once been tight, but he had no idea what it was like to have lost the only person in the world who had ever shown unconditional love.

Kinsley had witnessed firsthand the pain her mother had suffered at the hands of her womanizing father, who couldn't or wouldn't stop himself when it came to the ladies. No matter how her mother had cried and threatened to leave him, he would simply turn the tables on her and somehow manage to blame her mother for his own philandering. Even after her front-row seat for this cautionary tale, in college Kinsley had still been stupid enough to put her faith in a man who ended up proving himself as verbally abusive and faithless as her own father. In her studies she had learned that victims of abuse often unwittingly fell into the trap of falling for abusive partners.

She wasn't convinced that Christopher had abusive tendencies, but he sure did have an eye for ladies. That was enough to make Kinsley put on the breaks. It was clear that Christopher still had oats to sow. She wasn't going to fall into the same trap that her mother had suffered or repeat the same mistake she'd already made....

Last night was her last dance with Christopher Fortune.

Chapter Eight

Thursday night was ladies' night at Mendoza's. That's why Christopher was surprised his cousin Sawyer Fortune who was in town for the day, suggested that they meet there to discuss a fund-raising opportunity for the Foundation over a beer and a quick bite to eat.

Ladies' night didn't officially start until nine o'clock, so even though it was nearly eight o'clock, Mendoza's still had the air of a restaurant. The lights were a little brighter than they would be later on, and the music was much softer and less honky-tonk than it would be when the clock struck nine. So they had time to wrap up their business before the party overtook the place. Sawyer would be long gone before then, anyway, because he had to fly to Horseback Hollow before it got too late.

Sawyer was happily married to Laurel Redmond, had been since New Year's Eve. After the wedding, they had moved to Horseback Hollow to open a branch of Redmond Flight School and Charter Service. The operation was headquartered out of Red Rock, so Sawyer still came to town occasionally. Today, Sawyer had been involved in nonstop meetings all day and had suggested that the two of them grab a couple of Mendoza's famous tacos before he flew home that evening.

Whether they were talking business or not, Christopher was always glad for a chance to visit with his cousin because he hadn't really had the opportunity to get to know him very well before his own move to Red Rock. This was not only a good chance to spend time with him, but also a chance to discuss a way for the flight school to make a charitable contribution to the Foundation.

Christopher had asked Kinsley to join them, but she had her statistics class tonight and after that, she was attending a Lamaze class with a teenage girl she had agreed to help.

Kinsley had so much on her plate that Christopher didn't know how she handled it all. But working all day, going to class and then finding the energy to help this girl were just a few of the many reasons Christopher found her so amazing.

She had said she would text him when she was free so that he could fill her in on the details of what he and Sawyer had come up with. She had mentioned that she should be finished shortly after eight o'clock. Christopher found himself glancing at his phone, alternately checking the time and making sure he hadn't missed a text from her.

Nothing yet.

"Are you expecting a hot date?" Sawyer kidded.

"Nope. Not tonight," Christopher said as he clicked off his phone yet again.

Sawyer gestured to the phone. "You keep checking that thing. I thought maybe you were waiting for someone to call you."

"Actually, I'm waiting for Kinsley Aaron, my colleague, to text me so I can fill her in on how you're going to help us raise all kinds of money."

Christopher and Sawyer had discussed the possibility of having an air-show fund-raiser to benefit the Foundation's bully prevention program. Unfortunately, the date of the Spring Fling was too close for them to get something together, but the event was definitely a possibility for the future. In fact, it was probably best to do it as a separate experience, anyway, because it would be another opportunity to raise awareness for the cause.

"Just tell Kinsley not to get too excited yet," said Sawyer. "I need to run all this by Tanner and Jordana before we can give it the official green light. But I have a feeling they will be just as thrilled as I am about having the chance to help with this worthy cause."

Tanner Redmond and his wife, Jordana Fortune Redmond, owned and operated the Red Rock branch of Redmond Flight School and Charter Service.

"I'm sorry Tanner and Jordana couldn't be here tonight to discuss this," Christopher said.

The Redmonds were out of town. That was one of the reasons Sawyer had flown up for the day, to cover some meetings, check on the Red Rock office and make sure everything was running smoothly.

"I am, too," said Sawyer. "Later on, after they give me the thumbs up, we'll all get together and discuss everything. Maybe your Kinsley will be able to join us then, too."

Your Kinsley. If Christopher had anything to say

about it, next time Sawyer was in town, she *would* be his. Something intense flared inside him at the thought, and the sensation made him double his determination to make that so.

But the feeling was interrupted by a shapely brunette who slid into the seat next to Christopher.

"Hello?" Christopher said. "May I help you?"

The young woman looked familiar, but he couldn't place her.

"You don't remember me, do you?" she said, smiling as she twisted a strand of long dark hair around her finger.

Christopher darted a glance at Sawyer, who was watching them, in the off chance that the woman might be a friend of his. Christopher knew it was highly unlikely, though.

"I'm Crystal?" she said. "I seated you at Red for lunch the other day? And the time before that when you were in with the newlyweds?"

Crystal was pretty enough, but she seemed to have an annoying habit of turning every sentence into a question. Still, he didn't want to be rude.

"Right, I remember. Hello, Crystal. I'm Christopher Fortune. This is Sawyer Fortune, my cousin."

"Ooh," she said. This time it wasn't a question as much as an exclamation. She looked Sawyer up and down, her gaze lighting on his wedding ring. She turned back to Christopher.

"It's your lucky night. I'm going to let you buy me a drink."

Her question-phrasing was strike one. Strike two was calling him Chris. No one in Red Rock called him Chris.

Still, he played along. "Oh, you are, are you?"

Crystal nodded. "Yeah. And if you play your cards right tonight? I will make it very worth your while."

Christopher had gotten used to bold women, but this was the first time he had encountered someone who was downright carnivorous. He glanced at Sawyer, who looked as befuddled as Christopher felt, then he turned back to Crystal.

"Well, you're a very beautiful woman…and that sounds like an offer that would be hard for most men to refuse. But I'm right in the middle of a business meeting here."

At least he didn't have to ask her to leave. She scooted out of the booth. "Well, you come find me after you're done here, okay?" She blew him a kiss and tottered away in high heels and a short miniskirt that didn't look as alluring tonight as they had that first time he'd seen her.

Sawyer whistled under his breath. But it wasn't an appreciative sound; it was more the sound somebody made when they had witnessed a train wreck.

"Looks like someone's celebrating ladies' night a little early," said Christopher.

As he watched the woman walk away, he realized he wasn't interested. Not the least bit. Maybe he had finally had his fill of the pretty-girl smorgasbord. Or maybe he really did have standards when it came to women. How many other men had found it *worth their while* to buy her drinks? He really didn't want to know.

What he did know is that he wanted a woman with more substance.

As if right on cue a message from Kinsley flashed on his phone.

Just got home. How was the meeting?

Christopher picked up his phone and typed, Still with Sawyer. It's going well. A lot to tell you.

She returned, Good to hear. Fill me in when you're done?

He typed back, You bet!

"So, is your *colleague* back?" Sawyer asked.

"She is."

Sawyer took a long sip of his iced tea, then set the glass down on the table. "You seem pretty happy to hear from her."

Sawyer laced the words with insinuation. Christopher shrugged but couldn't hide his smile.

"Yeah, well…" He shrugged again.

Sawyer nodded. "Are you two dating?"

Christopher glanced at his phone again to see if Kinsley had responded. She hadn't.

"Why do you ask?"

"Well, I was just about ready to get on my way to Horseback Hollow so you could *make the night worth your while.* But I'm sensing you're not into that." Sawyer nodded toward the general area where Crystal waited.

Christopher didn't dare look over there for fear of sending her the wrong message. He really wasn't interested.

"It's complicated," he answered.

"It doesn't have to be," Sawyer said. "When it's right, it's the most uncomplicated feeling in the world. That doesn't mean things are always easy, or that in the beginning you don't have to fight the good fight. But when it's right you'll know."

Christopher weighed his words. He really didn't need to explain. In fact, there really wasn't anything to explain.

He and Kinsley were in limbo right now, but something told him to stay quiet.

"Okay, then, let's just say, I'm fighting the good fight right now."

Sawyer nodded, a knowing look in his eyes. "Good luck, man. I hope she's worth it. Not to say she's not."

Another text flashed on Christopher's phone. His gut contracted but then released when he saw it was from his buddy Joe.

Art and I are headed over to Mendoza's for ladies' night. See you there.

Christopher considered typing, *Already here,* but Sawyer said, "Are you concerned at all about dating someone you work with? I know a lot of people caution against it, but Laurel and I work together and Tanner and Jordana do, too. We might be the exception to the rule, but at least we're proof that it can work. If you have feelings for this woman, don't let being colleagues scare you off."

Christopher pushed his phone away. "I have to admit I've wondered how Uncle James would feel about workplace dating. She's important to me, but I don't want to rock any boats at work."

Sawyer made a *pffff* sound. "If you only knew how many Fortunes met their spouses on the job, you wouldn't be worried. The only thing you might need to keep in mind is if things don't work out, you can't let it get in the way of anything."

Christopher crossed his arms in front of him. "Of course not."

"Well, since you said Kinsley is important to you, I say go for it. You seem to have your priorities straight and a level head on your shoulders. Just use good common sense."

Sawyer looked at his watch. "It's getting late. I'd better get out of here so I can get home at a decent hour. I'm not going to lie. It's pretty nice to have someone to come home to."

Sawyer reached for his wallet, but Christopher held out a hand. "You came all this way. I've got the tab."

He was relieved that he hadn't seen Miguel tonight. Although it was generous of the guy to cover the bill the night he was there with Kinsley, Miguel's comment about Christopher's money not being any good there made him uncomfortable. He was perfectly prepared to pay his own way. He didn't want to seem like a moocher. In fact, even though he greatly appreciated Miguel's hospitality, he had to admit the thought of Miguel doing so in the future made him uneasy about hanging out at Mendoza's. Christopher's eyes darted back to the phone. Still no response from Kinsley. Then again, his response had been sort of closed-ended. He'd told her he would text her after Sawyer left, which was happening now.

Sawyer stood and so did Christopher. The two shook hands.

"It was great seeing you," said Sawyer. "And thanks for dinner. Next time it's on me."

Christopher clapped him on the back as he walked with him toward the entrance. "Next time, you bring me good news about the air-show fund-raiser and I'll not only buy you dinner, but I'll also throw in a bottle of champagne."

Sawyer laughed. "You better start chilling that bubbly because I'm pretty confident I'll have good news for you soon. Good luck with the girl."

As they were walking out to the parking lot, Christopher ran into Art and Joe, who were on their way inside.

Christopher introduced his cousin to his buddies and after quick small talk Sawyer said good-night and excused himself.

"Should've known you'd already be here," said Joe. "You get an early start on the night? So what are we waiting for? Bring on the ladies."

Funny thing, for the first time ever, Christopher wasn't in the mood to party. He was more eager to get to a quiet spot where he could write down all of the ideas that he and Sawyer had come up with and text Kinsley.

"Actually, I was here for a business meeting," he said. "It's been a long day. I'm beat so I think I'm just going to hit it." He gestured toward the exit.

"Oh, come on, man," said Art. "Just one drink."

Joe elbowed Art. "If we can get a drink down him, he'll start talking to the ladies and end up closing down the place. What do you bet?"

Christopher usually had a good time with these guys. He'd met them through a local men's pick-up basketball league and they'd hit it off straightaway. Maybe it was just his mood, but he really wasn't feeling it tonight. And he didn't like being pressured into staying.

Across the room, he saw Crystal. She looked up, saw him and waved. Then she got up and started walking toward him. Even stranger than not being in the mood to stay, he wasn't in the mood to deal with her tonight, either.

The thought actually made him do a mental double-take. What the hell was wrong with him? His buddies were ready to have a good time. And here was a woman who, for all intents and purposes, was a sure thing.

And he wasn't in the mood for any of it.

"Hey," said Crystal. "I see you finished with your business meeting. Come dance with me."

Joe and Art were standing there pretending to be cool, like they weren't watching him interact with Crystal. And Christopher was willing to wager that if he didn't go home with Crystal tonight, one of them would.

"Normally, I'd love to dance with you," he said to Crystal. "But I have more business I need to take care of. These are my friends Art and Joe. Joe, Art, this is Crystal. I'm sure one of these guys would love to buy you a drink." He dug his car keys out of his pocket and handed his friends a fifty-dollar bill. "Enjoy yourselves, everyone. First round is on me."

Kinsley had just finished washing up her dinner dishes when her cell phone rang at about 8:45 p.m. She knew it would be Christopher before she even looked.

Still, her heart leaped a little bit when she saw his name on her phone's display screen. She didn't even bother to dry her hands before she picked up the phone and accepted the call.

"Hello?" she said, taking care to keep her voice as level as possible.

"I hope I'm not calling too late." His deep voice was like sex. The thought made her blush. Where the heck had *that* come from?

Well, she knew where it came from; she just wished she could put it back in its box so that she could put the lid on tighter and ensure that thoughts like that never got out again.

Remember, last dance. Over. Done. Finito.

Good luck, said an impudent little voice that was probably responsible for unleashing the thought in the first place. *You know you want him.*

"Of course not," she said. "How did the meeting with Sawyer go?"

"The only way it could've gone better is if you would have been there."

"What? And miss all the fun of my statistics class and being a Lamaze coach? Actually, the Lamaze coaching is pretty cool. I'm glad I can be there for Tonya. She doesn't have anybody."

"You've got a really great way with kids, you know?"

She found herself smiling in spite of herself. "Thanks." She didn't quite know what else to say to that. She heard what sounded like a car horn in the distance.

"Are you in your car?" she asked.

"I'm sitting in Mendoza's parking lot."

She hated herself for it, but her heart sank. "Oh, that's right. It's Thursday—ladies' night at Mendoza's." She did her best to put a smile in her voice. "Listen, I won't keep you. Why don't we talk about this tomorrow at the office? Oh, wait, I'm going to be out most of the day. I'm going over to the high school to work with the advisory board and the kids in the Cornerstone Club to finalize the plan for their part at the Spring Fling. I really want them to take ownership of this program. If they do, it will stand a much better chance of taking hold. But listen to me blabbing on. I'm sure you want to get inside. I'll talk to you tomorrow."

"Kinsley, wait. I'm actually leaving Mendoza's. I'm not staying for ladies' night. Sawyer wanted to go there for the tacos. I figured I'd let him choose where we ate since he doesn't get to town very often."

Why was she so relieved to hear this? "Is ladies' night canceled?"

"Canceled? No, why?"

"Well, I can't imagine it going on without you there. I thought you always closed the place down."

He laughed. "No reason to since you're not there."

Against everything she knew was prudent and good for her, she melted a little bit inside.

"Contrary to your etched-in-stone thoughts of me, I'm really not a player," he said. "I don't know what I have to do to make you believe that."

She walked over to the couch and sat down, curling her bare feet beneath her. She was still in the gray skirt and white blouse she'd worn to work. Her apartment suddenly felt stuffy. She reached up and unbuttoned the top two buttons on her blouse.

"I'm not quite sure what I'm supposed to say to that," she said.

"What you can say is that you had as good a time dancing with me at Mendoza's as I had dancing with you."

Her hand fluttered to her throat, lingered there.

"You could say that maybe we could try it again. Say, maybe Saturday night?"

Her fingers pushed aside her blouse's cotton fabric and traced the line of her collarbone. She wasn't sure if it was his voice or his words that made her shiver a little…in a good way…with an anticipation that made her feel naked and vulnerable, that had her rethinking every reason why it was a bad idea to get involved with him.

"Christopher…"

"Yes, I'm here. And since you didn't say no, I'll consider it a yes."

* * *

Even though it was after four o'clock, Kinsley headed back to the office after finishing up with the kids at the high school. She could've gone home. She'd already put in an eight-hour day, but… Okay, if she was going to do this, she at least had to be truthful with herself.

She was going back with the hopes of running into Christopher. After all, if he had been serious about taking her out on Saturday night—tomorrow night—she needed to know where they were going and what they were doing, what time he would pick her up, all the details so that she could get ready. She played a crazy little game with herself when she found herself in a situation and was unsure of what she should do—and she still wasn't quite sure going out with him was such a good idea. After all, what happened at Mendoza's had happened by chance. If he picked her up on Saturday night and took her someplace purely social, it would be a date. Even though their date wasn't until tomorrow, she decided to toss everything up to fate: if it was a good idea to see Christopher socially—to go out with him tomorrow—he would still be at the office. If he wasn't there, well that meant it was not a good idea. If he wasn't there she would cancel the date and explain to him that they needed to keep things platonic. She was usually such a practical person that she only used the toss-it-up-to-fate method of decision-making on the rarest occasions. It was like flipping a coin to help her decide what to do on occasions like this, when her head was telling her one thing and her heart was insisting on another. On one hand, if she got involved with him, it could end in disaster. On the other hand, what if this could be the start of something good. He sure had been trying hard, and she needed to give credit where credit was due.

And there was the fact that she just couldn't stop thinking about him.

When she turned into the Foundation parking lot and saw his car in his reserved parking space, she couldn't breathe for a moment.

There was her answer. She should keep the date. And she was so relieved that she almost shook with joy. Before she got out of the car, she took her compact and lipstick out of her purse and touched up her makeup, then ran her fingers through her hair, gave herself a once-over in the rearview mirror and decided that was as good as it was going to get.

She let herself out of the car, feeling as giddy as a girl who had just been asked to the prom by the captain of the football team. As she walked toward the entrance, she contemplated her strategy—she would go to his office under the guise of discussing what she had accomplished at the high school today and ask him about the fund-raising idea that he and Sawyer had come up with last night.

She actually had a spring in her step as she emerged from the elevator into the third-floor reception area.

"Hi, Bev," she said to the young woman who looked as if she was already starting to pack up and head home for the weekend. But Bev was young and she would learn that when you got a job you really cared about sometimes you had to put in longer hours to get where you wanted to go.

Or you had to come back to the office to find out whether or not you were going to go anywhere that weekend, said the snarky voice in her head.

In the movie in her mind, she reached up and stuffed a sock in her doubting mouth.

"Oh, hey," Bev said. "What are you doing back here? It's nearly five o'clock."

"I know. I need to talk to Christopher. Is he available?"

Kinsley started walking toward his office before Bev had the chance to answer.

"I don't think you should go in there," she said. She looked around the office as if confirming nobody else was within earshot. Still, she lowered her voice to a stage whisper. "He has a woman in there. And she's really, really pretty. She just got here about fifteen minutes ago. I don't know that it's a business thing. But don't you dare say that I said that."

Kinsley's whole body tingled. And not in a good way. It was more like a pang of regret that was trying to undermine her confidence. She took a moment to put things in perspective. Sure it was Friday evening, but why would Christopher have a date meet him at the office? The woman could be a donor. She could be his sister. He had told her he had a sister. Two, in fact. If she stayed out here when the two of them came out of his office he would probably introduce her.

No, that would look contrived and desperate. A little stalker-ish. Instead, she would wait in her office and when she heard them come out she would grab her things and just happen to meet them at the elevator.

Yes, that plan would work.

"Hey, Kins," Bev said. "Could I ask a huge favor? It's like ten minutes to five and I have a date tonight. Is there any way you could cover the phones for me? Since you're gonna be here, anyway…?"

"Sure," Kinsley said. "Just forward the main line back to my office. But answer a question for me. What did she look like?"

Bev pressed some buttons on the phone, then stood there with her purse on her arm, her cell phone in her hand and a baffled look on her face. "I don't know…really pretty…really classy…like she has a lot of money…like somebody he'd take to the symphony or ballet on a Saturday night. You know, that kind of woman."

"Do you think she's here to donate to the Foundation?"

Bev was already edging toward the elevator. "I don't know…. She seemed to be kind of into him."

Bev pushed the elevator button and the door opened immediately. She backed into it. "I've got to go," she said. "Let me know what you find out. Maybe she's his new girlfriend?"

As the elevator doors closed and carried Bev away, Kinsley replayed in her head the conversation she'd had with Christopher last night. He had said that he wasn't staying at the night club because she wasn't there. He'd said that he wanted them to go out again. When she hadn't answered he'd said he would take that as a yes.

Given all that, why would he bring another woman he was interested in to the office? It just didn't make sense.

Kinsley went into her office, left the door open, settled herself at her desk and waited.

About fifteen minutes later, she heard laughter coming from the reception area. She stood and started to grab her purse so that she could go out and make the *accidental* meeting at the elevator happen, but something stopped her—something in the tone of their voices. Something in the way they seemed to be laughing intimately at a private joke…

She dropped her purse on her desk chair and edged her way to the door. She peeked out, hoping Christopher wouldn't see her. If he did she would just say she thought that she was the only one left in the office and… She looked just in time to see Christopher with his hand on the small of a very beautiful woman's back.

"Our dinner reservation is at seven," he said. "We should have time for a drink before they seat us."

As the elevator doors opened, his hand stayed there as he ushered her in. Kinsley ducked back inside her office so that they wouldn't see her when they turned around to face the front.

Standing there alone in the empty office on a Friday night, Kinsley suddenly felt like the biggest fool in the world. So she'd gone against her better judgment and had agreed to go out with Christopher tomorrow night. Here was proof positive that she was simply one of a string of women.

Her rational mind reminded her she had no right to be upset or jealous. She had known all along that this was his M.O. But she couldn't help the way her heart objected. Tomorrow night obviously meant something completely different to her than it did to him.

If she let herself fall for Christopher Fortune any more than she already had, she was setting herself up for a world of heartbreak. She'd grown up with a mother who had been so desperately in love with a man who treated her wrong. Her mom's love for her dad ended up killing her.

Even though Christopher had certainly given no signs of being physically abusive, his fickle ways, his seeming to want only the things that were out of his reach—and then abandoning them when he was finished toying with them—did not make Kinsley feel good.

If she invested any more emotion in him, she would be mentally abusing herself. That wasn't going to happen.

She forwarded the office phones to the answering service, gathered her purse and turned off the office lights, realizing that fate had given her the answer she'd been looking for earlier that evening.

Christopher Fortune had been in the building, but he was emotionally unavailable.

Chapter Nine

Okay, she was avoiding him.

She had been most of the week.

It was Thursday morning and she hadn't seen him in the office since she'd watched him leave with that woman on Friday. She admitted it was a little childish. But she felt a little burned and very foolish for letting her heart control her usually clear head. She needed to put space between them.

When he'd called her, she'd responded by text—except for Saturday and Sunday. She carefully avoided personal topics of conversation—such as *What happened to our date on Saturday? Didn't we have plans, tentative as they were?*

She hadn't bothered to explain that if he wanted to take her out he needed to firm up plans sooner than the day of—and not parade his Friday night date through the office.

Even if their relationship was casual, that was simply bad taste.

Oh, who was she kidding? If she hadn't seen him with that woman she probably would have overlooked his lax planning. But it didn't matter now. It was better that reality, the inconvenient interloper it was, crashed the party sooner rather than later. Now, she was intent on locating the silver lining in the gray cloud that she refused to let rain on her career.

This near miss had been fair warning that dating someone she worked with was simply a bad idea.

It wasn't that every man who took her out had to commit to exclusivity before the first date. But she realized—too late—that what she felt for Christopher was different. She should've known better than to let herself lose control. Playing with Christopher Fortune was like playing with fire. She knew who he was and what he was all about. She knew that she couldn't play by his rules.

It was best to keep their relationship strictly business. That way, no one misunderstood and no one got hurt.

Monday and Tuesday she had conveniently scheduled herself to be out of the office. With a little investigating, Kinsley learned through Bev that Christopher would be out of the office on Wednesday and today. That should be enough time to clear her head and regain her equilibrium. She was professional and she knew she couldn't avoid him forever. After all, the Spring Fling was on Saturday. But everything was in place. She had done her tasks and had discreetly followed up to ensure that he had taken care of everything on his list.

She wasn't surprised to discover that he had.

That's why she chose to focus on the good, the professional side of their relationship, the part that worked. She just needed to remember to not let herself get snared in Christopher's charismatic web.

She had the rest of the day to collect herself. Because he was supposed to be back tomorrow, she planned on emailing him later today and asking if he had time to meet at the fairgrounds Friday afternoon to do a walk-through and preliminary set up for the event. They would be so busy with their booth preparations there would be no time for personal talk. Plus, Christopher was a smart guy—he seemed to catch on quickly. Surely by now he understood that their relationship had been relegated to the "professional zone."

She printed out her to-do list and had just begun checking off items and making notes when she sensed someone standing in the doorway of her office.

Christopher.

Her stomach did a full-fledged triple gainer, and as much as she hated it she audibly inhaled. She bit the insides of her cheeks hard to get her emotions in check.

Act like a professional.

"Hey, stranger," said Christopher. "Just wondering if there's room for the putting green under the tent?"

Kinsley couldn't look him in the eyes. It wasn't very professional, and she knew it. But neither was the way his gaze seemed to be burning into her. She straightened a stack of paper on her desk. She put a few loose pens into her desk drawer. Aligned her coffee mug on the coaster on the edge of her desk.

"The putting green?" Good. Her voice was neutral. "Christopher, you know I was only joking when I suggested you bring it to the Spring Fling. You don't have to do that if you don't want to."

"I know I don't have to," he said.

She picked up her pen and circled an item on her list.

"I figured we could just have a raffle. The kids can put their name into a drawing for prizes when they sign the bullying prevention pledge card—"

"The raffle sounds great. But let's bring the putting green, too. It will be an active visual. We can use it to draw people in. Oh, hey, and I wanted to tell you that I got word earlier this week that not only is Redmond Flight School offering a couple of prizes for us to give away—a couple of glider flights, which the kids should really love—but also everyone over there is behind doing an air-show fund-raiser in the fall. And Susan Eldridge and Julie Fortune were able to snag some gift cards from some of the local restaurants and merchants for us to use as prizes. I'm just blown away by how great and helpful everyone has been. It's a great team, don't you think?"

"Of course. I've always found everyone here to be exceptionally helpful."

"I know. But good teams are hard to find." Something in his voice changed. "When you have one, you should hang on to it."

Oh, no. Here it came.

She decided to head it off before he could shift things into the personal.

"Yes, we are lucky to have such great coworkers, aren't we? And if you'll excuse me, I'm going to go talk to Hank in maintenance about getting some extra chairs for the tent."

She stood, but Christopher closed her office door.

"I called you on Saturday and Sunday, Kinsley. Did you get my messages?"

"I had to go out of town."

"If I didn't know better, I might think you've been avoiding me. We had plans over the weekend. Or so I thought."

"Well, you should have thought about that before you brought your Friday night date to the office. Christopher, you shouldn't have kissed me if you were involved with someone else." The words slipped out before she could stop them. Now she had no choice but to look him square in the eyes.

The sight of him completely upended her equilibrium. She fisted her hands at her side, digging her nails into her palms. It was supposed to distract her from how she always seemed to get drawn in simply by looking at him. Even now, as he stood there looking baffled.

Wow, not only was he a player, but he was a good actor too.

"I don't know what you're talking about," he said. "I'm not involved with anyone else."

Maybe *involved* was overstating it. "Well, you shouldn't have kissed me if you were even dating other people."

"Kinsley, I really have no idea what you're talking about. I mean, sure, I've dated other women in the past, but nobody seriously. You are the first woman I've even considered dating exclusively."

She suddenly felt claustrophobic. Hearing him say the words but knowing they were encased in a lie made her want to run. How could he stand here, look her in the eye and tell her she didn't see what she knew she saw?

At that moment, she realized just how different she and this man who was playing with her heart really were.

"Please don't, Christopher. Don't insult me. I saw you with that woman here at the office on Friday."

Confusion contorted his face. "Nora?"

And now he was going to try and change his tune, try to explain it away, but she wasn't going to have it.

"I have no idea what her name is, but she is beautiful. You have great taste in women—at least outward appearances. But what you don't seem to understand is that *Nora* and I are obviously cut from different material. Women like her might be fine with kissing and keeping it casual, but I'm not. I don't *give myself away.* Not even a kiss. Kisses are intimate, and I don't take intimacy casually."

She seemed to have struck him dumb because all he could do was stand there and stare at her, his lips pressed into a thin line.

"Since we have to work together," she said, "we have to keep things strictly professional, Christopher. Unlike you, I don't have family who can come to my rescue. My contacts aren't unlimited. I need this job."

Christopher looked taken aback, but there was a new light in his eyes.

"Kinsley, Nora Brandt is an etiquette coach. I hired her because I took your advice to heart. I was thinking about how I needed to get better at learning people's names, and that made me wonder about my other social and professional deficiencies. Nora and I went out to dinner Friday night so she could see me in action."

For the love of God, she wanted to believe him.

"But I saw you with your hand on the small of her back. That's pretty intimate."

"Apparently so. She told me as much when we were

in the elevator. Honestly, the entire night was pretty humiliating. I'm not good at this…this." He gestured with both hands, at her, around the office. "I was raised on a ranch. My role models were my buddies and my brothers. We hung out at The Grill and flirted with the same handful of girls who didn't know any better than we did. I have no idea what I'm doing. Sometimes I feel so far out of my element I feel like a total buffoon. So, I hired an etiquette coach to help me. You are so smooth and polished. You deserve to be with someone who is your equal. Someone who doesn't embarrass you like I would."

Kinsley was so stunned that her mouth actually hung open.

Christopher held up a finger.

"Wait just a moment. I can prove it to you."

He pulled a business card from his wallet and handed it to Kinsley. The card had Nora Brandt's photo on it. Sure enough she was the woman Kinsley had seen him with on Friday.

"You can call her if you want. She'll confirm everything."

Now Kinsley was the one who felt like the total buffoon.

"And just so you know, she's married. And even if she wasn't, *she's* not my type at all. There's no other woman in the world I'm interested in right now besides you."

Kinsley had been jealous.

The thought made Christopher smile as he filled the last helium balloon and tied a knot in the stem. Because if she was jealous, that meant she had feelings for him. Even though she was still keeping him at arm's length, the chill had thawed.

There was still a chance, he thought as he tied a ribbon to the balloon and added it to the bunch that would join its twin at the entrance to the tent.

He fully intended to seize that chance and make things work between them.

Today was the day of the Spring Fling. He and Kinsley had met at the fairgrounds early to get everything in place inside the white tents. Hank from maintenance had generously agreed to transport the putting green in his pickup truck. The guy had even taken it upon himself to build a wooden platform to keep the green out of the dirt.

Christopher made a mental note to get Hank a gift card to Red or something else he would enjoy. He had gone out of his way transporting the putting green on his day off. Building the platform was above and beyond.

But Christopher was beginning to learn that was how everything worked at the Foundation. They were all one big family. They helped and supported each other.

After he finished getting the balloons in place, Kinsley introduced him to a young pregnant woman named Tonya Harris who had agreed to help them today. He realized she was the teenager Kinsley was coaching through Lamaze.

Along with their anti-bullying message, the Foundation was also teaching self-esteem. The two went hand-in-hand. If a teen had low self-esteem, he or she might be more apt to fall prey to bullies. Bullies didn't all come in the same package. Sometimes the bully was the enemy. Other times the bully might be the boyfriend who pressured his girlfriend to have sex against her better judgment.

If they could save even one young woman from end-ing up pregnant and alone like Tonya, then he would consider this program a success.

He admired the way Kinsley spoke to the teenager like a friend, asking her advice on the placement of chairs and even entrusting her with manning the table where kids would pick up information and sign the anti-bullying pledge cards.

By the time the Spring Fling was open and running at nine o'clock, they actually looked as if they knew what they were doing. Music was playing from a sound system he had secured through one of his contacts. The putting green, which he was in charge of, looked pretty cool on its custom-made, green-painted plywood perch. Kinsley had wrapped a large rectangular box, where the kids would enter the drawing for the various prizes they were offering.

He thought back to Thursday when he'd been talking about what a great team they made. It was the truth. Look at everything that they had accomplished working together in such a short time. They seemed to have the same vision. There was a synergy between them, and if he had to spend an entire year proving himself to her, he would.

She was worth it.

As Christopher was demonstrating proper putting technique to a young boy who was frustrated because he couldn't seem to sink a hole in one, Lily Cassidy Fortune, who had created the Foundation in memory of her late husband, Ryan, who had succumbed to a brain tumor nine years ago, walked up and beamed at him, just as the boy sank his first putt. The kid let out a cheer and Lily clapped for him. After Christopher handed him his prize of two movie tickets and directed him to the table where Tonya could help him with the pledge card, Lily greeted Christopher as warmly as if he were part of her own family. It dawned on him that they actually were related somewhere down the line.

"I came over here purposely to shake the hand of the person who has been doing such a great job getting the word out to the community about the Foundation," she said. She gestured around the tent. "This is just magnificent. It's exactly the direction that I am proud to see the Foundation going. I know my Ryan would've been proud of this, too."

A pang of guilt spurred on by her genuine affection and appreciation stabbed Christopher. He glanced over at Kinsley and saw her helping a kid fill out an entry form for the drawing. There was no way he could stand here and take all the credit, especially when she was over there doing all the work.

"I appreciate you coming by, Mrs. Fortune," he said.

She put a hand on his arm. "Oh, please, do call me Lily. All my family does."

Christopher smiled at her generosity. "I would be honored to, thank you. If you have a moment, I want you to meet somebody who has been instrumental in putting together what you see here, and, I suspect, everything you've heard about the community outreach program."

"I absolutely have time."

Christopher motioned her over to the table where Kinsley sat with Tonya. Kinsley looked up and smiled at the two of them, genuine warmth radiating from her eyes.

"Lily Cassidy Fortune," he said, giving Kinsley a significant look. "I would like for you to meet Kinsley Aaron. She is an outreach coordinator for the Foundation and has tirelessly worked to put together everything you see today and more."

Christopher saw a faint hint of pink color Kinsley's cheeks as she stood and offered her hand to Lily.

"It is such an honor to meet you, Mrs. Fortune," she said. "I'm proud to work for such an incredible organization. The Foundation took a chance on me when I had very little experience—I'm still going to school. Their faith in me has made me want to work even harder to connect the Foundation with the Red Rock community. However, you need to know that this guy right here is doing incredible work. He is making a real difference. He has a great vision and nice way about him that everybody seems to love."

Kinsley's eyes sparkled good-naturedly, but the real meaning of what she said wasn't lost on Christopher. He smiled back at her and quirked a brow, sending a message that she was the only person he wanted to love.

Chapter Ten

Christopher was right—they had been working hard. The turnout at the booth had been better than Kinsley had ever dreamed it would be.

When they started, she was afraid they were going to have prizes to spare. But because of the fabulous response, they were having to tell the kids that they would do the drawings on the hour and that they had to be present to win. At the start of each hour, kids of all ages would cluster around the tent to hear the name of the lucky person whose name had been drawn from the box.

Each time a name was announced the crowd would cheer wildly. It struck Kinsley that even this was bringing the kids together. There seemed to be no rivalry or resentment from those who didn't win. Of course, Kinsley always made sure to announce that they could win prizes, like T-shirts, rubber bracelets and water bottles, instantaneously by signing the pledge card. Maybe these kids just needed a common meeting ground.

The crowd was dispersing after the most recent drawing, and for the first time since they had arrived Kinsley had a chance to step back and look around. Every single volunteer who had signed up to work the booth had shown up. Most of them were even hanging around after their shift was over. In fact, right now they had a plethora of help.

So when Christopher suggested that they take a break, she only hesitated for a moment. She was thirsty and what she wouldn't give for a bite of the cotton candy that she had seen the kids enjoying.

"Okay, but only if you promise we can go get some cotton candy," she said.

"Ahh, cotton candy. The way to Kinsley's heart."

She tried to ignore the butterflies that swarmed when he said that. She was beginning to realize he was an insufferable flirt. He couldn't help it any more than he could help the fact that his hair was blond and his eyes were a shade of blue that matched the clear spring sky.

She couldn't seem to help the fact that she noticed things like that about him. But what she had also noticed, she thought as they walked away from the Foundation tent, was that he had a much bigger heart than she had initially given him credit for. A lot of his bravado was to cover the insecurities of his upbringing.

She silently vowed to never judge another person until she learned their story. After all, who would've known that slick-dressing, fancy-car-driving Christopher Fortune had actually come from very humble roots? He may have been a Fortune by name, but his modest upbringing really was at the heart of everything he did.

After they grabbed some cotton candy to share, Christopher won her a giant teddy bear at the arcade shooting gallery.

"You surprise me every day," she said. "I never imagined that you'd ever even held a gun, much less that you knew how to use one. You're a pretty sharp shot."

"And that's just the start of my good qualities," he said, wiggling his eyebrows comically. "If you don't believe me, just give me a chance to prove myself."

His free arm, the one that wasn't holding the teddy bear, lightly brushed against hers as they walked side by side through the fair. The skin-on-skin contact made her shudder with a strange anticipation and an emotion that she couldn't remember ever feeling.

"You know what I've always wanted to do?" Christopher said.

"What's that?"

"Ride on the Ferris wheel with a beautiful woman," he said.

Kinsley rolled her eyes at him. "You are too cheesy for words sometimes," she said.

He laughed and and nudged her with his arm. This time the contact was on purpose. She couldn't help but wonder if he'd felt the same electricity the last time their arms brushed.

They made small talk as they made their way over to the Ferris wheel. By a stroke of luck the line was negligible. They were seated and the ride was in motion in less than five minutes.

With the giant teddy bear at her feet, the warm sun on her face and Christopher sitting next to her, Kinsley couldn't remember ever feeling so content or so free. When their car stopped at the top of the wheel, she felt as if she could see all the way to San Antonio. It was magical up there.

The car rocked a little and Kinsley gripped the safety bar that stretched across their legs.

"Don't worry," he said, stretching an arm around her and pulling her to him. "I'll keep you safe."

It was as if they were alone in their own little world. Kinsley leaned into Christopher, relishing how they seemed to fit so perfectly together. And when Christopher lowered his head to taste her lips, she didn't resist. In fact, she met him halfway.

All too soon, the car was moving again, breaking the spell and propelling them back into the real world. The only thing different was that Christopher did not remove his arm from around her shoulder until they stepped off the ride.

She wished that they could continue strolling around the fair hand in hand, stealing kisses and sharing cotton candy. But work called. They strolled back to the booth, not touching, looking as platonic as two coworkers ever looked walking with a giant teddy bear between them.

"You're an only child, right?" Christopher asked.

"Yes."

"How did you get to be so good with kids? You really are a natural. I thought only children were supposed to have a hard time empathizing with others. And that was supposed to be a joke but it didn't come out very well."

She smiled as he pretended to knock himself up the side of his head with the palm of his hand. "Just because I was an only child doesn't mean I can't relate to people, Christopher."

"What I'm trying so ineloquently to say is that I love watching you with the kids. They really listen to you and respect you. I think kids have a natural B.S. meter. They can tell when someone is sincere and when they're not. You're really good at what you do."

Her natural inclination was to make a joke out of his compliment or to spit out some snarky retort. But the words got caught in her throat. All she could manage was a choked "Thank you."

She cleared her throat. "I feel so lucky to do what I do, to have a job where I have an opportunity to make a real difference."

Christopher smiled. "Only-child anomaly number two—you're not selfish, either."

She felt her cheeks warming. "Would you stop with the compliments, already?" She shot him a smile so that he knew she was kidding. "Thank you. But good grief, if you keep this up my head is going to swell as big as the bouncy castle over in the kids' area."

"If it does, you'll have good reason."

"Christopher…"

"How did you meet Tonya?"

She smiled at the mention of the sweet teenage girl. "I met her at the high school a few months ago when I was there doing a presentation for Principal Cramer. She had just found out she was pregnant. Her parents had kicked her out of the house, and she really didn't have anywhere else to go. The boyfriend lives over in San Antonio and dumped her as soon as he found out they were going to be parents. She had slept at the bus station the night before and had almost gotten on a bus to San Antonio to try to talk to the boyfriend. The only thing that stopped her was that she didn't have enough money for a ticket. She went to school the next day because she didn't have any place else to go. I feel like it was divine intervention that I was there for her."

Christopher raked his hand through his hair. It wasn't a gesture of vanity as much as what seemed to be an expression of disbelief. The astonishment in his eyes spoke volumes.

"She broke down that day and cried and cried, right in my arms. I cried with her. And then I told her that she was allowed to have a twenty-four-hour pity party, but after that she needed to be strong for both her sake and the baby's. She stayed at my apartment that night and I went with her to talk to her parents the next day. They let her come back and that's where she is now. Her grades are good and she'll miss a little school when she has the baby in about three months, but I've already talked to the principal and we've arranged for her to do schoolwork while she's out. Her mother is going to watch the baby during the day, and she might have to get an after-school job to afford diapers, but she should be okay. I just keep telling her the most important thing is that she can't get behind on her schoolwork and she can't just give up. If she doesn't, everything will be fine."

Kinsley shrugged at a loss for what else to say.

"Isn't that what everybody needs sometimes?" Christopher said. "For somebody to tell them that they can do it? That the road ahead may be hard, but if they're persistent everything will be fine. Kinsley, you may have saved that girl's life. You helped her smooth things over with her family so that she has the support she needs until she graduates and gets a full-time job."

She didn't know what to say. So she didn't say anything for a long while as they walked. Then she identified one of the feelings knotted in her belly. It was shame.

"I meant what I said to Lily Fortune earlier. You really have done a good job. I didn't give you enough credit when you first started. I thought you were just trading on your name and your good looks."

"Oh, well, you've got to cut a guy a break in the trading-on-his-looks department." He shrugged and did a Justin Bieber-ish shake of his head, despite the fact that his close-cropped hair didn't move.

She knew he was kidding, but she couldn't resist egging him on. "And here I thought you were the humble Fortune—"

Her words were eclipsed by a commotion coming from the Foundation tent. She and Christopher exchanged a concerned glance and jogged over to the tent to see what was happening.

A sluggish-looking teenage boy was standing in an aggressive pose over Tonya, who was still seated at the table. The two were exchanging heated words. When Tonya stood and backed away from the guy, he reached out a hand, grabbed the back of her T-shirt and pulled hard. Tonya stumbled and immediately put her hands up, as if to shield herself from a blow. That's all it took for Kinsley to break into a sprint and put herself between Tonya and the boy.

"What the heck do you think you're doing?" she said to the guy. She got right in his face, determined to prove that she wasn't afraid of him. She looked the thug square in the eyes but kept her voice level and low as she spoke with authority. "You need to leave now. *Now.* Or I am going to call the police and have them escort you out of here."

A cocky sneer spread slowly over the guy's face. He was tall, but he was skinny. And although she didn't want to lay a hand on him, she was perfectly prepared to practice a few self-defense moves that she had learned over the years.

"I'm just here to talk to my baby mama," he said.

"It didn't look like you were talking to her. It looked like you were upsetting her."

"I don't need you interfering with me and my family," the thug said.

Kinsley sneered right back at him. "Oh, then you must be Jared. I've heard about you, Jared."

The kid seemed to flinch at the revelation that Kinsley knew him. "I think Tonya's dad would like to have a conversation with you. In fact, he's supposed to be stopping by any minute. Why don't you have a seat over there and wait for them?"

Kinsley could honestly say it was the first time she had seen all the blood drain from a person's face. Jared didn't say another word. He turned and sprinted away. It was only then that Kinsley realized that Christopher was standing right next to her, looking as if he was ready to spring into action if Jared had made one false move.

He squeezed her arm. "Why don't you see to Tonya? I'll deal with the crowd." He motioned with his head to the knot of onlookers that had gathered to watch the confrontation.

"Thank you," she said, giving him a squeeze back.

Tonya was huddled in the far corner of the tent, sobbing.

"Honey, I'm so sorry. Did he hurt you?"

Tonya shook her head as tears streamed down her face.

"What did he want?" Kinsley asked this question only to find out if Jared had been coming around other times or if this happened to be a chance encounter.

"Nothing," Tonya said. "He was just being disgusting. He's here at the Spring Fling with his buddies and he just wanted to act like a jerk."

And nobody had stepped in to help her.

"How long had you been standing there before I got back?"

Tonya shrugged as she swiped at her tears. Kinsley reached into her pocket and handed the girl a tissue. The girl blew her nose.

"He first saw me about ten minutes after you'd gone on break. He and his friends came up to me. I thought he wanted to say hi, but he called me a whore, asked me why I was here. He said they didn't allow whores at the Spring Fling. Then he walked away laughing with his friends. He came back just before you did."

Kinsley's mouth went dry.

"I'm so sorry this happened. But I don't think he's going to bother you anymore. If he does, you need to tell someone."

A dozen questions darted through her mind—at the top of the list was whether this was the first time she'd seen him since she told him about the baby and whether he had ever hit her in the past. His aggressive posture and Tonya's reaction made Kinsley wonder, but now wasn't the time to ask her. She gathered Tonya in her arms and let her cry on her shoulder, gently patting her on the back the same way she had the first day they'd met.

When Tonya's father arrived, she would let him know that Jared had been hassling her.

The girl needed to know she didn't have to put up with that kind of treatment. She needed to know she deserved better. Once she had calmed down, they would talk about that.

But there was one thing she needed to know right now. "Sweetie, did anyone try to help you? Did anyone tell him to go away?"

"No."

That was the crux of the matter. That's why they needed to educate people about taking a stand to help others. Kinsley focused on the clinical side of it because if she thought about all those people standing there looking on and no one caring enough to get involved, she would be sobbing as hard as Tonya was. How could people be so heartless? To stand there while an innocent girl was being verbally attacked. Who knows what might have happened if she and Christopher hadn't come back when they did.

She squeezed her eyes shut to dam the tears that were welling and to try and erase the image of her father swinging and hitting her mother when she had jumped between them, just as she had jumped between Tonya and Jared.

A few hours later, it was time for the Spring Fling to close. The booth was empty except for Christopher and Kinsley. Tonya's father had come to get her as soon as Kinsley had called him. She had sent home all of her volunteers after they had put in such a long day's work. There wasn't much to break down now, only the chairs and the tables, which they just needed to fold up and set aside so that Hank could come by tomorrow morning and load them along with the tent into his truck.

"What did Tonya's father say?" Christopher asked.

Christopher kept a respectable distance when Mr. Harris had come by to collect his daughter.

"He said he was going to talk to the sheriff about a restraining order," Kinsley said. "I think that's a good idea."

Her voice cracked on the last words. It was probably the combination of fatigue and the letdown after the adrenaline rush, but suddenly all the tears that she'd been able to contain while she was comforting Tonya threatened to break through. If they did, she was afraid she might not stop crying.

"You were the epitome of grace under pressure," Christopher said.

Kinsley opened her mouth to say, "No," but the words lodged in her throat as tears broke free and rolled down her cheek. She turned her head, hoping that Christopher wouldn't see.

"Hey—" he said, putting a gentle hand on her shoulder. "Everything is going to be okay."

She wished she could believe him, but for girls like Tonya and for women like her mother, nothing ever turned out okay. The tears crested and streamed. The harder she tried to stop them, the harder she cried.

The tables and chairs could wait.

Kinsley could not.

Christopher had to get her out of there and to a place where she felt safe enough to let out whatever it was that had her so tied up in knots. The episode with Tonya and Jared was upsetting, but she'd handled it well. However, it had obviously brought up something else.

He hoped she would let down her walls and trust him enough to let him help her.

He saw two boys who had been helping at the Foundation tent that afternoon. Now they were just hanging around. He offered to pay them twenty dollars each if they would stack the chairs and break down the tables and leave them over by the tree. The two jumped at the chance to make an easy buck, freeing Kinsley and him to leave.

She seemed much too upset to drive, so Christopher was relieved when she allowed him to take her home. He told her he would pick her up in the morning and they would come and get her car then. Just to ease her mind, he phoned the fairgrounds security office and informed them they would be back to get the car tomorrow.

By the time they had gotten to her apartment, Kinsley had composed herself. Even so, he tenderly helped her upstairs, but just as he expected, once they were inside, she tried to downplay what happened.

The walls were firmly back in place.

"Kinsley, you don't have to do this with me," Christopher insisted. "You're not an island. You don't have to go this alone—whatever it is that is torturing you. Haven't we gone beyond that?"

He reached out and tucked a strand of hair behind her ear.

"Talk to me," he said.

She was silent for a moment as they sat together on the couch. Christopher was determined to not fill the silence. It worked.

"I told you that both of my parents are dead," Kinsley said in a small voice.

Christopher nodded.

"It was my father's doing. Well, mostly. He drank himself to death, and my mother never recovered. It's as if she died from a broken heart. Not because she loved him. Her heart broke because of the way he had treated her. He was the quintessential bully, made her believe that she was worthless. No one should have to live that way."

Listening to the words, Christopher felt all the blood drain from his face. He reached out and took Kinsley's hand in silent support.

"I couldn't do anything to help her," she said. "I guess I thought she would heal, that her life would get better after he was gone. But she didn't, she just wasted away. And died. As I was growing up, as far back as I can remember my father always belittled my mother, and she was defenseless against his words—and sometimes his fists. He had such an anger problem. He thought I had a smart mouth when I would stand up for her, so he'd come at me, and my mother would put herself between us and bear the brunt of his anger so that I could get away. She just let him treat her that way."

He squeezed her hand and shut his eyes for a moment. When he opened them, he said, "Kinsley, I am so sorry."

She shook her head. "Please don't feel sorry for me. I don't want anyone's pity. Sure I wish I could've done things differently. I wish I could go back and force my mom to move out, to get away from him, but I can't and I know that. I made a decision long ago, Christopher, not to let my past define me. But it does inform my choices."

"Is that why you were so quick to put yourself in between Tonya and Jared?"

And why you tend to keep people at arm's length.

She nodded.

He pulled her into his arms and held her, just held her, for the longest time.

"I am so sorry for what you went through," he whispered in her ear. "But I'm not sorry for who you've become. You are one of the strongest, most amazing people I have ever met in my entire life."

He leaned his head in so that his cheek was on hers. The next thing he knew her mouth, soft, warm and inviting, had found his.

It vaguely registered that he shouldn't be doing this—

she was vulnerable right now. But he was kissing her and she was kissing him back.

Her lips tortured and tempted him more than they satisfied his craving for her. As he sat there with his arms around her, the feel of her lips on his urged him to lean in closer. Raw need swirled inside him, as if taking possession of her might bind them and fix everything that was broken.

A moan deep in his throat escaped as desire coursed through him, a yearning only intensified by the feel of her lips. His one lucid thought as Kinsley melted into him was the taste of her: sweet as spun sugar and candy apples and something warm...like cinnamon and sunshine.

It made him reel.

For a few glorious seconds he never wanted to breathe on his own again. He could be perfectly content right here with her in his arms for the rest of his life.

His hands slid down to her waist and held her firmly against him as his need for her grew and pulsed.

He slowly released her, staying forehead to forehead while the heat between them lingered, drawing him to her almost magnetically. He reached out and ran the pad of his thumb over her bottom lip.

"I'd better go," he whispered. "If I don't...you know what's bound to happen."

"I know," she said. "And I want you to stay."

Caught in the twilight between craving and clarity, he claimed one more kiss of her lips but knew this was as far as they should go. As much as he wanted her, it wouldn't be right.

"I don't want to force things," he said, his lips still a breath away from hers.

"You and I both know we've been moving toward this

moment for weeks—for months," she said. "Probably since the first moment we saw each other."

Her words, the nearness of her, sent heat rippling through his body. As she gently nipped at his bottom lip, he had to fight the desire to take her right there, right now, but in a way that would reach back through space and time and make right all the wrongs and ugliness that had ever darkened her world.

Tonight felt different.

This *thing* between them felt deeper and undeniably right. For the first time in a long time—maybe ever—his heart was no longer his own. Her essence had infused his senses. All the Fortunes' money couldn't buy what he'd found in her.

Then those lips that had been driving him crazy took possession of his once again, and he knew there was no turning back from what was about to happen.

They were inevitable.

Chapter Eleven

Kinsley got to her feet and took Christopher's hand. If this was going to happen, she was going to have to prove to him she wasn't simply seeking sanctuary in his body. She needed to show him that she was truly ready.

She led him to the bedroom.

It had been a long time since she'd allowed herself to fully want, to fully trust, but all that mattered was how she needed this man. His evident need for her made her feel powerful and desirable. Strong and beautiful. No one had ever made her feel like this before.

Piece by piece their clothes fell away until they stood naked in front of each other in the dim light of the bedroom lit by moonlight filtering in through the sheer curtains. His gaze searched her face as if he were giving her one last chance to protest.

Not a chance.

As if reading her mind, he walked her backward to the bed and lowered her onto it. Climbing in beside her, he stretched out, propping his head on his free hand to look into her eyes.

She rolled over to face him so that their lips were a whisper away. She wanted him to see that this was exactly what she wanted. He reached out and smoothed her hair away from her face, then traced a finger down to her breasts. He smoothed his palm over the sensitive skin, making her inhale sharply.

"You are so beautiful," he said. "I can't tell you how long I've wanted this...wanted us."

He closed the distance between them, allowing no room for doubt. Her lips were still swollen and tender from kissing him earlier, but still she opened her mouth to let him all the way in.

He responded by rolling her onto her back and gently nudging her legs apart. He covered her with his body as she ran her hands down his arms, then up his back as he settled himself on her, positioning himself so that his hips were square to hers. The feel of him on top of her released all the desire and longing that had been bottling up in her since the day she'd first realized that she wanted him.

She tried to stifle a groan that bubbled up in her throat as she savored the heat that coursed between them. She reveled in the feel of him, in the anticipation of the imminent joining of their bodies.

It had been such a long time since she'd felt this way about anyone, since she'd allowed herself to lose control and trust someone like she trusted him.

It was good that they'd talked tonight, that she'd opened up to him. It was cathartic, as if trusting him with her past had cleared a path to the future.

She wasn't sure what was going to happen after tonight, but she wasn't going to think about that now. All she cared about was the tender way he was kissing her neck as she lolled her head to the side to give him easier access. Now, his lips were trailing a path over her collarbones, then dipping down into the valley between her breasts.

One thing she had learned from Christopher was that you had to seize every moment, every opportunity and live. Until now, she hadn't been able to do that. But tonight she was in the here and now. Tonight, she intended to make love to him as if there would never be another moment like this one.

His kisses had found their way to her abdomen and were circling her belly button. Then he took a detour and kissed the insides of her thighs. She inhaled sharply and her eyes widened.

"Why did we wait so long for this?" Her voice was soft and breathless in the darkness.

"I don't know, but I can promise you it will be worth the wait." He flashed a wicked smile at her as he climbed back toward her. With a firm, quick move he pulled her on top of him. She could feel the hard length of him and she had to fight the urge to slide her body down and take him inside of her.

She drew in a jagged breath, determined to not rush things. Determined to savor every last delicious second of their first time together.

"But if you've changed your mind, I can stop," he said. "Are you sure about this?"

She nodded, then kissed him lightly on the mouth.

"I want you so badly, I can't think of anything else. So, if you're sure, then—"

"Shhh..." She pressed her finger to his lips. "I'm sure. Kiss me. Make love to me. Let's let what's in the past stay in the past. We can worry about tomorrow...tomorrow. Because tonight, I'm really glad we're right here."

He kissed her softly, then he slowly spread his hands over her breasts before gently cupping them. She was beautiful, all curves and legs and porcelain skin. He marveled at the ivory breasts in his hands and reverently closed his mouth over a nipple.

The sound of her sigh made him want her all the more.

He stretched out on top of her, gently nudging her legs apart with his knee. But then he felt her stiffen. She bit her lip and looked at him as if there was something she needed to say but couldn't find the words.

Had she changed her mind?

"What's wrong?" he asked, smoothing the back of his hand over her cheek.

She bit her bottom lip. "It's been a long time since I've been with anyone. So I'm not on birth control."

He bit back a curse. How could he have been so damn stupid? He was always cautious. He never had unprotected sex. It was a chance he wouldn't take for so many different reasons. Reasons that could justify a whole new division at the Foundation. Yet, tonight, being here with her so unexpectedly...wanting her as badly as he did, he'd pushed toward this coupling without thinking things through. Mainly because he hadn't been so presumptuous to think that he'd find himself in her bed.

"Oh...well...wow." He pulled himself off her and shifted onto his side so that he could look at her. He definitely needed some space, some room to cool off. "I don't have anything, either."

He cursed silently for not being prepared because he wanted her so much it almost caused him physical pain. He hoped it didn't show on his face as he stared into her beautiful, tormented blue eyes.

As she lay there illuminated by the moonlight filtering in through the slats in the plantation shutters, he realized he'd probably never seen her look quite so beautiful. That's when he knew…being here with her like this… holding her, feeling the warmth of her against him was all he needed.

"We don't have to make love tonight. We can just hold each other…or do other things. I can pick up some condoms tomorrow."

Never in her life had she experienced the perfect blend of euphoria and disappointment.

Euphoria because Christopher didn't have protection ready and waiting in his wallet or wherever grown men kept them these days. It meant that he wasn't prepared for a spur of the moment encounter, which put her mind at ease, and it showed that he cared about her and about his own health. He wasn't willing to have unprotected sex.

But she was also disappointed because she wanted him so badly that she… Okay, now she was blushing.

"So, here we are," he said, drawing in a deep breath. Clearly, this sudden one hundred miles per hour to zero stop was just as jarring for him as it was for her.

He made a pained noise as he adjusted his position on the bed.

"So, here we are," she said.

He raked his hand through his hair. "Not to bring up a sore subject, but does this prove to you that I'm not as big a player as you think I am?"

She ran her fingers over the hair on his chest. His perfectly natural chest was almost as sexy as his broad shoulders, which she touched appreciatively.

"Honey, if I still believed you were a player, you wouldn't be here naked in my bed."

"Touché."

He looked almost edible lying there propped up on his side, watching her with his sexy eyes. She didn't feel the need to cover up or hide from him. In fact, she loved the fact that, judging by his body language, he obviously liked what he saw.

"So I gather you must not have been a Boy Scout," she said.

He grinned. "Ahh, because I'm not prepared." He laughed. "Actually, I *was* a Scout, way back when. I guess I'm a bit rusty in the preparedness department these days. But don't tell anyone because I may have to give back my merit badge."

"You can always earn that badge back."

"Oh, yeah? Exactly what did you have in mind?"

She ran her hand down the length of his body until she found his manhood. She touched him, happy to see that he was still every bit as ready to go as he had been before they'd been forced to stop.

"How do you feel about going and getting something for us? There's a twenty-four-hour drugstore two blocks from here. Will you do it? Please?"

He pursed his lips, and at first he seemed uncertain. For a moment she thought he might say no. But then he leaned in and feathered a kiss onto her lips before he lifted himself off the bed and got dressed.

He was back within ten minutes.

While he was gone, Kinsley opened a bottle of wine and lit some candles.

She handed him a glass when he came into the bedroom. "I was going to say that this deed deserved another kind of merit badge," he said as he sat on the edge of the bed, "but I see that you're way ahead of me."

She smiled. "So kiss me."

He complied, kissing her for a long time. Leisurely and thorough kisses that had her wondering, once again, if he had changed his mind while he was out and decided to take things slowly. He was still dressed even though he was stretched out beside her on the bed.

She ran her hand along the waistband of his blue jeans, tearing at the fabric of his shirt until her fingers struck gold…bare skin. He helped her by drawing it up and over his head.

She sighed as she drank in the raw beauty of him. When she straddled him, she could feel his erection through his pants. The thought of his body—so sexy and large—moving inside her ignited a slow burn in her belly. She wanted him more now than when he'd first touched her.

She ran both hands over his abs, up his chest and out onto his well-defined biceps. And, hello, there were those shoulders. They were broad and ropy, making his torso taper into a manly vee that disappeared beneath the waistband of his jeans. Those jeans.

They were the only thing that still stood between them.

She inhaled sharply.

Pace yourself.

She steadied herself by allowing her hands to travel

back down over his abs, memorizing his form and the feel of the muscles under her hands.

She was so caught up in the beauty and feel of him, of his skin on her skin, that she was a little startled when he rolled her over and his hands did the exploring. They glided over her hips, down to her thighs and dipped between them.

This was really going to happen. She was ready and hyperaware of every breath, every kiss, every touch. When his hand found her most vulnerable spot, she shivered with anticipation. She noticed that his body seemed to tremble, too.

She put a little space between them and slowly unzipped his jeans. Together they got him out of his pants and his underwear. Finally, when nothing stood between them, she reached out and brushed her fingertips over his manhood. His body shuddered. He inhaled a sharp breath and his body arched slightly. Even though she'd already gotten a good look at him, she devoured his male glory with her eyes, from his flat, muscled stomach… up farther to his biceps and his shoulders…to his throat and the chiseled planes of his face. She stroked him and learned every inch of him, committing his body to memory, but he didn't let her linger for long. He pulled away and picked up the condom packet, ripping it open. As she watched him put the condom on the generous length of his maleness, she thought she would go over the edge before they'd even began. Once everything was in place, he settled himself between her legs. She welcomed him by opening her thighs so that their bodies could join.

The physical sensations of what was happening made her shudder with excitement. He entered her with a tender, unhurried push. The heat that radiated from him seeped into her. His body was stiff as he gently inched forward, going so very slowly and being so careful. As her body adjusted to welcome him, she joined him in a slow rocking rhythm.

"Christopher," she whispered. "Oh... Christopher..."

Her sighs were lost in his kiss. He touched her with such care and seemed to instinctively know what her body wanted.

Pleasure began to rise and she angled her hips up to intensify the sensation. Their union seemed so very right that she cried out from the sheer pleasure of it.

She wanted him to feel good, too. She needed to touch him, to give him the same pleasure he was giving her. So she slid her hand between their bodies, reaching for him, wanting to heighten his pleasure. But he grabbed her wrist and held her hand firmly.

"Not yet," he said.

"Why?" she asked.

"Because. Just...not...yet." His breathlessness matched her own. "When you touch me, you make me...crazy. And this...this time is for you."

He stretched her arms up over her head and held them there as he rocked her toward her first release. As spasms of ecstasy overtook her body, his lips reclaimed hers.

The gentle, almost reverent way he touched her proved that he had been worth waiting for...but his hunger for her was never so evident as when he came up for air and devoured her with voracious eyes.

She couldn't get enough of his touch. As if he read her mind, he drove into her with such intensity she fisted her hands into the bed sheets and gasped, arching against him, propelled by the pulsing heat that was growing and throbbing inside her.

"Let yourself go," he said, his voice hoarse and husky. "Just let go, Kinsley."

Maybe it was the heat of his voice in her ear; more likely it was the way he made her body sing with his touch, but the next thing she knew he had driven her over the edge for the second time that night.

Again, he wrapped his arms around her, holding her tightly, protectively, until she had ridden out the wave.

She buried her face in his chest, breathing in the scent of him, of their joining, needing to get as close to him as possible. He continued to hold her tight. She lost herself again in his broad shoulders and the warmth of his strong arms.

"How was that?" His voice was a throaty rasp.

When she lifted her head and looked at him, his eyes searched her face.

"It was great. Really, breathtakingly great."

He smiled. "And I'm not finished yet."

The feel of his bare skin against hers almost put her into sensory overload.

She was so aware of him, of the two of them fused so closely that it seemed they were joined body and soul.

Christopher buried his head in the curve of her neck and let out a deep moan.

She eased her palms down his back, kissed him hard and fast and then things got a little crazy as she wrapped her legs around his waist and dug her nails into his shoulders. He didn't seem to mind how tightly she was clinging to him. So she held him in place by the shoulders and shifted under him. The way he groaned was so delicious that she arched beneath him again, drawing him deeper inside.

* * *

At that moment, staring down into her clear eyes, his body joined with hers, Christopher felt the mantle of his life shift. All of a sudden, without explanation, everything was different.

How could that happen now when it had never happened before?

Because he'd never been in love before now.

He was in love with Kinsley's laugh and her mind and the way she was able to set him straight without making him feel as if he'd been lambasted. He loved the way she felt in his arms right now, the smell of her smooth skin and the way she gazed up at him with a certain look in her eyes that was equal parts courage and vulnerability. It was everything he already knew about her and all the things he had yet to discover. He wanted to be the first face she saw in the morning and the last face she saw before she closed her eyes and drifted off to sleep at night. He wanted to be the shoulder she cried on and the lips she kissed.

He wanted to prove to her that all men weren't like her father, and she deserved someone who was crazy about her, someone who adored her the way she deserved to be loved.

He wanted to show her that love didn't have to hurt. The only problem was the prospect of doing that, rendering his heart that vulnerable, leaving it in someone else's hands, scared him to death.

But it was too late now. Judging by the way he felt, he had a feeling he'd already passed the point of no return.

"Christopher?" Kinsley's eyes searched his face. "Are you…okay?"

"I am absolutely better than okay." He kissed her

deeply, pulling her to him so tightly that every inch of their bodies were merged. He hadn't particularly cared how close he'd felt to other women he'd been intimate with. But as he built up to the pace that would simultaneously transport Kinsley and him to nirvana, he wanted to see her face. He needed a one hundred percent connection. Not just body to body, but eye to eye and soul to soul.

It didn't take long before their bond, coupled with the rhythmic motion of their bodies, carried them over the edge together. As he lay with her, sweaty and spent, he cradled her against him.

As they'd made love, three words had been darting around inside his head. Now they'd somehow found their way to the tip of his tongue.

Oh, man.... Don't do that, he thought. *You're caught up in the moment. Don't say things you don't mean.*

The problem was, he did mean it. With all his soul.

Even so, meaning it and following through with the implications of *I love you* were two very different things.

Kinsley rolled over onto her stomach and looked up at him. "Are you really okay?"

He wanted to tell her exactly how he felt. Except when he opened his mouth all that came out was, "I've never been better."

Christopher wasn't used to being in this position of vulnerability. Since he'd been in Red Rock, he'd been used to being in command. But this woman lying in his arms had changed everything.

Frankly, it scared him to death.

Chapter Twelve

Christopher didn't find his way home until late Sunday night. And that was only because he didn't have any suitable work clothes over at her place.

Once he was at home, with a little space to digest what had happened between them, he realized two very important things about himself: that he was in love with Kinsley, even if he didn't know how to tell her, and that he needed to be the one to reach out to his father and set their relationship on the road to right.

Funny, last week if someone had told him that falling in love would change him so much that he'd be willing to extend the olive branch to Deke, he would've told them to go to hell.

But here he was, at nine o'clock on Sunday night, staring at his cell phone as he dialed his parents' number.

He had to do it now before he changed his mind or the spell that Kinsley had cast on him wore off.

Somehow, he didn't believe that this call would do any good. His old man was as stubborn as a bulldog that had clamped down on a stick. Once Deke sank his teeth into something there was no prying it loose. Everything in his world was black-and-white. He wasn't about to change his mind about his son.

How his sweet mother had put up with him all these years was a mystery. As he listened to the phone ring two-three-four times, the realization washed over Christopher that the reason he had decided to be the one to reach out and try to make amends was so he could know in his heart that he had done everything in his power to not be like his father.

Good, bad or indifferent, it had taken him a while to realize that. And it had taken the childhood experiences of a great woman to help him reframe his situation and see his family with a new appreciation. Kinsley was right, the family you took for granted wasn't going to be there forever. Having lost both of her parents within a one-year period, Kinsley was living proof of this.

Her father sounded like a monster. While Deke could be difficult, the old coot had never emotionally or physically abused his family. Sure he was hard on them. You could say a lot of things about Deke Jones, but he always did right by his family. Or at least, his version of right.

Wasn't that something to hold on to? Something to focus on? Because when he put it all into perspective, Christopher knew his upbringing could've been a whole lot worse.

It was probably too late to call the house on a Sunday night, anyway. Deke, the creature of habit he was, had probably been in bed for a good half hour.

Maybe, subconsciously, he'd known that and that was

the reason he'd decided to call…or maybe he shouldn't overthink it. He could try again tomorrow.

Christopher had just pulled the phone away from his ear, when he heard a craggy voice grunt and gruff, "Hello?"

Hesitating, Christopher drew in a breath as he brought the phone to his ear.

"Hello?" the man repeated, the irritation in his voice mounting.

Deke and Jeanne Marie didn't have caller ID so there was no way he would've known it was his son. In his mind's eye Christopher could see Deke giving the phone a dirty look before he slammed the receiver back into the cradle.

"Pops? It's Chris."

Silence answered him. For a moment he wondered if Deke had already hung up. But then the old man said, "Son?" His voice was so soft, it was barely audible and most un-Deke-like.

"Yeah, Pops, it's me. Is this a good time? I hope I'm not calling too late."

Christopher waited for Deke to cut him off at the knees as he was so fond of doing. The old man had had two months to stew on his anger at Chris for abandoning the ranch to take a desk job pushing papers, for disassociating himself from the Jones name, moving to Red Rock and surely a plethora of other sins real or imagined of which he had found Christopher guilty.

"You can ring this house at midnight and I would take your call, son. It's good to hear your voice."

As Deke's positive response registered, Christopher exhaled a breath he didn't realize he'd been holding. On the other end of the line, he heard his father call to his mom. "Jeanne, it's Chris on the phone. Get in here."

"Chris, it's ladies first. Talk to your mama and then she'll give me the phone."

His mother was her usual, sweet, unconditional self, saying how much she and the family had missed him but that they all understood that he was making a nice life for himself in Red Rock.

"I do wish you would come home to visit soon," she said, her voice a little wistful. "You don't know what I'd give to hug you."

Christopher made noises about being busy at work but promised that he would see what he could do about arranging some time off for a visit. He thought about telling her that she and Deke were always welcome in Red Rock but decided against it. Deke would never hear of making the trip. Not even if it was his wife's dying wish— Christopher stopped himself from tumbling down the path of negativity that he usually traveled when he conversed with his father. Old Deke had started the conversation off nicely enough. Even though it raised his hackles, Christopher forced himself to take the high road and not instigate an argument…and to refuse the invitation if Deke invited him to one.

"I got the photo album you made for me, Mama. I really appreciate it."

"I wanted you to have some pictures from Toby and Angie's wedding. We all missed you. It was a beautiful day, but it would've been even better if you had stood up with your brother."

A pang of guilt stabbed Christopher right in the heart. He grabbed the album off the end table where it had been hidden under a stack of magazines and financial newspapers since he'd brought it home from the office.

He opened it to a page featuring a five-by-seven photo of the smiling bride and groom. He flipped the page and saw another of the entire family—minus him, of course—gathered around his brother and his new sister-in-law.

It really had been ridiculous and selfish to miss such an important occasion. But with the frame of mind he'd been in then and as mad as Deke had been at him, there was no way he was going to cast a dark shadow over his brother's big day.

He heard Kinsley's voice in the back of his head saying, *Don't dwell on things you can't change. Look forward and spend that energy on things that matter.*

Toby understood why he'd stayed away and that was all that mattered. Still, a funny feeling circled in his gut like a shark poised to attack.

"It was great to see Toby when he and Angie were here in town. Will you please be sure and tell him I called?"

"I sure will, honey. But I'm going to hand the phone over to your dad now. He's getting a little antsy waiting to talk to you."

Right. That would be the day the sky fell when Deke stood antsy with anticipation waiting to talk to his black-sheep son. Christopher wanted to snort, but he didn't. Instead, he told his mother he loved her and promised her one more time that he would do his best to make it home for a visit as soon as he could manage.

Then he put on his emotional armor and prepared for Deke to shoot him like a sniper poised and ready high atop a building.

"Well, now it's my turn," Deke said.

Christopher held his tongue, unsure if that was sarcasm or sincerity in his dad's tone.

"You made your mama really happy by calling tonight, son."

Oh. Okay. Could it have been sincerity? Or was it a verbal trap designed to lure Christopher into a false sense of security so that Deke could turn around and sucker punch?

He closed the photo album and set it on the coffee table, scooting forward so that he was sitting on the edge of the couch.

"It was good to hear her voice," Christopher said. In a split second he decided to stick to his original plan and play nice. "It's good to hear yours, too, Pops."

The words hung out there for a few beats before Deke answered, "I'm glad to talk to you, too. Son, I have a confession to make. I regret the way we parted when you took off for Red Rock. You and I have had our differences over the years, but we've never left things so badly between us."

The old Christopher would have quipped, "You regretted it so much that you waited for me to call so you could tell me." But from his view on the high road, he could see that this was a hard confession for Deke to make.

"I've regretted it, too, Pops. I'm… I'm sorry."

As soon as the words escaped Christopher clamped his mouth shut, gritting his teeth so hard he could feel it all the way up to his temples.

"That's right big of you to say that, boy. To be the first one to apologize." Deke's voice sounded small and… humble? So much so that Christopher wasn't even sure it really was his father on the other end of the line.

"How's that job of yours going?" Deke asked.

So in the end his father couldn't bring himself to say the two little words that would have gone such a long way toward healing them…reuniting their family. Then again, maybe this was Deke's version of an apology. Christopher swallowed his pride and decided it was.

"It's great. I'm really enjoying it. Working for the Foundation is giving me a lot of opportunities to do some good in the community."

And that was as far as he was going to justify what he did for a living.

"That's what I hear. James has been in touch with your mama and he's had a lot of good things to say about you. He bragged about you, saying that you have a great work ethic and a real creative head for business. He says you've been such an asset to the Foundation, he would've hired you even if you weren't a blood relative. I'm really proud of you, son."

Proud of you, son.

Christopher fell back against the couch cushions so hard it knocked some of the air out of his lungs in a *whoosh.*

For the first time in his life, his father had told him he was *proud* of him. Christopher had a hard time hearing the rest of what his father said because of the blood rushing in his ears.

Family could be the most amazing people in your life while simultaneously being the most exasperating.

If an apology was gold, the words that had just passed from Deke's lips and traveled four hundred miles through the phone line were platinum.

No, they were priceless.

* * *

What was the Foundation's policy about fraternizing with a superior?

As Kinsley flipped through the employee handbook, she silently chastised herself. *Now was a heck of a time to worry about that.*

Still, for her own peace of mind she needed to know. After Christopher left her on Sunday evening, Kinsley had fallen back to earth with a terrifying awareness of her vulnerability.

She'd decided when she saw Christopher again, it should be business as usual. If they were going to work together, they had to keep their emotions (and libidos) in check.

Or at least *she* had to.

That sounded like common sense, but it was easier said than done. Now she was having a hard time keeping her mind on work when she knew Christopher was right across the hall.

That was the problem. He sat right. Across. The hall. And that's where he'd been, holed up in his office, for the better part of the day Monday.

Now it was midday Tuesday and he hadn't come into the office yet, which was no big deal. Before things had *changed* between them, she hadn't felt it necessary to know his schedule. They had never checked in with each other. Why should they do that now? It was a ridiculous thought.

Yet every time she heard a deep voice in the reception area she looked up, hoping to catch a glimpse of him.

To no avail.

He was acting as if nothing had happened between them. He wasn't exactly avoiding her. Or maybe he was…

she wouldn't know because she hadn't seen him except for late yesterday afternoon, when she'd run into him as she was on her way out and he was on his way in. He'd held the elevator door for her, and he had acted like the same old Christopher—the "before sex" Christopher. After the initial exchange of hi-how-are-yous, he'd mentioned that he had the germ of a wonderful idea for educating people on how to intervene when they saw someone being bullied. He had been saddened and inspired by what had happened to Tonya at the Spring Fling.

"Maybe we can talk about it soon?"

"Absolutely," she'd said, trying to figure out if he had run with the idea because he knew how important the cause was to her. Then again, adding another leg to the bullying prevention campaign would reflect well on him, too.

Although she hadn't expected him to kiss her at the elevator, she had wished for a little more. A whispered *Saturday night rocked my world;* a *Let's do it again soon;* or even better, *What are you doing for dinner tonight?*

He looked as if he was about to say something, but the elevator had buzzed, scolding them for holding the doors open too long.

He'd simply said, "Don't let me keep you," and she'd answered, "Good night," and had gotten into the elevator…alone with her pride.

She wasn't about to let herself appear needy because at that point, weren't his feelings pretty clear?

Today, after paging through the handbook no fewer than five times, she still couldn't find the answer to her question about superior/subordinate relationships. Did that mean there was no policy? And why wasn't there one? Probably because not sleeping with your superior/

subordinate was common sense—something every savvy professional knew.

Instead of driving herself crazy dwelling on it, she busied herself doing something more productive: polishing the recap of the Spring Fling event for the staff meeting next week.

As she was reading through her draft, her mind drifted. Maybe she should call him and ask him where they stood?

And maybe she should just stamp the word NEEDY on her forehead.

Stop it.

She had two choices. She could talk to Christopher about it, or be confident that things would turn out the way they were meant to be.

She had always prided herself on being confident. She had never obsessed over things she couldn't control, and she wasn't going to start now.

Realizing that her eyes had been scanning the recap but her mind had been thinking about Christopher and nothing of what she had just read had registered, she started back at the top of the page and forced herself to focus.

Bev buzzed her phone.

"Hey, Kinsley," she said. "Sawyer Fortune is on line one for you."

Sawyer Fortune?

"Thank you, Bev."

She pressed Line One.

"This is Kinsley Aaron."

"Hi, Kinsley, it's Sawyer Fortune. Am I catching you at a good time?"

"Absolutely, Sawyer," she said. "How can I help you?"

"I've been trying to reach Christopher today, but he seems to be unavailable. When I met with him the last time I was in town, he mentioned that the two of you worked closely in the community relations department, so I thought I would run it by you."

Sawyer went on to tell her about possible dates for the air-show fund-raiser that would benefit the Foundation. She assured him that she would talk to Christopher today and make sure he got back with Sawyer as soon as possible to reserve the date.

So, Christopher had even been unavailable to Sawyer.

That shed a new light on things. Something was up. Maybe that meant he wasn't avoiding her.

She was about to hang up with Sawyer when he said, "Oh, and, Kinsley, thanks for talking Christopher into calling his father. When I last spoke to Christopher, he said he had talked to Deke and that you were the one who had urged him to do so."

A knot of emotions formed in Kinsley's stomach as she mumbled something to Sawyer, then hung up the phone. He had called his father. That was great, a true breakthrough for him. He had told Sawyer that he had done so at her urging. That was tremendous, especially because he had mentioned her to Sawyer yesterday. She could let her mind go in all sorts of directions, imagining what he had said about her to his cousin.

But why did there always have to be a qualifier? If she had been the one who convinced him to take such an important step, why hadn't he shared the news with her? It was pretty important. He could've said something when they were standing at the elevator.

A cold, prickling realization settled around Kinsley.

Maybe he hadn't shared this personal news with her because it was *personal*.

Maybe she needed to take a hint from his lack of communication over the past day and a half.

A bubble of laughter escaped, but the sound was dry and devoid of humor. Despite Christopher's claims to the contrary, he had a love-'em-and-leave-'em reputation. Facts were facts. She had put too much stock into their night together. Their…liaison.

Oh, God. That was all it had been.

Icy hot humiliation settled around her. She bit her lip until it throbbed in time with her pulse. She sat there—just sat there—for several long minutes, letting reality seep into her pores, flogging herself with I-told-you-sos.

You knew this was a very plausible outcome. Whenever she violated her gut instinct, she always lived to regret it.

Now, if she knew what was good for her, she'd get herself together. No moping. No sniping at Christopher. No looking back with regret.

She would not let this interfere with her work.

Because in her work, she would find the solidity that would distract her and camouflage the despair that colored everything in sight.

For what must've been the hundredth time, Kinsley reminded herself that the Fortunes considered blood thicker than water. She didn't want to chance losing her job should someone disapprove of her affair with Christopher. Or worse yet, if talk started around the office that Kinsley was attempting to sleep her way to the top, Christopher might see her as a burden and decide the office would be better off without her.

If she had learned one thing growing up in an abusive

home, it was that the less attention you drew to yourself, the better off—the safer—you were in the long run. That meant no more jealous outbursts like the time she thought he was dating his etiquette coach.

From this moment forward, she would put a smile on her face and it would be business as usual.

Good thing, too, because when she looked up, Christopher was standing in her doorway smiling and holding a big presentation board.

Christopher was simply flat-out scared to fall in love. He recognized that but had no idea what to do, besides stop hiding and acting like a child. Kinsley deserved better than that.

He knew he had been distant, using the excuse that he had been immersed in work, busy coming up with a plan for them to use as a follow-up to the initiative that they'd started at the Spring Fling.

But if he were completely honest with himself, he had been avoiding Kinsley. By doing so, he didn't have to face his feelings.

Why could he analyze so easily, but he had no idea what to do with it?

He had been heartened by his father's newfound respect and bolstered by his uncle's good report.

With this newfound support system, in a day and a half he had managed to outline the basics of the follow-up program. His initial reaction had him wanting to involve Kinsley, but fear caused him to back away. He simply needed a cooling-off period, time to put things into perspective and remember how to be her colleague without wanting to undress her and lay her flat across his desk.

But seeing her at the elevator yesterday, he knew that

his silence was hurting her. Hell, it was hurting *him*. But last night he'd decided that in a similar way that he'd reached out to Deke, he needed to break the ice with Kinsley.

He thought the best way to do that—at least, for starters—was to ask her opinion on the new idea.

As he stood in her office doorway, gripping the presentation board, he felt the same pull of attraction that he felt every time he looked at her.

"May I come in?" he asked.

Her blue eyes looked wary as she smiled at him. Her professional smile. He recognized it.

"Sure," she said.

He left the door open on purpose, to discourage the conversation from veering off on a personal path.

"Remember how I told you yesterday that I had come up with a new plan for us to use in the schools?"

She nodded. Yep. Her wall was up. He recognized that, too.

"This is intended as a tool for school guidance counselors to use." Damn, this was harder than he had expected. The way she was looking at him…it was more like she was staring right through him. "I hope that it will help kids remember to not just stand there when someone is in trouble, but to act."

He realized that he was nervous as he turned the board around, showing her the acronym GET INVOLVED. Each letter of the words stood for an element of the program.

Christopher watched Kinsley as she read the board, her lips pressed into a thin line.

When she was finished, she simply nodded and said,

"Get Involved, huh? That's good advice. Even if it is a little ironic coming from a man who seems to do everything in his power to avoid doing exactly that."

Chapter Thirteen

On Wednesday morning, Christopher still couldn't get Kinsley's face out of his head. The way she'd looked as she'd read the GET INVOLVED acronym.

She'd had good reason for looking so upset. The words obviously hit home.

Sitting at his desk, he rested his forehead on his palm. He was such an idiot. How could he not have seen the irony of the message before he brought it to her?

As soon as she'd read it, he'd seen it in her eyes. Sure, she kept a professional poker face, but she couldn't disguise the hurt. She'd told him it was perfect and then excused herself, saying she had a lunch engagement.

She'd walked out, leaving him sitting there with his presentation board on the desk and his foot in his mouth. He needed to practice what he preached.

GET INVOLVED?

His problem was that he was too afraid to get involved. So ridiculously terrified—of what? He had better figure it out because his fear was going to cost him the best thing that had ever happened to him.

They needed to talk about this. Even if he didn't know what to say. He needed to let her know it wasn't her; it was him. That she was smart and beautiful and deserving of so much more than he could offer.

He picked up the phone to call her office. But then he put it back down in the cradle. Maybe he should just go talk to her. Common sense told him he should wait until after work. He didn't want to upset her, but that seemed as though he wasn't giving her enough credit.

He got up from his desk and made his way into the reception area, but before he could get to Kinsley's office, Bev intercepted him.

"Mr. Jamison just called," she said. "He wants to see you in his office right away."

Christopher made his way to Emmett Jamison's wing of the building. His administrative assistant, Clara, was expecting him.

"Oh, good, there you are," she said. "He wants to see you but he has another meeting at 10:30." She glanced at her watch. "Oh, no problem. You have plenty of time. Go right in."

As Christopher walked toward Emmett's door, he heard Clara inform him that Christopher was on his way in.

For a fleeting second, he wondered if this had to do with the talk he had had with his father. But then that gave way to the guilt he felt over how things had turned out with Kinsley. Surely, she wouldn't have lodged a complaint against him, would she?

No, that would be completely out of character for her. But he couldn't ignore the little voice that jabbed at him and said she would be completely within her rights. He should've been stronger and not taken advantage of her while she was vulnerable, even though that's not at all what he had intended.

The same jabbing voice brought up words like love and feelings, but he ignored it as he rapped on Emmett's door.

"Come in."

Christopher opened the door and stepped inside. He was immediately set at ease by the broad smile that graced Emmett's face.

"Just the man I wanted to see," Emmett said. "Have a seat, please." He gestured to a chair in front of his desk.

Christopher complied.

As soon as he was settled Emmett picked up the display board that outlined the GET INVOLVED program. He tapped it with his finger.

"This is good work."

He paused, as if letting the praise ring in the air.

"You have done some impressive work in your short time here at the Foundation. I'm not the only one who has taken notice. But before I tell you what I have in mind, let me ask you, are you happy with what you're doing? Because you sure are doing a good job."

"I love what I'm doing. I truly feel like I've found my calling here at the Foundation."

"Great, that's exactly what I was hoping you would say. I have an opportunity I would like to talk to you about. We have discovered the need for a presence in New York City. I know New York is very different than Red Rock, but the work would be similar. We—the board, your uncle James, Lily and I—were hoping that you would be willing to take on the challenge. How would you feel about relocating to New York City and opening that office for us? We would love for you to be the man in charge. If anyone can do it, you could."

Emmett's offer caught Christopher so off guard, he couldn't even answer for a moment. He was truly stunned.

New York City? They wanted him to move out there and open the office?

But what about Kinsley?

"Would anyone else be in the office with me?" he asked. "Would I have a staff?"

Emmett steepled his fingers. "Not right off the bat. We would have to make sure that the new office was up and running and self-sustaining, of course—there's no mission without margin—before we could fully staff the office. But don't worry. We would pay to relocate you and give you a salary increase and housing allowance that would allow you to live comfortably in the city."

Of course, it would mean leaving behind everybody he had come to care so much about.

Kinsley's face was the first to flash in his mind again. Even before his newfound relatives and all the friends he had made since moving to Red Rock.

It was a tempting offer. It meant that they trusted him. It meant that they respected him and appreciated his vision. Uncle James, Lily and Emmett were the first people who had truly believed in him.

That inappropriate voice piped up inside him and reminded him that Kinsley had once believed in him too.

"I realize that this is a lot to think about," said Emmett. "I will have Clara draw up the specifics and get them to you by the end of the day. Why don't you take a few days to think about it before you let me know your answer? The sooner we can get you there, the better."

Christopher cleared his throat. "I want you to know how much I appreciate your confidence in me. I am greatly honored and humbled that you would entrust me with this position. I'll look forward to reviewing the details."

Emmett stood and offered Christopher his hand. Christopher stood and accepted it. What would Deke and Jeanne Marie think of this? His father had had a conniption when Christopher had accepted the job in Red Rock. If his father had thought this place was highfalutin, what in the world would he think of his son moving to New York City?

But Christopher reminded himself not to get too far ahead. He hadn't seen the offer yet. He had no idea what they intended in terms of dollars and cents.

Even though he wasn't anywhere close to making up his mind, he knew one of the biggest sacrifices he would be making would be leaving Kinsley behind.

Suddenly everything that had been so muddled and tentative seemed to snap into sharp focus. This job was everything he had ever wanted, except it didn't include Kinsley. But maybe time away from her in a place where he could focus on his job and not be distracted by her full lips and the way their bodies fit so perfectly together that it drove him nuts to even catch a glimpse of her in the office hallway was a good thing.

Maybe putting some distance between them was exactly what he needed. Then again, maybe this opportunity would cost him the one woman he had ever loved. But maybe that was case in point why he should go and not look back.

* * *

That evening Christopher sat at his desk reading—for the fifth time—the details of the generous New York City relocation offer that Clara had delivered to him just before five o'clock.

Among other perks, they were offering him nearly twice his current salary and a housing allowance that would afford him a comfortable apartment in Manhattan.

It was a far cry from Horseback Hollow and the life sentence on his family's ranch. This offer was a dream come true. And more than that, it was validation that he was good at his job. The board could've chosen anyone to head up this project, but they'd put their faith in him.

Christopher closed the file and leaned back in his leather chair, stretching his feet out in front of him and looking around his office. When he'd first gotten here, he'd thought this place was the be-all and end-all with its paneled walls, living room furniture and that view.

Now, he'd been handed the chance of a lifetime to write his own ticket.

So why was he hesitating?

The numbers checked out. It would be a long time before a chance like this would come along again, much less be dropped into his lap.

He needed to think about it. Sleep on it. Even if Emmett was pushing for a fast answer, Christopher needed a few hours to process everything. Then maybe this uncertainty would sort itself out.

In his head it was a no-brainer: only idiots passed up the chance of a lifetime for a woman. Especially when he'd had trepidations about their relationship before the deal was on the table.

However, now that the deal was on the table, his head and his heart were at odds.

He'd have to sort that out, and fast.

He put the file in his briefcase and clicked off his desk lamp.

It was after 6:30 p.m. The sun was painting the Western landscape outside his window in shades of gold and amber. Everything looked a little different in the light of this offer. As Christopher headed toward the elevator, the light that was still on in Kinsley's office drew him like a moth.

She was completely engaged in whatever it was she was reading on her computer screen. He stood there watching her, wanting to memorize the way she looked right now with her guard down and her hair hanging in soft curls around her shoulders. He owed it to her to tell her about the offer before she heard it from someone else.

"Don't you ever go home?" he said.

She startled and looked up at him. "Oh, Christopher. I didn't realize anyone else was still here."

"Just you and me," he said, his heart compressing at the words. "Do you have a minute?"

She pushed her mouse away and angled her body toward him. "Sure, come in."

He settled himself in the chair across from her.

"Everything okay?" she asked. Her hand fluttered to her blouse collar and she fidgeted with the top button, which, as always, was buttoned up tight.

Despite everything, he had to resist the urge to reach out and undo it and all the others and pull her into him so that he could lose himself in the Nirvana that was her.

And that was exactly why he needed to distance himself. He couldn't even think straight when he was with her. It was his own fault. Yep, it was all on him, and he needed to do something to regain his equilibrium.

"Everything is fine. More than fine, actually. I got a job offer today."

Her expression remained neutral. "Really? Where?"

"New York."

He told her how Emmett had called him into his office earlier.

"It's great money, and such an opportunity I can't see how I can refuse."

For a split second he thought he saw a flicker of regret flash in her blue eyes, and in that same split second he knew that if she said, "Don't go," he wouldn't. He'd turn down the offer and he'd take her home and make love to her until they'd finally figured out that this complicated thing between them didn't have to be so—

"How wonderful for you," she said, verbally slapping the sense back into him. "When do you leave for New York?"

Kinsley was happy for Christopher. Truly, she was.

And she had told him that yesterday when he stopped by her office. She said it with her most genuine smile.

She wanted him to be happy.

Really, she did. And if she kept telling herself how happy she was that he was leaving, maybe she would start to believe it.

Even though she hadn't seen the specifics of the offer yet, Kinsley knew he would take it. The Fortunes were generous with their compensation. There was no way he would turn it down.

His leaving was probably the very best thing that could happen to both of them. He would relocate to a place

where he could steep himself in big city, sophistication.
She could keep her job here and maybe regain her concentration…and her heart.

Of course it would end up this way. Of course it would.
This proved that it really was best that they hadn't committed to each other.

It was hard enough to know that he didn't want a relationship with her. The only thing that might've been harder was knowing that he did want a relationship and then him having to choose between her and his dream job.

She laughed to herself as she realized she had gotten it wrong. Women weren't Christopher's mistress; his work was.

She sat there trying to convince herself that this really was the best thing for both of them. If she said the words enough, surely she would begin to believe it. If not now, maybe by the time he made the move. Just then an email popped up in her computer inbox. Kinsley sat up a little straighter when she realized it was from Lily Cassidy Fortune.

The subject line read Surprise party for Christopher.
Kinsley clicked on the email.

Hello, Kinsley, I am calling on you for a rather large favor.
Since you seem to be the colleague closest to Christopher, would you please take on the task of organizing a surprise going-away party for him? I was hoping we could do something nice for him—something a touch sentimental? I will leave it in your capable hands as I'm sure you will know exactly what to do to make Christopher realize how much he means to us and how grate-

ful we are that he has accepted this challenge. We were hoping to have the party tomorrow, as he will be making the move this weekend. I know this is all terribly fast, but I'm sure Beverly will be happy to assist you with anything you need.

Kinsley fell back against her chair and her breath rushed from her lungs.

So it was official.

And he was leaving this weekend?

Christopher was leaving *this* weekend?

Her heart cracked open and filled with a leaden dread.

She wasn't surprised that he had accepted it. He'd all but made up his mind when they'd talked last night. She just hadn't realized he would leave so soon.

She fought the sudden urge to cry, blinking back the unwelcome tears that clouded her vision. There was no use getting emotional. It was for the best.

Really, it was.

She needed to treat this the same way one would rip off a bandage—the faster the better. The sooner Christopher got on with his new life, the sooner she could get on with her life here in Red Rock without him.

She sat there for several minutes in her quiet office, listening to the whirr of the air conditioner and the hum of her computer. Now that the tears were at bay, a strange numbness had overtaken her.

She picked up the phone and called Bev.

They had less than twenty-four hours. They would have to get this party planning rolling as soon as possible if they were going to pull it off.

The sooner they started planning, the sooner it would be over.

Chapter Fourteen

"*Surprise!*"

The chorus of voices rang out when Emmett opened the conference room door and ushered Christopher inside.

Christopher blinked once, twice, three times as he looked around at all of his coworkers who had crowded into the conference room, surrounded by streamers and helium balloons.

"What the heck is this?"

His uncle James stepped forward and clapped him on the back. "This is your party, son. We wanted to give you a good sendoff on your last day here in the Red Rock office."

A surprise party?

He glanced at Emmett and murmured something unintelligible. Emmett grinned back at him, obviously proud that his paper-signing ruse had worked to get him to the conference room.

Christopher *was* surprised. Surprised and genuinely touched that everyone would gather on a Friday afternoon—just for him.

There were steaming covered chafing dishes in the middle of the conference room table being tended to by catering staff in uniforms with the Red logo. His stomach growled as he inhaled the delicious aroma of Red's Mexican food—a mélange of savory dishes blending with the aroma of fresh corn tortillas, chilies and spices. There were platters of Red's famous corn roasted in the husk stacked on platters which were next to the biggest cake he had ever seen in his life. And there was champagne.

That's when he realized that everyone was raising a glass toward him. Lily stepped forward and handed him and Emmett each a flute, too.

Emmett and James, who were flanking Christopher, simultaneously touched their glasses to his.

"I would like to propose a toast," said James. "To Christopher Fortune, our golden boy. May you shine in the city as brightly as you do here."

"To Christopher!" someone shouted and everyone raised their glasses a little higher, then took a sip.

Christopher glanced around the room, taking in his family, friends and coworkers: Miguel and Marcos Mendoza were there. So was their cousin Sierra Mendoza Calloway. Standing next to her was Emmett's wife, Linda Faraday. She was talking to Susan Fortune Eldridge and Julie Osterman Fortune. Nicholas and Jeremy Fortune were there. Then he saw Tanner and Jordana Redmond and Sawyer and his wife, Laurel—had they come all the way from Horseback Hollow to be here just for him?

As people surrounded him, offering handshakes, high fives and fist bumps, he realized how much he truly cared for these people.

It was a bit overwhelming.

Funny, before he got here, when he had first taken on the Fortune name, he had imagined them all to be so different than they had turned out to be. Not in a bad way. In fact, they were better than he could've ever imagined. They were all warm, loving, family-oriented people, and he was proud to be one of them.

And when Sawyer came over and shook his hand, Christopher experienced an inexplicable pang of homesickness for his immediate family in Horseback Hollow. Even Deke.

Especially Deke.

As the good wishes continued and people rallied around him—it was a good thing he wasn't claustrophobic—he found himself craning his neck searching for the one person he was desperate to see.

Finally, he saw Kinsley standing by the table with the champagne, refilling glasses, doing what she was so good at—helping other people.

His gaze was drawn to her like a pin to a magnet. He drank her in, trying to take a mental snapshot of her gorgeous face, her blue-blue eyes that were framed by eyebrows a few shades darker than her sun-streaked blond hair. Her finely chiseled cheekbones. The delicate slope of her neck. Her full lips.

He could still feel those lips on his. He could feel the way their bodies had fit so perfectly, as if they were made for each other. A surge of longing so deep and fraught with desire for her consumed him.

It was as if he were seeing her for the first time.

Through new eyes. Now he wanted her even more than he had the first time he'd seen her.

Why was it that he never really appreciated what he had when he had it? Why did he always wonder if something better was around the corner? Standing here in the midst of the crowd, among all these well-wishers, his heart spoke loud and clear: there wasn't a better woman in the world for him than Kinsley Aaron.

He had to tamp down the urge to fight his way through the crowd and pull her into his arms. His heart ached for her.

As much as he loved the attention and the accolades and the thought that his uncle James and Lily Cassidy Fortune trusted him—*him,* the guy who never seemed to have the capability to do anything right back in Horseback Hollow—with opening their satellite office in a city like New York, and even though they had been more than generous with the compensation and benefits package that they had given him, moving to New York would mean losing touch with everyone that mattered to him.

And it would mean losing Kinsley.

Suddenly his future flashed before his eyes in a crystal-clear vision: he would have the money and the dream job and the prestige and everything he could ever want at his disposal in a big city where the world would be his oyster, but it would never be enough. He would never be satisfied with all of that because it was empty. Well, the work had proved to be fulfilling, but all the money in the world couldn't replace what he had found in Red Rock.

Being here, he had learned how to go home again.

He had learned the value of everything money couldn't buy.

Was he really willing to give up everything for...emptiness?

He excused himself from his colleagues and made his way over to Emmett and James, who were standing with Linda and Lily.

"This is a fabulous party," Christopher said. "I can't thank you enough."

Lily set a slender hand on his arm. "Oh, honey, I wish we could all take credit for this party. But this is all Kinsley Aaron. Is there anything that woman can't do? Didn't she do a lovely job?"

"There is absolutely nothing she can't do," Christopher said. "She's even taught me a thing or two since I've been working with her. So I'm not at all surprised to learn that she is the one responsible for this."

Christopher watched Kinsley as she cut the cake and put small squares on the colorful party plates. He watched her as she worked while everyone else was enjoying themselves. She was always willing to go the extra mile for somebody else. Always willing to sacrifice even if it meant standing back while somebody else shined.

How could he have been such a damn fool?

How could he have been willing to let go of the only woman in this world he would ever be able to love?

Christopher turned to James and Emmett. "If you don't mind, I need to speak to the two of you privately."

Both men did a double-take.

"Right now?" asked James. "In case you didn't notice, son, there's a party going on. Rumor has it it's in your honor."

"That's exactly why I need to talk to you now," said Christopher. "This can't wait."

* * *

Just keep yourself busy and it'll be over faster.

Kinsley was not in the mood to party. But she sure was good at playing the role of the hostess.

She reminded herself that this was not about her. It had nothing to do with her. She needed to keep smiling and keep her eye on the light at the end of the tunnel.

It would all be over soon.

So, Kinsley refilled the tortilla platters and the water pitchers. She brought out extra bottles of soda and champagne and replenished the paper goods, cups and the plastic utensils.

As she looked around, she caught a glimpse of Christopher. He was talking to Mr. Jamison, Lily Fortune and James Marshall Fortune. She looked away but not before she felt the heat of his gaze on her.

But then, when she glanced back, he was gone. Probably hidden by one of the one hundred balloons in the room. She breathed a sigh of relief and moved around the chafing dishes the catering staff had just replenished.

Good grief, these people were tough customers. From the way they were devouring the food you would think they hadn't eaten in days. But who could blame them? Red prided itself on delicious food. Today they offered beef brisket enchiladas, chicken mole and spicy lobster tacos. She was having to hustle now, but the more they ate, the less she and the staff would have to clean up later.

And the more work she would have to keep her hands busy and her mind off the reason for the party.

Christopher. The mere thought of him made her chest tighten and her heart squeeze.

Stop it.

But what good did fighting it do? She kept her head

down and allowed herself to switch over to autopilot. To let the thoughts and feelings come and go as they would. Maybe if she leaned into the emotions she'd have an easier time of it.

Or maybe she would break down into a heaping, sobbing mess and really humiliate herself. She took a deep breath and released it slowly.

No, it seemed that the thoughts and feelings were hidden deep enough under the surface. Even so, everyone else in this room was so convivial and having such a good time that no one had a clue that her heart was breaking.

Scratch that. Her heart had already broken. Past tense. For days, she had been carrying around a bunch of bits and pieces of broken heart that she knew would never be able to fit back together again.

That was okay. She didn't have any use for her heart anymore. She just hoped the pieces didn't rattle.

Stepping outside of herself, she had to admit that Christopher had seemed astonished. It was always nice when a surprise party went off the way it was planned.

That's right. Focus on the good. There you go.

She resisted the urge to look up and search the crowd for him. So far, playing caterer had helped her to not moon over him, to not watch what he was doing or who he was talking to. It just hurt too much.

Plus, the last thing she needed was for someone she worked with to discover her secret: that she was brokenhearted because had slept with Christopher and the affair had gone horribly, disastrously wrong. *That* could be misconstrued in so many ways.

Normally, she didn't care what people thought of her. But this was a different case. She may have lost her heart, but it was imperative for her to walk away with her integrity and dignity intact. Because what had happened between Christopher and her hadn't been like that. She wasn't using him to get favors or a boost up the corporate ladder.

It was…

Yeah, it was.

And it was over now. She needed to get over it. But it had only been a week since she had given herself—body and soul—to him; her heart still felt tender and her pride was pretty raw.

What had she expected? She knew what she had wanted. But what you want and what you get were sometimes two entirely different things.

What she had gotten was a lesson. She didn't give her heart away easily. And she wouldn't do it again anytime soon. After all, who would want the bag of broken pieces she stored in the place where her heart had once lived?

She would feel better someday. It would just take time. Right now she needed to keep her chin up.

Chin up, buttercup. Her mom used to say that when they'd hit a rough patch. God, what she wouldn't give to be able to go to her mother right now. Not for advice, but for a shoulder. For the shelter of her hugs. She had been the one person in whom Kinsley had found unrequited love.

And if she'd learned one thing from watching her mother it was that sometimes when you loved too much your generous spirit became your undoing.

Unlike her mother, she had a second chance to reclaim herself. Rather than mooning, she would embrace the blessing in this narrow miss.

Right…

Forcing herself to look up, she glanced around the

room admiring her handiwork—not looking for Christopher. Everyone was chatting, and the buzz of convivial energy filled the room. The helium balloons she had procured did a fairly decent job of hiding her—or hiding him. Either way, because they were clustered in the area where she had been hiding out, she had to make an effort to look for him. As if blatantly defying her, her eyes swept the room looking for him, but before she could pick him out she came face-to-face with a giant yellow balloon…well, what better caution sign could a girl ask for?

She was running the risk of driving herself crazy, so she made another conscious effort to refocus. She scanned the food tables in search of something to distract her, but it appeared that everyone was finally slowing down. Nothing needed refilling or replenishing or replacing.

She picked up a couple of empty cups and plates, realizing if she felt like the hired help, it was because she had put herself in that position. The catering staff would take care of this. She swiped the back of her hand across her forehead, then tucked an errant strand of hair behind her ear.

Maybe she would have a glass of champagne. She didn't really feel like celebrating, but that was no reason to boycott the bubbly. In fact, looking on the bright side, she should celebrate the fact that she'd pulled this off.

Who would've thought that planning a party would be one of the hardest assignments she'd ever faced?

The old adage what doesn't kill you makes you stronger definitely applied here.

She had just poured herself a glass of champagne when Mr. Jamison called everyone in the conference room to order.

"May I have your attention, please? Everyone, please settle down and listen. Christopher has something he would like to say."

Oh, boy. Here we go.

The room quieted down and everybody turned their attention to Christopher. For the first time that afternoon, Kinsley stopped what she was doing and gave him her ears.

Mr. Jamison turned to Christopher and murmured, "Are you sure this is what you want to do?"

Christopher nodded. "Actually, I've never been so sure about anything in my life." He glanced at Kinsley, and their gazes locked. She wanted to look away, but she couldn't. "Well, maybe I've been that sure about one other thing, and she's a big part of the reason that I'm going to say what I have to say. I appreciate this party. I appreciate everybody gathering here to wish me well and to give me such a great sendoff. However, turns out a funny thing happened on the way to the cake table. I realize I won't be moving to New York, after all."

Kinsley was frozen in place, desperately pulling back on the reins of her heart, which was hopefully anticipating a preposterous turn of events that would surely never be.

So just stop it.

Audible gasps mixed with surprised murmurs and astonished glances, but Christopher's gaze didn't waver from hers.

"It's always been important to me to be respected and regarded as an intelligent man. But it took a party like this, a gathering of my family and friends and one hell of a party planner—everybody please give Kinsley a round of applause for the wonderful job she did to bring us all together—to clarify some things for me."

Her hand fluttered to her collar. *Oh, why did he do that?*

She finally broke their gaze and glanced around at the people who were clapping for her. She really wished they wouldn't do that.

When they quieted down, Christopher continued. "Today I realize that I love Texas too much to leave. I have just gotten to know my Fortune family, and quite frankly I'm not ready to put that much distance between us. But most of all, there is someone special here I simply can't bear to leave behind."

Kinsley's heart stopped beating for what seemed like an eternity. When it resumed, it picked up double time.

"She has made me a better person. I haven't quite figured out how this happened, and I'm pretty sure I don't deserve her. But I love her. I love her with my entire being, and I can't imagine my life without her."

Kinsley's gasp was audible, surprising even herself. Heat crept up her neck and fanned across her cheeks as every gaze in the place turned to her.

She wasn't sure if she wanted to cry tears of joy or crawl under the table to escape scrutiny. The tears of joy definitely won out. This unusual proclamation of love certainly wasn't what she had expected when she thought about Christopher declaring his love, but had Christopher Fortune ever done anything by the book?

"I wouldn't blame Kinsley if she killed me right now," Christopher said, hoping he hadn't gone too far with this workplace pronouncement. "So if you see me with a piece of cake smashed in my face, it probably doesn't mean we've gotten married. It probably means she simply smashed that cake in my face, which I suppose I would deserve."

He was relieved when everyone laughed.

He couldn't quite see Kinsley, who had gradually worked her way to the back of the room. Hell, he didn't blame her—he probably shouldn't have gotten so carried away. It would serve him right if she told him to take a hike.

He remembered his initial vow to win her over no matter what. He fully expected to have to work harder than he'd ever worked his entire life to get her to commit to him. He'd never looked so forward to a challenge. Speaking of challenges, he still owed everyone the rest of the explanation. He turned back to the group and continued.

"Plenty of folks right here in this room are probably better qualified than I am to open an office in the Big Apple. I was thinking about that while I was standing here enjoying everyone's company. So I offered Emmett, James and Lily a new proposal for the Fortune Foundation, but this one hits a little closer to home. With their blessing, I will be opening a satellite office of the Foundation in Horseback Hollow, with an anti-bullying/GET INVOLVED initiative. I will split time between Horseback Hollow and Red Rock. So, I'm sorry to say that you haven't gotten rid of me yet."

As his family and coworkers applauded this news, Christopher scanned the room for Kinsley, wanting to gauge her reaction, but he didn't see her. He wanted to go find her, but people approached and started the whole process all over again of shaking his hand, slapping him on the back and congratulating him—on the satellite office and on falling in love with a wonderful woman.

They all seemed genuinely pleased for him. It was very moving, but he was starting to get a little anxious over Kinsley's absence.

Had she left?

He wouldn't blame her if she'd walked out. But if she had, he would fix it.

If it was the last thing he did, he would fix things between them.

He excused himself again from the knot of well-wishers and went to look for her.

He found her in the reception area standing quietly gazing out the window. It was a similar view as from his office, the one that had captivated him from the start. He'd thought the south Texas landscape couldn't look more beautiful. But he'd never seen it as a backdrop to Kinsley.

"I meant what I said in there," he said. "I'm in love with you. I may have changed my mind about the job, but I'm not going to change my mind about you. All I need to know is do I even stand a chance after all I've put you through?"

She turned and met his gaze. Her beautiful eyes were brimming with tears. In that instant he knew everything was going to be okay.

He walked over to her, pulled her into his arms and reached up and brushed a tear off her cheek.

"Don't worry," she said. "They're happy tears. I love you, too."

Kinsley was never so happy to leave a party—even one she'd planned. But she knew the two of them would have a much better time at the after party—in Christopher's bed.

With him, she was home, even amid the partially packed boxes that would now need to be unpacked. Yes, she was more than happy to help him with this task. It was the packing and the goodbyes she couldn't bear.

They spent a long, luxurious evening making love and snuggling and making love and snuggling. She couldn't tell if they were making up for lost time or living in the moment, but it didn't matter. They didn't need to define it. They already had when they had exchanged those three precious words that even twelve hours ago she feared she would never hear cross his lips.

If she had learned one thing about Christopher it was that when he said something he meant it. His word was golden, and Kinsley basked in the glow of it as he held her.

She splayed her hand across his chest, reveling in the downy-soft feel of his chest hair.

"So, speaking of being the last to know…" she said.

He pulled her closer, as if he were afraid she would get away.

"Oh, hell…here we go." He smiled and pretended to roll his eyes before he kissed her soundly. "I knew there would be hell to pay for what I did. May I make it up to you…again? Because I am perfectly willing to make love to you until you fully understand just how much I love you."

He shifted her to the side and then rolled on top of her.

"Oh, you have no idea how much trouble you are in, mister." She kissed his neck and then nipped at his earlobe as he nudged her legs apart and entered her again.

After they were spent and breathless, she managed to catch her breath. "As I was saying, I had to hear through

the grapevine that you called your father. And that the
two of you had a good talk."

He did a double-take. "Oh, yeah? Who is spreading
such rumors?"

"I'm not telling."

He grinned at her slyly. "I thought we promised that
there would be no secrets between us. Am I going to have
to assign you penance?"

"Please do. I could be a very happy woman doing
atonement with you." She traced his lips with her index
finger, getting momentarily lost in the mix of masculine
strength and male beauty that was Christopher.

She swallowed around a lump of love and gratitude
that had settled in her throat.

Or maybe it was her heart that was so full it was spilling over. Whatever the case, she never wanted it to go
away. She wanted it to keep bubbling up like a fountain.

She settled into the crook of his arm and rested her
head in that place on his shoulder that seemed to be made
just for her.

"Actually, it's not a rumor," he said. "I did call my dad.
Deke said to tell you hello."

"Really?" she asked.

"No, but I do want to take you home to Horseback
Hollow so that you can meet him and my mother. I know
she'll love you. They will all love you. Maybe not quite
as much as I do, but I don't know that that's humanly
possible. But I digress.

"The call went great. Better than great. I underesti-
mated my father. I learned that he and I are two different men, but that's okay. We have finally come to the
point where we accept that and respect each other for
who we are."

"I'm so glad," Kinsley said.

Gently, he rubbed her back in a slow, rhythmic motion that was almost hypnotizing. She couldn't remember the last time she had been this relaxed.

"I might not have called him—or at least not so soon—if not for you. Thank you for that. Thank you for always seeing the best in me."

"Well, not *always*— Remember, you still have a lot of penance before you're completely redeemed. But I can assure you that I do love what I see."

They were quiet for a moment. The air-conditioning clicked on. Somewhere out in the world, outside the snug cocoon that had become their universe, a car door shut and a dog barked.

"So, who do you look like—your mom or your dad?"

"Everyone says I take after my dad. In looks and personality. My brothers say that's why Deke and I butt heads so often. That we're too much alike."

"I'd love to see a picture of him sometime. He must be a good-looking guy."

Christopher stretched. "My mama thinks so. She's stuck with him for forty years. Can you believe they've been married that long?"

"I think that's wonderful."

"Maybe that gives you a little hope for me. I don't commit easily, but once I do, I'm sort of like gum on your shoe."

"That's *so* romantic."

They laughed. She loved the way they didn't take themselves too seriously.

"At least I think I'll be the gum on your shoe. I've never loved someone enough to be their gum."

"Wow. How did I get so lucky?"

They laughed again, and when they stopped, she lost herself in his sigh of contentment.

"So, now, tell me again, how many brothers and sisters do you have?"

"I'm one of seven."

"Holy cow. Your poor mother."

"Nah, Mama loved her children. There are two girls and five boys, including me. A handful."

"Sounds like your mother should be canonized."

"Yup, pretty much. Wait—" he said sitting up suddenly. "I want to show you something."

Kinsley enjoyed watching him walk from the bed to the bedroom door.

"What a fine specimen you are, Mr. Fortune."

When he returned he was holding a photo album. The one she remembered seeing in his car that night they went to Mendoza's.

The night everything started.

"What's that?" she asked as he climbed back into bed beside her.

"It's a photo album my mother sent me to remind me of where I came from."

"And you're letting me look now? Remember that night before we went to Mendoza's? I thought you were going to smack my hand away from it."

He looked at her solemnly, momentarily sobering. "Besides loving you for the rest of your life, the other thing I can promise you is that I will never, ever raise a hand to you."

She inhaled sharply and nodded.

In that moment, she sensed that her mother was with her. That her mother, the angel, had quite possibly sent Christopher to watch over her. The kind of man she should have, rather than the kind of bad example her father had set.

Everything is going to be all right, Mom. Everything is fine now.

"Here," said Christopher. "Look at this picture. Here's my dad when he was about my age."

Wrapped in the sheet, Kinsley scooted up and sat next to Christopher on the bed.

She studied the picture, loving this new window into her love's world. "Wow, you do look like him."

"My dad's name is Jones. Deke Jones. I'm going to start using Jones in my name again. How would you feel about being part of the Fortune Jones family?"

"Hmm… Kinsley Aaron Fortune Jones," she said. "That's a mouthful. But it sounds like poetry to me."

When Christopher leaned in and kissed her. She knew that she was home, that she had finally found her family at last.

* * * * *

New York Times bestselling author **Allison Leigh**'s high point as a writer is hearing from readers that they laughed, cried or lost sleep while reading her books. She credits her family with great patience for the time she's parked at her computer, and for blessing her with the kind of love she wants her readers to share with the characters living in the pages of her books. Contact her at allisonleigh.com.

Books by Allison Leigh

Harlequin Special Edition

One Night in Weaver...
A Weaver Christmas Gift
A Weaver Beginning
A Weaver Holiday Homecoming
A Weaver Baby
A Weaver Wedding
Fortune's Prince
Fortune's Perfect Match
Fortune's Proposal

Visit the Author Profile page at
Harlequin.com for more titles.

FORTUNE'S PRINCE

Allison Leigh

For all the Fortune Women.
As always, it is an honor to be among you.

Chapter One

He stopped cold when he heard a faint rustle. The only light there was came from the moonlight sneaking through the barn door that he'd left open behind him.

Standing stock-still, Quinn Drummond listened intently, his eyes searching the black shadows around him. He'd built the barn. He knew it like the back of his hand. He knew the sounds that belonged, and the ones that didn't. Animal or human, it didn't matter. He knew.

He reached out his right hand, unerringly grabbing onto a long wooden handle. He'd prefer his shotgun, but it was up in the house. So the pitchfork would have to do.

This wasn't some damn possum rooting around.

This was some*one*. Someone hiding out in his barn.

He knew everyone who lived in his Texas hometown. Horseback Hollow was the polar opposite of a metropolis. If someone there wanted something, they'd have come to his face, not skulk around in the middle of the night inside his barn.

His hand tightened around the sturdy handle. His focus followed the rustling sound and he took a silent step closer to it. "Come on out now, because if you don't, I promise you won't like what's gonna happen."

The faint rustle became a scuffling sound, then the darkness in front of him gathered into a small form.

His wariness drained away. His tight grip relaxed. Just a kid.

He made a face and set aside the pitchfork. "What'd you do? Run away from home?" He'd tried that once, when he was seven. Hadn't gotten far. His dad had hauled him home and would have tanned his butt if his mother hadn't stepped in. "Never works, kid," he advised. "Whatever you think you're running from will always follow."

The form shuffled closer; small, booted feet sliding into the faint moonlight, barely visible below the too-long hem of baggy pants. "That's what I'm afraid of," the shadow said.

Forget wariness. The voice didn't belong to a child. It was feminine. Very British. And so damn familiar his guts twisted and his nerves frizzed like they wanted to bust out of his skin. A runaway would have been preferable to this. To *her*.

Amelia.

Her name blasted through his head, but he didn't say a word and after a moment, she took another hesitant step closer. Moonlight crept from the dark boots up baggy pants, an untucked, oversize shirt that dwarfed her delicate figure, until finally, *finally,* illuminating the long neck, the pointed chin.

The first time that he'd seen her had been six months ago on New Year's Eve, at a wedding for one of her newly discovered cousins, right there in Horseback Hollow. Her long dark hair had been twisted into a knot, reminding him vaguely of the dancers at the ballet that his mom had once dragged him and his sister to. The second time that he'd seen her months later at the end of April, had been at another wedding. Another cousin. And her hair had been tied up then, too.

But that second time, after dreaming about her since New Year's, Quinn hadn't just watched Amelia from a distance.

No.

He'd approached her. And through some miracle of fate—or so he'd thought at the time—later that night, he'd taken the pins from her hair and it had spilled down past her shoulders, gleaming and silky against her ivory skin.

He blocked off the memory. He'd had enough practice at it over the past two months that it should have been easy.

It wasn't. It was the very reason he was prowling restlessly around in the middle of the night at all when he should have been sleeping.

"What the hell'd you do to your hair?"

She made a soft sound and lifted her hand to the side of the roughly chopped short hair sticking out from her head. She'd have looked like a boy if her delicate features weren't so distinctively feminine. "It's lovely to see you, too." She moved her hand again, and it came away with the hair.

A wig. It was stupid to feel relieved, but he did.

She scrubbed the fingers of her other hand across her scalp, and her hair, the real stuff, slid down in a coil over one shoulder, as dark as the night sky. "It's a wig," she said, stating the obvious. Her voice was unsteady. "The second one, actually. The first was blond, but there were reporters at the airport, and—" She shook her head, breaking off.

That night—the night he'd twisted his hands in her hair and thought he'd tasted perfection on her lips—she'd talked about the reporters who had dogged her family's footsteps for as long as she could remember. How she hated being in a fishbowl. How her life felt claustrophobic. How she envied his life on a ranch; the wide-open spaces, the wind at his back when he rode his horse.

Again, he pushed away the thoughts. He shoved his fingertips into the pockets of his jeans, wishing he could wipe away the memory of her silky hair sliding over his chest as they'd made love. "What are you doing here?"

"In your barn? Proving I'm better at remembering a Google Map than I thought." She let out a nervous sound that was maybe supposed to be a laugh but could have been a sob.

"Not my barn," he said tightly. *"Here."*

She took a quick, audible breath. She was young. Seven years younger than his own thirty. Practically a girl. Except she wasn't a girl. She was full-grown. Self-possessed. Aristocratic.

And now, she was hiding in his barn, stumbling around for words.

"Amelia," he prompted sharply. He couldn't pretend her unexpected appearance didn't make him tense. Any more than she could hide the fact that she was clearly nervous. The way she kept shifting from one foot to the other, almost swaying, told him that.

"Yes. Right. The, um, the last time we spoke—"

"*What* are you doing here?" He didn't want to rehash that phone conversation. It had been nearly two months ago. He didn't want to think about what had precipitated it. Didn't want to think about it and damn sure didn't want to feel anything about it. Not that conversation, or whatever was making her so skittish now.

Her lips moved again but no sound came out. She lifted her hand to the side of her head again. Swayed almost imperceptibly.

And pitched forward.

He let out an oath, his heart nearly jumping out of his chest, and barely caught her limp body before it hit the ground at his feet.

He crouched beside her, carefully holding her. He caught her chin in his hand. She felt cold. And was out cold. "Amelia!"

Dim light or not, he could see that her lashes, so dark against her pale, pale cheeks, didn't so much as flicker.

He rose, lifting her in his arms. It was easy. He routinely tossed around hay bales that weighed more than she did, and she seemed even thinner now than the night he'd replaced her fancy gown with his hands. She was neither short, nor tall. Pretty average height. But that was the only thing average about Amelia Fortune Chesterfield.

Everything else—

He shook his head, blowing out a breath and carried her out of the barn, not even bothering to pull the door closed though he'd likely come back in the morning to find that possum taking up residence there again. He aimed for his truck parked up by the house, about a hundred yards away, his stride fast and gaining speed as he went. The moonlight shone down on her, painting her face an even whiter hue, and her gleaming head bounced against his arm as he ran.

He could hardly breathe by the time he made it to his truck, and it wasn't because he was out of shape. It was because the nearest hospital was in Lubbock, a good hour away.

He could deal with a lot of minor medical emergencies.

He couldn't deal with an unconscious Amelia Fortune Chesterfield.

Adjusting his grip beneath her, he managed to get the door open with one hand and settled her on the seat.

Her head lolled limply to the side, quickly followed by her lax shoulders.

"Come on, princess," he whispered, gently situating her again, holding her up long enough to get the safety belt clipped in place. The chest strap held her back against the seat and he started to draw his hands away from her waist and her shoulders so he could close the door, but her arm shifted slightly. Then her hand. Sliding over his, lighter than a breath but still enough to make the world seem to stop spinning.

"I'm not a princess," she whispered almost inaudibly.

He exhaled roughly. She'd said the same thing *that* night, too.

Only then she'd been looking up at him through her lashes; a combination of innocence and sexiness that had gone to his head quicker than the finest whiskey.

Maybe she wasn't a princess. But she was still the youngest daughter of Lady Josephine Fortune Chesterfield and the late Sir Simon John Chesterfield. And since it had come out last year that Horseback Hollow's own resident Jeanne Marie Jones was a long-lost sister of Lady

Josephine, the Chesterfield family was officially one of the town's hottest topics. Even Quinn's own sister, Jess, usually practical and definitely down-to-earth, had been struck royal-crazy. It had gotten so bad lately that he'd pretty much avoided her whenever he could, just so he wouldn't have to listen to her jabber on about the latest news from across the pond.

And for the past few months, particularly, he couldn't even visit the Superette in town to pick up his weekly milk and bread without seeing a magazine on the racks that mentioned Amelia in some way.

He took her hand and set it away from him, backing away to slam the truck door closed. He strode around the front and got in behind the wheel, not wanting to look at her, yet not being able to stop himself from doing so. The dome light shining on her face was more relentless than the moonlight, showing the dark circles under her eyes.

She looked ill.

He swiftly turned the key and started the engine. "I'm taking you to the hospital in Lubbock," he said flatly.

She shifted, her hand reaching for his arm again. Her fingertips dug into his forearm with surprising strength for someone who'd nearly face-planted in the dirt. "I don't need a hospital," she said quickly. "Please." Her voice broke.

"You need something." He shrugged off her touch and steered the truck away from the house. "And you won't find it here."

She sucked in an audible breath again and even though he knew he was in the right, he still felt like a bastard.

"You fainted. You need a doctor."

"No. I just… It's just been a long trip. I haven't eaten since, well since Heathrow, I guess."

He wasn't going to ask why. Wasn't going to let himself care. She was just another faithless woman. He'd already graduated from that school and didn't need another course. "First-class fare not up to your standards?"

She ignored his sarcasm. "I was in economy." She plucked the collar of her shirt that was mud-colored in the truck's light. "I was trying not to be noticed." She turned away, looking out the side window. "For all the good that did. I managed to lose Ophelia Malone before I left London, but there were still two more photographers to take her place the second I landed." She sighed. "I lost them in Dallas, but only because I changed my disguise and caught a bus."

He nearly choked. "You rode a bus? From Dallas to Horseback Hollow?" It had to have taken hours. On top of the flight, she'd probably been traveling for nearly twenty-four hours. "You have no business riding around on a bus!"

She didn't look at him, but even beneath the rough clothes that dwarfed her slender figure, he could tell she stiffened. "It's a perfectly convenient mode of transportation," she defended.

Sure. For people like him. He was a small-town rancher. She was *the* Amelia Fortune Chesterfield. And since the day she'd returned to England after her night dabbling with Quinn—after making him believe that she was going back to London only to attend to some royal duties and would quickly return to Horseback Hollow— she'd become one half of the engaged couple dubbed "Jamelia" by the media that dogged her steps.

Amelia Fortune Chesterfield was to marry James Banning in the most popular royal romance since the Duke and Duchess of Cambridge. *Lord* James Banning. A viscount, whatever the hell that was. A man who was her equal in wealth and family connections. A man who was slated for an even higher title, evidently, once Amelia was his wife. Earl something of something or other.

His sister had talked about it so many times, the facts ought to be tattooed on his brain.

His fingers strangled the steering wheel. "Wedding plans becoming so taxing that you had to run away from them?" He didn't wait for an answer. "Never mind. I don't want to know." He turned through the overhead arch bearing the iron Rocking-U sign and pressed harder on the gas. The highway was still a fair piece away, but once he hit that, it'd be smooth sailing. He'd leave her in capable medical hands and wash his hands of her, once and for all.

Somewhere inside his head, laughter mocked the notion. He'd been doing that so-called washing for the past two months and hadn't gotten anywhere. There had to be something wrong with him that he couldn't just file her away as a one-night stand where she belonged and be done with it.

"*Please* don't take me to Lubbock," she said huskily. "I don't need a doctor. I just need some sleep. And some food." She reached across as if she were going to touch his arm again, but curled her fingers into a fist instead, resting it on the console between their seats. "Drop me on the side of the road if you must. I'm begging you. Please, Quinn."

He ground his molars together. Would he have had more resistance if she hadn't said his name? "I'm not gonna drop you on the side of the damn road."

He should take her to Jeanne's. Recently discovered

family or not, the woman was Amelia's aunt. Jeanne would take her in. Even if it *was* the middle of the night.

He muttered an oath and pulled a U-turn there on the empty highway.

Maybe Amelia wouldn't mind Jeanne's questions, asked or unasked, but Quinn would. Particularly when he had unanswered questions of his own.

He didn't look at her. "I'll take you back to the Rocking-U. And then you can start talking."

His voice was so hard.

His face so expressionless.

Amelia wrapped her arms around herself and tried to quell her trembling. She was so, so tired.

She'd foolishly thought that once she got back to Horseback Hollow, once she saw Quinn in person, everything would be all right.

She could explain. And he would understand.

He would take her in his arms, and everything would be perfect and as wonderful as it had been the night of her cousin Toby's wedding. Quinn would know that there was only him. That there had only ever been him.

It had been the single thing keeping her going throughout the dreadful ordeal of getting to Horseback Hollow.

"You can start—" Quinn's deep voice cut through her "—with explaining why you came to the Rocking-U at all."

"I wanted to talk," she whispered.

He gave her a long look. Animosity rolled off him in waves, a stark contrast to the tender warmth he'd shown her just six weeks earlier. "Yet so far you haven't said anything new."

She wanted to wring her hands. Such a silly, naive girl

to think that her presence would be enough to make up for everything she hadn't said that she should have. For everything she hadn't done that she should have.

"What did Banning do? Disagree over china patterns? So you run away again to the States to bring him to heel? Your last trip here was pretty effective. Ended up with a royal engagement the second you got back home. Or maybe you're just in the mood for one more final fling before the 'I do's' get said."

"I told you weeks ago that there's no engagement," she reminded carefully. After a week of the frantic telephone messages she'd left for him once she'd arrived in London, he'd finally returned her call. She'd tried to explain to him then about the media frenzy that had greeted her at the airport when she'd returned from Toby's wedding.

Reporters shouting their congratulations on her engagement to James. Cameras flashing in her eyes. She'd been blindsided by the unwanted attention as much as she'd been blindsided by news of an engagement she and James had discussed, but had never agreed to.

He grunted derisively. "And I don't believe you any more now than I did when you said it the first time. You came to Horseback Hollow two months ago and you had sex with the poor dumb cowboy who didn't know enough to recognize things for what they were. Your little walk on the wild side, I guess, before settling down all nice and proper with the English earl."

"James isn't an earl yet." Which was the furthest thing from what she wanted to say.

"I don't give a damn what he is or isn't." He slowed to make the turn through the iron archway, but the tires still kicked out an angry, arching spit of gravel. "He's your fiancé. That's the only thing I have to know. And as good as you were in the sack, princess, I'm not interested in a repeat performance."

She bit down on her tongue to keep from gasping and stared hard out the side window until the tears pushing behind her eyes subsided. They hadn't ever made it to a "sack," as he so crudely put it. They'd made love under the moonlight in a field of green, surrounded by trees, singing crickets and croaking frogs. She'd slept in his arms under the stars and wakened at dawn to chirping birds and his kisses.

It had been magical.

"It was six weeks ago," she whispered.

He still managed to hear. "Six. Eight. Whatever it was, it no longer matters to me. You want to screw around with a cowboy, do it on someone else's ranch."

She snapped her head around, looking at him. Even though it was dark as pitch, and the only light came from the glow of his pickup truck's instrument panel, she still knew every inch of his face. Every detail. From the dark brown hair springing thickly back from his sun-bronzed forehead to the spiky lashes surrounding his hazel eyes to his angular jaw. She knew his quiet smile. The easy way he held his tall, muscular body.

"Don't do that," she said sharply. "Don't cheapen what we had."

"What we had, prin*cess*—" he drew out the word in a mocking British accent "—was a one-night stand. And the next day, you returned to the loving arms of your intended. Poor bastard. Does he know what he's getting?" He pulled to a stop in front of a modestly sized two-storied house and turned off the engine. "Or maybe he doesn't care. Maybe he's just happy to merge one highfalutin' family with another and fidelity doesn't matter one little bit."

"He's not my fiancé!"

"And that's what you came all the way here to talk about," he said skeptically. "To claim that he's not your fiancé? While every newspaper and trashy tabloid in print, every gossipy website that exists, is dissecting the great 'Jamelia' romance. If he's not your fiancé, why the hell aren't there any quotes from you saying *that*? Everything else about the two of you has been chronicled across the world. Seems to me there have been plenty of opportunities for you to state otherwise." He stared into her face for a long moment, then shook his head and shoved open his truck door. "We had this same conversation two months ago on the phone." His voice was flat. "Should have saved yourself a ten-hour flight in coach." He slammed the door shut and started walking toward the house.

"Six weeks ago," she whispered again

But of course he didn't hear her this time.

Chapter Two

Amelia finally got out of the truck and headed slowly toward him. Quinn watched only long enough to assure himself that she wasn't going to collapse again, before he turned toward the house once more. He wanted her in his home about as much as he wanted holes drilled into his head.

It was hard enough to forget about her when she'd never stepped foot in his place. Now she was going to do just that. And his need to keep her out of his thoughts was going to become even more impossible.

He shoved open the front door and waited for her to finish crossing the gravel drive. Her dark hair gleamed in the moonlight, reminding him of the last time. Only then the long strands had been fanned out around her head, and her face bathed in ecstasy.

He clenched his teeth and looked at the scuffed toes of

his leather boots. The second she crossed the threshold, he moved away. "Close the door behind you."

His steps sounded hollow on the wood floor as he headed through the house to the kitchen at the back and he heard the soft latch of the front door closing behind him.

He slapped his palm against the wall switch, flooding the kitchen with unforgiving light, and grabbed the plastic-wrapped loaf of bread from where he'd last tossed it on the counter. He yanked open a drawer, grabbed a knife, slammed the drawer shut and yanked open the fridge. Pulled a few things out and slammed that door shut, too.

None of it helped.

She was still in his damned house.

Another woman he'd let himself believe in.

Didn't matter that he knew he was to blame for that particular situation. He'd barely known Amelia. And he'd known his ex-wife, Carrie, for years. Yet he'd made the same mistake with them both.

Trusting that he was the one.

The only one.

He carelessly swiped mayonnaise on the two slices of bread, slapped a slice of cheese on top, followed by a jumble of deli-sliced turkey.

Every cell he possessed knew the minute Amelia stepped into the kitchen behind him, though she didn't make a sound. She was as ghostly quiet as she was ghostly pale.

He dropped the other slice of bread on top of the turkey and managed not to smash it down out of sheer frustration. He tossed the knife in the sink next to his elbow and it clattered noisily.

He turned and faced her, choking down the urge to take her shoulders and urge her into a chair.

She looked worse than ill.

The shadows under her eyes were nearly purple. The oversize shirt—an uglier color than the contents of his youngest nephew's diaper the last time he'd been stuck changing it—had slipped down one of her shoulders and her collarbone stuck out too sharp against her pale skin.

It wasn't just a day of traveling—by means he damn sure knew she wasn't used to—taking its toll.

"What the hell have you done to yourself?"

Her colorless lips parted slightly. She stared up at him and her eyes—dark, dark brown and enormous in her small triangular face—shimmered wetly. "You're so angry," she whispered.

Angry didn't begin to cover it. He was pissed as hell. Frustrated beyond belief. And completely disillusioned with his judgment where women were concerned.

Especially this woman, because dammit all to hell, there was still a part of him that wanted to believe in her. Believe the things she'd said that night. Believe the things she'd made him feel that night.

And he knew better.

"I should have taken you to the hospital," he said flatly. "Have you had the flu or something?" God forbid she was suffering anything worse.

Her lashes lowered and she reached out a visibly unsteady hand for one of the wood chairs situated around his small, square table. But she only braced herself; she didn't sit. "I haven't been sick. I told you, I just need food and a little rest."

"A little?" He snorted and nudged her down onto the chair seat. A nudge is all it took, too, because her legs folded way too easily. He would have termed it collapsing, except she did even that with grace.

As soon as she was sitting, he took his hand away, curling his fingers against his palm.

Whether to squeeze away the feel of her fragile shoulder, or to hold on to it, he wasn't sure.

And that just pissed him off even more.

He grabbed the sandwich, and ignoring every bit of manners his mom had ever tried to teach him, plopped it on the bare table surface in front of her. No napkin. No plate.

If she wanted to toy around with a cowboy, she'd better learn there weren't going to be any niceties. He almost wished he chewed, because the notion of spitting tobacco juice out just then was stupidly appealing.

She, of course, not-a-princess that she was, ignored his cavalier behavior and turned her knees beneath the table, sitting with a straight back despite her obvious exhaustion. Then she picked up the sandwich with as much care as if it were crustless, cut into fancy shapes and served up on priceless silver. "Thank you," she said quietly.

He wanted to slam his head against a wall.

Every curse he knew filled his head, all of them directed right at his own miserable hide. He grimly pulled a sturdy white plate from the cupboard and set it on the table. He didn't have napkins, but he tore a paper towel off the roll, folded it in half and set it next to the plate. Then, feeling her big brown eyes following him, he grabbed a clean glass and filled it with cold tap water. She was surely used to the stuff that came in fancy tall bottles, but there was no better water around than what came from the Rocking-U well. Aside from water, he had milk and beer. He wasn't sure the milk wasn't sour by now, and she definitely wasn't the type to drink beer.

"Thank you," she said again, after taking a long sip of the water. "I don't mean to put you to any trouble."

He folded his arms across his chest and dragged his gaze away from the soft glisten of moisture lingering on her full, lower lip. "Shouldn't have gotten on the airplane, then." Much less a bus.

She looked away.

For about the tenth time since he'd found her hiding in his barn, he felt like he'd kicked a kitten. Then ground his boot heel down on top of it for good measure.

"Eat." He sounded abrupt and didn't care. "I'll get a bed ready for you."

She nodded, still not looking at him. "Thank—" Her voice broke off for a moment. "You," she finished faintly.

That politeness of hers would be the end of him.

He left the kitchen with embarrassing haste and stomped up the stairs to the room at the end of the hall. He stopped in the doorway and stared at the bed.

It was the only one in the house.

It was his.

"You're a freaking idiot," he muttered to himself as he crossed the room and yanked the white sheets that were twisted and tangled and as much off the bed as they were on into some semblance of order. He'd have changed the sheets if he owned more than one set.

Once she was gone, he'd have to burn the damn things and buy different ones. For that matter, he might as well replace the whole bed. He hadn't had a decent night's sleep since learning she'd gotten engaged to that other guy within hours of leaving his arms. He was pretty sure that sleeping was only going to get harder from here on out.

He realized he was strangling his pillow between his fists, and slapped it down on the bed.

It was summertime, so he hadn't personally been bothering with much more than a sheet, but he unearthed the quilt that his mother had made for him years earlier from where he'd hidden it away in the closet after Carrie left him, and spread it out on top of the sheets. It smelled vaguely of mothballs, but it was better than nothing.

Then he shoved the ragged paperback book he'd been reading from the top of the nightstand into the drawer, effectively removing the only personal item in sight, and left the room.

He went back downstairs.

She was still sitting at the table in his kitchen, her back straight as a ruler, her elbows nowhere near the table. She'd finished the sandwich, though, and was folding the paper towel into intricate shapes. Not for the first time, he eyed her slender fingers, bare of rings, and reminded himself that the absence of a diamond ring didn't mean anything.

When she heard him, she stood. "I should go to Aunt Jeanne's."

"Yes." He wasn't going to lie. She'd already done enough of that for them both. "But it's after midnight. No point in ruining someone else's night's sleep, too. And since Horseback Hollow isn't blessed with any motels, much less an establishment up to your standards," he added even though she was too cultured to say so, "you're stuck with what I have." He eyed her. "Bedroom's upstairs. Do you have enough stuffing left in you to make it up them, or do I need to put you over my shoulder?"

Her ghostly pale face took on a little color at that. "I'm not a sack of feed," she said, almost crisply, and headed past him through the doorway.

His house wasn't large. The staircase was right there to the left of the front door and his grandmother's piano. She headed straight to it, closed her slender fingers over the wood banister and started up. The ugly shirt she wore hung over her hips, midway down the thighs of her baggy jeans.

He still had to look away from the sway of her hips as she took the steps. "Room's at the end of the hall," he said after her. "Bathroom's next to it."

Manners might have had him escorting her up there.

Self-preservation kept him standing right where he was.

"Yell if you need something," he added gruffly.

She stopped, nearly at the top of the stairs, and looked back at him. Her hair slid over her shoulder.

Purple shadows, ghostly pale and badly fitting clothes or not, she was still the most beautiful thing he'd ever seen and looking at her was a physical pain.

"I need you not to hate me," she said softly.

His jaw tightened right along with the band across his chest that made it hard to breathe. "I don't hate you, Amelia."

Her huge eyes stared at him. They were haunting, those eyes.

"I don't feel anything," he finished.

It was the biggest lie he'd ever told in his life.

Amelia's knees wobbled and she tightened her grip on the smooth, warm wooden banister. Quinn could say what he wanted, but the expression on his face told another story.

And she had only herself to blame.

No words came to mind that were appropriate for the situation. Even if there *were* words, she wasn't sure her tight throat would have allowed her to voice them. So she just gave him an awkward nod and headed up the remaining stairs. Because what else was there to do but go forward?

There was no going back.

He'd made that painfully clear more than once and her coming to Horseback Hollow to see him face-to-face hadn't changed a single thing.

At the landing, the room he spoke of was obvious. Straight at the end of the hall.

The door was open and through it she could see the foot of a quilt-covered bed.

She pushed back her shoulders despite her weariness, and headed toward it. If she weren't feeling devastated to her core, she would have gobbled up every detail of his home as she walked along the wooden-floored hallway. Would have struggled not to let her intense curiosity where he was concerned overtake her. Would have wondered how each nook and cranny reflected Quinn. The man she'd fallen head over heels in love with on the foolish basis of a few dances at a wedding reception.

And a night of lovemaking after.

The thought was unbearable and she pushed it away.

She'd deal with that later.

She stopped at the bathroom briefly and shuddered over her pallid reflection in the oval mirror that hung over a classic pedestal sink when she washed her hands. It was no wonder he'd stared at her with such horror.

She looked hideous.

Not at all the way she'd looked the night he'd stopped next to her at Toby's wedding reception, smiled quietly and asked if she cared to dance. She'd looked as good that day as her gawky self was capable of looking.

But when Quinn took her in his arms and slowly circled around the outdoor dance floor with her to the croon of Etta James, for the first time, she'd felt beautiful. All because of the way he'd looked at her.

Tears burned behind her eyes again and she quickly left the bathroom behind, hurrying the remaining few feet into the bedroom. She shut the door soundlessly, leaned back against it and slid down it until her bottom hit the floor.

Then she drew up her knees and pressed her forehead to them.

He believed their lovemaking had been some sort of last fling for her, before settling down with Jimmy, whom she'd been seeing during the months before she'd spontaneously attended Toby's wedding. Quinn had accused her of that during that dreadful phone conversation. In the weeks since, he'd obviously not changed his opinion.

So how was she ever going to be able to tell him that she was pregnant?

With *his* child?

If he accused her of lying about that, too, she wasn't sure she could survive it.

She sat there, her sorrow too deep for tears, until her bottom felt numb. Then feeling ancient, she shifted onto her knees and pushed herself to her aching feet. The boots she'd borrowed from Molly, one of her mother's junior secretaries whom Amelia trusted, were too wide and too short. They, along with the ill-fitting jeans and the shirt, belonged to Molly's teenage brother as had the other set of clothes she'd started out in. They'd been left, shoved deep in the rubbish, at the airport in Dallas alongside the blond wig and the knapsack in which she'd carried their replacements.

She dragged her passport out of the back pocket and set it on the rustic wooden nightstand. Even though Molly had helped with the disguises, neither one of them had been able to think of a way around traveling under Amelia's own name. Not with security standards being what they were. All she'd come with had been the passport, her credit card and a small wad of American currency tucked among the well-stamped pages of her passport. Molly had insisted on the credit card, though Amelia had wanted to leave it behind. She knew cash was untraceable, while a credit card wasn't, and she'd stuck to it. The only thing she'd purchased had been the bus fare from Dallas. Once she'd reached Lubbock, she'd hitched a ride with a trucker as far as the outskirts of Horseback Hollow. Then, using the directions she'd memorized from Molly, she'd walked the rest of the way to what she'd hoped was Quinn's ranch. But in her exhaustion and the darkness she hadn't been certain. So she'd hidden in the barn, intending to rest until daylight.

Her head swam dizzily and she quickly sat at the foot of the bed, the mattress springs giving the faintest of creaks. She closed her eyes, breathing evenly. She didn't know whether to blame the light-headedness on pregnancy or exhaustion. Aside from her missed period, she hadn't experienced any other signs that she was carrying a baby. And if it hadn't been for Molly who'd suggested that her irregularity might *not* be a result of stress as Amelia had believed at first, she probably wouldn't know even now that she was carrying Quinn's baby. She'd still be thinking she was just stressed over the whole engagement fiasco.

Why, oh, why hadn't she spoken up when those reporters greeted her at the airport six weeks ago, clamoring for details about her engagement to James? Why had she just put up her hand to shield her face and raced alongside her driver until reaching the relative sanctuary of the Town Car? She hadn't even dared to phone James until she'd gotten home because she feared having her cell phone hacked again. Even though it had happened well over a year ago, the sense of invasion still lived on.

If she'd only have spoken up, denied the engagement to the press right then and there, she wouldn't be in this situation now. After the initial embarrassment, James's situation with his family would have ironed itself out in time.

Most important, though, Quinn wouldn't have any reason to hate her.

She would have returned to him weeks ago exactly as they'd planned while lying together atop a horse blanket with an endless expanse of stars twinkling over them. Then, learning she was pregnant would have been something for them to discover together.

If only.

Her light-headedness was easing, though she really felt no better. But she opened her eyes and slowly pulled off the boots and socks and dropped them on the floor next to the bed. She wiggled her toes until some feeling returned and flopped back on the mattress.

The springs gave a faint squeak again.

It was a comforting sound and, too tired to even finish undressing, she dragged one of the two pillows at the head of the bed to her cheek and closed her eyes once more.

Things would be better in the morning.

They had to be.

When there were no more sounds, faint though they were, coming from his room upstairs, Quinn finally left the kitchen where he'd been hiding out. He left the house and walked back down to the barn with only the moonlight for company. He closed the door and even though there'd be endless chores to be done before the sun came up and he ought to be trying to sleep the last few hours before then, his aimless footsteps carried him even farther from the house.

But he kept glancing back over his shoulder. Looking at the dark windows on the upper story that belonged to his bedroom. Amelia had eaten the sandwich. But did that really mean anything?

If she fainted again how would he even know?

She'd been raised in the lap of luxury. First-class flights and luxury limousines driven by guys wearing suits and caps. Not economy class and bus tickets and God knew what.

Clawing his fingers through his hair, he turned back to the house. It wasn't the house that he and Jess had grown up in. That had burned nearly to the ground when Quinn was fifteen, destroying almost everything they'd owned. The same year his dad had already succeeded in literally working to death on the Rocking-U, trying to prove himself as good a rancher as the father who'd never acknowledged him. Jess, five years older, was already off and married to Mac with a baby on the way. Ursula, his mom, would have sold off the ranch then if she'd have been able to find an interested buyer other than her dead husband's hated father. But she'd only been able to find takers for the livestock.

Despite Quinn's noisy protests, she'd moved the two of them into a two-bedroom trailer on the outskirts of town and there they'd lived until Quinn graduated from high school. Then she'd packed him off to college, packed up her clothes and moved away from the town that had only ever seemed to bring her unhappiness. Now she lived in Dallas in one of those "active adult" neighborhoods where she played bridge and tennis. She had a circle of friends she liked, and she was happy.

Not Quinn. The moment he could, he'd headed back to Horseback Hollow and the fallen-down, barren Rocking-U. He'd had a few years of college under his belt—gained only through scholarships and part-time jobs doing anything and everything he could pick up—and a new bride on his arm.

He was going to do what his father had never been able to do. Make the Rocking-U a real success.

At least one goal had been achieved.

He'd built the small house, though it had cost him two years and a wife along the way. He'd had his grandmother's piano restored and the dregs of the old, burned house hauled away. He'd shored up broken down fences and a decrepit barn. He'd built a herd. It was small, but it was prime Texas Longhorn.

He'd made something he could be proud of. Something his father had never achieved but still would have been proud of and something his father's father could choke on every time he thought about the people he liked to pretend never existed.

And when Quinn had danced with Amelia at a wedding reception six weeks ago, he'd let himself believe that there *was* a woman who could love his life the same way that he did.

All he'd succeeded in doing, though, was proving that he was Judd Drummond's son, through and through. A damn stupid dreamer.

He went back into the silent house. He had a couch in the living room. Too short and too hard to make much of a bed, but it was that or the floor. He turned off the light and sat down and worked off his boots, dropping them on the floor.

He couldn't hear anything from upstairs.

He stretched out as well as he could. Dropped his forearm over his eyes.

Listened to the rhythmic tick of the antique clock sitting on the fireplace mantel across the room.

What if she really was sick?

"Dammit," he muttered, and jackknifed to his feet. Moving comfortably in the darkness, he went to the stairs and started up. At the top, he headed to the end of the hall and closed his hand around the doorknob leading into his bedroom.

But he hesitated.

Called himself a damned fool. He ought to go back downstairs and try to redeem what little he could of the night in sleep.

Only sleeping was a laughable notion.

He'd just glance inside the room. Make sure she was sleeping okay.

He turned the knob. Nudged open the door.

He could see the dark bump of her lying, unmoving, on his bed. He stepped closer and his stockinged toes knocked into something on the floor. They bumped and thumped.

Her shoes.

It was a good thing he'd never aspired to a life of crime when he couldn't even sneak into his own bedroom without making a commotion. He'd probably been quieter when he'd found her in his damn barn.

Despite the seemingly loud noise, though, the form on the bed didn't move. He ignored the sound of his pulse throbbing in his ears until he was able to hear her soft breathing.

Fine. All good.

He had no excuse to linger. Not in a dark room in the middle of the night with another man's fiancée. There were lines a man didn't cross, and that was one of them.

It should have been easy to leave the room. And because it wasn't, he grimaced and turned.

Avoiding her shoes on the floor, he left the room more quietly than he'd entered. He returned to the couch. Threw himself down on it again.

He'd take her to her aunt's in the morning. After she woke.

And what Amelia did after that wasn't anything he was going to let himself care about.

Chapter Three

Quinn stared at the empty bed.

Amelia was gone.

It was only nine in the morning, and sometime between when he'd left the house at dawn and when he'd returned again just now, she'd disappeared.

If not for the wig that he'd found on the ground inside his barn door, he might have wondered if he'd hallucinated the entire thing.

It didn't take a genius to figure out she'd beat him to the punch in calling her aunt. One phone call to Jeanne, or to any one of the newfound cousins, and rescue would have easily arrived within an hour.

He walked into the bedroom.

The bed looked exactly the way it had when he'd tossed the quilt on top of it, before she'd gone to bed. Maybe a little neater. Maybe a lot neater.

He'd also thought her presence would linger after she was gone. But it didn't.

The room—hell, the entire house—felt deathly still. Empty.

That was the legacy she'd left that he'd have to live with.

He tossed the wig on the foot of the bed and rubbed the back of his neck. He had a crick in it from sleeping—or pretending to—on the too-short couch.

It shouldn't matter that she'd left without a word. Snuck out while his back was essentially turned. He hadn't wanted her there in the first place. And obviously, her need to "talk" hadn't been so strong, after all.

"Gone and good riddance," he muttered.

Then, because he smelled more like cow than man and Jess would give him a rash of crap about it when he showed up at his nephew's baseball game in Vicker's Corners that afternoon, he grabbed a shower and changed into clean jeans and T-shirt.

In the kitchen, the paper towel that he'd given Amelia was still sitting on the table where she'd left it, all folded up. He grabbed it to toss it in the trash, but hesitated.

She hadn't just folded the paper into a bunch of complicated triangles. She'd fashioned it into a sort of bird. As if the cheap paper towel was some fancy origami.

I have lots of useless talents.

The memory of her words swam in his head.

She'd told him that, and more, when they'd lain under the stars. How she had a degree in literature that she didn't think she'd ever use. How she spoke several languages even though she didn't much care for traveling. How she could play the piano and the harp well enough to play at some of the family's royal functions, but suffered stage fright badly enough that having to do so was agonizing.

He pinched the bridge of his nose where a pain was forming in his head and dropped the paper bird on the table again, before grabbing his Resistol hat off the peg by the back door and heading out.

He paid Tanya Fremont, one of the students where Jess and Mac taught high school, to clean his house once a week and she'd be there that weekend.

She could take care of the trash.

"Aunt Jeanne, *really?*" Amelia lifted a glossy tabloid magazine off the coffee table where it was sitting and held it up. "I can't believe you purchase these things."

Her aunt's blue eyes were wry as she sat down beside Amelia on the couch. She set the two mugs of herbal tea she was carrying on the coffee table and plucked the glossy out of Amelia's hands. She spread it over the knees of her faded blue jeans and tapped the small picture on the upper corner of the cover. "It had a picture of you and Lucie," she defended. "You and your sister looked so pretty. I thought I'd clip it out and put it in my scrapbook."

Amelia was touched by the thought even though she deplored being on the magazine cover. The photo was from the dedication of one of the orphanages her mother helped establish. Amelia recognized the dress she'd worn to the ceremony. "I don't even want to know what the article said." Undoubtedly, it had not focused on the good works of Lady Josephine or Lucie's latest accomplishments, but the pending nuptials of Amelia and Lord James Banning, the Viscount St. Allen and heir apparent to the Earl of Estingwood.

"No article," Jeanne Marie corrected. "Not really. Just

a small paragraph from *close friends*—" she sketched quotes in the air "—of 'Jamelia' that the wedding date had been set, but was being kept under wraps for now to preserve your and James's privacy."

"There *is* no wedding date," Amelia blurted. She slumped back on the couch.

"Oh?" Jeanne Marie leaned forward and set the magazine on the coffee table. She picked up her tea and studied Amelia over the rim of the sturdy mug with eyes that were eerily similar to Amelia's mother.

That was to be expected, she supposed, since Josephine and Jeanne Marie were two thirds of a set of triplets. What wasn't the norm, was the fact that the siblings had only recently discovered one another. Amelia's mother hadn't even known that she'd been adopted until she'd met Jeanne Marie Fortune Jones and their triplet brother, James Marshall Fortune. He was the only reason the trio had found one another after having been separated as young children. There was even another older brother, John Fortune, to add to the new family tree.

Amelia realized her aunt wasn't gaping at her over the news there was to be no wedding. "You don't seem very surprised."

Jeanne Marie lifted one shoulder. "Well, honey. You *are* here." And again, even though her words were full of Texas drawl, her mild, somewhat ironic lilt was exactly the same as Josephine's entirely proper Brit would have been.

It was still startling to Amelia, even after meeting her aunt nearly a year ago.

"I'm assuming you have a good reason for not announcing you broke things off with your young man in England?"

"It's complicated," she murmured, even as she felt guilty for leaving her aunt under the impression that there had ever been something to break off in the first place. James had been as much a victim of their supposed engagement as she, since the presumptuous announcement had been issued by his father. But once it had been, and Amelia hadn't denied it, James had been doing his level best to convince her to make it a reality. Under immense family pressure to make a suitable marriage, he'd given up hope of a match with the girl he really loved—Astrid, who sold coffee at the stand in his building—and tried giving Amelia a family ring in hopes that she'd come around, though she'd refused to take it. "Jimmy and I have known each other a long time."

While she really only knew Quinn in the biblical sense. The irony of it all was heartbreaking.

"Sometimes a little distance has a way of uncomplicating things," Jeanne said. "And as delighted as I am to have you here, it does tend to raise a few questions. Particularly havin' to get you from Quinn Drummond's place practically before sunup. And havin' you dressed like you are."

Amelia's fingers pleated the hem of the oversize shirt. "I was trying to avoid paparazzi."

"So you said while we were driving here." Jeanne Marie finally set down the mug. She was obviously as disinterested in her tea as Amelia was. "What's going on between you and Quinn?"

"Nothing." She felt heat rise up her throat.

"And that's why you called me from his house at seven in the morning. Because nothing is going on between you two." Jeanne Marie's lips curved. "In my day, that sort of *nothing* usually led to a shotgun and a stand-up in front of a preacher whether there was another suitor in the wings or not."

Amelia winced.

Her aunt tsked, her expression going from wry to concerned in the blink of an eye. "Oh, honey." She closed her warm hands around Amelia's fidgeting fingers. "Whatever's upsetting you can be worked out. I promise you that."

Amelia managed a weak smile. "I appreciate the thought, Aunt Jeanne. But I grew up with my father always telling us not to make promises we couldn't keep."

Jeanne Marie squeezed her hand. "I wish I'd have had a chance to meet your daddy. Your mama says he was the love of her life."

Amelia nodded. Her father had died several years ago, but his loss was still sharp. "He was." She couldn't contain a yawn and covered it with her hand. Despite having slept several hours at Quinn's, she still could hardly keep her eyes open. "I'm so sorry."

"I'm the sorry one," Jeanne Marie said. She patted Amelia's hand and pushed to her feet. "You're exhausted, honey. You need to be in bed, not sitting here answering questions."

It took all the energy Amelia possessed to stand, also. "Are you certain I'm not imposing?"

Jeanne Marie laughed. "There's no such thing as imposing among family, honey. Deke and I raised seven kids in this house. Now they're all off and living their own lives. So it's nice to have one of those empty rooms filled again."

"You're very kind." She followed her aunt along the hall and up the stairs to a corner bedroom with windows on two walls. Amelia remembered the room from her first visit to Horseback Hollow six months ago, though it had been her mother who'd been assigned to it then. It was obviously a guest room. Simply but comfortably furnished with a bed covered in a quilt with fading pastel stitching that was all the lovelier for its graceful aging, a side table with dried cat's tails sticking out of an old-fashioned milk bottle, and a sturdy oak wardrobe. White curtains, nearly translucent, hung open at the square windows and moved gently in the warm morning breeze.

"This used to be Galen's room," Jeanne Marie said. "Being the oldest, there was a time he liked lording it over the others that he had the largest room." She crossed to the windows to begin lowering the shades. "Would have put you in here back when you came for Toby's wedding in April, but James Marshall and Clara were using it."

"Leave the windows open," Amelia begged quickly. "Please."

"The sunlight won't keep you awake?"

She self-consciously tugged at her ugly shirt. Light was the least disturbing thing she could think of at the moment. And better to have sunlight than darkness while the memories of the last time she'd been at her aunt's home were caving in on her. "The breeze is too lovely to shut out."

Jeanne Marie dropped her hands. She opened the wardrobe and pulled out two bed pillows from the shelf inside and set them on the bed. "Bathroom is next door," she reminded. "I'll make sure you have fresh towels. And I'm sure that Delaney or Stacey left behind some clothes that should fit you. They might be boxed up by now, but I'll try to scare up something for you to wear once you're rested."

Her welcome was so very different than Quinn's, deserved or not, and Amelia's eyes stung.

She cried much too easily these days. "Thank you." She sat on the foot of the bed and tried not to think about sitting on the bed at Quinn's.

She'd thought that had been a guest room, too. Until she'd awakened early that morning and had gone looking for him. She'd done what she hadn't had the energy for the night before. The rooms upstairs were spacious and full of windows and nothing else. Almost like they were stuck in time. Waiting for a reason to be filled with furniture. With family. Downstairs, he had a den with a plain wooden desk and an older style computer on it. The living room had a couch, a television that looked older than the computer, and a gleaming black upright piano. She'd drawn her fingers lightly over the keys, finding it perfectly tuned.

What she hadn't found was Quinn. Not only had he been nowhere to be found inside the two-story house, but she'd seen for herself that his home possessed only a single bed.

Which, regardless of his feelings, he'd given up for her.

Jeanne Marie watched the tangled expressions crossing her new niece's delicate features and controlled the urge to take the girl into her arms and rock her just as she would have her own daughters. "We've got most of the crew coming for supper tonight. But you just come on down whenever you're ready," she said comfortingly. "And don't you worry about me spilling your personal beans to your cousins. You can do that when you're good and ready." Then she kissed Amelia's forehead and left the room, closing the door behind her.

She set out fresh towels in the bathroom, then headed downstairs to the kitchen again and stopped in surprise at the sight of her husband just coming in from the back. "I thought you'd be out all morning."

"Thought I could get the engine on that old Deere going, but I need a couple more parts." He tossed his sweat-stained cowboy hat aside and rubbed his fingers through his thick, iron-gray hair before reaching out a long arm and hooking her around the waist. "Which leaves me the chance for some morning delight with my wife before I drive over to Vicker's Corners."

Jeanne Marie laughed softly, rubbing her arms over his broad shoulders. How she loved this man who'd owned her heart from the moment they'd met. "We're not alone in the house," she warned.

His eyebrow lifted. "I didn't notice any cars out front. Who's come this early for supper? Can't be Toby and his brood." He grinned faintly. "Those kids've been coming out of their shells real nice lately."

"And they'll continue to do so," Jeanne agreed, slightly distracted by the way Deke's wide palms were drifting from her waist down over the seat of her jeans. "As long as no more hitches come up to stop Toby and Angie adopting them." Their middle son and his new wife were trying to adopt three kids he'd been fostering for the past eight months and the process hadn't exactly been smooth so far.

Her blood was turning warm and she grabbed his wide wrists, redirecting his hands to less distracting territory. "Amelia's here."

His brows pulled together for a second. "Amelia? Josephine's youngest girl?"

"We don't know another Amelia," Jeanne Marie said dryly.

His hands fell away. He leaned back against the coun-

ter and folded his arms over his chest. "Fortunes are everywhere," he murmured.

She knew his face as well as she knew her own. She
had happily been Jeanne Marie Jones for forty years. But
learning that she had siblings out there, learning that she
had a blood connection to others in this world besides
the children of his that she'd borne, had filled a void inside her that Deke had never quite been able to understand. Even though her adoptive parents had loved her,
and she them, not knowing where she'd come from had
always pulled at her.

And now she knew.

And though Deke hadn't protested when she'd added
Fortune to her own name, she knew also that it hadn't
been entirely easy for him. When their kids followed suit,
it had gotten even harder for him to swallow.

No. The advent of the Fortunes to the Jones's lives
hadn't been easy. And maybe it would have been easier
if James had gone about things differently when he'd
tracked her down. Her newfound brother was a self-made
business tycoon used to having the world fall into place
exactly the way he planned and he'd not only upset his
own family in the process, he'd sent Jeanne Marie's family reeling, too, when he'd tried to give her part of his
significant fortune.

She'd turned down the money, of course. It didn't matter to her that all of her siblings turned out to be ridiculously wealthy while she was not. She and Deke had
a good life. A happy life. One blessed with invaluable
wealth for the very reason that it had nothing to do with
any amount of dollars and cents.

Convincing her pridefully suspicious husband that the

only fortune that mattered to her was the *name* Fortune, however, had been a long process.

One that was still obviously in the works, judging by Deke's stoic expression.

"How long's she staying?" he asked.

"I have no idea. The girl came here to figure some things out, I believe." Because she always felt better being busy, she pulled a few peaches out of the basket on the counter and grabbed a knife. She'd already made a chocolate cake for dessert for that evening, but Deke always loved a fresh peach pie. And even after forty years of marriage, a man still needed to know he was in the forefront of his wife's thoughts. "Do you think she should stay somewhere else?"

He frowned quickly. "No. She's family." His eyes met hers. "I get it, Jeanne Marie."

Her faint tension eased. He might not exactly understand the way she'd taken on the Fortune name, but he did get "it" when it came to family. Nothing was more important to him, even if he didn't always have an easy time showing it.

"She'd been at Quinn Drummond's," she added. Then told him everything that had happened since Amelia had called. She pointed the tip of the paring knife she was using to peel the peaches at Deke. "I don't care what everyone's saying about her and that Banning fella." She deftly removed the peach pit and sliced the ripe fruit into a bowl. "There's definitely something going on between her and Quinn."

"I'd think Quinn's too set in his ways to be interested in a highbred filly like Amelia." Deke reached past her to filch a juicy slice. "'Specially after the merry chase that ex-wife of his led him on. She was a piece of work, remember?"

She did and she made a face. "That was years ago."

"Yup. Having your wife leave you for her old boy-friend leaves a stain, though. Least I think it would. Now he's interested in a girl the world thinks is engaged?" He stole another slice, avoiding the hand she batted at him.

"You keep eating the slices, I won't have enough left to make a pie for you," she warned.

His teeth flashed, his good humor evidently restored. He popped the morsel in his mouth and gave her a smack-ing kiss that tasted of him and sweet, sweet summer. It melted her heart as surely now as it had the first time he'd kissed her when they were little more than kids.

Then he grabbed his hat and plopped it on his head again. "I'll stop at the fruit stand on my way back from Vicker's Corners," he said, giving her a quick wink. "Replenish the stock." He started to push open the back screen door.

"Deke—"

He hesitated.

"You're the love of my life, you know."

His smile was slow and sweeter than the peaches. "And you're mine. That's what gets me up in the morn-ing every day, darlin'."

Then he pushed through the screen door. It squeaked slightly, and shut with a soft slap.

Jeanne Marie pressed her hand to her chest for a moment. "Oh, my." She blew out a breath and laughed slightly at the silliness of a woman who ought to be too old for such romantic swooning.

Then she looked up at the ceiling, thinking about her young niece. Amelia was running away from something, or running to something. And she needed to figure out which it was.

Jeanne Marie was just glad that she was there to provide a resting place. And that she had a man of her own who could understand why.

Quinn had no intention of going by Jeanne Marie and Deke's place later that evening. But he ran into Deke at the tractor supply in Vicker's Corners before the baseball game and the man—typically short on words and long on hard work and honor—asked after Quinn's mom. That brief exchange of pleasantries had somehow led to Deke casually tossing out an invitation to come by for supper.

"Havin' a cookout," Deke had said. "All the kids're coming. And you know how Jeanne Marie always cooks more'n we need."

Quinn had wondered then if it was possible that Deke didn't know his wife's new niece was there. And then he had wondered if it was possible that Jeanne's new niece *wasn't* there.

Which had led to him poking at that thought all through the ball game, same way a tongue poked at a sore tooth, even though it hurt.

He ought to have just asked Deke.

Instead, here he was at six o'clock in the evening, standing there staring at the front of Jeanne and Deke's place.

He could smell grilling beef on the air and hear the high-pitched squeal of a baby laughing. Ordinarily, the smell of a steak getting seared really well would have been enough to get his boots moving. He didn't even mind the babies or the kids much. He'd had plenty of practice with Jess's batch, since she popped one out every couple of years.

His reluctance to join them now annoyed him. He'd had plenty of meals at the Jones's place over the years. He'd been in school with the older ones and counted them as friends. He'd danced at Toby's wedding. *With Amelia.* Right here, in fact, because Toby and Angie had been married out in back of the house.

Quinn hadn't been back since.

Muttering an oath, he grabbed the short-haired wig, slammed the truck door and headed around the side of the house. He knew they'd all be out back again and he was right.

This time, though, instead of rows of chairs lined up like white soldiers across the green grass and a bunch of cloth-covered tables with pretty flowers sitting on top arranged around the space, there were a couple of picnic tables covered with plastic checked tablecloths, a bunch of lawn chairs and a game of croquet in the works.

He spotted Amelia immediately and even though he wanted to pretend he hadn't been concerned about whether she had or had not sought haven with her aunt, the knot inside him eased.

She was off to one side of the grassy backyard where Toby's three kids were playing croquet, and talking with Stacey, Jeanne's and Deke's second youngest. The two females were about the same age and the same height, but Stacey was as sunny and blonde as Amelia was moonlight and brunette.

Both women were engaged, too, he thought darkly, though only one of those engagements caused him any amount of pleasure. He was just a little surprised that Colton Foster, who was Stacey's fiancé, hadn't gotten her to the altar already. As he watched, Amelia leaned over and rubbed her nose against Piper's, Stacey's year-old daughter, who was propped on her mama's hip.

He looked away and aimed toward Deke where he and Liam were manning the grill. "Smells good," he greeted. "Would only smell better if that was Rocking-U beef."

Liam snorted good-naturedly. Horseback Hollow was dotted with small cattle ranches and all of them were more supportive than competitive with each other. "You got yourself a new pet there? Looks like a rat."

Quinn wished he'd have left the wig in the truck. He'd only thought as far as returning it to its owner so he wouldn't have the reminder around. He hadn't thought about the questions that doing so would invite. "It's a wig. Thought maybe one of Toby's kids might want to keep it around for Halloween or something." The excuse was thin and he knew it. "My sister's kids outgrew it, I guess," he improvised and felt stupid even as he did. He'd never developed a taste for lying. Anyone who knew Jess's brood would also know the five boys were hellions who wouldn't be caught dead wearing a wig.

Liam was eying him oddly, too. "Whatever, man." He grabbed a beer from an ice-filled barrel and tossed it to him. "Crack that open and get started. Maybe it'll soften you up before we get to dickering over that bull of yours I want to buy."

Despite everything, Quinn smiled. He tossed the wig on one of the picnic benches nearby. "Rocky's not for sale, my friend."

"Even if I paid you twice what he's worth?"

They'd had this debate many times. Quinn knew Liam wouldn't overpay and Liam knew Quinn wasn't selling, anyway. "That bull's semen's worth gold to me."

"Oh." The word was faint, brief and still filled with some shock.

The knots tightened inside him again and Quinn turned to see Amelia standing beside him.

Chapter Four

Her fragility struck Quinn all over again, like a fist in his gut.

The red dress that she was wearing was pretty enough, he guessed. But it was loose. And the straps over her shoulders couldn't hide the way her collarbones were too prominent.

She looked like she needed to sit at a table and stuff herself for a month of Sundays.

As if she read his disapproving thoughts, her cheeks were nearly as red as the dress.

The day of Toby's wedding, she'd worn a strapless ice-blue dress that ended just above her perfect knees, and a weird little puff of some feathery thing on her head. When they'd ended up sneaking off for a drive in his truck, he'd teased her about it. She'd promptly tugged it off, and plopped his cowboy hat on her head, where it had slipped down over her eyes, and said she was in the market for a new look, anyway.

His lips twisted, his eyes meeting hers. "You're going to hear words like *bull's semen* if you're going to play around cowboys, princess."

Stacey, standing beside Amelia, rolled her eyes. "Good grief, Quinn. Manners much?"

"It's quite all right," Amelia said quickly. She lifted her chin a little. "This is Texas, for goodness' sake. Cattle ranch country. I certainly don't imagine anyone stands around discussing tea and biscuits. Or, cookies, I guess you call them."

He nearly choked. Because they'd laughed together about that, too. Only she'd been naked at the time, and throatily telling him that she'd bet he'd enjoy teatime perfectly well if she served it up for him after making love.

"Depends on whose cookies you're talking about," Deke said. "Jeanne Marie makes some oatmeal peanut-butter deals that are the talk of three counties." His dry humor broke the faint tension. "Stacey girl, you wanna grab a tray for these steaks? They're 'bout ready."

"Sure."

"I'll take her," Amelia offered quickly, reaching out her hands for Piper, and Stacey handed her over. She settled the wide-eyed toddler on her hip and tickled her cheek, making Piper squeal and wriggle. "Who is the prettiest baby girl here, hmm?"

For some reason, Quinn's neck prickled.

He twisted the cap off his beer and focused on Liam. "Where's your better half, anyway?" There was no sign of his friend's red-haired fiancée.

"Julia's meeting with one of the suppliers over at the Cantina. She'll be here as soon as she finishes up."

"Is the restaurant still going to open on schedule?" Amelia asked.

Liam nodded. "Two weeks from now, right on track."

The Hollows Cantina was a big deal for their little town. It was owned and to be operated by Marcos Mendoza and his wife, Wendy Fortune Mendoza, who'd relocated all the way from Red Rock, a good four hundred Texas miles away. They'd hired Julia as an assistant manager and the establishment promised upscale dining that was intended to draw not only the locals from Horseback Hollow and nearby Vicker's Corners, but as far away as Lubbock. Considering the Mendozas' success with Red, a fancy Mexican food restaurant in Red Rock that was famous even beyond the state lines, Quinn figured they had a decent shot of success at it.

He was reserving judgment on whether that all would be a good thing for Horseback Hollow or not. He wasn't vocally opposed to it like some folks, nor was he riding around on the bandwagon of supporters, though he was glad enough for Julia. She'd always been a hard worker and deserved her shot as much as anyone did.

He, personally, would probably still choose the Horseback Hollow Grill over the Cantina. Even on a good day, he wasn't what he would call "upscale" material.

"My mother has the grand opening on her calendar," Amelia said. "I know she's looking forward to it. Not only is Uncle James going to be there, but Uncle John, as well. It should be quite a family reunion."

Quinn stopped pretending an interest in his beer and looked at her. Ironically, the British Fortunes seemed too upscale for the Cantina. "And you? Is it on your calendar, too, princess? Maybe you'll drag your fiancé along for the trip."

Amelia's chocolate-brown eyes went from her cousin's face to Quinn's and for the first time since he'd met her, they contained no emotion whatsoever. "I'm not sure what I'll be doing by the end of the month." Her voice was smoothly pleasant and revealed as little as her eyes did.

Her "royal face," he realized.

She'd talked about having one. Having had to develop as a little girl the ability to give nothing away by expression, deed or word.

He'd just never seen it in person before. And not directed at him.

Piper was wriggling on her hip and Amelia leaned over to set the little girl on her feet. She kept hold of Piper's tiny hands as the girl made a beeline toddle for the wig sitting on the picnic bench next to them.

"Keekee," she chortled, and reached for the wig.

Amelia laughed lightly and scooped up the wig before Piper could reach it and brushed the short thick strands against the baby's face. "That's not a kitty, darling. It's a wig."

She'd crouched next to Piper and while the child chortled over the hairy thing, she glanced up at Quinn. "There was no need to return the wig to me, Quinn," she told him. "You could have tossed it in the trash bin."

He really wished he would have.

Liam tilted his beer to his lips but not quickly enough to hide his faint grin. "Thought the rat belonged to your sis's kids."

"Here's the tray," Stacey announced, striding up with a metal cookie sheet in her hand that she set on the side of the grill.

She was also carrying a big bowl of coleslaw under her other arm, and, glad of an escape route, Quinn slid his hand beneath it. "I'll put it on the table before you drop it." He turned away from the lot of them and carried it over to a folding table that had obviously been set out to hold the food.

Trying not to watch Quinn too openly, Amelia continued entertaining the sweet baby with the wig while everyone else seemed to suddenly spring into action organizing the food onto plates and the people onto picnic benches.

Though she tried to avoid it, she somehow found herself sitting directly across from Quinn. He was hemmed in on one side by Delaney, Jeanne Marie and Deke's youngest daughter, and Liam on the other. Amelia was caught between Jeanne Marie and Deke.

If she didn't know better, she almost would have suspected her aunt and uncle of planning it.

Judging by the way Quinn noticeably ignored her, he was no more comfortable with the seating plan than she was. Fortunately, his friendship with Liam was evident as the two men dickered over the issue of Rocky's studding abilities and whether or not the summer season would be wetter or drier than usual.

"Have some more corn bread," Jeanne Marie said, nudging a basket of the fragrant squares into her hands.

Amelia obediently put another piece on her plate, and managed a light laugh when Deke tried to talk her into another steak, though she'd only eaten a fraction of the one on her plate. "If I ate all this, I'd pop," she protested.

"So, Amelia," Delaney drew her attention. "What are you doing in Horseback Hollow, anyway?" Her eyes were bright with curiosity as she grinned. "Are you planning some secret meeting with your wedding gown designer?

Texas has our very own Charlene Dalton. She's based in Red Rock and I hear she did Emily Fortune's gown."

"Delaney," Jeanne Marie tsked, handing the corn bread across to her daughter. "You're sounding like one of those nosy reporters."

Delaney made a protesting sound. "That's not fair. None of us expected to find ourselves family with *The* Fortunes. If you can't share some secrets among your own family, who can you share 'em with? It's not like I'll go tattling to the newspapers. And besides. I didn't get to see Emily's gown outside of pictures, 'cause she got married before we even knew we all were cousins!"

"It's all right," Amelia said quickly. Not only could she sense her aunt's sudden discomfort, but she was painfully aware of Quinn across from her. "I'm not…not planning any designer sessions." She was loath to discuss her personal business in front of everyone, even if they *were* family. That just wasn't the way she'd been raised. Even among her four brothers and sister, she didn't get into whys and wherefores and the most personal of emotions. She hadn't even divulged all the facts to her own mother about her "engagement," though she knew Josephine had her suspicions.

She tried not looking at Quinn, but couldn't help herself. "I'm not planning anything." It wasn't exactly a public admission, but since she'd discovered she was pregnant with his child, it was entirely truthful.

"'Scuse me." He suddenly rose and extricated himself from the picnic bench and the human bookends holding him there.

Amelia's fingernails dug into her palms as she watched him carry his plate over to the table of food and make a point of studying the display.

"Getting a microphone stuck in your face or a camera flash blinding you every time you go out in public would be a pain in the butt," Deke said, as if nothing had happened. Then he looked around at the silence his unexpected input drew. His eyebrows rose. "Well. Would be," he drawled in conclusion.

And that seemed to be that.

Nobody else broached the subject about Amelia's unplanned appearance. Nor did the topic of the wedding come up again.

And Quinn never returned to their picnic table.

He stuck around long enough to have a piece of the three-layer chocolate cake when Jeanne Marie presented it, along with a peach pie that was so picturesque it might have come out of the kitchens at the Chesterfield estate. But whenever Amelia entered his vicinity, he exited hers.

It was so plainly obvious that he was avoiding her that she felt herself receiving looks of sympathy from Stacey, Delaney *and* Liam's fiancée, Julia, who'd arrived in time for dessert.

She didn't want sympathy.

She wanted Quinn's love.

In the absence of that, at least his understanding.

But clearly he wasn't going to offer that, either.

She saw him shake Deke's hand, drop a kiss on her aunt's cheek and exchange easily a half-dozen goodbyes with some of the others, without a single glance her way. And then he was walking away, heading out of sight around the corner of her aunt's house.

She swallowed and sucked all of her feelings inward until she felt reasonably confident that her expression was calm. She listened in on Toby and Angie's conversation as they talked about the difficulties they kept encountering trying to adopt the three Hemings children Toby had been fostering ever since she'd first met him, and knew she made the appropriate nods and sounds when she should have. But a portion of her mind was wondering if she could get back home again without drawing undue media attention.

Which was rather laughable to worry about now.

The attention she'd draw once word of her pregnancy got out would thoroughly eclipse what she'd already garnered.

And poor James. Instead of dealing with the embarrassment of a broken engagement, he would have to endure speculation over being the baby's father. It wouldn't matter that he wasn't. It wouldn't matter what statements were issued or what proof was given.

Forever on, people would whisper. Every time either one of them did something to draw the attention of the media, the scandal would be dug up all over again, regurgitated on the internet or on gossip networks.

They'd all pay the price and none more dearly than her and Quinn's innocent baby.

Her head swam dizzily and she excused herself, walking blindly. She instinctively followed the path that Quinn had taken, heading around the side of the house and away from all of the noisy gaiety.

Going home was as impossible as staying in Horseback Hollow would be.

The thought came over her in a wave and her knees went weak. She stopped, bracing herself with one hand against the side of the house.

"Are you going to pass out again?"

She nearly jumped out of her skin at the sound of Quinn's voice. He was standing a few feet away, his hazel eyes alert, as though he was ready to leap forward if he had to.

At least he didn't hate her badly enough to allow her to collapse flat on her face.

She let out a choking laugh at the thought, which only had him closing the distance between them, his expression even warier as he clasped her bare arms.

She shivered, looking up into his face. The night they'd danced, she'd felt as if they'd known one another for all their lives. "I think I'm losing my mind, Quinn." Even her voice sounded unhinged, shaking and pitched too high.

He made a rough sound. "You're not losing your mind."

Where was her dignity? Her self-control? Her throat tightened even more, her voice almost a squeak. "But you don't know—"

"Shh." His big warm hand slid around the back of her neck and he pulled her against his chest in a motion that felt both reluctant and desperate. "You're going to make yourself collapse again. Is that what you want?"

Her forehead rubbed against the front of his soft plaid shirt as she shook her head. She could feel the heat of his hard chest burning through the cotton. Could hear the rhythmic beat of his heart when she turned her cheek against him.

He was holding her, though not cradling her. But her ragged emotions didn't care. They only wanted her to burrow against him while he safely held everything that didn't matter at bay.

She'd never felt even a fraction of this need when she was with James. If only she had, things wouldn't be in such a mess.

Her fingers twisted into Quinn's shirt lapel. "There's something I need to tell you."

"Well it's gonna have to wait." His hands tightened around her arms as he forcibly set her back a foot. "I only came back to warn you that there's an SUV parked maybe a hundred yards down the road that's not from around here. Has a rental car sticker on the bumper." His fingertips pressed into her flesh and his gaze, as it roved over her face, was shuttered once more. "It's probably nothing, but the strangers that've been coming around the Hollow these days usually stick to town. They don't traipse out onto private property and park off the side of the road half-hidden behind the bushes."

She grasped at the shreds of her composure and came up with threads. His thumbs were rubbing back and forth over her upper arms and she wondered if he even realized it. "You think it's a reporter." Maybe even that dreadful Ophelia Malone had managed to catch up to her. The young paparazzo had sprung from nowhere after Amelia's "engagement" and seemed determined to earn her stripes on Amelia ever since.

"All I'm thinking is that the car doesn't belong." His thumbs stopped moving. He still held her arms to steady her, yet managed to put another few inches between them. "But I don't figure any of the Joneses—*Fortune* Joneses," he corrected himself, "deserve their lives intruded upon."

"Whereas this Fortune Chesterfield does?"

His lips twisted and his brows lowered. "Don't make me feel sorry for you, princess."

"I'm not trying to!" Despair congealed inside her chest and she lifted her palms to his face. She felt his sudden stillness and mindlessly stepped closer. "Please give me a chance to make things right, Quinn." Feeling as powerless as a moth flying into a flame, she stretched up on the toes of her borrowed sandals and pressed her mouth to his jaw. The hard angle felt bristly against her lips. "That's all I want. A chance." She stretched even farther, pulling on his shoulders, until her lips could reach his.

And for a moment, a sweet moment that sent her hopes spinning, he kissed her back.

But then he jerked away.

His hands felt like iron as he held her in place and took another step back, putting distance between them yet again. "Finish making one bed before you try getting in another." His voice was low. Rough.

"I was never in James's bed," she whispered. Her lips still tingled. "I'm not in it now. What can I do to make you believe me?"

A muscle worked in his jaw. "Walk out to that SUV and see if it's a reporter, and if it is, tell 'em what you told me. That the two of you aren't engaged. Never were."

She swallowed. "And that would make everything all right? Between you and me?"

He didn't answer and her stomach sank right back to her toes.

Of course it wouldn't.

He'd made up his mind where she was concerned and that was the end of it.

It didn't matter who was to blame for what as far as the "engagement" was concerned. James's father had precipitated everything by announcing they were engaged. And she'd compounded the problem by not denying it when she could have.

By talking to the paparazzi now, all she would succeed in doing would be hurting James, embarrassing his family, and by extension, her own.

And in the process, she wouldn't gain a thing where Quinn was concerned.

She drew herself up. Lifted her chin. She was a Chesterfield. A Fortune Chesterfield. Even if her world was disintegrating around her, she needed to remember that fact. "That would be throwing James to the wolves."

His eyes flattened even more. "So?"

She exhaled, praying for strength. It was obvious that he wouldn't welcome hearing any defense of the other man. "An announcement like that needs to come through official channels, not some random gossipmonger on the side of the road. *Don't!*" She stared him down. "Don't look at me like that. Whether you want to believe me or not, it's true. Otherwise it would be just one more rumor tossing around among the flotsam."

"Even though it came from you."

She nodded. "Even though." This time, she was the one to put more space between them, though she had to force herself to do it. But it was enough to make his hands finally fall away from her arms. It took every speck of self-control she possessed not to clasp her arms around herself to hold in the feel of his touch. "James and I had been dating nearly a year when you and I—" She drew in a shuddering breath. "When I came here for Toby's wedding," she amended. "The…advantages of us marrying had come up a few times. I never lied to you about that."

"No, princess. Your lie was in pretending you weren't going to bring those advantages to reality. You said you weren't in love with him. And that I did believe. Or there's no way we'd have ended up out in that field that night." His lips thinned. "Wouldn't have happened."

"Are you trying to convince me of that or yourself?" The muscle in his jaw flexed. Once. Twice. Then it went still. His expression turned stoic and he didn't speak.

She realized she'd pressed her hands to her stomach and made herself stop. "And…and after I went back home to all that—" she waved her hand, trying to encompass the indescribable media storm that had greeted her "—and you made it plain once you finally deigned to speak with me that there was no…no hope for us—" Her voice broke and she stopped again, gathering herself. "James suggested we go on with the illusion. His father is in very poor health. For an assortment of reasons, he wants to see James married and pass on his title to him while he's still alive. We weren't the great romance everyone wants to make us out to be, but we *were* friends and, given time, he hoped we might be more." Her vision glazed with tears as she stared at him. "I didn't have you. So, yes. I made no public contradictions. I'd had one night of magic and I let it slip through my fingers. Maybe a life with him was the best I could expect after that. But then I—"

"Enough!" He slashed his hand through the air between them. "Enough of the fairy-tale bull, princess. I've been down this road before. I already know how it goes." His smile was cold and cutting. "I made the mistake of marrying the last woman who was selling a story like this. I am not in the market to buy it again."

Then, while she was frozen in speechless shock, he turned on his boot heel and strode back to his truck parked nearby.

Chapter Five

The next morning it was Quinn's sister, Jess, who saw the photograph first.

It was grainy. It had obviously been taken from a considerable distance and the subjects' faces weren't entirely visible, or even entirely clear.

But it was enough for Jess.

She slapped the piece of paper on Quinn's kitchen table in front of him and jabbed her finger at the image. "That's you." She jabbed again. "That's Amelia." Then she propped her hands on her hips and stuck her face close to his, wholly, righteously in big-sister mode. "What the *hell,* Quinn? They've already coined a nickname for you!"

Annoyed, because even though she was five years his senior, he was a grown man and not in the least interested in being called on her metaphorical carpet, he pushed her aside and picked up the sheet of paper that she'd obviously printed off her computer. "They who?"

Her arms flapped as she gaped at him. "It doesn't matter who! You've got eyes. You can read reasonably well, last time I checked. The caption is right there!"

Is this the end for Jamelia? Who is the tall, dark Horseback Hollow Homewrecker caught in a passionate clinch with England's own runaway bride?

He let out a disgusted sound and crumpled the thin paper in his fist. "You have five kids, a husband and a full-time job at the high school. When the hell do you have time for hunting up this sort of crap on the internet?"

"Summer vacation," she returned. "And obviously you've never acquainted yourself with internet alerts." She waved her cell phone that she seemed perpetually attached to under his nose, then shoved it back in her pocket.

He wasn't sure if she was more disgusted with the photograph itself or with his seeming ineptitude where technology was concerned. The only thing he kept a computer for was ranch records and he detested using it even for that. He'd rather be out in the open air than sitting in the office pecking at computer keys.

"That picture is everywhere," she added. "All this time and you never said *anything* about her to me! How long has this been going on?"

"There's no *this*." He opened the cupboard door beneath the sink and pushed the wad of paper deep into the trash can stored there.

"Please. Don't try saying that isn't you and Amelia in the picture. Where were you, anyway?"

Standing to one side of the Joneses' house, not as hidden from view as he'd thought.

He didn't voice the words. Just eyed his sister. "It's Saturday morning," he said instead. "Shouldn't you be at a soccer game or something instead of cornering me in my own kitchen?"

She pointed her finger at him, giving him the stink eye that she'd had perfected since she was a superior eight years old and didn't like him coming uninvited into her room anymore. "She's an engaged woman, Quinn."

It wasn't anything he didn't know and hadn't been tarring himself for. But that didn't mean he welcomed his sister's censure, too. And, he justified to himself, the photograph hadn't caught him kissing Amelia; it had caught *her* kissing *him*. "Engaged isn't married."

He scooped up a Texas Rangers ball cap and tugged it down over his eyes before shoving through the wood-framed screen door leading outside. For her, Saturdays were chock-full of squiring one kid or another hither and yon.

For him, Saturdays meant the same chores that every other day meant and he fully intended on getting to them. If he kept acting normal, sooner or later, things would be normal. It had worked that way when Carrie left. He had to believe it would work again now, or he might as well order up a straightjacket, size extra-large-tall, right now.

Amelia woke early the next day after yet another fitful night of sleep. She could smell the heady aroma of coffee wending its way from downstairs and she rolled out of bed, donning the robe that Jeanne Marie had loaned her. Downstairs, she found her aunt sitting at the kitchen table. Her silver hair—usually pinned up—was hanging in a long braid down her back and she had a pair of reading glasses perched on her nose as she perused a newspaper.

When Amelia walked into the room, she looked over the top of her eyeglasses and smiled. "Aren't you the early bird this morning," she greeted. "Would you like coffee?"

Amelia waved her aunt back into her seat when she started to rise. "Don't get up." She wanted coffee in the worst way, but had read that caffeine was something pregnant women were supposed to avoid. "Water's all I want." To prove it, she pulled a clean glass out of the dish rack where several had been turned upside down after being washed, and filled it from the tap. Then she sat down across from her aunt. She was determined not to think about Quinn for the moment.

She'd spent enough time doing that when she'd been unable to sleep. She'd thought about him. And the fact that he'd once been married. Something he hadn't shared before at all.

"I need some clothes of my own," she said. "I can't keep borrowing." It was something she'd never done in her entire life. And she needed underwear. She'd been washing her silk knickers every night, but enough was enough.

"Well." Jeanne Marie looked amused. "You can, you know. But a pretty girl like you doesn't want to keep walking around in things two sizes too large." She adjusted her glasses and glanced at her newspaper again. "Guess you already know you won't find much in the way of clothes shopping here in Horseback Hollow."

"I know." Much as she loved the area, Horseback Hollow only consisted of a few small businesses. "I thought perhaps Vicker's Corners." She hadn't been to the nearby town, but she'd heard mention of it often enough and knew it was only twenty miles away. "When I was talking to Stacey yesterday, she mentioned that there are a few shops there."

"Yes," Jeanne Marie agreed. "You'll find more of a selection in Lubbock, though."

She didn't want to go to Lubbock. She wanted to avoid all towns of any real size. Vicker's Corners was probably pushing it as it was. "I just need a few basics," she said. "I'm sure Vicker's Corners will suit." She chewed the inside of her lip for a moment. "I also ought to purchase a cell phone." Molly had called it "a burner." One that nobody—namely Ophelia Malone and her ilk—would know to track. "Do you think I'd be able to find one there, as well?"

"Imagine so. There's a hardware store that carries everything from A to Z." Jeanne Marie turned the last page of the newspaper and folded it in half. "I'd drive you myself, but I have to go to a baby shower my friend Lillian is giving her niece this afternoon. I can call one of the kids or Deke to drive you."

"I don't want to put anyone out." She'd sprung her "visit" on them uninvited. She certainly didn't expect them to rearrange their plans because of her. "I don't suppose I could hire a car around here? I have some experience driving in other countries."

Jeanne Marie's smile widened. "We're not exactly blessed with car rental companies," she said mildly. "But if you want to drive yourself, there's no problem. You can use my car and drop me off at Lillian's. Her place is on the way to Vicker's Corners."

Amelia hesitated. "I don't know, Aunt Jeanne. It's one thing to rent a car, but to impose—"

Her aunt waved her hand. "Oh, hush up on that im-position nonsense, would you please? Would you think your cousins were imposing if they came over to England to visit y'all there?"

"Of course not."

"This is about money, then."

Dismayed, Amelia quickly shook her head. "No," she lied. Because it was exactly about money. Her aunt and uncle had an undeniably modest lifestyle in comparison to the Chesterfields. The whole lot of Jeanne and Deke's family could visit their estate and they'd still have room to spare.

Jeanne Marie just eyed her.

Amelia's shoulders drooped. "Mum'll want to put me in chains if I've offended you."

Her aunt's lips twitched. "I'm not offended, Amelia," she assured. She propped her elbows on the table and folded her hands together, leaning toward her. "There are all kinds of wealth, honey. I have no problem whatsoever with the type of wealth I've been blessed with. I love my life exactly the way it is. A husband who loves me, kids we both adore and the opportunity to see them starting on families of their own. Just because we're not millionaires like my brothers and sister, doesn't mean we don't have all that we need." She tapped her fingertip on the table and her eyes crinkled. "And if I want to lend my niece my car, I will."

Amelia studied her for a moment. "Did you always know that this was the life you wanted?"

"Pretty much. I was only twenty-two, but I knew I wanted to marry Deke almost as soon as I met him." She chuckled. "Depending on the day, he might not necessarily admit to the same thing."

Her chest squeezed. She'd felt the same way about Quinn. "I'm a year older than you were then, and I don't feel half the confidence you must have felt."

Jeanne Marie rose and began puttering around the kitchen. She was wearing an oversize plaid shirt that looked like it was probably Deke's and a pair of jeans cut off at the knees. "Comparing us is as silly as comparing apples and oranges, sweetheart. I was learning how to be a good rancher's wife. You're out there establishing orphanages and dedicating hospital wings and such."

"Mummy's the one who gets those things done. I just—" She broke off and sighed. "I don't know what I just do." She made a face. "Maybe the media's right and the only thing I was perfectly suited for was being a proper wife for the future Earl of Estingwood."

"Which you've already admitted you're not planning to do," Jeanne reminded. "So *you* know you're not suited."

Her aunt had no idea just how unsuited.

She rose and restlessly tightened the belt of her borrowed flannel robe. "You really don't mind lending me your vehicle?"

Jeanne Marie smiled. "Just make sure you drive on the right side of the road."

Unfortunately, after Amelia had let off her aunt later that afternoon at her friend's home, she discovered driving on the right side was a task easier said than done.

Her aunt had told her that it was a straight shot down the roadway to Vicker's Corners. What she hadn't said was that the roadway wasn't, well, *straight.*

It was full of curves and bumps and dips and even though there was hardly any other traffic to speak of, more than once Amelia found herself wanting to drift to the other side of the road.

By the time she made it to the quaintly picturesque little town of Vicker's Corners, her hands ached from clenching the steering wheel so tightly, and she heartily wished she'd just have waited until her aunt was available to bring her into town.

Which was such a pathetic, spoiled thought that she was immediately disgusted with herself. Back home, more often than not, she used the services of a driver. It was simpler. And as Jimmy had so often told her, it was safer.

But that privilege also came as part and parcel along with public eyes following her activities. And that was something she'd always hated. Growing up was difficult enough without having an entire country witnessing your missteps.

She didn't care what the supposed advantages were of being raised a Chesterfield. No matter what happened with Quinn, she was not going to raise their child in that sort of environment. It was fine for some.

But not for her. Not for her baby.

When she saw the way several cars were parked, nose in to the curb between slanted lines, she pulled into the first empty space she spotted and breathed out a sigh of relief. She locked up the car and tucked the keys inside the pocket of her borrowed sundress. It was the same red one from the day before because the other clothes from Stacey and Delaney that Jeanne Marie had found had been from their earlier years. It was either wear the slightly oversize sundress once more, or skintight jeans and T-shirts with the names of rock bands splashed in glitter across her breasts.

Even though she was the only one who cared about what she wore, the sundress was preferable.

Looking up and down the street, Amelia mentally oriented herself with the descriptions that Jeanne Marie had given her of the town. Her impetuously chosen parking spot was directly in front of the post office. Across the street and down a bit was the three-story bed and breakfast, identifiable by the green-and-white-striped awnings her aunt had described. Which meant that around the corner and down the block, she would find the hardware store her aunt recommended.

She waited for two cars to pass, then headed across the street. Her first task would be to secure a phone and then she'd check in with her mother. Amelia had instructed Molly to let Josephine know her plans once she'd left the country.

It wasn't that she'd been afraid her mum would talk her out of going. It was that Amelia didn't entirely trust everyone on her mother's staff to have the same discretion that Molly did. Someone had been feeding that Malone woman details concerning Amelia's schedule and the only ones who kept a copy were her mother's staff and James's assistant.

She reached the hardware store and went inside. There was a girl manning a cash register near the front door and she barely gave Amelia a look as she continued helping a customer, so Amelia set off to find what she needed.

The aisles were narrow; the shelves congested with everything from hammers and industrial-sized paint thinners to cookware. But she didn't see any electronics. She returned to the clerk who'd finished with the customer. "Do you offer cell phones?"

The girl chewed her gum and looked up from the magazine lying open on the counter. "Yeah." She jerked her chin. "Over on aisle—" She broke off, her eyes suddenly widening. "Hey, aren't you that fancy chick related to Jeanne Jones who's marrying this guy?" She lifted the magazine and tapped a photo of James Banning astride one of his polo ponies, his mallet midswing. "He is *so* hot."

"Jeanne Marie is my aunt." She managed a calm smile. "The phones?"

"Oh, yeah. Right." The girl slid off her stool and came around the counter. "I'll show you." She headed toward the rear of the store. "Keep alla that stuff on this aisle over here 'cause the only way out is back past the counter. Cuts down on shoplifting." She gave Amelia a quick look. "Not saying *you* would—"

"I know you're not." Amelia spotted several older-style cell phones hanging from hooks. They were generations away from the fancy device she was used to using. But then that fancy thing had been hacked.

She grabbed the closest phone. It was packaged in the kind of tough, clear plastic that always seemed impossible to open.

The girl snapped her gum. "Are you gonna want a phone card, too?" She gestured at the rack next to the small phone selection. It held an array of colorful credit-card-sized cards. "You pay for the minutes up front," she added at Amelia's blank look. "You know. Otherwise you gotta get a contract and all that."

Feeling foolish, Amelia studied the cards for a moment. Contracts were certainly something to avoid. "Do they cover international calls?"

"Yeah." The girl looked over her head when a jangling bell announced the arrival of another customer.

Then she tapped one of the cards. "That one's the best value for your money," she provided as she backed away. "I've gotta get back to the register," she excused herself.

"Thank you." Amelia looked at the display. She wasn't going to use her credit card. Just the cash. Which meant, for now at any rate, she needed to use it wisely. She chose the card the girl suggested and flipped it over, reading the tiny print on the back. Not once in her life had she ever needed to concern herself with such details.

She carried the phone and the card back to the register, but stopped short at the sight of the young blonde woman standing there with the clerk.

Ophelia Malone.

Amelia ducked back in the aisle with the cell phones where she couldn't be seen. There was country music playing over a speaker and she couldn't hear what they were saying, but she didn't need to. There was only one reason why Ophelia would be in that store at that moment and Amelia was it.

She quickly returned the phone and the card to their places on the racks and scurried around the opposite end of the aisle, looking for an escape even though the girl had said there wasn't another way out. She discovered the reason quickly enough. There *was* another exit. But it was a fire exit and she knew from regrettable experience in similar situations that going through it would set off an alarm. Gnawing on her lip, she edged to the end of the aisle again and peeked around the racks toward the front.

Ophelia wasn't there. But the door hadn't jangled, meaning she was still in the store somewhere.

She felt like the fox in a hunt and that never ended well for the fox. She continued sneaking her way around the aisles, keeping to the ends because there was less chance of getting caught, hearing the door jangling periodically. When the urge to look grew too great, she held her breath, darting up the empty row next to her where she could see the entrance just as another customer came in.

She quickly backed out of sight again, then nearly jumped out of her skin when the clerk appeared.

"There you are," she said. "Your friend's looking for you."

"She's not my friend," she corrected, keeping her voice low. Feeling increasingly hemmed in, she grabbed the clerk's hands and the girl's eyes widened. "She can't find me. Is there another way out or an office where I can wait until she's gone?"

"Too late, Lady Chesterfield." Ophelia stepped into sight. Her green eyes were as sharp as her smile, and in a move she'd probably practiced from the womb, she deftly lifted her camera out of her purse.

Chapter Six

Amelia could hear the clicking whirr of the shutter even before the lens aimed her way and she wanted to scream in frustration.

"Any comments on Mr. Tall, Dark and Nameless you were kissing yester—" Ophelia broke off when a shrieking alarm blasted through the store, making all three of them jump. "What the bloody hell is *that?*"

"The fire alarm." The salesclerk waved her hands, looking panicked. "You have to leave the store."

"Oh, come on," Ophelia said impatiently.

"There are flammable items everywhere, ma'am. We don't take chances." The clerk pushed the reporter toward the aisle where a half-dozen other customers were jostling around the displays in the narrow aisle toward the front door.

Seizing the opportunity, Amelia dashed instead for

the fire exit in the rear. The alarm was going off already so what did it matter?

She hit the bar on the door and it flew open, banging against the wall behind it, and she darted out into an alleyway. Her heart pounding, she shoved the door closed behind her. The fire alarm was noisy even through the door, pulsing in the air and making it difficult to think straight. Could she make it back to Aunt Jeanne's car without Ophelia seeing her?

"Hey. Over here." A tall, dark-haired woman dressed in cutoffs and a tank top beckoned from one side near a large, metal trash bin. "They won't see you over here."

Amelia didn't stop to question the assistance and her sandals slipped on the rough pavement as she took off toward her. She caught herself from landing on her bottom and hurried, half jogging, half skipping after her rescuer who set off briskly away from the hardware store. "*You* set off the alarm?"

"Yes, but if they try to fine me for it, I'm denying it. Already had to pay a few of them thanks to my oldest boy." They reached the end of the alley and the woman held up a warning hand as she cautiously checked the street. A fire truck, siren blaring and lights flashing, roared past. She waited a moment, then beckoned. "Come on. You need to get off the street before more people see you."

"How'd you—"

"Never mind." The woman grabbed her arm and tugged her out into the open. Amelia could see her aunt's car still parked in front of the post office down the street, but they didn't head that way. Instead, the woman pulled Amelia through the propped-open door of the bed-and-breakfast.

A teenager wielding a dust cloth across a fake Chippendale desk looked at them, clearly surprised. "Mrs. O'Malley. What're you doing—" her eyes landed on Amelia and widened with recognition "—here," she finished faintly. She pointed her dust rag at Amelia. "You're...you—"

"Yes, yes. She's her." The brunette—Mrs. O'Malley, obviously—nudged the teen's shoulder to gain her attention again. "You have any guests today, Shayla?"

Shayla shook her head and her wildly curling orangey-red ponytail bounced. "Not yet, but Ma's expecting some newlyweds t'night."

Mrs. O'Malley boldly stepped around the desk and grabbed an old-fashioned hotel key off a hook. "Gonna use number three for a while, then. Keep quiet about that, though, if anyone comes asking, all right?"

Shayla's lips moved, but no words came.

"All right?"

The ponytail bounced again, this time with Shayla's jerky nod. "Yes, ma'am."

"Good girl. Now come on." Mrs. O'Malley tugged Amelia toward a lovely staircase with a white painted banister and dark stained wood treads and started up. "Shayla's a student of mine," she said over her shoulder. "Her mother owns this place."

Thoroughly discomfited, Amelia followed. "You're a teacher?"

"High school English." The other woman turned on the landing and headed up another flight, her pace never slowing. "Better hurry your tush, hon," she advised.

Amelia grasped the banister and quickened her pace. Her head was pounding from the adrenaline rush. "Why did you set off the alarm?"

"Figured somebody needed to do something." She glanced over her shoulder. "I went in to buy paint for my youngest's room—the sweetest shade of pink you ever saw—and I saw that woman showing Katie your picture and asking about you."

"I should have tried Lubbock," Amelia muttered. "You didn't get your paint and I didn't get my phone." They'd reached the top of the stairs and Mrs. O'Malley unlocked the only door there, pushing it open to reveal a cozy-looking guest suite.

They went inside and Mrs. O'Malley immediately crossed to the mullioned window and looked out. "Talk about the nick of time," she said.

Amelia shut the door before joining her, and keeping to one side of the window, looked down. She could see Ophelia marching up the street, her stride determined as she systematically went in and out the doors of each business until she disappeared beneath the striped awning over the B and B's front door.

Hoping she hadn't jumped from the pot into the fire, Amelia sank down on a white wicker rocking chair situated near the window and eyed the other woman. "What do you want out of this? If it's money, you'll be sorely disappointed. My family's dealt with more embarrassing situations than shopping for a discount cell phone."

Mrs. O'Malley didn't look calculating, though. If anything, her light brown eyes turned pitying. "Never heard of a Good Samaritan?"

Amelia's lips twisted. "I apologize for my suspicions, but lately helpful strangers have been in rather short supply."

The woman sat on the corner of the bed that was covered in a fluffy white duvet. "Not as much a stranger as you think. Doesn't seem fair for me to know who you are when you don't know me." She held out her hand. "I'm Jess O'Malley," she said.

Amelia shook her hand. "It's nice to make your acquaintance, Mrs. O'Malley."

"Jess'll do." The woman's lips quirked. "I'm Quinn's sister," she added meaningfully.

Amelia's mouth went dry. "Oh."

Jess shifted and pulled a fancy phone from her back pocket, tapped on the screen a few times then held it out.

Amelia warily took the phone.

The sight of herself in Quinn's arms on the display didn't come as a shock. Since her supposed engagement, she'd become almost numb to the existence of such photographs. The fact that she'd drawn Quinn into the mess, though, caused a wave of grief. "Where'd you find this?"

"It's all over the internet."

She scrolled through the image then handed back the phone. Her mouth felt dry. "Has he seen it?"

"My brother? Or your fiancé?"

Amelia tucked her tongue behind her teeth, gathering her wits. Jess pulled as few punches as her brother. "Quinn."

"He's seen it." Jess sat forward, her arms on her knees. Her eyes—hazel, just like Quinn's, Amelia realized—were assessing. "He doesn't need his heart broken again, Lady Chesterfield. Once was bad enough."

"Amelia," she said faintly. She loathed the courtesy title of "Lady" when she hadn't done a single thing to earn it. "I'm not trying to break anyone's heart. Quinn—" She swallowed and looked away from his sister's eyes. "Your brother hates me, anyway."

"Hate and love are two sides of the same coin, hon."

"Not this time." One corner of her mind wondered if she'd have been better off facing Ophelia than Quinn's sister. And another corner of her mind argued that she would probably get her chance momentarily, because she had significant doubts that any teenager would be able to hold up under the determined paparazzo, no matter how devoted she was to her high school English teacher.

The rest of her mind was consumed with Quinn.

It didn't take a genius to know it was Quinn's ex-wife who'd caused his heartbreak. She pressed her numb lips together for a moment but her need overcame discretion. "What exactly did his ex-wife do to him?"

"Cheated on him with her ex-boyfriend." Jess's voice was flat and immediate. She clearly had no reservations about sharing the details. "Got pregnant and left him for her ex-boyfriend."

Amelia felt the blood drain out of her head. She sat very still, listening as Jess went on, oblivious to Amelia's shock.

"They're still married, living right here in Vicker's Corners. Didn't even have the decency to get out of Horseback Hollow's backyard." Her tone made it plain what she thought of that.

"I haven't cheated on anyone," Amelia said. Her voice sounded faraway. "Least of all Quinn." No matter what he believed right now, six weeks ago, she had been nothing but honest with him. As for James, she'd never made any promises to him either before or after her night with Quinn. And when she'd returned to all the engagement commotion, she'd told him about the man she'd met in Horseback Hollow. The man she'd intended on returning to.

Only that man had said in no uncertain terms that her return was no longer wanted at all.

How would Quinn react once she informed him of her pregnancy?

Trying not to cry, she stood and looked out the window again. There were a few vehicles driving up and down the street. A young family pushing a stroller was walking along the sidewalk, looking in the shop windows. The cars on either side of her aunt's in front of the post office had been replaced by different ones. The fire engine siren had gone quiet.

Ophelia hadn't come pounding up the stairs, her camera whirring away.

"D'you mind if I ask what you're doing in Texas?"

Amelia laughed silently and without humor. Learning she was pregnant had changed everything. She could no longer remain in England actually considering marriage to a man she didn't love. Regardless of what Jess had revealed about Quinn's ex-wife, he still needed to know he was going to be a father. And she had to learn how to become a mother.

She blinked hard several times before looking at Jess, more or less dry-eyed. "Yes." Even that one word sounded thick.

Jess's eyes narrowed for a moment. Then she smiled faintly. "Well, at least that's honest."

Amelia's eyes stung all over again. She looked away. "I'm not a Jezebel."

"No." Jess sighed audibly. "I want to say you're a twenty-three-year-old kid. But that'd be ironic coming from me since Mac and I already had two babies by the time I was your age." She rose also. "Stay here. I'll see if your nosy gal-pal is still snooping around downstairs."

Amelia waited tensely until Quinn's sister returned. "Shayla says she doesn't know you're up here, but she checked in to the room downstairs anyway," she said. "Unfortunately, that room opens right onto the lobby. And there's no convenient fire exit this time."

Dismayed, Amelia could do nothing but stare.

"Yeah." Jess rubbed her hands down the sides of her cutoff denims. "I didn't expect her to check in, either," she grumbled.

"What am I going to do?" Amelia stared at the room around them. "I can't stay here! I have to get my aunt's car back to her."

Jess patted her hands in the air, obviously trying to calm her. "I'll figure something out." She made a face. "Shayla couldn't very well turn down a paying customer. There are only three rooms here. But she said she'd try to let you know if your fan heads out to look for you. If not, just be glad there's an entire floor between you with a newlywed couple expected to occupy it." She gave her a wry smile. "Maybe they'll make enough noise you can sneak out without anyone noticing."

Try as she might, Amelia couldn't prevent heat from rising in her cheeks.

"Wow." Jess eyed her flush openly. "Just how sheltered *were* you growing up?"

Amelia blushed even harder. She thought of the private schools. The tutors. The chaperones. There were days when she and Lucie had felt like the only thing they were being raised for was to become a pristinely suitable choice for a noble marriage. Something their mother had vehemently denied since *her* first marriage had been just that type. Arranged. And terribly unhappy despite the production of Amelia's half brothers, Oliver and Brodie.

Jess looked at the sturdy watch on her wrist and made
a face. "I'm going to have to leave you here. Just for a
bit," she assured quickly. "I've got to pick up my two oldest from baseball and drop off my middle at karate class.
But I'll be back in an hour, tops. And, I'll, uh, I'll make
sure Shayla keeps quiet in the meantime. At least the
room's comfortable and it has its own bathroom, right?"

Amelia wanted to chew off her tongue. "The room's
comfortable," she allowed. But a prison was still a prison.
"My aunt's car—"

"I promise. It's my fault you're stuck up here and I'll
figure something out," Jess said again. "Just hang tight
for a little bit. Here." She handed Amelia her cell phone.
"I'll leave that with you to prove I'll be back quickly.
Everyone knows I don't go far without my cell. Quinn's
always complaining about it."

"Fine." Amelia took the phone only because Jess
seemed so intent on it and once the other woman left,
she set it on the narrow dresser against the wall across
from the bed and went back to the window. She saw Jess
hurry out from beneath the striped awning a few minutes
later and heartily wished that it was Ophelia Malone who
was the one departing.

It was warm in the room and she figured out how to
open the window to let in some fresh air. Then she sat
back down on the wicker rocker.

She didn't even realize she'd dozed off until the buzz-
ing of Jess's phone startled her awake. She had no intentions of answering the other woman's phone, and she
ignored the ringing until it stopped. She used the bathroom and turned on the small television sitting on one
corner of the dresser and flipped through the meager
selection. Black-and-white movies, a sitcom repeat and

an obviously local talk show. She smiled a little when the hostess with a helmet of gray hair talked about the buzz surrounding the Horseback Hollow Cantina slated to open in two weeks, and switched the telly off again just as Jess's phone began ringing again.

She picked it up, hoping to find some way of silencing it. But the sight of Quinn's name bobbing on the phone's display stopped her. Her thumb hovered over the screen almost, *almost,* touching it.

But she sighed and turned the phone facedown on the dresser instead. The ringing immediately stopped and she went back to stare out the open window. The street outside was undeniably picturesque with its streetlights shaped like old-fashioned gas lamps and big pots of summer flowers hanging from them. Her aunt's car was now the only one in front of the post office. Everything looked peaceful and lovely and on any other day, she'd be perfectly charmed by the town.

When there was a bold knock on the door, she went rigid, feeling panicked all over again.

She wouldn't put it past Ophelia Malone to go door-to-door looking for her. She looked out the window. There was plenty of space for her to climb out, but nothing to climb onto. No terrace. No fire escape ladder. Just the awning below her window that hung over the front entrance.

She'd never jumped out of a window onto an awning but she'd jumped out of plenty of trees. Now she was pregnant, though, so that option was out no matter *how* badly she wanted to avoid the reporter.

The knock came again. Followed by a deep voice that she would recognize anywhere. "Open up, princess."

Not Ophelia.

Shaking more than ever, she ran to the door and pulled

it open, looking up at Quinn for only a second before dragging him inside. "Are you *crazy?* What if someone saw you?"

He was wearing faded blue jeans that hugged his powerful thighs, a plain white T-shirt stretched over his broad shoulders and he needed a shave. Badly. And even though his lips were thin as he looked down at her, he still made her knees feel weak. "If answering a phone wasn't beneath your dignity, you wouldn't have missed an opportunity to get out of here."

"What?"

"Your camera-toting friend went to the sandwich shop next door."

"How do you even know what she looks like? I didn't see her leave." She reached around him for the door. "If we're quick—"

"She's already back," he cut her hopefulness short. "And there aren't a lot of people browsing around Vicker's Corners with that sort of camera clenched in their hands."

"Shayla was supposed to let me know if Ophelia left!"

"Yeah, well, Shayla's a seventeen-year-old kid and her mom sent her out on an errand."

"How do you know that?"

His expression turned even darker. He crossed to the window and glanced out. "Because I heard them when I came in to see why the hell you weren't answering the damn phone."

Her head swam and she leaned back against the door for support.

He crossed to the window and glanced out. "Jess called me from the park where her boys play baseball. She got tied up there with the coach trying to keep the guy from kicking Jason off the team for fighting. For some unfathomable reason she was worried about you."

She winced. "You can return her phone to her, then." She'd have to take her chances with Ophelia whether the prospect nauseated her or not.

She was a grown woman carrying a baby. She shouldn't need rescuing. Maybe that was one of the ways she was supposed to start acting like one. "You might have gotten up here without Ophelia seeing you, but try not to be caught on camera when you leave again." She reached behind her and closed her hand over the doorknob. "I appreciate your…efforts…but I need to get my aunt's car back to her. I'm sure the baby shower she's attending is over by now."

He looked impatient. "Jess told me about the car. I already got hold of Deke. He's got Jeanne covered."

Amelia exhaled. At least that was something, though it didn't alleviate her anxiety over Ophelia, much less Quinn. "That was—" *unexpected* "—very good of you."

"Jess also told me she's the reason you're stuck here."

"*Ophelia*'s the reason. I never imagined that woman would go to these lengths for a few pictures to sell." Her stomach churned and her palm grew sweaty on the doorknob. "Regardless, you shouldn't have come."

"Afraid your fiancé'll find out?"

She strongly considered opening the door and walking out. Only the fact that she'd brought this on herself by not addressing the press—the legitimate press—straight-on from the beginning kept her from doing so.

She took her hand away from the doorknob and wiped it down the side of her borrowed sundress. "Insult me all you want. I still don't want Ophelia taking after you, too. Right now—" her lips twisted "—assuming she doesn't find us here *together,* all you are is a faceless man with dark hair. She's still focusing on me, and it's best to keep it that way."

"You'd prefer hiding out here on your own until she gives up and goes away?"

"If I confront her, she'll somehow use that for her own gain. I know how these people work, Quinn. She's not breaking any laws—"

"Yet. Or have you forgotten already about the ones who did when they hacked into your phone calls?"

She sighed. She would never forget. "Ophelia doesn't know for certain that I'm here. And she can't stay cooped up in this B and B forever. She's not gaining anything unless she has photos to sell."

Or a story.

And Amelia's pregnancy would be a whale of a tale. It would put the detestable woman's career on the map, at least until the next scandal came along.

"I'm just grateful your sister happened to be in the hardware store at the right time to provide a distraction." It was at least one thing that had gone her way.

His lips curled derisively. "Don't kid yourself, princess. My sister never *happens* to do anything."

"She was there to buy pink paint for her daughter's room!"

"Jess doesn't *have* a daughter. And I can promise you that none of my nephews would be caught dead in a pink room."

"But—"

"Don't try to figure it out," he suggested darkly. He paced around the room as if he found it as cagelike as she. "Jess is a law unto herself. She's just as infected with royal-fever as the rest of the people around here."

Except for him. He'd been fully vaccinated, courtesy of an engagement that didn't exist.

"I don't care why she was there," Amelia said abruptly. "Facing your sister, whatever her reasons, is always going to be preferable to Ophelia Malone. At least she's—" She broke off.

"At least she's what?"

Family. Amelia stared at him, the word she'd been about to blurt still alarmingly close to her lips.

Just tell him.

She'd wanted a chance to speak with him alone, and now she had it.

Just tell him!

Her mouth ran dry. She started to speak. "O-only trying to protect you," she finished, instead.

His eyes narrowed, studying her face so closely she had to work hard not to squirm.

"I wish I had another disguise," she said. "We could just get out of here. Even if Ophelia doesn't discover us, Shayla's mother probably will."

"We don't have to worry about her." He pulled something from his pocket and tossed it on the bed.

She eyed the old-fashioned key.

"I rented the room for the night," he added flatly.

Amelia's stomach hollowed out. "We're *both* stuck here?"

Chapter Seven

Quinn paced across the room, putting as much distance as he could between them. "I'm not the one who's stuck," he corrected.

The bed with the puffy white comforter loomed large between them. Particularly when she sank down on the corner of the mattress.

With the red dress and her dark, dark hair, she looked like she might have been posed there for an advertisement. If not for the fact that her face was nearly as white as the bedding.

He ruthlessly squashed down his concern.

"I can come and go any time I want," he continued. "You're the one who isn't supposed to be here."

"Right. Silly of me to forget," she murmured.

He exhaled roughly. "Maybe she'll want to go out for dinner later and we'll be able to get out of here."

Before morning.

Before they spent an entire night together in a room with only one freaking bed.

He pinched the bridge of his nose and sat on the rocking chair. The wicker creaked a little under his weight, sounding loud in the quiet room.

He cleared his throat. "How many times have you had to do this?"

"Hide out from paparazzi?" She pushed her hair behind her ear. "I have no idea. Lucie and I've been doing it since we were teenagers, I guess."

Lucie, he knew, was her older sister. "She doesn't seem to be in the news as much as you."

"That's just because nobody thinks she's marrying a future earl right now. We've always been in a fishbowl, but never as bad as the last several weeks have been." She rubbed her hands nervously over the bed beside her hips.

He looked away. Whether she looked terrifyingly fragile or not, imagining her hair spread out over all that white was way too easy and the effect it was having on him wasn't one he needed just then. "It's a first for me," he muttered.

She spread her hands, smiling without any real amusement. "Welcome to my world." Then even the fake smile died. "You didn't tell me before—" Her lashes swept down. "In April I mean, that you were married."

It was the last thing he expected to hear and as a cold shower, it was pretty effective.

"It was a long time ago," he finally said.

"How long?"

"Why does it matter?"

"Because you're painting me to be just like her."

His jaw tightened. Knowing she was right didn't mean that he was wrong. "History tends to repeat itself."

Her long throat worked. "You have no idea," she murmured.

The hairs on the back of his neck stood up and he sat forward. The chair creaked ominously. "What's *that* supposed to mean?"

She pushed off the bed and pressed her hands together. "Look, despite you trying to help me here, I understand that things are...are over between us. You've been more than clear about that. And no matter what I say I don't expect that to change. You are not under any obligation—"

His jaw tightened. "Amelia—"

She moistened her lips. Her dark brown eyes met his, then flicked away again. Her tension was palpable.

"I'm pregnant," she said in a low voice. "I came back to Horseback Hollow to tell you."

He stared at her. There was a strange, hollow ringing inside his head. "You're...pregnant."

She chewed her lip. "Keep your voice down. Who knows how thin the walls are."

"You're *pregnant*," he repeated, a little more softly, but no less incredulously.

"And saying it a third time won't change that fact." She went into the adjoining bathroom and returned with a glass of water. She pushed it into his hand. "Drink."

The kind of drink he felt in sudden need of came out of a bottle and was strong enough to put down a horse. He set the glass on the windowsill. "How do you know?"

She paced across the room again. "The usual way."

"You missed your period?"

A tinge of color finally lit her cheeks. She didn't look at him. "Yes."

"And you're saying its mine."

"Yes." The word grew clipped.

"Even though you're engaged to someone else."

She thrust her fingers through her hair and tugged. "I am *not* engaged!" She dropped her hands and sank onto the foot of the bed again. "And before you accuse me, I know this baby is yours because you're the only man I've ever slept with," she added in a flat voice.

He shook his head once, sharp enough to clear it of the fog that had filled it. "You expect me to believe you were a virgin? And I didn't happen to notice?"

Her cheeks turned bright. "I don't care what you noticed or not. That night with you was the only time I—" She broke off. "This baby is not James's," she said crisply. "What earthly reason would I have for being here—" she lifted her arms "—if it were? You think I like facing you and, and telling you—" her voice grew choked "—knowing how you feel about me?"

"Calm down."

"Easy for you to say." She rushed into the bathroom and slammed the door behind her.

He sat there, hearing his pulse pounding in his head. Remembering that April night. The dawn following.

She'd been shy, yes. At first. But he'd never suspected—

He shoved to his feet, crossed the room and pushed open the door.

She was sitting on the closed lid of the commode, tears sliding down her cheeks. And her jaw dropped at his intrusion. "What—"

"It's only been six weeks." He bit out the fact that she'd been so careful to point out to him. "How can you be certain? Do you have any other symptoms? Have you seen a doctor?"

Her expression went smooth, her eyes remote. "I did a home pregnancy test."

"Sometimes they come back false." He grimaced when she just looked at him. "Another experience from my regrettable marriage." Before the "I do's" Carrie's test had been positive. After, the test was negative. But he couldn't even accuse her of lying about it, because at that point, he'd still believed she loved him and he'd been right beside her when they'd looked at those test results.

Carrie had been relieved.

He hadn't been. Not at that point, anyway. He'd built their house with a family in mind. A family that had never come. Not for him.

"Two years later she got pregnant for real," he added abruptly.

"With her ex-boyfriend's child."

He studied her for a long moment but could see nothing in her expressionless eyes. "Either you've been listening to really old gossip or my sister's got a big mouth."

She didn't respond to that. "I'll agree to whatever tests you want." Her tone was still cool.

He really, really hated that "royal" face of hers. "Another pregnancy test will do for starters."

Her brows lifted, surprise evidently overcoming remoteness. "I meant paternity tests."

"I know." He could only deal with so much at once. "When you arrived in my barn, you were worn out. Exhausted and full of stress. You collapsed, for God's sake. Let's just make certain there's a pregnancy to begin with."

She sucked in her lower lip for a moment. "I don't

think now's a good time for me to stroll into a pharmacy to buy a test kit."

He stifled an oath. For a moment there, he'd managed to forget the very reason they were in the guest room at all. "After we get back to the Hollow," he said. "My sister's pregnant so often she's probably got a stockpile of tests."

As far as humor went, it fell flatter than a pancake.

Turning slightly, she swiped her hand over her cheek. As if he couldn't see perfectly well that she was crying.

"First things first," he said gruffly. "Sooner or later, your stalker downstairs will have to eat. Or sleep. And then we'll get the hell out of this place."

"Here." Several hours later, Shayla handed Quinn a set of keys on a key chain with a plastic heart hanging from it. "Mrs. O'Malley said to give these to you, too."

It was finally dark and Ophelia had left the B and B, presumably for dinner, though Shayla reported that she'd had her camera with her when she'd gone.

The teenager—who clearly thought she was taking part in an exciting adventure—had also delivered a knapsack much like the one Amelia had ditched in the airport restroom, filled with clothing and a long blond wig.

"Those are the keys to Mrs. O'Malley's van?"

The girl nodded, looking conspiratorial. "It's parked at the end of the block in front of the bar. You could see it from your window if you looked out."

The bar, Amelia knew, was O'Malley's and it belonged to Jess's father-in-law. She looked at Quinn. Aside from working out their escape plan with his sister and Shayla, he hadn't said much in the past few hours.

He hadn't done much except watch Amelia, leaving

her to imagine all manner of dark thoughts he was having about her.

"I can just as easily drive my aunt's car," she argued not for the first time.

"Ophelia probably already knows it belongs to your aunt," he returned, also not for the first time. "It's been sitting there all day even though the post office closed at noon."

As long as Ophelia didn't spot them together, there was no reason for him not to drive his own pickup truck back to Horseback Hollow.

Her stomach was churning. The longer they'd waited in the pretty guest suite, the crazier she'd felt. The news that Ophelia had left the B and B on foot had been a relief, but it didn't mean the end of her problems.

Not by any stretch of the imagination.

"I'll change into the clothes then." It wasn't as if she had many options. She looked at Shayla. "You've been a big help, Shayla."

The girl bounced on her toes. "Are you kidding? Nothing interesting ever happens here! I'm just glad my ma's out on a date tonight. I love her, but if she knew *you* were here, so would the rest of the town. She can't keep anything a secret." Holding her finger to her lips, she slipped out the door and closed it behind her.

Amelia exhaled and, avoiding Quinn's gaze, took the clothing into the bathroom. She changed into the diminutive bandage of a skirt that was as bright an orange as Shayla's hair and the white V-neck shirt that came with it. Amelia wasn't wearing a bra and when she pulled the thin cotton over her head, she cringed at her reflection. The neckline reached midway down her chest and the shadow from her nipples showed clearly through the fabric.

If she asked for another blouse, though, they'd be delayed even longer. And they had no idea how long a window Ophelia was unwittingly allowing them. So she swallowed her misgivings and wound her hair into a knot on her head before pulling on the cheap wig that Shayla had provided. The hair was synthetic and an obviously false platinum blond. But it covered Amelia's dark hair and reached down to her waist.

As a disguise, she decided she far preferred the boy look she and Molly had attempted.

She kept the sandals on that she was already wearing. There was nothing distinctive about them and the platform wedges that Shayla had stuck in the knapsack were too small anyway. Then she zipped the discarded dress inside the pack and, hauling in a steadying breath, opened the door to face Quinn.

"Jesus," he muttered.

"I look like a tart," she said before he could.

"You look like jail bait." His gaze was focused on her chest.

Flushing, she dragged the cheap blond hair over her shoulders so it covered her breasts. "Are you ready to leave or not?"

In answer, he opened the door and handed her the heart-shaped key ring. "Like we agreed. You first. I'll follow in a few minutes. We'll meet up at the Rocking-U. You remember how to get there?"

"I got there on foot. I imagine I can get there by van." Squeezing the hard metal heart in her fist, she left the room.

This wasn't her first rodeo, as they said, when it came to avoiding the paparazzi, but it was the first time she'd done so as a scantily clad teenage girl. Even when she'd *been* a teen, she'd never dressed like this. Her parents wouldn't have allowed it.

She encountered no one on the stairs between the third and second floors. On the second, she could hear music coming from behind the door of the honeymooners who had arrived a short while ago. On the last flight, she descended more gingerly.

But Shayla, dusting again though there was surely no need for it, caught her eye and quickly nodded. "All clear, Lady Amelia," she whispered loudly.

Resisting the urge to look back up the staircase to see if Quinn was watching, Amelia skipped down the rest of the stairs and sailed across the small lobby and out into the night air. She turned left, walking briskly to the end of the block, waiting with every footstep to hear a camera shutter clicking or see a camera flash lighting the night.

But there was nothing.

And soon she was jogging. Then running flat out, the knapsack bouncing wildly against her backside, until she reached the green van right where it was supposed to be. Her heart was pounding in her chest as she fumbled with the keys, nearly dropping them, before managing to unlock the door and climb inside. Once there, she worked the knapsack free and tossed it behind the seat before fitting the key into the ignition.

The engine started immediately and she cautiously drove away from the curb. She hadn't been accustomed to her aunt's car and the van—considerably larger—felt even more unwieldy to her.

She drove around the corner, then the next and the next until she was right back where she'd begun the day, near the post office. She waited for a car to pass, then turned again and headed out of town. Back to Horseback Hollow.

Going from one fire into the next.

* * *

Amelia was sitting at Quinn's piano, rubbing her fingers over the keys but not really playing anything, when he arrived. He walked over to the piano and deliberately closed the lid on the keys as if he couldn't stand the idea of her touching it.

"Here." He tossed her a small white sack. "I stopped at the drugstore on the way back."

She dumped out the contents on her lap.

A three-pack of pregnancy test kits.

Evidently, he *really* wanted to be certain.

"Decide you didn't want to let your sister know?"

His smile was thin. "Something like that."

She dropped the paper sack on top of the discarded blond wig sitting on top of the piano and turned the box over, pretending to read the instructions on the back, but not seeing any of the words.

She'd been waiting nearly an hour alone at his home before he got there. He'd told her the door wouldn't be locked, and it hadn't been. Only the fact that she needed the loo had made her go in, though.

Otherwise, she would have just sat in his sister's van and waited.

It wasn't as if he truly wanted her in his home, after all.

"You weren't followed?"

He shook his head once.

She pressed her lips together and rose. "I suppose you want me to do this now?" She waved the box slightly.

"You want to wait until morning?"

She wanted to turn back the calendar six weeks and do things right. She wanted the warm, tender man back that he'd been the night they'd made love.

Her eyes burned. Not answering, she walked past him and down the hall to the bathroom there. When she was finished, she put the cap back on the stick and left it sitting on the bathroom counter.

She opened the door to find him standing on the other side and heat ran up under her cheeks. "Two minutes."

He lifted his hand and she realized he was holding a pocket watch.

"My father used to carry a pocket watch," she murmured.

He crossed his arms and leaned back against the bathroom door, his hooded gaze on the test stick. "So did mine. This one." He dangled the watch from the chain. "One of the few things the fire didn't take. This and the piano." He could have been discussing the weather for all the emotion in his voice.

She chewed the inside of her lip.

Never had two minutes passed so slowly.

When finally it had, he picked up the stick and studied it silently. Then he flipped it into the little trash can next to the cabinet.

"It's late," he said, walking past her. "You need to eat."

Amelia's throat tightened.

Even though she knew, she *knew* what the test would show, she plucked the plastic stick out of the empty can and looked at the bright blue plus sign.

Tears slid out of her eyes and she dropped it in the trash once more.

She turned on the cold water and splashed it over her face until her cheeks felt frozen. Then she dried her face and followed him.

He was in the kitchen. Just as he had been the night he'd found her in his barn.

Only this time the sandwich was sitting on a plate, and a glass of milk sat next to that.

Her stomach lurched. Whether from a sudden attack of morning sickness-at-night or from the horrible day it had been she didn't know. But the thought of choking down any kind of food just then made her want to retch.

She forced herself to sit down, though, in front of the plate. He, however, remained standing by the window, looking out into the night. "Aren't you going to eat?" He had spent nearly as much time cooped up in the B and B as she had.

"We'll go to the justice of the peace on Monday." He didn't look at her. "Unless you want a minister. It'll be more complicated that way, but—"

"A *minister.*" She pushed aside the plate and stared at his back. "What are you suggesting?"

He turned, giving her a narrow look. "What do you think? My kid's not going to be born without my name."

Her jaw went loose. "So," she said with false cheer, "now you magically believe it's yours?"

His lips twisted. "Don't push me, princess."

She shoved back from the table so abruptly the chair tipped over and crashed to the tiled floor. "Don't push *you?* I can't believe I ever thought I—" She broke off, grasping for some semblance of self-control even though she wanted to launch herself at him, kicking and screaming. Which was altogether shocking, because she never lost her temper like that. "If I wanted a marriage without love, I could have stayed in England and married Jimmy! It certainly would have been easier than this!"

"That—" he pointed toward her midsection "—changes things."

She lifted her chin, channeling her mother at her most

regal. "It doesn't change the fact that I won't be arranged into a convenient marriage. I've done a lot of things in my life purely for propriety's sake, but not this."

He swore and planted his boot on one leg of the up-turned chair and kicked it away from her.

She gasped as it slammed against the wall.

"Next time you give me that royal face, I'll put you over my knee." He leaned over her, tall and furious. "And I won't let you take *my kid* back there to be raised by another man!"

Shocked to her very core, she stood there frozen. "I wouldn't do that."

A muscle ticked angrily in his jaw and his eyes raked over her face.

"I swear to you, Quinn." She stared into his eyes, wishing with all of her heart that he'd just take her in his arms the way he had six weeks ago. "I would never do that," she finished hoarsely.

"Then you can prove it on Monday in front of the JP."

She hauled in an unsteady breath. Marriage to Quinn Drummond was something she'd dreamed about since they'd made love. Since they'd unknowingly created the baby inside her.

But not this way.

Not ever this way.

"No."

Then she retrieved the chair, turned it upright and tucked it under the table and walked out of the kitchen.

Chapter Eight

When he heard the front door open and close, Quinn bolted after her, catching her at the bottom of the porch steps. "Where the *hell* do you think you're going?"

She yanked her arm out of his grasp and gave him a glacial look. "Where I go is not *up* to you."

"You wanna strut out to the highway and hitch a ride, princess?" His lips twisted as he looked her over. "Imagine a trucker will go by eventually. Depending on what sort of guy he is, he might or might not stop for someone looking like you."

She gave a futile yank down on the hem of the skirt that showed nearly every inch of her gloriously God-given stems. "You are *not* the man I thought you were," she said through her teeth.

"And you aren't the woman I thought, either," he returned.

She turned on the heel of her little sandals, her hair flying around her shoulders and started walking away, her sweet hips swaying.

He cussed like he hadn't cussed since he was fifteen and his mom had washed out his mouth with soap. "You're not going anywhere, princess." In two long steps, he reached her and hooked her around the waist, swinging her off her feet before she had a chance to stop him.

Her legs scissored and he slid her over his shoulder, clamping his arm over the back of her legs before she could do either one of them physical damage. "Cut it out."

She drummed her fists against his backside, trying to wriggle out of his hold. "Put me *down* this instant," she ordered imperiously.

"I warned you," he said and swatted her butt.

She pounded his back even harder. "You...cretin."

"Yeah, yeah. Sweet nothings won't get you anywhere, princess." He stomped back into the house and into the living room. He lifted her off his shoulder and dumped her on the sofa.

She bounced and tried scrambling away, but he leaned over her, pinning her on either side with his hands. "Stay," he bit out.

She glared at him through the hair hanging in her face. "I. Don't. Take. Orders." Her chest heaved.

He didn't move.

Didn't do a damn thing even though he should have, because she was there, in his house and she was pregnant with his kid and he didn't want to ask for a polite dance or gentle, moonlit kisses.

He just *wanted*.

With a need that was blinding.

She suddenly went still.

A swallow worked down her long, long throat and the glint in her eyes shifted to something else entirely.

She moistened her lips. "Quinn," she whispered.

And then her hands weren't pushing at him, they were pulling.

At his shirt that he ripped off over his head.

At his belt that slid out of his belt loops with a loud slither.

"Hurry," she gasped, squirming beneath him as she yanked his fly apart and dragged at his jeans, nearly sending his nerves out the top of his skull.

He reached under that excuse of a skirt and tore her panties aside. She was wet and hot and she gasped when he dragged her closer and drove into her.

He let out a harsh breath, trying to slow down, get some control, get some sanity, but she wrapped her lithe legs around his hips, greedily rocking. And then she was shuddering deep, deep inside, her body clutching at him and her lips crying out his name.

And he was lost.

Every cell Amelia possessed was still vibrating when Quinn silently rolled away. She felt like they'd just been tossed out of a tornado.

The night they'd made love had been magical. Tender. Sweet.

This was…raw. Most assuredly not sweet.

And every bit as powerful.

She let out a shuddering breath, knowing that if he touched her again, she'd welcome him just as wantonly. "Quinn—"

"This shouldn't have happened." He sat up and slid

off the sofa. He didn't look at her as he fastened his jeans and his voice was low. "Did I hurt you?"

She caught her breath, aching inside. "No," she whispered honestly. "Did…did I hurt you?" She dimly recalled her nails sinking into his flesh while pleasure exploded inside her.

He looked over his shoulder at that, genuinely surprised. His gaze raked over her and she trembled, muscles deep inside her still clenching. The thin cotton shirt felt rough against her agonizingly tight nipples and she tugged the skirt down where it belonged. She had no idea what had become of her underpants.

"No," he said gruffly. "You didn't hurt me." He leaned over and picked up his T-shirt. The neckline was nearly torn right out of it. He looked at it for a moment, then bunched it in his fist. "I'll get you something to put on."

She sat up, curling her legs to the side. "Thank you."

The roping muscles defining his strong shoulders seemed to tighten when she spoke. He went up the stairs and returned in minutes with a button-down shirt. "You still need to eat," he said evenly, handing it to her. "And decide if you want a minister or not."

Then he turned and went into the kitchen. Through the doorway she could see him readjusting the chair.

Her eyes stung.

She didn't know what she was going to do.

But she knew she was not going to marry Quinn Drummond without his love.

Swiping her cheeks, she stood on legs that felt as insubstantial as candy floss. The shirt he'd given her was clearly a dress shirt but it definitely wasn't the one he'd worn to Toby's wedding. That one had been stark white while this one was a pale gray with an even paler pinstripe. When she unbuttoned it and found a tag still attached to the collar inside, she realized it was new. Never been worn.

She'd have preferred something he'd worn. At least she'd have been able to take a little comfort from it. And she wouldn't be wondering who'd bought the shirt for him because it looked too fancy for anything he'd have chosen for himself.

She removed the tag and pulled the shirt over the one she already had on. New or not, there was something very intimate about wearing his shirt. She needed all the barriers against that feeling that she could get.

She buttoned it up, then folded the long sleeves over several times until they didn't hang past her wrists. She spotted her panties and picked them up. The thin silk was torn in two.

Thank goodness the shirttails reached her knees, though just thinking why that was a good thing made her cheeks hot and her stomach hollow out.

She toed off the one sandal that she was still wearing, blushed some more over that as well, then hurried down the hall to the bathroom, the ruined silk bunched in her fist.

She washed up, dropped the panties in the trash next to the test stick, and tried to restore some order to her tangled hair with her fingers. Finally, with no other excuses remaining, she returned to the kitchen.

The sandwich was still there on the plate.

He was sitting in the chair opposite it, his long legs stretched out across the floor, a dark brown bottle propped on his hard, tanned abdomen.

She ignored the curling sensation inside her belly at the sight and sat down. Unlike earlier, she was suddenly famished, but she cringed a little when she picked up the sandwich, because the bread hadn't even had an opportunity to grow stale while they'd been…been—

"Don't think about it," he said abruptly and she jumped a little.

"I beg your pardon?"

"You're thinking about what we just did on the couch." His hazel eyes were hooded and unreadable. "My suggestion is don't." He lifted the bottle to his lips and took a long drink. "Safer that way," he added when he set the bottle down again. The glass clinked a little when it hit the metal tab still unfastened at the top of his jeans.

She dragged her eyes away and took a bite of the sandwich. For something that had transpired in a span of minutes, she was quite certain *not* thinking about it wasn't going to be as easy as he made it out to be.

"I didn't have anything but peanut butter and jelly," he said.

She chewed and swallowed. "I like peanut butter."

His lips twisted a little. "So do my nephews. They go through a jar every time they're here."

She gingerly took a sip of milk. On a good day, she didn't much care for it, and now was no exception. She slid out of the chair and saw his eyes narrow. "I prefer water," she said quickly, lifting the glass. She dumped the milk down the drain, rinsed the glass and refilled it from the tap then sat down again to the sandwich. "Your sister really doesn't have a daughter?"

"She really doesn't," he said evenly.

"How old are her boys?"

"Fifteen, thirteen, nine, six and two."

"Goodness." She toyed with the water glass. He might not have told her before about an ex-wife, but he had talked about his family. The death of his father. The fact that he had only one older sister.

"Who else knows you're pregnant?"

She looked at him quickly, then back at the sandwich. "Just, um, just Molly." She tore off a tiny piece of crust. "She's one of my mother's secretaries."

He bent his knees and shifted forward, setting the bottle on the table. "You told a *secretary?* Not a friend or your sister?"

"Molly is a friend. And Lucie—" She shook her head. "Lucie's busy with her own issues. Besides, we've never exactly shared secrets."

"Thought you were close in age?"

"We are. She's only two years ahead. But—" She shrugged. "We've all had our responsibilities growing up. Some more than others." She smashed the tidbit of crust between her thumbs. "Mostly, mine has been to provide window dressing at my mother's events."

"You pulled together the companies who funded that last orphanage. That's a little more than window dressing."

She looked at him and it was his turn to glance away and shrug. "I can read," he muttered. "And Jess was yammering on about it not too long ago."

In other words, don't get excited thinking he'd been following her activities. She wondered how impressed he'd be if he knew the companies she'd been able to pull together for the funding were all controlled by the Earl of Estingwood, and took another bite of the sandwich.

The peanut butter and jelly stuck to the roof of her mouth, reminding her of the sandwiches she used to beg off their cook when she was a little girl. "Well—" she swallowed it down with another drink of water "—speaking of reading. We might have avoided Ophelia Malone for now, but I doubt she'll go quietly into the night."

"She got lucky with one photo," he dismissed.

"Sometimes one photo is all it takes to set off a firestorm."

"Afraid your—" he hesitated for a moment "—future earl is going to see it?"

She was certain he'd been going to say *fiancé*. Undoubtedly, James and his staff had already seen the photo and were organizing the appropriate damage control. But she didn't share that fact because Quinn wouldn't want to hear about it. "May I use your phone?" she asked instead.

He looked at the pocket watch he'd left earlier on the table. "Nearly eleven. Your aunt figures we're still in Vicker's Corners."

"I'm not calling my aunt." It would be early in London, but James always rose early. "I'm calling James."

His hazel eyes went flat. "Missing Lord Banning already?"

"If I didn't know better, I'd think you were jealous," she said sweetly. Of course he wasn't. He'd have to feel something other than reluctant lust and duty for him to be jealous. "May I use your phone or not?"

He picked up his bottle and gestured with the bottom of it. "It's right there on the wall, princess."

And he wasn't inclined to give her any privacy. That was more than apparent.

She went over to the phone that was, indeed, hanging on the wall just inside the doorway. Even though she knew Quinn had built the house within the past ten years, the phone was an old-fashioned thing with a long coiled cord tethering the receiver to the base. She plucked the receiver off the hook and punched out the numbers she knew by heart. After a number of clicks and burps, the line finally connected and James answered.

"It's Amelia," she greeted. She could feel Quinn's eyes boring holes in her backside. "How's your father?"

"Amelia! Where the bloody hell have you been? The media here is going mad. Not even your mother knew you were leaving. Are you all right?"

"I know. And I... I'm fine." She absently worked her finger into the center of the coiling phone cord. "You've got to issue a statement that we're not being married."

Even across the continents, she could hear his sigh. "You're back with that fellow, then."

She didn't know how she'd describe the situation with Quinn, but "back with" wouldn't be it. "I know what you'd hoped, Jimmy, but you've got to trust me. It's better to come from you. And the sooner the better." She looked over her shoulder when she heard a scrape on the floor.

Quinn had pushed back his chair and he walked past her, leaving the room.

"Ophelia's been hunting me around," she said into the phone, wanting to laugh a little hysterically because there was a gun rack containing several rifles attached to the wall above the doorway.

"If you hadn't given her something to find, she'd have had to give up," James returned. "You let her catch you kissing that man."

She exhaled, pressing her forehead to the cream-colored wall for a moment. "Just tell your father the truth," she said. "Tell him you're not in love with me. You never were!"

"Father doesn't care about love. He cares about bloodlines and he decided a year ago that yours was the right one."

"A marriage between us would be a disaster." She said the same thing she'd been telling him for months, ever since the whole idea of a union between them had come up. "You're in love with Astrid and I'm—"

"In love with your Horseback Hollow rancher," he finished and sighed again. "Father's condition is worse. He's home still. Refuses to go to hospital. Says there's no point alerting the vultures and he wants to die in his own bed."

She exhaled. "I'm so sorry, Jimmy." For all the earl's faults, he thought he knew what was best for his son. "How's your mum?"

"A rock, like always. Can you just hold on a few more days, Amelia? That's what the doctors have told us he has left. Days." He cleared his throat. "Once father is… gone… I'll issue a statement. You won't come out looking badly. I'll blame it on my increased duties or something. Mutual decision and all that."

She knew his request wasn't because of the Earldom he'd inherit. It was because, despite the problems between them, he wanted his father to die in peace, believing his son was on the track he'd laid.

"A few days," she agreed huskily.

"Thank you. You've been a good friend, Amelia." She heard him speaking to someone in muffled tones, then he came back. "I have to go. Take care of yourself. And look out for Ophelia Malone."

"I will." The line clicked, going dead and she unwound her fingers from the cord and replaced the receiver. She left the kitchen, thinking that Quinn would be in the living area. But he wasn't. Nor was he upstairs.

She went to the window and pulled up the blinds, looking out. She could see a light on inside the barn and she pushed her feet back into the sandals and went outside. The night air was balmy and quite a bit warmer than it had been six weeks earlier, and it smelled earthy and green.

He'd parked his pickup truck next to where she'd left his sister's van and she walked around them as she headed toward the barn. Unlike the house, which he'd built not so long ago, the barn looked like it had stood there for generations and in the dark now, with gold light spewing out the opened doorway, it looked almost medieval. She stepped inside.

Quinn, still shirtless, was stacking bales of hay against one wall.

She pulled in a soundless breath at the sight of him, entirely too aware of her lack of undergarments beneath the shirttails.

Her sandals scuffed the hard packed ground and he looked at her.

"I, um, I would have been much less nervous the other night had I known there were lights in here," she said, gesturing with her hand toward the row of industrial looking fixtures hanging high overhead.

He turned his back and tossed another bale into place. She wasn't sure why. To her, it looked as if he were just moving the stack from one spot to another.

She rubbed her damp palms down her thighs. "James will issue a statement in a few days."

He just kept working. "Why the wait?"

She hesitated and saw the way his lips twisted as if she'd done exactly what he expected.

Annoyed, she walked across the barn, feeling bits of straw and grit crunching beneath her shoes. "I told you James's father is in poor health. He's also been hiding that fact because, in addition to being the Earl of Estingwood, he is head of Estingwood Mills."

"The textiles."

She wondered if he'd learned that courtesy of his sister, or if he'd found out on his own. "James has been running the company in his father's stead and fending off a takeover bid by one of their competitors. If the earl's health was made public it would endanger their hold. Once James succeeds his father, that will no longer be the case. The mill will be safe, as will the hundreds of people it employs."

"Again, why the wait?" His tone was hard.

"The title is passed on at the earl's discretion during his lifetime, or to his son upon his death which, according to James, sadly is fairly imminent. Before now, he's insisted that James be married to an appropriate mate before receiving the title and had been doing his best to see that happened."

He tossed another hay bale and turned to her. "So the old man was yanking Banning's strings."

"I suppose it might look that way." Sweat gleamed across his broad chest and she looked away, shocked at how badly she wanted to press her mouth against that salty sheen. "Lord Banning's not a bad man. He just has very traditional expectations where his family is concerned. You behave suitably. You marry suitably."

"Fine. The old man kicks the bucket in a few days. So which is it going to be? Justice of the peace or a minister?"

Stymied, she just stared. "Your callousness aside, regardless of what announcements James makes, I'm still not marrying you like this!"

He tugged off the worn leather gloves he'd been wearing and grabbed the shotgun she hadn't even noticed leaning against the wall.

"I've heard of shotgun weddings," she said, smiling weakly, "but this is taking it too literally."

"I've got a possum."

She blinked. "Excuse me?"

"A possum," he repeated with exaggerated care. "It's raiding my feed."

She grimaced. "And you want to shoot it?"

"I don't want to make it a pet," he drawled. "Ranching, princess." He dragged the leather gloves beneath her chin and flicked her hair behind her shoulder. "It's not fine linens and sidesaddles."

Fine linens had their place, but she was just as happy sitting in the kitchen with a peanut butter and jelly sandwich. "I've never once sat sidesaddle," she said with a cool smile. "Some of the Chesterfields are champion riders. I do know what manure smells like."

"You'll get even more familiar with it." He smiled, too, but it was fierce-looking and dangerous. "Along with the stench of branding and the mess of castrating. JP or minister?"

Her smile wilted. Her stomach lurched more alarmingly than ever before and she suddenly knew it wasn't going to go away so easily this time.

She whirled on her heel and barely made it outside of the barn before she leaned over and vomited right onto the dirt.

Quinn came up beside her.

"This is the most humiliating moment of my life," she managed miserably. "Please, *please* just leave me alone."

He carefully gathered her hair behind her shoulders. "Not a chance in hell, princess."

Chapter Nine

"There you are!" Jeanne Marie waved her hand from the window of her car and pulled up alongside Quinn's pickup truck. She got out quickly and strode across the gravel, a wide smile on her face.

Even though Amelia had gotten a few hours of actual sleep after tossing her cookies the night before, her stomach still felt rocky half a day later. She gingerly pushed out of the porch chair where she'd been sitting, soaking up the fresh afternoon air while Tanya, the teenager Quinn paid to clean his house, worked inside, and went down the three steps to greet her aunt. "I'm so sorry about the car."

"Oh." Jeanne Marie waved her hand. "These things happen." Then she laughed. "Well, not exactly *these* things. Nobody around here has ever had to hide out from the paparazzi before. But it turned out perfectly convenient for me. After church, Deke dropped me off in Vicker's Corners and was able to go back home rather than waiting around while I browsed the shops for you. Which made him a very happy camper." She gave Amelia a quick, squeezing hug. "And I'm glad that you didn't go to church this morning. That woman with the camera was there asking questions about you." She sniffed. "Not that *anyone* gave her the time of day."

"A fine churchlike attitude," Amelia said wryly, though she was glad the citizens of Horseback Hollow were showing some discretion, even if it was only because of loyalty to her aunt.

Jeanne Marie laughed again. "Now. Shall we discuss this *nothing* going on between you and Quinn?" She looked over Amelia's head at the ranch house behind her.

Amelia assumed her aunt didn't know about the internet photograph or she would have mentioned it. And she was glad for that. "Something is going on. I'm just—" she tugged at the red sundress that she'd pulled on yet again that morning "—not ready to say exactly what that is."

Her aunt's eyes narrowed a little, studying her. "At least you don't look quite like the whipped puppy that you did last week, so I'll give you a pass for now. Have you spoken with your mother?"

Amelia nodded. She'd called Josephine that morning and told her that the false engagement was over, though not the entire reason why. She wasn't ready to share her pregnancy with anyone other than Quinn, though she knew she'd need to sooner rather than later. She couldn't very well wait until she was round as a house. Her mum had been glad to hear about the pretense coming to an end, but Amelia wasn't so sure how she'd react to having another grandchild. Her brother Oliver had little Ollie already, but at least he'd been born *before* Oliver and his wife divorced.

Amelia could be married before her baby arrived, too, if she were willing to marry a man who didn't love her.

"She's really looking forward to coming for the Cantina's grand opening," Amelia told Jeanne Marie. "She hinted that she might be able to stay a few days longer than she expected."

"That would be marvelous." Jeanne turned back to her car and opened the back door. She pulled out a plastic shopping bag and handed it to Amelia. "Whatever doesn't fit can be returned," she said. "I made sure of that."

Amelia peeked inside the bag, seeing a couple T-shirts, a skirt and a package of white cotton underpants. "Perfect," she breathed. "Thank you so much, Aunt Jeanne." She carried the bag up onto the porch and set it on the wooden rocking chair and her aunt followed.

"Where's Quinn?"

"Off doing chores," she said vaguely. She wasn't entirely sure, because she'd been giving the man a wide berth since he'd insisted she take his bed the night before.

She'd been as wary of instigating another episode that led to torn panties as she was finding herself weakly admitting that she preferred a minister over a justice of the peace.

And her cheeks heated just thinking of panties and a minister in the same thought.

She realized her aunt was watching her thoughtfully, and quickly plucked the receipt for the purchases out of the bag. She drew a couple folded bills to cover the amount out of her sundress pocket and handed them to her aunt.

"All right now," Jeanne Marie said, tucking the cash

in her own pocket. "Can you and Quinn come for dinner later? Christopher and his gal, Kinsley, will be there. You know he's opening a branch of the Fortune Foundation here."

Amelia smiled. "I know you're excited about that, but I suspect it's more because Christopher's moving back here from Red Rock."

"It was hard when he was gone," Jeanne Marie admitted. "When he left, there was such turmoil between him and Deke. All came to a head because of that darned money James Marshall wanted to give me." She let out a huge sigh as if she were dismissing all her bad thoughts and smiled again. "The important thing is our boy is coming home. Kinsley will be a beautiful wife for him and he's happier than he's ever been. He's finally found his niche with the Foundation."

"Tell me again how we're all connected to it?"

Jeanne Marie leaned against the porch rail, her expression bright. "Chris could tell you far more than I ever could since he works there, but it was founded in memory of Ryan Fortune who was a distant cousin of ours. They have all sorts of community programs and they help fund clinics and—oh, just bunches of good things for people. Having a branch in Horseback Hollow is going to mean so much. It'll be jobs, it'll be aid for those who need it—" Her eyes sparkled as she focused on Amelia's face. "Where was I? Oh, yes. Ryan's cousin William Fortune—he used to have a business in California—is married now to Lily, who was Ryan's widow and they're in Red Rock. I know it sounds scandalous, but it really wasn't. And then there are the Atlanta Fortunes—John Michael is our oldest brother, then James Marshall and your mama and me."

Amelia chuckled. "I need a map."

"I know." Jeanne Marie laughed merrily. "And they all have grown children and some of them are starting families, and it's just… Well, I hit the mother lode in family when I grew up with none except my adoptive parents."

Amelia smiled. It was hard not to let her aunt's delight infect her as well. "And to answer your question, yes, I'd love to join you all for dinner." She wasn't going to speak for Quinn.

Jeanne Marie glanced at her watch and tsked. "Speaking of, I've got to get the roasts in the oven or we'll be stuck eating at the Horseback Hollow Grill. Come by anytime. Food'll be on around six." She kissed Amelia's forehead and went back down the steps, briskly returning to her car.

Amelia watched her drive away, then jumped a little when Quinn appeared around the side of the house.

He was wearing a white T-shirt covered in sweat and dirt, multi-pocketed cargo shorts, heavy work boots and had a tool belt slung around his lean hips.

And he still needed a shave.

She felt heat gather inside her and dug her fingernails into her palms as a distraction.

It failed miserably, particularly when he spotted her hovering there on the front porch. It felt as if his gaze saw right through her dress to the sum total of nothing that she wore beneath it.

She pulled the strap that kept slipping off her shoulder back into place and snatched up the bag of clothes that Jeanne had delivered. "My aunt played personal shopper," she said.

The top rail surrounding the porch was chest high to him and he dropped his arm over it before tipping back the bill of the ball cap he wore. Throwing up in front of him may have been excruciatingly embarrassing, but it had served to break *some* of the tension.

At least he didn't have accusation clouding his eyes every time he looked at her.

"Guess you're wishing you'd have had her do that in the first place," he said

The bag crinkled in her fingers. "It would have been easier," she allowed. The memory of the way his T-shirt had torn the night before taunted her, and she focused instead on the dirt covering the one he was wearing now. "What, um, what have you been doing?"

He lifted his arm off the rail again and tilted his head. "Come on. I'll show you."

Surprised by the invitation, she squeezed the bag again. "I should, uh, probably change."

His lips quirked and he plucked his dirty shirt. "What for?"

She dragged her eyes away from his chest. "Aunt Jeanne invited us for dinner later."

"Nice of her. S'pose you want to go."

"Christopher will be there. I haven't seen him since Sawyer's wedding over New Year's. He's engaged now."

"I heard."

It wasn't an answer of whether *he* wanted to go. "So?"

He smiled faintly. "I generally don't turn down a meal cooked by someone else."

She didn't know if she was relieved or not. But she left the porch anyway.

He waited until she reached him before turning and heading away from the house and the barn and the antique-looking windmill beside it that stood motionless in the still summer air. They passed several pens, all empty and fenced in by round metal rails, following a path that was more dirt than gravel with a strip of grass growing down the center.

He kept to the dirt part and puffs of dust rose around his sturdy boots as he went and he eyed her when she moved to the grassier strip and shook one foot then the other to get out the grit that had worked its way into her sandals.

"These boots aren't made for walking," she said wryly.

"I could toss you over my shoulder," he deadpanned.

She flushed and continued walking. "I don't think so," she said primly.

He laughed softly.

Something in her stomach curled, and it was not morning sickness.

She stared ahead at the land. It seemed more covered in scrubby bushes and wild grasses than anything. And the horizon seemed to stretch forever. "Don't you have fences to pen in your cattle?"

"There's fence. Just can't see it from here."

"What about your horses?"

"We're getting there."

She moistened her lips. "It's, uh, it's very warm today, isn't it?"

He shot her an amused look. "Probably close to ninety. 'Bout average for this time of year. Be glad there's air-conditioning in the house. The one I grew up in didn't have it. Probably just as well that shack burned down. Made tearing down what was left easy."

"You told me back in April you were very young when it happened."

He shrugged. "Fifteen." The hammer hanging from his tool belt made a soft brushing sound against his khaki-colored cargos with each step he took and she realized her steps had slowed, intentionally or not, allowing her an excellent view of his backside.

She picked up her pace again, skipping a few times until she was level with him once more.

He didn't seem to notice.

"Same year my dad died," he added.

She studied his profile. The night of Toby's wedding, they'd talked about everything under the sun. But he hadn't told her that he'd been married. Or that the fire had happened the very same year he'd also lost his father. "That must have been devastating."

"You lost your dad, too."

"And it was horrible," she murmured, "but we still had a home."

"The Chesterfield estate," he drawled.

Her nerves prickled at his tone. "Yes."

He stopped. Propped his hands on his hips and stared out. "Lot different than this place, no doubt."

She continued forward a few steps and turned until she was facing him. "Yes," she agreed. "But, like the Rocking-U, it has been in the Chesterfield family for generations. I understand ancestral ties to one's land."

His lips twitched again.

"What?"

"Just listening to you talk, darlin'." He shook his head. "Kills me."

She huffed. "There is nothing wrong with the way I speak. *You* are the one who's all…all…drawly." Had he really called her *darlin'?*

"Drawly." His smile stretched. "That some grammatical term they taught you in those fancy schools you attended?" He shook his head again, then started walking once more, brushing past her since she was standing right in his path.

Wholly bemused, she turned and followed and shortly, the road began descending and she realized his house and his barn were positioned on the top of a ridge. "There's a river!"

"That's like calling a mosquito an eagle. It ain't a river, but it's a decent creek. The Rocking-U always had water and thank God it still does since Texas has been drying up around our ears for too damn long." He headed for the trees and the grass growing lush and thick alongside the glittering water.

She hurried after him. Several horses were grazing contentedly, barely even giving a flick of their tails at their approach. "It's beautiful down here."

He pointed at an enormous oak tree. "That is what I've been doing."

Confused, she walked toward the tree, feeling the coolness its shade provided. She had no idea how tall it was, but it was *huge,* with a trunk so wide not even Quinn could have circled it with his arms. "Pruning the tree?"

"Nah. Nature prunes that beast. Even lost a couple limbs during a lightning storm when I was a kid." He closed his hand around her upper arm and moved her around to one side, pointing up into the canopy above them. "You can still see the scar there."

She couldn't see anything because her entire being seemed focused on the feel of his fingers. "Right," she said faintly.

"Figured I'd build it back up."

"Hmm?"

He was still pointing and she mentally shook herself, looking. She saw the healed over slash on the trunk, nearly hidden among the leaves. And then she saw the pieces of lumber a few feet above that, forming the frame for a floor. "You're building a *tree house?*"

"Rebuilding." He let go of her, circling the base of the tree where she realized he'd fastened fresh boards for a ladder. "The one my dad put up was about like everything he put up." He looked wry. "Half-assed and half-done," he murmured. "But the guy never stopped trying."

Quinn's efforts were half-done, too, but that was the only comparison she could see. "I used to love climbing trees. I'd go as high as I could and feel like I was flying. My mother didn't agree. She used to send me to the nursery as punishment. Since I considered myself much too mature as a teen for that, it seemed a fate worse than death." She eagerly placed her foot on the first foothold.

"No way, princess. You're not climbing up there."

She huffed. "I'm perfectly capable!"

"You were perfectly capable of riding a bus all the way from Dallas, too, and look what state you were in once you got here."

He closed his hands around her hips and she went breathless, her nerves vibrating. But all he did was lift her away from the tree and set her feet on the thick grass. "You're pregnant," he added. "You're not going up there. The floor isn't close to being finished. What if you fell?"

Her lips parted. Why hadn't she realized that herself? "But I want to go up there." She craned her head back and studied the tree house. It wasn't complete, of course, but when it was, she could tell it would be magnificent. "I think you have a bit of Peter Pan in you."

His expression sobered. "I grew up a long time ago."

"Why are you build—*re*building this now?"

He looked back up into the branches. "It was a good place to be when I was a kid."

She chewed the inside of her cheek, watching him. "And you think it'll be a good place for—"

"Our kid." His hazel gaze slid over her. "Yeah."

She was melting inside. There simply was no other description for it. "It'll be years before he—"

"Or she—"

"—is ready for that," she finished huskily.

"Yeah, well, it's also a good way to burn off some energy. And lately, I have a lot of—" He suddenly tugged the strap that had slipped from her shoulder back into place. "Energy."

Her mouth went dry and breathing became an effort. She stared up at him, feeling the warmth of him sliding around her, through her.

"What's this?" He dragged his finger along her collarbone where her skin was faintly irritated.

Her heart lurched. "I think it's, um—" She moistened her lips. "From your beard."

Something came and went in his eyes. He abruptly turned away and slapped his palm against the tree as he walked around it, heading toward the stream. "It'll be a good tree house," he said briskly.

She actually felt herself sway and was glad he was looking elsewhere. She hauled in a soundless breath and pressed her hand to her heart, willing it to calm. She'd blame the effect he had on her on pregnancy hormones if she could, but he'd had the same effect on her from the very beginning.

It's the reason she was pregnant in the first place.

"You coming?" He'd taken off his tool belt and sat

down on the grass and was unlacing his boots. "Might as well cool off in the water for a few minutes."

She knew the water wasn't deep enough to swim; she could see right through the crystal clear water to the rocky bottom.

No skinny-dipping here.

She held back a nervous giggle at the shockingly disappointing thought and started toward him, only to trip a little when he tossed his cap aside and pulled his T-shirt over his head.

He glanced her way. "You all right?"

She balled her fists in the folds of the dress at her sides and smiled brightly. "Just shoe… Just caught my, uh, my shoe. In the grass."

He looked away but not before she saw his smile and she knew she was turning as red as the borrowed, too-oft-worn dress.

Pressing her lips together, she crossed the grass purposefully and sat down beside him. "Would serve you right if I whipped *my* dress over my head," she said crossly.

He laughed outright, tossing his T-shirt behind him. "Darlin', if you're expecting a protest from me, you're dreaming. Unless you took to stealing boxers from my drawer, I know what all you *don't* have on under there so feel free to get naked as a jaybird. No telephoto lens in the world strong enough to spot you out here."

Flushing even harder, she slid her feet out of the sandals and stuck them in the water. "Whoa!" She just as rapidly jerked them back. "Cold."

"Refreshing," he countered, and tugged off his boots and socks. Then he stood and stepped into the creek. The water swirled around his strong calves, only a few inches below the bottom of his long shorts. "Come on." He held out his hand and beckoned.

"What if I slip and *fall?*"

He smiled faintly. "I'm getting the sense you were pretty spoiled growing up. You're the baby of the lot, right?"

"Yes. And I was not spoiled," she grumbled and pushed to her feet, stepping gingerly into the water, bunching the dress in one hand above her knees.

After the initial shock, the water was possibly more refreshing than frigid, though she wasn't going to admit it. She was glad for his hand, though, because the rocks littering the bottom of the creek were smooth and slick.

"If you start to fall *here,*" he said calmly, "I would catch you." He squeezed her free hand.

And her heart squeezed right along with it.

They walked quite a distance and he kept to the center of the creek which she quickly discovered was far less rocky and far more sandy and she was able to let go of his hand and walk unaided.

When he finally stopped, he swept his arm from one side to the other. "All Rocking-U land right up to there." He pointed. "That water tower over there is the eastern border."

She could see the structure well off in the distance across an expanse of unyielding looking red earth peppered with stubby trees, wild grasses in every shade from olive to straw, and lazy-looking cattle in just as many hues from yellow to black with horns that looked deadly even from a distance. And the blue sky overhead went on and on, without a single cloud in sight.

In her mind's eye, she pictured him on horseback, riding out there. Open and free. "It's no wonder you came back," she breathed. "Built your house. Built your herd." She looked up to find him watching her.

"This life isn't for everyone."

She wasn't sure if he was warning her, or remembering. In April he'd told her how his mother had been happy to leave this place. "Maybe your mum couldn't bear staying after losing your dad."

"She wasn't the only one who didn't like it here." He touched her elbow but she didn't want to take the hint that it was time to turn back.

"You mean your ex-wife," she said instead. "She didn't go far," Amelia added boldly. "Jess told me she lives in Vicker's Corners."

His eyes were narrowed against the bright sun. "Might not seem like it to you, but there's a big difference between Horseback Hollow and Vicker's Corners."

Yes. Horseback Hollow possessed a single main street with a handful of businesses, though that was already changing with the coming Hollows Cantina and Fortune Foundation office. For now, Vicker's Corners, while still small and quaint, was considerably more developed.

"I like Horseback Hollow," she said evenly and sloshed her feet through the water, her toes squeezing into the sandy bottom as she started back the way they'd come.

For how long?

The question stuck in Quinn's head though he didn't voice it. He watched her walking in front of him. She was holding up the dress, but the back of it had still dragged in the water below her knees, and it trailed behind her, dark and wet. Her hair was tangled around her shoulders that were turning pink from too much sun.

Right now, she might want to be there.

But she didn't know how hard his life could be. Didn't know that sometimes there could be as many bad years as good. That's what had driven his dad to his early grave.

Ahead of him, Amelia leaned down and swiped her hand through the water, then splashed it over her head.

She looked young. And carefree and ungodly sexy.

He blew out a harsh breath and leaned over, cupping water to throw over his own face. It was cold.

But it wasn't enough to douse the heat.

It wasn't ever going to be enough to do that.

Chapter Ten

"I was getting used to the red dress."

Amelia smiled ruefully as she entered the kitchen. Once they'd returned from their walk, Tanya was finished, so while Quinn paid the teenager, Amelia had gone upstairs to shower and change into the clothes that her aunt had procured for her while Quinn headed into the barn.

"This isn't going to fit me for long," she told him now and twitched the skirt that reached her ankles. The light gray knit hugging her hips before flaring out loosely had wide black stripes angled across it and was much livelier than her usual taste, but she'd toned it down with a white T-shirt with a deep scooped neck and snug cap sleeves. She knew the second she developed a bump, it would show. "The sundress was roomy enough to last awhile."

He was sprawled at the kitchen table wearing jeans

and a black T-shirt. He'd obviously used the downstairs bathroom to shower as well; his hair was wet and darker than ever. He'd also shaved.

She nearly told him she'd been getting used to the ridiculously sexy stubble.

"Not that it matters," she blathered on. "I'll have my own wardrobe soon enough."

He didn't move, but his gaze sharpened. "Is it being shipped here?"

She had the sense to realize she'd just stepped right into a minefield. All because she obviously couldn't think sensibly when she was near him.

"No," she said cautiously. "But I can't stay here forever."

"Here." His jaw canted slightly to one side for a moment. "Rocking-U here? Horseback Hollow here?" His eyes narrowed and he rose. It was like watching a cobra uncoil. "*United States* here?"

She stood her ground though the desire to back up was strong. "I do have responsibilities at home. I can't avoid them forever."

"I told you, I'm not letting you take my child away from here."

"Actually, to be specific," her tone cooled, "you said you weren't going to let another man raise your child."

He slowly pushed the chair back into the table. "What did I tell you about pulling that royal face with me?"

A jolt shot through her from her head to her toes.

She wisely took that step back after all, only to find her spine against the countertop. "I'm not pulling anything," she attempted reasonably. "I'm not saying I intend to return to the UK permanently."

"You want to go back, you can go. After we visit the justice of the peace."

"I don't have the choice of a minister anymore?" Her smart question fell flat and she exhaled. "At least you seem to believe me about James," she muttered.

He snorted. "Honey, I don't give a goddamn anymore if you were engaged to the man for real." He stepped up to her and pressed his palm flat against her abdomen. "The second you told me you're pregnant with *my* kid, that no longer mattered."

She braced herself against the shudder that rippled through her.

He angled his head toward hers. But all he did was speak softly next to her ear. "I may not be some fancy-pants future earl with money and connections, but there is no way on this earth I will let my child grow up without me." He suddenly straightened and dragged his palm upward until it was pressed flat between her breasts. Then he spread his fingers, rubbing them pointedly over the stab of her nipple through the white fabric. "I'll use every advantage I've got."

She couldn't very well deny the fact that she was weak where he was concerned. She'd slept with the man after only a few dances, something she'd never once been remotely tempted to do even though she'd been squired around by suitable matches since she was sixteen.

But neither could he hide the fact that he was equally aroused by her.

"Is that a threat?" she asked evenly. "Or a promise?"

His eyes darkened. "Don't pull an animal's tail, princess. Even the most patient one'll eventually turn on you."

The man who'd counted stars on a magical April night with her was the same one who was building a tree house, and the same one who was standing here now, she reminded herself, and she lifted her chin.

"You already turned on me," she reminded boldly. "When I didn't immediately deny the engagement stories." Her heart was thundering so hard in her chest he couldn't fail to notice. "And whether that was wrong or not, you obviously didn't care about me as much as I'd believed, or you wouldn't have mistrusted me as easily as you did. And you *still* don't trust me, only this time it's because you think I'll take your child away from you."

Instead of trying to pull away, she leaned into him until her breasts were pressed against his chest, his hand caught between them. "I am not your ex-wife," she said evenly. "No matter what you thought, or still think for that matter, I didn't betray you with anyone. And I have no intention of keeping you from being this baby's father." She went onto her toes until her mouth was only inches from his. "Using sex," she whispered slowly, "still isn't going to make me agree to a loveless marriage."

Then, taking advantage of the fact that he'd gone still as a statue, she shimmied out from between him and the cabinet and deliberately lowered her gaze to the hard length of him clearly evident behind his zipper. "Now, are we going to my aunt's for dinner, or do you have something else in mind?"

His eyes narrowed until only a greenish-brown sliver showed. His jaw flexed. And for a breathless moment that seemed to last an eternity, she was afraid he would call her bluff.

But he finally moved and the sound of his boot against the tile floor seemed loud. "Be glad there's hardly any food in the fridge," he said, and pulled open the kitchen door, stomping outside.

Her shoulders sank and she brushed her hair behind her shoulders with shaking fingers.

"You waiting for a pumpkin carriage or something?" he called from outside.

She pressed her lips together, lifted her chin and joined him.

Deke and Jeanne Marie's place was so packed inside with people when Quinn and Amelia arrived that, at first, their entrance wasn't even noticed.

But then Piper, half crawling and half walking, latched on to Amelia's leg and she chuckled, picking up the little girl and stepping into the crowd of family, leaving Quinn behind.

He couldn't seem to drag his eyes away from her. The shirt she was wearing hugged her lithe torso like a lover, and the skirt was just as guilty around her narrow waist and slender hips. It hardly seemed possible that she was sheltering a baby inside her.

"You going to stand there and drool or do you want a beer?" Liam stood beside him looking amused.

Quinn took the beer bottle and twisted it open. He nodded toward Liam's younger brother, Christopher, who seemed to be holding court in the middle of the parlor, his arm around a pretty blonde. "Guess your family's going to be having a lot of weddings in the near future."

Julia, Liam's fiancée, tucked herself under Liam's arm. "We might have to draw dates out of a hat," she said humorously. But then she looked stricken, looking from Quinn's face to Amelia and back again.

He pretended not to notice.

All of Jeanne Marie and Deke's offspring were engaged except for Galen and Delaney. The oldest and the youngest. And Toby, as well. He and Angie had already gotten hitched.

He finally managed to pull his gaze away from the swell of Amelia's hips where she'd pulled the hem of her snug T-shirt over the long, flowing skirt. As a teenager, he'd always been more preoccupied with the front of a woman.

But the perfect sweep of Amelia's back, nipping into her waist then flaring out again was enough to bring him to his knees.

He chugged a little more beer. The front door was open, but the room was still too warm thanks to all the bodies. He asked the first thing he could think of. "Toby and Angie get their adoption approved yet?"

"Not yet." Almost absently, Liam brushed his lips against Julia's forehead as he looked over at his middle brother. He was sitting on the couch with Kylie on his knee, watching over the checker game that Brian and Justin were playing.

Quinn hadn't been around the Hemings kids all that much, but it was the quietest he'd ever seen them. "Never thought adoption proceedings took this long. Toby was already taking care of them for months before he filed."

"I don't think all adoptions have the challenges that Toby and Angie have had," Julia murmured.

"You'd think learning we're Fortune-connected would have made it easier," Liam added, even though Quinn could remember a time when his buddy hadn't been remotely thrilled about that particular connection. He'd been suspicious the Fortunes were invading Horseback Hollow, throwing their moneyed weight around and making too many changes. "Instead, the social worker's got some bug about the kids' safety *because* of it."

Christopher joined them, holding Kinsley's hand. "Yeah, well, there've been times over the years when being a Fortune was sort of like having a target painted on your chest. The stories I learned while I was in Red Rock—" He pursed his lips and blew. "Lot of history there. Some serious stuff."

"That was years ago," Liam dismissed.

"Tell that to Gabriella," Julia reminded. "She only came to Horseback Hollow to take care of her dad after his plane accident. And those anonymous letters to the post office, saying it wasn't an accident? That it was sabotage and the *Fortunes* were the target and not Mr. Mendoza at all?" She made a face. "You'd think people around here would be grateful your cousin Sawyer and his wife opened their flight school and charter service in Horseback Hollow instead of somewhere else. I'm sure the investigators will get to the bottom of things, but what a horrible business."

"You gonna let that scare you off of marrying me? My mama's a Fortune, too," Liam goaded lightly, clearly not afraid of any such thing.

Julia's eyebrows rose. "Oh, no," she assured. "You're not getting off the matrimonial hook, mister, any more than Jude is with Gabi."

Quinn sucked down half the beer. Everyone around him seemed as happy as pigs wallowing in mud. He wished he found it revolting.

Instead he just found it…enviable.

His gaze strayed back to Amelia. She was perched on the arm of her aunt's chair, still holding Piper on her lap and trying to untangle the kid's fingers from her long hair.

She couldn't be accustomed to gatherings like this.

Nearly twenty people jammed into the front parlor of an old ranch house. The night they'd spent together she'd told him about the huge house where she'd grown up. The servants. The carefully orchestrated public functions.

What reason would be strong enough to keep her in Texas when she had *ancestral lands* and a family estate and God knew what else waiting for her back home?

It wasn't love.

She'd already said as much. No loveless marriages for her.

One small sliver of his mind kept listening to the conversation around him.

"Has Toby been able to find out who made that donation to him yet?" someone asked.

"Don't think he cares. That anonymous money'll go a long way to raising those kids. There's enough for college funds even."

"Must be nice," Quinn murmured. Generally speaking, there weren't too many packed into that parlor who'd been able to go to college at all. Or, like him, they'd had to scrimp and save and pray for every scholarship that came their way.

Not Amelia, though.

She'd gone to the finest schools that her family's money and position could buy.

Through no effort of his, her baby—his baby—would never want for anything.

He'd finished his beer and needing escape he excused himself, heading into the kitchen that was nearly as congested as the parlor. Jeanne Marie was at the center of things, giving out orders to her helpers with the precision of a master sergeant. She caught his eye with a smile as he continued right on through until he'd escaped out the back where Deke and Galen were hanging over the opened hood of an old pickup truck.

He joined them. "You still trying to keep this old thing running, eh?"

"Never get rid of something that still works." Deke's hands were covered in grease as he worked.

"*Works* being the operative word here," Galen said wryly. His hands weren't quite as filthy as his dad's but they were close. Quinn still shook the man's hand when he stuck it out, then propped his elbows on the side of the truck to watch them tinker.

"Guess that reporter girl has been making the rounds in town," Galen said. "Has she found her way out to the Rocking-U yet?"

Quinn grimaced. "Don't expect her to. She only knew to find Amelia here because it's no secret Jeanne's her aunt." He absently grabbed a hose that Deke couldn't quite reach and held it in place.

"What's going on between you two?" Deke pinned Quinn with a look. "Jeanne Marie's real fond of that gal. Do I need to ask your intentions?"

Galen laughed silently and lifted his hands up. "Good luck, bro. I'm outta here." He turned on his heel and strode away.

Deke's brows rose. "Well?"

"You don't need to ask," he said flatly.

"Recognize the side of my own house when I see it," the other man said.

He damned the heat rising in his neck. "Jeanne know about the photo, too?"

The other man's eyebrow rose. "Who d'ya think showed it to me?"

Quinn grimaced. "She's not engaged to that other guy."

"Heard that, too. Amelia 'fessed up on that score to Jeanne Marie right off," he added at Quinn's surprised look.

"She comes from a different world," Quinn said after a moment.

"Yup," Deke agreed, drawing out the word. He scratched his cheek, leaving behind a streak of black. "You worried about that?"

Quinn started to deny it but the older man's steady gaze wouldn't let him. "Yes, sir."

"Yeah." Deke's piercing gaze finally flicked past Quinn to look at the house behind them. "Jeanne Marie coulda bought anything her heart desired if she'd kept that money her brother wanted to give her. Clothes. New car. New furniture. Coulda traveled around the world a dozen times and stayed in the fanciest hotels there are. Hard to figure why a woman wouldn't care about those things but she says she doesn't." He pursed his lips for a second and scratched his cheek again.

"Deke Jones!"

They both looked back to see Jeanne Marie hanging out the screen door. "You get your hands outta that rust bucket and wash up for supper!"

Deke straightened and wiped his hands on a thin red rag he pulled from the back pocket of his jeans. He smiled a little at Quinn and tossed the rag to him. "All comes down to trust," he said and headed toward the house.

It was easy for Deke to trust Jeanne, Quinn thought, wiping his hands and following. They'd been married longer than he'd been alive.

The first time he'd set eyes on Amelia had been six

months ago. And he could count on his fingers how many actual days they'd spent together in the time since.

He pulled open the screen door and went inside. Jeanne Marie was smiling up into Deke's face, rubbing a dish towel over the black streak on the man's weathered cheek. "What am I going to do with you?" he heard her murmuring.

"Don't you want to be like them after forty years together?"

Startled, Quinn found Stacey and Colton standing behind him and he realized her words had been for her fiancé. He gave them a dry look.

"Considering the two of you can't look at each other without a besotted expression on your face, I'd say your chances are pretty good," Quinn said.

Colton chuckled and Stacey smirked, jerking her chin toward the doorway opening up to the dining room where Amelia was standing, talking to her cousin Jude and Gabriella. "Get out a mirror whenever you're looking *her* way," Stacey suggested smartly.

"Dishes, dishes," Jeanne Marie called out. "If you are standing in *this* kitchen, and your hands are empty, then grab something and take it into the dining room," she ordered. "Meal's not going to get onto the table by itself!"

Quinn grabbed the closest thing—a basket of fragrant, yeasty rolls—and escaped into the dining room.

They'd had to set up folding card tables on either end of the actual dining room table to accommodate everyone but they were covered with tablecloths. None of them matched. Some had colorful flowers stitched on the corners. Some didn't. But they were all crisply ironed and Quinn had a sudden memory of the way his mom had stood at an ironing board doing just the same thing before every Thanksgiving and every Christmas. The plates weren't all matching, either, nor were the glasses, but they were Jeanne's best.

She had all of her family home and it was obvious that she was celebrating that fact with all the finery she had.

She bustled in to the crowded room, pointing and directing and soon everyone's butt was in their designated chair. Deke at the head of the pushed-together tables. Jeanne Marie at the opposite.

Quinn and Amelia were situated midway down, next to each other. The chairs—another mixture of real dining room chairs, folding chairs and even the picnic table bench from outdoors—made for cozy seating, and there was barely two inches to spare between them and that, only because Amelia was as narrow and slender as she was.

Deke said the blessing and the dishes started passing. Quinn was relieved to see Amelia pile on the food for once. She was too thin as it was, and now she was eating for two. And fortunately, there were so many simultaneous conversations going on that nobody seemed to notice the fact that they were barely participating.

Her arm brushed his when they both reached for the cucumber salad at the same time and she quickly drew back. "Excuse me."

He grabbed the bowl and held it for her. "Go ahead."

Her gaze flicked over his, then away again. She scooped some of the salad onto her plate. "I feel like a glutton," she murmured as she handed him the handle of the serving spoon.

"It's about time you're finally eating more than a few bites." He dumped some of the cucumber and onion mixture on his plate. His mom made the same thing every time he visited her in Dallas. "Were you the one who gave that money to Toby for the kids?" He kept his voice low so only she would hear.

She blinked, looking genuinely surprised. "No." She looked across and down the tables. Toby's brood was surrounding one of the folding tables, with him and Angie on either side.

Supervising referees, he figured.

"Even if I'd wanted, *I* don't personally have that kind of money," she said quietly. "From what Aunt Jeanne told me, it was quite a large sum. It wasn't my mum, either. Aunt Jeanne asked her outright."

"How much money do you have?"

She let out a soft sound and gave him another quick look. "Why are you asking?"

He just eyed her. "Why do you think?"

Her soft lips compressed. "This is hardly the time, Quinn."

"Preacher or justice of the peace?" He waited a beat. "If you can't make up your mind, we could put it out for a vote right here. See what everyone else has to say."

Beneath the edge of the starchy white tablecloth, she dug her fingertips into his thigh. "You wouldn't dare."

He damned the heat collecting in his gut and closed his hand over her wrist, pushing her hand away. "Don't tempt me." The warning worked on all counts. Outing her pregnancy to the entire family all at once. Pulling her hand up to his fly despite sitting in the middle of that very family.

She twisted her wrist free. "I have a personal account that I control," she said after a moment. "It allows me a comfortable existence."

"Comfortable's a subjective term."

"Comfortable," she repeated evenly. "Not extravagant. Then there are family trusts as well from both my mother's and my father's sides that my brothers and sister and I all come into at various ages. It's all managed and very secure, and frankly I haven't ever much thought about it." She speared a green bean with her fork and smiled tightly. "Does that answer your question?"

Enough to underline the differences between their worlds.

Even if he sold every acre of Rocking-U land, and every hoof that ran on it, he wouldn't be able to match the resources she had at her disposal.

Amelia suddenly grabbed his hand beneath the table and pressed it against her belly. "I am not taking him away," she murmured, sliding him a look. "Now, quit looking shocked and eat your supper."

Chapter Eleven

By the time they returned to the Rocking-U it was late.

Quinn parked where he usually did halfway between the house and the barn and turned off the engine. "Your aunt's a good cook," he said after a moment and felt the look Amelia gave him.

"Maybe she'll give me lessons," she said. "It'd be more useful than most of the other lessons I've had." She pushed open the door herself and got out, heading around the truck toward the house.

His neck prickled, though he didn't really know why and his eyes searched out the shadows of the barn and the windmill.

But there was nothing to see.

That's what came from studying every unfamiliar car he spotted. Every unfamiliar face. He was letting paranoia get the best of him.

He left the keys hanging in the ignition like always and caught up to her. "Let me turn on a light first." He went up the front steps and inside. Turned on the porch light and held the door open for her. His gaze roved over the porch. The two rocking chairs his mom had given him a few Christmases ago were in their usual spot. Nothing out of place.

Amelia slipped past him. "What's wrong?"

He rubbed the back of his neck and closed the door. "Nothing." He hit the wall switch again, turning on the light that hung over the small foyer.

"You should take the bed tonight." She folded her arms around herself. "It's your bed. And the sofa is too short for you."

The simple answer squatted like a fat elephant in the middle of the room.

Share the bed.

"I'll live." Once she was gone—and he was convinced she would be sooner or later—he'd need to get rid of the couch, too. Like the bed, it would be riddled with memories. "I'm gonna take a look around outside."

Amelia studied him for a moment. He was still rubbing the back of his neck. "Seriously, Quinn. What's wrong?"

"Nothing," he said again and went into the kitchen to retrieve the shotgun from the rack over the door. "Just want to check if that possum's rooting around again." He went outside before she could comment.

Sighing, Amelia wrapped her hand around the banister and dragged herself upstairs.

She'd never felt so tired in her life and wanted to blame it entirely on being pregnant. But feeling like she was on one side of a war with Quinn on the other was not helping.

She washed her face and cleaned her teeth—blessing her aunt who'd had the forethought to include some basic toiletries among the clothes—and pulled on the pinstriped shirt of Quinn's again for something to sleep in. She bundled up the quilt—it was warm enough that a person didn't need any covering but a sheet anyway—and carried it downstairs, along with one of the bed pillows.

She didn't care what Quinn said. He was over six feet tall and couldn't possibly stretch out comfortably on the sofa. He needed his own sleep, too.

She spread the quilt out on the brown cushions, then flopped down on it, bunching the pillow under the back of her neck. She yawned hugely and pressed her hands to her belly.

How long would it be before it was no longer flat?

Before her secret—*their* secret—was visible for anyone and everyone to see?

How long would it be before Quinn would trust her?

She flexed her toes against the arm at the end of the sofa, and yawned again before turning on her side, cradling the pillow to her cheek, and slept.

She didn't even wake when Quinn came in a while later and spotted her sleeping on the couch.

He hadn't found the possum, though the evidence it had been there was obvious thanks to the trash can it had upended and strewn across the ground in back of the barn.

He'd cleaned up the mess, slammed the lid back on the can and weighted it down again with a concrete block. He should've remembered to warn Tanya to do the same when she was cleaning.

Now, looking at Amelia's defiant possession of the couch, he debated the wisdom of carrying her upstairs and putting her in bed where she belonged.

Some remaining cells of common sense inside his brain laughed at that. There *was* no wisdom in carrying Amelia anywhere. He'd already proven that.

Sleeping in his own bed without her—now that she'd occupied it twice—held zero appeal but it was safer than the alternative.

He returned the shotgun to its rack, turned on the light over the stove so it wouldn't be completely dark if she woke, then turned off the foyer light and went upstairs.

Evidence of her was everywhere.

In the damp hand towel she'd folded neatly over the rack next to the sink

In the inexpensive clothes she'd folded and stacked on the top of his dresser in the bedroom.

For someone who'd grown up with servants at her beck and call, she was a whole lot neater than he was.

He flipped off the light and peeled out of his clothes, pitching them in the general direction of the hamper. It was stupid to be avoiding his own bed, but there was no denying that's what he was doing when he went to the window and fiddled with the blinds. Pulling them up. Letting them down. Tilting them until they were just so and then repeating the whole damn process again.

Finally, he gave up. He pulled on a pair of ancient sweatpants and went back downstairs and scooped Amelia off the couch.

She mumbled unintelligibly, turned her nose into his neck as trusting as a babe and slept on.

He carefully carried her upstairs and settled her on the center of his bed. It let out its faint, familiar squeak. He started to back away, but she made a protesting sound and caught his arm.

Not asleep after all.

"I wish we could start over," she whispered.

So did he.

But he was afraid he wouldn't know how to do anything differently the second time around.

She pulled slightly on his arm. "Quinn."

He exhaled roughly and nudged her. "Move over."

She quickly wriggled over a few inches.

He lowered himself onto the mattress. "Come here." His voice was gruff.

She scooted back, until she was tucked against his side, her arm sneaking across his chest.

He stared into the dark. "We're getting a marriage license tomorrow." He wasn't sure if he said it to piss her off or to remind himself how adamantly opposed to marrying him she was.

She shifted slightly, but surprised him by not moving away. "Did your parents love each other?"

"What?"

"I always knew my parents loved each other," she whispered. "It was obvious in everything they did. He'd walk in a room and she'd light up. She'd smile at him when he was upset about something and place her hand on his chest, and everything would be all right." Her palm slid over his skin, leaving a trail of heat in its wake.

He steeled himself against it. "Get to the point, Amelia."

"That's what I want," she finished huskily. "The whole package. Can you give me that?"

His jaw was tight. "My father was illegitimate. I know that stuff doesn't matter these days, not like it used to.

But it mattered to his mother. It mattered to my old man. And it matters to me. You're having my kid. He's going to come into this world with my name. Nobody's going to steal that right from me. Not even you."

Pressing her hand against his chest, she levered herself up until she was half sitting. He could feel the weight of her gaze just as clearly as he could feel the long ends of her silky hair drifting over his ribs. "I'm not trying to steal anything, Quinn."

"Then prove it. Minister or justice of the peace?"

Her fingertips flexed against him with frustration, but only succeeded in sending heat through his veins.

"That's all marriage is to you? A means of legitimizing our baby? It has nothing to do with love?"

"Love's never been a friend of mine."

She was silent for so long he hoped she'd drop it.

But she didn't.

"If I said yes, what happens after the baby is born? What then? We live our separate lives? Passing the baby back and forth on what? Alternate weekends and holidays?"

His jaw went so tight it ached. "If that's the way you want it," he said stiffly. "You're used to a life that I won't ever be able to give you. Things I'll never be able to provide."

She was silent again for a long, long while before speaking, and when she did, her voice was husky. Careful. "I told you before that none of those…trappings… mattered to me. Did you…never believe me?"

"It's one thing to talk about it. It's another to actually live it."

Her fingers curled against him, then pulled away. "Be

glad I'm too exhausted to fight." She lay back down on the bed, her back to him.

Fighting was safer than making love.

He threw his arm over his eyes, grimly aware that there was no point in doing either.

And equally aware that it would only take a nudge, and he'd be ready for both.

He didn't expect to sleep, but eventually he did and when he woke it was only because his arm was going to sleep where it was tucked beneath Amelia's cheek and the rest of him was wide-awake thanks to her warm thigh tucked between his.

For a while, he stared at the sunlight streaking through the slats in the window blind. It had been years since he'd slept past dawn.

Then he carefully extricated himself, arms and legs, grabbed a pair of jeans and a shirt and left the room, quietly pulling the door closed after him.

He showered, letting the cold water pour over him, then pulled on his jeans and went downstairs. His mind consumed with the woman upstairs, he went through his usual routine by rote. Started water running through the coffeemaker. Dumped cereal into a bowl and ate it, standing in the back doorway, looking out over his land while it brewed. He had stock to check, horses to feed. Same things as every other day. Day in. Day out.

It was a life he loved. A life he knew he couldn't exchange for anything else, not unless he wanted his soul to shrivel up and die.

He heard a faint noise and looked back to see Amelia shuffling into the room, her eyes soft with sleep, her hair tangled and the shirt Jess had given him for his last birthday wrinkling around her bare thighs.

"Coffee smells so lovely." Her bare feet crossed the kitchen floor and she leaned over the coffeemaker, inhaling deeply.

The shirttails had climbed a few inches as she'd leaned against the counter and he dragged his eyes away from the smooth thighs and the tender spot behind her knees that he knew from experience was ticklish.

He knew his sister didn't drink any caffeine when she was pregnant. She also always gave up the margaritas she loved, and she'd complained often and long about that fact. Particularly since her husband, Mac, hadn't had to give up either.

"Sorry." He crossed the room and yanked the plug out of the outlet. The gurgling continued for only a moment before sputtering to a stop. "I'll quit making it."

She pushed her hair out of her face. Her gaze roved over his face. "You don't have to do that."

"Because you don't plan to be around?"

She tucked her hands behind her, leaning back against the counter. Unplugged and half-brewed or not, the scent of coffee filled the room. Same as her beauty shined through whether she was clothed in designer dresses or a man's wrinkled shirt.

"Because there's no reason for you to give up something you enjoy just because of me." She tucked her hair behind her ear. She wore no earrings. Didn't even have pierced ears at all. He knew, because he'd spent enough time kissing his way around her perfect earlobes to know there were no holes marring them. "There's no—" She broke off when there was a loud knocking on the front door.

He didn't want to answer it. Didn't much care who was out there, because he wasn't expecting anyone.

But she'd pressed her soft lips together and her lashes had swept down and whatever she'd been about to say was obviously going to go unsaid.

Particularly when the knocking continued, intrusively annoying and noisy as hell.

He left the kitchen and strode to the front door. "Cool your jets," he said, yanking it open.

He barely realized there were at least a half dozen people crammed onto his porch because of the cameras suddenly flashing and the microphone that was shoved close to his face.

"Do you have anything to say about your involvement with Amelia Chesterfield when her fiancé is reportedly sitting by his father's deathbed?"

Amelia suddenly raced up behind him and slammed the door shut on the words that just continued shouting through the wood.

Her eyes were huge in her face and she was visibly shaking. "How do they keep *finding* me?"

"I don't—" He broke off, because they were pounding on his door again and one of 'em—a guy with spiky hair and wide-lensed camera—was even peering through the unadorned front window.

Quinn grabbed Amelia's arm and steered her toward the staircase which was out of view from the window. "Stay."

"Don't aggravate them," she insisted, though she backed up several steps before sinking down onto one and hugging her arms around her knees. "It only makes them behave more outrageously." Her teeth were chattering and she'd gone white. "Did you tell anyone I was pregnant? Your sister? *Any*one*?* If that gets out—"

"I haven't told anyone," he said flatly.

The pounding and questions hadn't ceased and he stomped into the kitchen. He grabbed his shotgun off the rack above the doorway and loaded it with birdshot.

"What are you doing?"

She bolted to her feet and her huge eyes engulfed her entire face. They were the haunted eyes she'd had when she'd fainted in his barn.

And they made him want to string somebody up from the nearest tree.

"Getting rid of the vermin."

She shook her head rapidly. "Don't, Quinn. You have to ignore—"

"They're trespassing. Maybe they should've concerned themselves with aggravating *me,*" he finished harshly.

Then he yanked open the door, greeting the intruders with the business end of the shotgun. "Get off my land."

Like cockroaches hit with the light, they scrambled off his porch, but only so far as to shield themselves.

He stepped out onto the wood porch and cocked the gun. It sounded satisfyingly loud and threatening. "Get."

"How long have you been sleeping with her?" some fool called out and Quinn swung the barrel toward the voice, finding the gel-haired guy who'd had the nerve to aim a camera through his front window.

"You're trespassing," he said coldly. "And I'm a real good shot." He met the man's eyes. At least he had the good sense to take a nervous step backward. "You want to test it out?"

"Lord Banning's a powerful man," someone else

yelled in a shrill voice. "You're not afraid of retribution for trying to steal his bride?"

He aimed beyond them where the vehicles they'd arrived in were parked every which way all over his gravel, and planted a load of shot exactly six inches from the front tire of the closest car. The noise was shockingly loud and gravel spewed, pinging against the car.

The roaches scattered even faster.

"Next one goes in the car!"

He had no intention of shooting anyone, but they didn't need to know that. There were seven of them, three men and four women, and he wondered which one, if any, was the Ophelia who'd plagued Amelia.

He eyed them each before cocking the gun again. *"Get off my land."*

They scrambled for the cars, nearly colliding among themselves as they poured into doors, gunned engines and spun tires.

Only when the last of them was nearly out of sight and the clouds of dust were starting to die did his grip on the gun relax.

And it was several minutes after that before the rest of him relaxed enough that he could go back inside the house.

He closed and locked the door, unloaded the rest of the birdshot and left the gun propped against the door.

Amelia was no longer huddled and hiding on the staircase.

She was pacing around the living room, looking agitated. "You couldn't have just *ignored* them? You had to go all…all Texas Ranger on them?" She sank down on the couch and clawed her fingers through her hair. "You may know ranching, Quinn, but I know the paparazzi.

There will be pictures of you on every network by the evening news." Just as fast as she'd sat, she shoved off the couch. "I have to phone my mother. Warn her." She laughed, sounding on the verge of hysteria, and her face was white. "If she hasn't already been treated to the same sorts of questions."

He caught her arms before she made it to the kitchen. "Calm down," he said. "You're going to make yourself sick again."

"Calm down?" She shook off his hands. "Would you feel calm if you knew you were causing nothing but embarrassment to the people you love?"

The words felt like blows.

"That's what involvement with me is. An embarrassment."

She looked stricken. "No! I never said that. I—I—" She broke off hugging her arms tightly around her. Her eyes turned wet. "I don't like being the cause of scandal. That's all."

"I don't believe you."

Her lips parted. She seemed to sway a little.

Then her face smoothed, though her eyes still gleamed, wet and glassy. "Of course you wouldn't," she said expressionlessly. "You haven't believed me about anything I've said yet. You just want to maneuver me into marriage to protect *your* interests. Same thing James wanted to do."

"You're gonna compare our baby to a textile company?"

She just shook her head, looking weary, and walked over to the stairs.

There was no phone upstairs. The only one inside the house hung on the wall in the kitchen.

"Thought you were calling your mother."

She didn't answer him. Just kept going up the stairs.

He was still standing there, rooted in place, when she came down a few minutes later.

She'd twisted her hair into a knot at the nape of her neck and pulled on a black T-shirt with the same striped skirt she'd worn the day before. The clothes were inexpensive. Hardly fancy. Yet she still managed to look untouchably elegant.

Her eyes didn't meet his. "If you'd be kind enough to drive me to Aunt Jeanne's, I would be grateful."

His hands curled into fists. "Aren't you afraid the vultures will be waiting?"

"I'm sure they will be." Her triangular chin lifted. "I'll handle it."

Unlike him.

She didn't say it.

But she didn't need to.

Chapter Twelve

"When is this going to die down?" Jeanne Marie fretted, and turned off the television and yet another gossipy tidbit on the morning news speculating about the most intimate details of Amelia's, Quinn's and James's lives while a silent video ran in the background showing Amelia, dressed only in Quinn's shirt slamming his front door shut on the photographers' cameras. "It's been a week already."

This time, the commentator—Amelia refused to call the vapid woman an actual reporter—had even dug up ancient stories about her mother's first marriage to Rhys Henry Hayes and even more ancient stories about King Edward's abdication of the throne for the woman he'd loved. Trying to manufacture out of thin air similarities where there were none at all.

"It's because of the funeral," Amelia said on a sigh.

James's father's funeral service had been held in London that morning and the timing made it a prime topic for the morning's national news shows. "The story will lose traction eventually, once something more interesting in the world comes along." She made a face. "Horrible of me to wish for a slew of natural disasters somewhere in the world."

Jeanne Marie squeezed her hand and sat down beside her. "Have you spoken with Quinn?"

Just the sound of his name caused a pang inside her and she shook her head.

Since he'd dropped her off at her aunt's home that dreadful morning a week ago, he hadn't tried to reach her once.

To be fair, she hadn't tried to speak with him, either. The only thing she'd been able to do was unleash threats of a lawsuit against the offenders who'd trespassed on the Rocking-U.

Only because her family had won the last suit they'd brought against the phone hackers a year ago had there been enough teeth behind the threat to encourage many of the pests to finally move on. Amelia wished that were true of Ophelia Malone, but the woman was still taking up residence at the B and B in Vicker's Corners. She was a freelancer, according to the sketchy information Molly had been able to unearth. She didn't have publishers keeping her on a leash they could retract when necessary.

"You're going to want to talk to Quinn sooner or later," her aunt said gently.

"I know." Amelia plucked the knee of her jeans. She just didn't know what she was going to say when she did. He'd had an up close and personal taste of the sort of things she'd had to deal with almost daily back in London.

Who would blame him for wanting no part of it?

For the past week, she'd lived in the seclusion of her aunt and uncle's house. Avoiding going outdoors in case there were still remaining telephoto lenses aimed their way. Avoiding all but the most necessary of phone calls. She'd even been careful not to find herself standing or sitting near windows.

It wasn't fair to burden her aunt and uncle with that sort of behavior, but they'd both been adamant that she remain with them. Even Amelia's mother had agreed that Amelia should stay in the States while she and James— now the Earl of Estingwood himself—dealt with the official media back home.

Everyone around her was taking care of her.

And she was heartily tired of it.

"I need a good solicitor," she said abruptly. "An attorney. Is there anyone you recommend? Someone you trust?"

Jeanne Marie looked thoughtful. "We haven't had a lot of need for attorneys, but Christopher once mentioned an attorney in Red Rock he knew through people at the Fortune Foundation. Or I can contact James Marshall. He surely has his own legal department at his company."

Amelia knew that JMF Financial was located in Georgia. Red Rock, though, was only four hundred or so miles away. "Would you mind calling Christopher for me?"

"Of course not." Jeanne Marie hesitated a moment. "Do you want me to call him right away?"

Now that Amelia had brought it up, she did.

In fact, she was suddenly impatient to do *something*.

"If you would. I need an appointment as soon as possible. Preferably before Mum arrives in a few days. I can call Sawyer Fortune and arrange for a charter flight to Red Rock." Until her latest escape from London and subsequent trek making her way to Quinn's, she'd used the flight service her cousin ran to get from Dallas to Horseback Hollow the other times she'd visited.

"You're ready to go out in public?"

Amelia made a face. "No," she admitted. "But the longer I hide out, the harder it will get. And I'd rather get used to it now than wait until the Cantina's grand opening this Friday." She followed her aunt into the kitchen and found herself looking out one of the windows at the picnic table and benches sitting on the grass.

But she wasn't really seeing them.

She was remembering dancing with Quinn out there on a portable dance floor.

He'd put his arms around her, and even though it was the first time he'd touched her, the first time they'd ever done anything but see each other from a distance really, she felt like she'd come home.

Her throat tightened and her nose burned with unshed tears.

Now, she feared that home was nothing more than a fantasy. A silly girl's romantic longing.

"Pour another." Quinn tapped the empty shot glass sitting on the bar in front of him. At seven in the evening, he hadn't expected the Two Moon Saloon to be entirely empty, even on a Tuesday. But he'd been the only one there for a good hour now.

He'd had no particular desire to go out at all, but Jess had nagged him into meeting up at the Horseback Hollow Grill for burgers with her family. He'd been avoiding her, like he'd been avoiding most everyone else in town for the past week. But he'd been sick of his own company, and since the paparazzi that had plagued him for most of the week since the whole shotgun incident had finally gone off for greener pastures, he'd agreed.

And even though, for once, his sister had wisely showed the good sense not to bring up anything to do with Amelia or the fact that his image—shirtless and brandishing a shotgun like some kind of madman—was all over creation thanks to the magic of the worldwide web and nonstop news services, he'd been glad when the meal was over.

While his sister and brother-in-law had corralled their sons out the door to go home, he'd just gone next door to the saloon that was attached to the grill.

He was sick of his own company, true. But he also wasn't in the mood for socializing.

Nor was he in the mood to hide out inside his own damn house because everywhere he looked, he saw Amelia.

One night last week he'd even slept out on the porch.

Damned pathetic.

He eyed the pretty bartender who was pouring him another shot of bourbon. "You're new." She had brown hair and brown eyes, just as dark as Amelia's, and was slender as a reed, also like Amelia.

And he didn't feel the faintest jangle of interest.

"What's your name?"

"Annette."

"Why'd you come to Horseback Hollow, Annette?" He tossed back the drink and clenched his teeth against the burn that worked down his throat. "Nothing going on in this place." He set the shot glass down on the wood bar with a thud.

She swiped her white bar towel over the wood. "Wouldn't say that, Mr. Drummond," she countered.

He narrowed his eyes, studying her while his fingers turned the small glass in circles on the bar. "How'd you know my name?"

She smiled faintly. "How d'ya think? I have a television." She lifted the bottle. "Another?"

He moved his hand away and she filled the glass, then set the bottle on the counter behind her and returned to her polishing.

"It wasn't as bad as it looked," he muttered.

"It looked like a man trying to protect what's his," she said calmly. "What's so bad about that?"

He lifted the glass, studying the amber-colored contents. The deputy sheriff who'd come calling about the matter had agreed with that notion and it'd been plain from the ample video coverage that Quinn hadn't tried shooting at anyone.

But that didn't change things for Quinn.

Amelia *wasn't* his. She'd made it plain she didn't want to be his. The only thing that *was* his was the baby she carried.

His chest tightened and hating the feeling, he put the glass to his lips. The liquor burned again, but brought no relief. No blurring of reality. No softening of the facts.

Amelia came from one world. He came from another.

"Send us over a round of margaritas and a couple a' waters, would you, darlin'?"

He realized that a group of people were coming in through the street-side entrance and glanced over to see Sawyer and Laurel Fortune coming in along with a few of the folks he knew were working for them over at their charter service. He lifted his hand, returning the greeting they sent him, then turned back to his solitude.

He quickly realized, though, that Sawyer and his group weren't cooperating with that notion, insisting that he join them as well.

Quinn had no desire to be among the Fortunes, but Orlando Mendoza was with them, and his daughter Gabriella was marrying Jude Fortune Jones, whom he'd known all his life. The new bartender was noisily scooping ice into margarita glasses with one hand and pouring tequila into a pitcher with the other so he reluctantly left his empty shot glass and moved over to their table.

"Y'all look like you're celebrating," he greeted.

"We are." Sawyer gestured to his companions. "You know everyone here, don't you, Quinn?"

"Some, more 'n others." Quinn gave a general nod, sticking out his hand to Orlando and the older man shook it. "Glad to see you're up on your feet again."

The pilot grinned. "Needed to if I'm going to be able to walk Gabi down the aisle and give her away when she and Jude get married. Glad to get the casts off at last. Things were itching me like crazy."

The bartender delivered the tray of waters and ice-filled, salt-rimmed glasses and set the margarita pitcher in the middle of the table before returning behind the bar.

"Broke my arm once." Quinn shook his head when Laurel started pouring out drinks and offered him one. "Couldn't stand the cast so bad I ended up cutting it off myself a week before the doctor said. Are you cleared for flying again?"

The salt-and-pepper-haired man nodded, looking relieved.

"That's what we're celebrating," Sawyer said. "That and the fact that the investigators have finally closed the case about the accident." He held up one of the glasses and waited while the others did the same. "No sabotage. No pilot error—" he gave a nod toward Orlando at that "—and no maintenance insufficiencies."

"So what happened?"

"Aircraft design," Orlando supplied.

"The plane's been recalled," Laurel added. She clinked her glass against her husband's and the others. "Just wish the manufacturer could have caught their error before people got hurt."

"Manufacturer is wishing the same thing," Sawyer said. "Not saying we're planning to, but it's a given that someone will bring lawsuits against them about it all."

Laurel looked at Quinn. "Speaking of lawsuits, is that what Amelia's planning?"

His skin prickled. "What do you mean?"

Orlando sat forward. He was the only one around the table drinking only water. "I flew Miss Chesterfield to Red Rock this morning. She was meeting with one of my cousin Luis's boys. Rafe's a lawyer over there. Told her she could've just waited until this weekend to talk to him, since he'll be in town for the opening of his brother's restaurant, but she was anxious to go now. I'll be picking her up again tomorrow afternoon."

Was she just adding on another layer of protection against more media invasions like they suspected? Or was she really laying the groundwork to keep his child away from him? "You'd have to ask Amelia what she's planning," he said abruptly and started backing away from the table. "I'll leave y'all to your celebrating. Congratulations." Not leaving them an opportunity to respond, he peeled a few bills off his wallet and dropped them on the bar.

Annette tucked the bills in the cash register. "You want some coffee before you head out, Mr. Drummond?"

He had never felt more stone-cold sober but to keep her satisfied and quiet about it, he told her to give him one to go, and then he went on his way, a foam cup of hot coffee in his hand. He was parked on the other side of the grill, so instead of leaving on the street side, he walked through the doorway separating the bar from the grill.

Only a few people were still sitting at the old-fashioned tables positioned around the ancient tiled floor. The little game room where his nephews always fought over playing the race car game was silent, the light turned off.

The coffee smelled bitter, like it was a day old by now, and his first sip confirmed it tasted that way, too.

The coffee still reminded him of Amelia.

He dumped the cup in the trash can next to the pay phone that hung in one corner of the diner and pulled out the thick phone book that was stuffed on the shelf below the phone. He paged through the yellow pages, finding the section he wanted. He tore out the first page of law firm listings, pushed the book back on the shelf and left.

Amelia paged through the agreement that Rafe Mendoza had sent with her and read through the paragraphs yet again. The attorney had tried talking her out of some of the stipulations that she'd wanted included, but she'd been adamant.

"You may change your mind," he'd argued. "You want to stay in Texas now, but there's no reason to sign away your choice of moving away later on." His dark eyes had been kind. "You're only twenty-three, Amelia. At least think about it."

"I won't change my mind," she'd told him. But she'd agreed to give it a day and had picked up the agreement that afternoon on her way to the Red Rock regional airport for her return charter to Horseback Hollow.

She closed the document and tucked it back inside the folder Rafe's secretary had provided with the custody agreement and then she climbed out of her aunt's car that she'd borrowed and walked past Quinn's truck toward the house.

It was the middle of the afternoon, so she wasn't particularly surprised when he didn't answer her knock. When she tried the knob and found it locked, though, she was.

A lesson learned from the paparazzi, she assumed with a pang of guilt. Once your privacy was invaded, it was hard to trust that it wouldn't happen again.

Carrying the folder with her, she walked down to the barn and found it empty. There were six horses standing around in the corral next to the barn, their long tails swishing against the heat of the day. She held out her palm over the metal rail and the nearest one nuzzled her palm, obviously looking for a tidbit.

"Sorry, girl," she murmured and rubbed her hand down the horse's white blaze. "Next time I'll bring a treat."

If she'd be allowed a next time.

Following the road with the grassy strip in the center, she kept walking until it began to dip and she could see Quinn's tree house tree in the distance. When she drew closer, she heard the distinctive beat of a hammer.

And even though she'd been gearing herself up for the

past twenty-four hours to see him, her mouth still went dry and her chest tightened.

She tucked the folder under her arm and smoothed back a strand of hair that had worked free from the chignon at her nape. She aimed toward the tree while the hammering grew louder and more distinct, and soon she was standing beneath the shady leaves.

She moved around to where the footholds were and tapped the lowest one with the toe of the Castleton cowboy boots she'd purchased while killing time in Red Rock. Since her whereabouts weren't remotely a secret, she'd also visited Charlene's boutique with her credit card, and stocked up on clothing, including a black silk dress for the Cantina's grand opening. She'd also had lunch with her cousin Wyatt and his wife, Sarah-Jane. And even though Amelia had found Red Rock surprisingly sophisticated and quite lovely, she knew she still preferred the rugged, much smaller Horseback Hollow.

"Fancy boots. You buy them before or after meeting up with that Red Rock lawyer?"

She looked from the detailed stitching over her toe up into the leaves and met Quinn's hazel gaze. "As usual, news is traveling at the speed of light." She ran her palm over the rough tree bark. "Can you come down?"

He swung down from the floor he was constructing and climbed down several footholds before jumping the rest of the way to the ground. He straightened and looked down at her, his expression unreadable. "You going to tell me anything I want to know?"

"I don't know," she said huskily and handed him the folder. "Considering everything that happened last week, you might not welcome anything to do with me."

His lips thinned and he made no attempt to open the

folder. "A hundred reporters camped out on my front porch wouldn't change the fact that you're pregnant with my baby."

"They didn't cause you any more problems, did they?" She tucked her hands in the front pockets of the narrow, black trousers she'd bought at the boutique. There'd been a small selection of delightful maternity clothes, though she hadn't had the nerve to purchase any. Not with the other customers there who'd watched her, somewhat agog, as she'd shopped.

"Guess you'd have seen it on the news if they had." His tone was flat. He gestured with the folder. "You bring this here to settle the fact I can't prevent you from going back to England? Already found that out myself from three different attorneys over in Lubbock."

A pang drove through her. "If that's what you think, you really don't know me at all."

"Saw your earl's press conference."

"Evidently not," she countered, "if you still have the impression that James is *my* anything."

"'Amelia Fortune Chesterfield's support during this difficult time has been steadfast,'" Quinn said, quoting almost verbatim the brief statement that James's staff had released. "'And though we are not betrothed,'" his lips twisted, "'we remain loyal friends.' Didn't exactly say you were never engaged to marry him in the first place."

"People in James's positions don't explain," she said. "They don't complain to the media and they never lend credence to speculation by commenting on anything that smacks of scandal. Which is not to say they won't use the media if it serves their purposes. James's father certainly proved that." She exhaled. "I didn't come here to talk about him." She nodded toward the folder. "I came here to give you that."

Looking even more grim, he flipped open the folder.

His eyes narrowed as he read, his frown coming and going as he flipped slowly through the pages.

"It's a shared custody agreement." Of course he could read for himself what it was, but his silence was more than she could bear. "With stipulations that the baby will bear your name and be raised here in Horseback Hollow."

He finally looked at her. "Why would you do this?"

She lifted her chin. "Why wouldn't I? I've told you more than once I don't want that life." She unconsciously pressed her hand to her abdomen. "I didn't want it for myself and I don't want it for our child. I don't know how else to prove it to you."

"You've already signed it."

"Yes. Duly witnessed by the appropriate individuals." She pressed her tongue to the back of her teeth, hunting for strength. "Go back to your Lubbock attorneys and have them review it. They'll tell you it's exceedingly fair. And once you sign it, there'll be no need for a justice of the peace or a minister."

His jaw canted to one side. He closed the folder and tapped it against the side of his jean-clad thigh. "You *really* don't want to marry me."

"No." She suddenly jabbed her forefinger into his unyielding chest. "*You* really don't want to marry *me*. You're stuck in the past with the one who did betray you. The only reason you want to marry me is to ensure the baby has your name." She gestured at the folder. "Well, happy tidings. Sign it and neither one of us need worry about that a moment longer."

"I don't have a pen."

She felt like her heart was turning to dust inside her chest. She looked up into the leaves above their heads.

He'd build a magical place for their child.

But he wouldn't let himself believe in love.

At least not love with *her*.

"I'm sure you'll find one somewhere," she managed. "You can send me a copy of the agreement once you do."

"And then?"

"And then I guess we'll figure out what to do next." She lifted her hands, feeling helpless. "At least things can't possibly get any worse."

Then she turned on her boot heel and walked away.

Chapter Thirteen

But Amelia was wrong.

Things could get worse.

And they did.

"She is *pregnant?*" Jess's screech could have been heard around the world.

It was certainly enough to wake Quinn from his stupor where he was sprawled on his couch, and he bolted upright, rubbing his hands down his face as his sister stormed into his house brandishing a magazine over her head.

"What?"

She slapped the glossy tabloid on top of Amelia's custody papers that were sitting on the coffee table and picked up the bottle of whiskey he'd tried working his way through the day after Amelia had left him. "Oh, my God." She was clearly disgusted. "You're drunk."

"No. I was drunk." He pinched the bridge of his nose. "Now the term would be *hungover*. So if you'd take your hysterics and leave me the hell alone, I'd appreciate it. And give me back your key to my front door while you're at it."

She sat down on the coffee table in front of him and caught his chin in her hand, giving him a look that was unreasonably similar to their mother's. "You're a grown man who's going to be a father," she tsked. "Start acting like it!"

He brushed her hand aside. The fact that she knew about Amelia's pregnancy was seeping into his throbbing brain. "How'd you find out?"

She shifted and tugged the magazine from under her hip and waved it in front of his face. "Same way everyone on the planet did."

He snatched it from her and stared at the cover of the international tabloid. It contained only a single photograph of a positive pregnancy test stick, with a question mark and the words The Real Cause Behind the End of Jamelia? superimposed over the top.

Disgusted, he threw it aside and shoved off the couch. "Why the *hell* won't everyone just leave her alone!"

Jess narrowed her eyes and studied him. "It's true, then. Amelia is pregnant."

"Whatever happened to people's right to privacy?"

"Privacy's an illusion," Jess said. "I think somebody famous said that. Or the government did. Or—" She shook her head. "Doesn't matter. I'm asking you, Quinn. Is that story true?"

He raked his fingers through his hair. "I didn't read the damn story."

She made a face and straightened. She tilted her head slightly, studying him. "Quinn."

"Yes," he said grudgingly.

"Is it yours?" She quickly lifted her hands peaceably when he glared at her. "I'm just asking!"

"It's mine."

"How do you know? I mean, a week and a half ago, she was supposedly engaged to marry Lord Banning."

"She wouldn't lie to me." His head was clanging and he headed blindly into the kitchen. There was still coffee in the pot from the day before and he dumped it in a mug and drank it cold and stale. Amelia wouldn't lie, yet how many times had he accused her of it, anyway?

Jess had followed him into the kitchen. Her eyes were concerned. "What are you going to do?"

"Not much I can do," he said wearily. "She won't marry me."

His sister's eyebrows disappeared up her forehead. "You, Mr. Never-Get-Married-Again, *proposed*?"

"She refused." More than once and the memory of each time felt engraved on his throbbing brain. He turned on the faucet and stuck his head under the cold water.

When he came up for air, Jess stuck a dish towel in his hand. "Did you tell her you loved her?"

He jerked. "This isn't above love."

"Oh, Quinn." Jess shook her head, looking disgusted all over again. "When it comes to a woman, particularly a pregnant woman, everything is *always* about love."

"Maybe for you." He ran the towel over his face and tossed it aside. "And Mac." His brother-in-law had grown up in Vicker's Corners. "You two've been together since high school. You're the same. Hell, you even teach together at the same school!"

"So? Carrie and you had the same backgrounds, too, and that wasn't exactly a stellar success!"

"There's no comparison between Carrie and Amelia." His voice was abrupt. Carrie had never made him feel half the emotion that Amelia did.

She gave him a look. "Well, duh. It's about time you realized it."

He shoved his fingers through his hair, slicking the wet strands back from his face. He hadn't been talking about the other similarities, despite what his sister obviously thought. "Where'd you see the tabloid?"

"It's front and center on the racks in the Superette."

He exhaled. "This'll send her off the rails." He reached for his Resistol and headed for the door, but his sister grabbed the back of his shirt.

"Hold on there, Romeo," she drawled. "Might want to at least brush your teeth before you go after the fair maiden."

He yanked away. "You're a pain in the ass, you know that?"

"Yeah." She patted his cheek like he was ten. "But nobody loves you like I do. And I kinda fancy the idea of getting some blue blood in our family gene pool." Then she shoved his shoulders, pushing him toward the living room. "And clean clothes wouldn't go amiss, either."

The fact that she was right annoyed the life out of him. He headed toward the steps. "I don't know how Mac puts up with you."

"He loves me," she assured blithely and patted her flat belly. "Which is why we're trying for a girl again." Her eyes were revoltingly merry. "According to that tabloid, your baby and mine will be born right around the same time next January."

Quinn squinted. "You're pregnant, too? Again?"

Jess smiled. "Isn't life grand?"

Amelia stared at the cover of the magazine that her mother had presented the second she'd walked into Aunt Jeanne's house.

The pregnancy stick in the picture was not the same brand Amelia had used either time, but some portion of her mind knew that it didn't really matter.

The message was still the same.

"Well?" Josephine propped her hands on her slender hips and raised her eyebrows. She'd arrived a full day earlier than expected because of the dreadful magazine, and her blue eyes were steely. "Is it true?"

Amelia rubbed her palms down the thighs of her cropped slacks and nodded. Then she gestured at the cover. "I don't know how they found out. Were you contacted for a comment?"

Her mother just gave her a look. "As if we would have offered one to such a disreputable publication? My senior social secretary gave me a copy when no one else on my staff seemed to have the nerve to show it to me." She sighed and sat down on the couch next to her. They were alone in the house only because Jeanne Marie and Deke had gone to see Toby and his crew for a while. "We'll have to release something officially at some point, but I wanted to see you for myself, first. Darling, why didn't you *tell* me?"

Amelia's throat tightened. "I was going to. I just wanted to clean up some of the mess I made after the whole Jamelia business exploded."

Her mother closed her cool hands around Amelia's

and squeezed gently. "Are you feeling all right? I hate knowing you've been dealing with this all on your own."

"It's about time I finally dealt with something on my own," she murmured thickly. She met her mother's eyes. "I'm sorry I've done such a poor job of it."

"Amelia." Josephine sighed. "I love you. The only thing I am concerned about is that you're happy. I knew you weren't happy in London even before this ridiculous betrothal business with James came about." She tucked Amelia's hair behind her ear the same way she'd been doing since Amelia was a tot. "Had you confided in me, perhaps we could have prevented some of this outrageous publicity."

Amelia chewed the inside of her cheek. "Molly knew," she whispered. "She's the only one other than Quinn who knew I was pregnant."

Josephine's expression cooled. "*My* Molly?"

Amelia nodded miserably. "I don't want to believe she would have said something, but who else was there?" James hadn't known she was returning to Horseback Hollow, much less that she was pregnant with Quinn's baby, so the information couldn't have come from his quarter.

"And your Quinn," Josephine said gently. "He wouldn't have—"

"No." Amelia shook her head, adamant. He might have threatened that one time to out her pregnancy during Jeanne Marie's and Deke's family dinner, but he never would have gone beyond that. Certainly not to the very type of strangers he'd threatened off the Rocking-U. She reached for the hateful tabloid and flipped it open to the main article that turned out to be only a few paragraphs, accompanied by two pages of photographs obviously meant to chronicle the rise and fall of her and James's supposed romance.

There were also a startling number of images of Quinn that had to have taken some effort to collect. One was even of him as a solemn boy, standing next to an easily recognizable Jess and a woman she could only assume was their mother, given the casket they were looking at. She trailed her fingertip over his young face then made herself look at the text.

"'Sources close to Amelia Fortune Chesterfield and her baby daddy, Horseback Hollow Homewrecker Quinn Drummond, confirm that the stick turned a big, positive blue,'" she read aloud. Then she made a face and flipped the magazine closed, tossing it aside. "Ophelia Malone finally gets her big payday," she muttered. "And Quinn didn't do a thing to deserve her trashy comments."

"I'll have to deal with Molly." Josephine rose and paced around the parlor. Her silver hair was immaculately coiffed and despite her day of travel, she looked impeccable in a black and white pantsuit. "I'll have Jensen look into her finances." She referred to Amelia's third-eldest brother. "If there's proof she was compensated, we can take her to court since it's a violation of her confidentiality agreement. Jensen knows how to be discreet."

"Whereas I don't."

Her mother sent her an exasperated look. "Stop reading between the lines, Amelia. I wasn't implying any such thing."

"I want it all to go away." She twisted her hands together. "You always said if we ignored rumors and gossip, they'll die of starvation."

"Well, that used to be truer than it is nowadays. People don't depend on news to come from reputable newspapers and the nightly news." She sighed. "It's become quite exhausting in the past few years." She brushed her hand down her silk sleeve. "Either that, or I'm just getting too old to want to put up with it."

"You're not old, Mum."

Josephine's lips twisted a little. "I'm sixty-two, darling. I've divorced one husband and buried another. Now I'm going to be a grandmamma again, and maybe I would like to slow down my schedule and enjoy that more this time around than I was able to do with Oliver Junior."

She sat down beside Amelia again and hugged her arm around her shoulders. "I don't want you worrying about Molly. She's my secretary and I'll see that matter is handled appropriately. In the meantime, you can tell me more about your Mr. Drummond."

Amelia's nose burned. "Quinn is anything but *my* Mr. Drummond," she said thickly.

"Do you love him?"

Amelia nodded. "I knew he was special the first time I saw him. When we were here for Sawyer's wedding. Remember?"

"I remember."

"I couldn't get him out of my head. When I came for Toby's wedding, I made the excuse that I just wanted some space from James pressuring me about marrying, but I had to see Quinn again."

Her mother smiled softly. She rested her head against Amelia's. "I felt the same way the first time I saw your father."

Tears collected and squeezed out her eyes. "He'd be so ashamed of me," Amelia whispered.

Josephine tsked. "He'd have been ready to put Quinn's head on a spike," she allowed, gently teasing. "Because you were his baby girl. But then he'd have come to his senses, the way Simon always did, and start campaigning for the baby to be named after him."

Amelia smiled through her tears. "Yes." She wrapped her arms around her mother's neck. "Yes, he would have. I love you, Mum."

"I love you too, darling." Josephine squeezed her back. "And everything is going to be all right. You'll see."

They both heard the crunch of tires from outside and Josephine stood again while Amelia swiped her cheeks. "Sounds like my sister and Deke are back already. I hope they have good news finally about Toby and Angie's adoption."

Only it quickly became apparent that it wasn't Amelia's aunt and uncle, when her mother looked out the window. "Oh, my." She turned and eyed Amelia for a moment, then picked up her suitcase that was still sitting near the front door where she'd left it upon arriving. "I'm going to go upstairs and get settled."

Amelia started to tell her that she was using the room her mother was accustomed to, but broke off when she spotted Quinn crossing in front of the window.

A moment later, he was pounding on the front door. "Open up, Amelia," he said loudly. "I saw you sitting in there."

She nervously tucked her hair behind her ears and moved to the door, waiting until her mother was gone before tugging it open.

His hazel eyes were bloodshot and they raked over her face. "Was that your mother I saw?"

She nodded. "She's a day earlier than I expected," she said inanely.

He brushed past her, entering the house even though

she hadn't exactly issued an invitation. "Are you all right?"

He was looking at the magazine lying on the coffee table.

Dismay sank through her belly and her shoulders bowed. "You've seen it." She could tell by the lack of shock on his face.

"Jess brought a copy by."

"I'm sorry," she said huskily. "If I would have just stayed in London, you would never have been dragged into any of this."

"And I wouldn't know you're having my baby." His voice was flat. "Regretting the papers you had drawn up already?"

"No!" She lifted her hands. "I don't know what else to do, Quinn." She waved at the tabloid. "Thanks to that nastiness, every last bit of privacy we might have had is lost."

"I don't give a rip who knows about us," he said impatiently. "But I also don't want you working yourself up into a state over it."

Her lips parted. "You were worried about me?"

His gaze raked over her again. "That's my baby you're carrying. You think I want anything endangering that?"

She pressed her lips together, her hopes sinking yet again. Of course his concern would be for the baby. "As you can see, I'm fine."

"Suppose your mother wants to take you back."

"Actually, no." Her voice cooled even more. "I've made it more than clear to you that I intend to remain in Horseback Hollow and raise our child here where he—"

"She—"

"—will have both parents in his life." She stepped

closer to him, looking up into his face. She'd seen him just the day before when she'd left him the agreement, but he looked like he hadn't slept in weeks. "Why are you so insistent that the baby is a girl?"

He picked up the magazine and flipped it open to the article. "Got enough boys in the family," he muttered. "Little girl would be a change of pace."

Her throat tightened. How easy it was to imagine him holding a baby girl. Their child would succeed in wrapping him around a tiny finger.

He would love the baby. He just wouldn't love her.

She rubbed her damp palms down her thighs again, banishing the image before she started crying like a baby herself. "Did you consult an attorney about the, uh, the agreement?"

He tossed the magazine down again. "I don't need to consult anyone. And I haven't signed it."

"Why not? It gives you everything you wanted!"

His lips twisted. "You'd think."

Her head felt light in a way that it hadn't since she'd first arrived in Horseback Hollow. She thought about how many times he'd seemed stuck on the idea that she'd be happier back in London. "Do you *want* me to go back to London?"

His brows pulled together. "No."

Her hands lifted, palms upward. "Then what, Quinn?"

"I want to know I can protect you from crap like that!" He gestured at the magazine. "And I know I can't."

Her heart squeezed and she had to remind herself that feeling protective wasn't the same thing as feeling love. "I wanted to protect you, too," she said huskily. "And I didn't do a good job of it, either. I confided in Molly—"

She broke off and shook her head. "I shouldn't have trusted anyone but my own family. And you."

"You know for sure it was her?"

"Who else?" She sat down on the arm of the couch and held her arms tightly around her chest. "You said nobody saw you buy the test kit I used here. I know you didn't tell anyone. That just leaves Molly. You think you trust someone and they betray—" She broke off. "I don't want to think about it anymore." She watched him for a moment. "I thought I'd, um, speak with Christopher about volunteering at the Fortune Foundation office once he gets it up and running here. I could offer music lessons or something."

"Thought you didn't like playing in front of people."

"I don't like performing. But one-on-one? I told you once I liked working with children." She wished she wouldn't have brought it up, because it only made her remember that perfect April night when she'd talked about her life and he'd actually seemed to listen. "I... I have to do something to fill my days."

"You'll have a baby to fill your days." He waited a beat. "Or are you planning to hire some nanny to do that? That's what people like you do, right?"

"People like you," she repeated, mimicking his drawl. "I was born into a family that happened to have money," she said crisply. "It doesn't make me a different species than you!"

His jaw flexed. "People with your financial advantage," he refined. "That's what my dad's father's *real* family did. Hired...nannies."

She studied the fresh lines creasing his tanned forehead. He'd said his father was illegitimate but hadn't offered anything else about it. Only had used it as a reason why she ought to marry him. "What do you mean?"

"Baxter Anthony." He practically spit the name. "My grandfather. He had a wife. He had kids. His *real* family. The ones who lived in comfort on a big old ranch in Oklahoma. While my grandmother—whom he fired as one of those nannies after knocking her up—and my dad eked out a life in Horseback Hollow. Baxter's real family had nannies. They had private schools. They had everything that my old man didn't."

"I don't want a nanny," she said after a moment. "It never even entered my mind. But the baby won't be here for months yet, and I'm not exactly used to sitting around, whiling away my days waving a lacy fan and eating bonbons."

"You could use a few bonbons," he muttered. "You're still too thin."

"Gawky, skinny Amelia." She sighed. "Lucie got all the grace in the family."

"What the hell are you talking about?"

She shrugged dismissively. "It doesn't matter."

"You're the most graceful thing I've ever seen," he said in such a flat tone she couldn't possibly mistake it for a compliment. More like an accusation. "You're so far out of my league it's laughable. I still can't believe you danced with me that night, much less—" He broke off and shoveled his fingers through his hair, leaving the thick brown strands disheveled.

She tucked her tongue between her teeth, trying to make sense of his words. "You're the one who seemed out of reach to me," she finally said. Self-assured. Quietly confident. A man who'd held her and made her feel safe and beautiful and wanted.

His brows were pulled down, his eyes unreadable. "Baxter was the only one who wanted to buy the Rocking-U when my old man died." His lips thinned. "He'd buy it now, too, if I'd let him. Just so he could finally succeed in wiping away the evidence that anyone with his blood ever existed here."

"Forget about him! The man sounds hideous. And why would you want to sell the Rocking-U? That ranch is—" She broke off, trying to make sense of the nonsensical. "It's who you are," she finally finished and knew she had it right. Ranching wasn't merely something Quinn did. It was entwined with everything he was. The ranch was an extension of him just as much as he was an extension of it.

"It's the only way I can bring something equal to the table," he said through his teeth.

She pushed to her feet. "Let me get this straight," she said slowly. "You think the only thing you can offer this baby is *money?*" She laughed, but it sounded more hysterical than anything. "Money doesn't matter, Quinn! Good Lord, how can you think it would?"

"Because you've always had it," he said roughly.

"If I gave it all away would that make you happy?" Her voice rose. "Would that soothe your…your *ego?*" She swept out her arms, taking in the room around them. "How can you stand in this home that *love* so obviously built and talk that way?"

She snatched up the tabloid and threw it at his chest. "You should have sold the story," she said icily. "At least then you would have been the one to make a fortune on it. You know what? *Don't* sign the custody agreement. I'd rather take this baby back to London than have him be raised by a man who can't recognize what's right in front of his face!"

Then, because tears were blinding her and her stomach was heaving, she fled upstairs.

Quinn started after her. She'd walked away the other day when she brought him that custody agreement and he wasn't going to let her walk off again.

He got to the top of the stairs just as she slammed the bathroom door shut and he started to reach for it.

"I would give her a little time," a calm voice said.

He looked from Amelia's mother, standing in a bedroom doorway, to the bathroom door. On the other side, he could hear Amelia retching, and his sense of helplessness made him want to punch a wall.

"Come." Lady Josephine walked toward him and tucked her hand around his arm, drawing him away from the door. "No woman wants to be overheard when they're in Amelia's state. Morning sickness is never fun." She smiled at him with unexpected kindness.

But he also noticed the way she subtly placed herself between him and the door.

"She's in there because of me." He wasn't only talking about her pregnancy. "She's upset."

"Yes." Lady Josephine's expression didn't change. Nor did her protective position or the steel behind her light touch on his arm. "It's been upsetting business. Come."

He reluctantly went with her back down the stairs and followed her into the parlor. She glanced out the window, then sat on the edge of a side chair, her hands folded in her lap, her long legs angled to one side. It was such an "Amelia position" that he had to look away.

"Mr. Drummond, please sit."

He exhaled and feeling like a kid called in front of the principal, sat on one end of the couch. "Call me Quinn. Lady Josephine," he tacked on hurriedly. Was it supposed to be Lady Chesterfield? Lady Fortune Chesterfield? He wished to hell he'd listened more to Jess's yammering about all that.

A faint smile was playing around the corners of the woman's lips. "And you may call me Josephine. We are a bit of family after all."

He could feel heat rising up his neck. "I suppose I should apologize for that. I wouldn't blame you if you wanted my head."

Her head tilted slightly. "Are you saying you took advantage of my daughter?" Before he could answer, she shifted slightly. "Amelia has a kind heart," she said. "She's always hated the attention our family is given back home. As if we're celebrities of some sort. Unfortunately, this business with Lord Banning got quite out of control and in hindsight, I wish I would have interfered early on. Perhaps I could have saved us all some of this embarrassment. But I've actually never witnessed Amelia allowing herself to be taken advantage of. In fact, she can be quite headstrong at times." Her blue gaze didn't allow him to look away. "I feel certain she was an equal participant in this situation."

"Lady—"

"Josephine."

"Josephine." He rubbed his hands down his jeans and stood, because just sitting there had his nerves wanting to jump out of his skin. "No disrespect, ma'am, but I'm not going to talk about that." He wasn't going to talk about having sex with Amelia to her mother. He wasn't going to talk about it with anyone.

"I've always thought that when two people who belong together are not, it's one of the saddest things there is."

He stared. "You think she belongs with *me*. I'm a

small-town rancher, ma'am. I don't have a pot of gold. I've got one failed marriage and pots of cow manure."

Her lips twitched. "I forget how refreshingly frank you Americans can be." She rose gracefully. She was taller than Amelia, but no less slender, and Quinn knew when Amelia was her age, she'd be just as beautiful. "I had an unsuccessful marriage as well, Quinn. And then I met Amelia's father and I had a very, very successful one. I loved Simon with all of my heart and knew that he loved me equally. I want that for Amelia. I want that for all of my children. The past is past. And if you'll forgive an unintended pun, fortune isn't in gold. I hope you'll realize that for both your sakes."

She patted his arm as she passed him and pulled open the front door. "You don't have to love Amelia to be a good father to your child together. But if you don't love Amelia, be decent enough to allow her space to find someone who will."

Chapter Fourteen

"Come on." Jess dragged Quinn by the arm, pulling him toward the brightly lit building.

The Hollows Cantina was having its grand opening celebration and everyone in town seemed to have turned out for the festivities.

"Mac reserved a table for us," Jess continued, "and is waiting, and you are *not* getting out of coming just because you're a flaming idiot."

"Amelia's going to be there."

"No kidding, Sherlock." She dug her fingernails into his forearm the same way she'd done when she was an equally irritating teenager. "Maybe if you weren't so clueless when it comes to wooing a woman, you'd be with her instead of playing third wheel to me and my husband."

"I don't want to be here with you, either," he reminded.

But she'd driven out to the Rocking-U and made it plain she wasn't leaving unless he came with her.

For the sake of a little peace and sanity, and only because he really didn't want to upset yet another pregnant woman, he had pulled on the only suit he owned and gone with her.

"I'll be just as happy to go back home again," he finished. There were strands of white lights strung around the Cantina's building, outlining not only the second story's open-air terrace, but the market umbrellas lining the street in front of it, and country music spewed out from inside. The festive atmosphere was the last thing he was in the mood for.

"Over my dead body," Jess raised her voice over the music and even though there were a couple dozen people lined up outside the entrance waiting to get in, she pulled him into the throng, waving at the familiar faces they passed. He knew everyone in Horseback Hollow, too, but she knew everyone from Vicker's Corners who was there as well, which made for slow going. But they finally reached the small table deep inside the first floor of the restaurant where Mac was already seated.

She slipped behind the table to sit next to her husband who shoved out the chair that had obviously been added to what should have been a two-person table for Quinn. He gestured with his half-empty beer mug. "Place is a madhouse," he said, leaning across the table so he could be heard above the noise. "Already put in orders for a beer for you."

Jess made a face and reached for her glass of fruit juice. "Some men might forgo alcohol in support of his pregnant wife having to abstain."

Mac grinned at her, obviously unfazed. "Baby, you're

pregnant so often, I'd never have another beer again if I gave it up whenever you're knocked up." He bussed her cheek. "I ordered you some hot crab dip," he added. "You can eat yourself silly on it."

Jess looked slightly mollified. "At least I know I won't have to share it with either one of you." Both Mac and Quinn detested crab. "You wouldn't know there had ever been any protests in town about this place opening." She was craning her neck around, openly gawking at the people crowded inside. "This is amazing!" She wriggled a little in her seat, clearly delighted. "I think every person from Horseback Hollow *and* Vicker's Corners must be here tonight."

Quinn was looking around, too, hopefully less noticeably than his sister.

But he hadn't spotted Amelia.

He knew she hadn't left town. Jess would've reported it.

A waitress wearing a stark white blouse and a black apron tied around her hips stopped next to their table and delivered a steaming crock of crab dip and crackers as well as two freshly frosted mugs filled with beer. "We have a special menu tonight," she told them as she dealt three one-page menus on the table. "Because of the grand openin' and all. I'll give you a chance to look it over and be back if you have any questions."

Quinn's only question was where Amelia was.

Not that he knew what he would say to her if he saw her. She was making a habit of walking away from him. The fact that he deserved it wasn't something he was willing to look at real closely.

And he was still feeling the bruises from her mother's velvet-over-steel dismissal the day before.

He lifted the beer mug, and angled in his seat so he could see around the restaurant more easily.

The staircase that led to the second floor was situated close to the center of the room; a wide iron and rustic wood thing that was as much a focal point as it was functional and the mayor, Harlan Osgood, was holding court at the base, recounting the steps taken to bring such a fine establishment to their little town as if he hadn't ever had his own doubts about it. Privately, Quinn figured it was a good thing Harlan's main job was as the town's barber, because a natural politician, he wasn't.

Marcos and Wendy Mendoza, the owners, were working the room, too. The young couple was eye-catching, to say the least. Wendy in particular looked more like she belonged on the cover of magazines than making the desserts that Julia claimed were out of this world. Quinn had to give the couple credit for seeming to give equal attention to everyone they stopped to speak with. They gave just as much time to Tanya and her folks, sitting at a table as crowded as Quinn's across the room, as they did the mayor.

"Mac, what are you going to have?" Jess was asking, tapping the crisp edge of her menu against the table. "I'm starving. I haven't had a speck of morning sickness in two days, and I am going to take advantage of it."

Mac chuckled. "I think I'm having whatever else it is you want to order so you can eat it, too."

Was Amelia still plagued with morning sickness?

Quinn pushed out of the chair.

Jess looked at him. "You're *not* leaving."

He leaned over her. "Stop bossing," he warned.

Then he kissed the top of her head and made his way toward the staircase. He knew the entire extended Fortune family was supposed to be there that night, and if they weren't on the bottom floor, maybe they were up top.

Getting there proved as slow-going as getting into the restaurant in the first place, though, because of all the people standing around on the stairs blocking the way. He could hear bursts of laughter coming from the upper floor and barely controlled the urge to physically move some of the roadblocks out of his way.

"Mr. Drummond!"

He looked over the side of the staircase to see Shayla waving at him excitedly, her orange ponytail bouncing, and he sketched a wave. But she was already worming her way around the mayor and up the steps until she was only a few below his position midway up. "It's so cool to see you," she gushed. "Is Lady Amelia here, too?"

The girl had helped them avoid Ophelia Malone in Vicker's Corners, so Quinn swallowed his impatience to get upstairs. "I'm looking for her now," he admitted. "How've you been? Do you still have a particular guest staying at the B and B?"

She widened her eyes dramatically. "Right? Miz Malone finally left this morning. My ma's not so happy—" she waved her hand behind her, presumably to indicate the presence of her mother somewhere in the madhouse "—'cause she paid the room on time and all, but I was glad to see her go. I can't believe what she got printed the other day." She wrinkled her nose. "So gross."

It was as good a definition as any and a lot milder than what Quinn still thought about the tabloid cover. "Did you and your mom already have dinner?"

"Nah. Not yet." She twisted her head around, looking down on the patrons below. "Ma's over there talking to the Fremonts. They're all on the graduation committee for high school next year."

He automatically glanced over at the table he'd noticed earlier where Tanya sat with her parents. Shayla's mother's hair was just as orange as her daughter's. Either the color was real or they shared the same bottle of hair dye.

"Can't believe she did it," Shayla was babbling on. "Just so stupid, you know?"

He frowned. "What?"

"Tanya." Shayla rolled her eyes, looking disgusted. "Believe me, she's not one of *my* friends anymore."

God save him from teenage girl angst. He managed to edge up another step when the person in front of him moved slightly. "That's too bad," he said vaguely. Tanya had always been a hard worker for him and the dozen or so other people she also cleaned for in order to help supplement her family's strained income.

"Wow. You're nicer than I would be," Shayla was saying. She was practically shouting to be heard above the music. "Blabbing about your personal business to Miz Malone and all."

He went still, her words penetrating.

He went back down the step. "What did you say?"

Shayla looked suddenly nervous. "Uh—"

He nudged her to one side of the stairs so one of the servers carrying a stack of menus could get past them. "What do you mean about personal business, Shayla?" But he had the sinking feeling he already knew.

He'd tossed Amelia's pregnancy test in the trash.

Tanya cleaned his house.

Shayla shot a look toward the table below and Quinn caught the pale expression on Tanya's face even from a distance.

"I don't think she meant to," Shayla said hurriedly. She might be willing to eschew Tanya's friendship, but she was obviously afraid of tossing her under the bus. "It's just Miz Malone kept talking to everybody and…and—" She lifted her shoulders. "Well, Tanya needed that car in the worst way or she's not gonna be able to get back and forth to Lubbock for school when she graduates next year and the money she gets cleaning houses is already used up on her ma's medicine. I thought you already knew."

Quinn sucked down his fury.

"I don't think she knew how bad it would be," Shayla finished. "Still." She made a face. "*I* wouldn't want her cleaning around my stuff. You're prob'ly pretty mad, huh."

Amelia's friend Molly hadn't done a single thing to betray her.

"It's okay, Shayla." He squeezed her shoulder and managed a smile even though he wanted to kick both Ophelia Malone and Tanya Fremont off the planet altogether. "I'm glad to hear the truth."

"Quinn!"

He looked toward the top of the stairs to see Liam beckoning.

"Go on and enjoy your dinner," Quinn told Shayla. "Once I find Amelia, I'll let her know you're here. I'm sure she'll want to say hello."

Shayla beamed. "You think?"

He nodded and started edging up the stairs again while she slipped through the people on her way down.

Liam clapped him on the shoulder when he finally made it to the top. "Julia's done a helluva job here tonight with the Mendozas, hasn't she?" The man's face was proud. "We've got the whole family up here."

Suspicions confirmed, Quinn looked beyond Liam to the crowded tables spilling out onto the open terrace. Jeanne and Deke were sitting with Josephine and their brother, James Marshall Fortune. There was also another older couple sitting with them and he was pretty certain the man was the threesome's older brother, John. Which, according to Jess who always needed to know who was who, made him Wendy Mendoza's father. Aside from Jeanne and Deke's crew, spread out among the rest of the tables were a bunch of other faces he recognized from Sawyer and Laurel's New Year's wedding.

But Amelia was not among them.

"We've got extra reason to celebrate," Liam was saying. "Angie and Toby's adoption was finally approved."

His head was still banging with Shayla's news, but Quinn glanced at the man who seemed deep in conversation with his uncle James. Happiness radiated from his face. "That's great," he said. "Where's Amelia?"

Liam looked surprised for a moment, then glanced around. "Don't know, man. She was here earlier." He raised his voice even more. "Aunt Josephine, where'd Amelia go?"

In addition to Amelia's mother, Quinn suddenly found himself the focus of way too many eyes.

Josephine said something to her companions, then rose and worked her way through the tables toward him.

"I didn't mean to interrupt your dinner," Quinn said.

"You're not interrupting," she assured. She smiled slightly at her nephew. "Liam, I haven't had a chance yet to applaud your fiancée's efforts tonight. Is Julia going to be able to join us, or is she on duty all evening?"

"She's not on duty at all," Liam said, grinning. "But she can't keep from checking on things. She'll be 'round soon enough." He headed after the waitress that was circulating throughout the room with a tray laden with drinks. "Hey there, darlin', lemme take one of those off your hands."

Josephine looked back at Quinn. "I wasn't sure we would have the pleasure of seeing you tonight."

He wondered what she'd really like to say if she weren't so polite. Probably something more along the lines of hoping he wouldn't have the gall to show his face that night.

"I wasn't going to come," he admitted. He was glad he had, though, if only to hear what Shayla'd had to say. "Is Amelia all right?"

Josephine's expression was the same as it had been the other day when she'd essentially told him to put up or shut up. Calm. Seemingly gracious, yet still reserved.

"She's unhappy." She didn't attempt to raise her voice above the music to be heard, yet her words somehow managed to carry through anyway. "As are you, I believe." Then she sighed a little, her gaze following Sawyer and Orlando Mendoza as they moved among the tables. "I keep having to remind myself how entwined the Fortune and Mendoza families are," she murmured then looked back at Quinn again. "She went outside a short while ago. She said she needed some fresh air."

He stifled an oath. How had he missed her leaving the restaurant when he'd been on the damn stairs?

"Thank you." He started to turn and go back the way he'd come, but stopped. "La— Josephine."

She lifted her eyebrows, waiting.

"It wasn't Molly," he said abruptly. "You know. Who spilled the beans." He told her briefly about Tanya cleaning his place.

When he was done, he couldn't tell if she was relieved or not. He'd thought that Amelia's "royal face" was bad, but in comparison to her mother's, her expressive face was an open book.

"What do you plan to do about your young employee?"

"Fire her," he said flatly.

"Hmm." She nodded once. "Is that why you're anxious to see my daughter? To share this information?"

He could lie and say it was, even though he'd been looking for Amelia before Shayla's disclosure. As far as he was concerned, what went on between him and Amelia *was* between him and Amelia. "I don't know why I'm anxious to see her," he finally said truthfully. "I just know I have to."

It wasn't any sort of answer, but it seemed enough for her to smile just a little as she nodded once and headed back to her table.

He went down the stairs again where the sounds of celebration weren't as raucous, though the music was, and pretended he didn't see his sister trying to flag him down as he worked his way toward the entrance.

Once he got past the crowd still waiting to get in, he felt like he'd been shot from a noisy cannon into blissful peace.

The music was still loud. There were still dozens of people surrounding the tables beneath the colorful market umbrellas. But it was still *open* and he yanked off his suit jacket and hauled in a deep breath of fresh air.

The Hollows Cantina might well be bringing new jobs and new revenue to the area, and it wouldn't be crazy busy in the days to come like it was for the grand opening, but he was pretty sure he wouldn't be in any hurry to go back, no matter how good the food might turn out to be.

Bunching his jacket in one hand, he scanned the tables outside the restaurant. Amelia wasn't at any of them, so he walked past them until he reached the side of the building. She wasn't there, either, so he walked all the way around the building. And even then, he didn't spot her.

"Dammit, Amelia. Where are you?"

The whole of Horseback Hollow's businesses were contained in just a few short blocks and trying not to imagine her passed out cold in some shadowy corner, he started down the street, and then nearly missed her altogether where she was sitting on a bench in front of the mayor's barbershop.

The soles of his boots scraped against the street when he stopped in front of her and peered at her in the dark. Her skin looked white in the moonlight, her hair, eyes and clothing as dark as midnight. "You're not easy to find."

"I didn't know you were looking." She shifted slightly, given away only by the slight rustle of her clothes. "You've been in the restaurant?"

"Yeah." It was a warm night and he tossed his jacket on the bench beside her and started rolling up his sleeves. "It's a zoo."

She made a soft sound. "Yes. Too many people and too much noise for me."

"Were you feeling sick?"

She shifted again. "Not in the way you mean," she murmured. "What do you want, Quinn?"

"Molly didn't rat us out," he said abruptly. "It was Tanya. When she cleaned the house—"

"She found the test," Amelia finished slowly, dawning

revelation clear in her tone. "Of course she did. I can't believe I never thought of that."

"I can't believe she talked to that woman," he said flatly. "I wouldn't have known if Shayla hadn't said something. Would've just kept paying the kid every Sunday to clean the bathrooms and mop the damn floors, never knowing any better."

"She's a girl," Amelia murmured.

"She talked about *our* business for the price of a car," he countered. "She won't be stepping foot in my house again. Or any others, if I can help it."

"Didn't you ever make a mistake when you were young?"

His lips twisted. "Why are you being so understanding? You were pretty upset thinking it was your mother's secretary."

"It's just all so…so sad, isn't it?" Her voice was soft. Oddly musing. "I'd say it was tragic except there are so many other real tragedies occurring every day." She sighed. "The press has been vilifying us ever since I came to Horseback Hollow. Ophelia used Tanya like a tool, no differently than she'd use a long-distance lens. Have you ever noticed how random it all is?" she asked abruptly.

He peered at her face but even though his eyes were becoming accustomed to the dark, he still couldn't tell if she was looking at him or not. "What's random?"

"If I hadn't decided to come to Horseback Hollow with Mum for Sawyer's wedding over New Year's. If you and I hadn't danced when I came back again for Toby's. If James's father hadn't announced an engagement-that-wasn't. If any one of those things hadn't occurred, everything would be so different today."

"Maybe that's not random." His chest felt tight. "Maybe that's fate."

She shifted, her dark dress rustling. "You believe in fate." She sounded skeptical.

"I don't know what I believe, Amelia. Except I know I don't want you going back to London."

"I've told you and told you, you needn't worry about your place in the baby's life."

"What about a place in your life?"

She went silent for a moment, then slowly stood, walking closer to him until he could smell the clean fragrance of her hair and see the gleam in her dark eyes.

"Did you really want me to come back to Horseback Hollow after the night we shared? You said you did. And I… I thought you meant it. But maybe that's just what a person is supposed to say after a one-night stand. Protocol, if you will."

"It wasn't protocol," he said flatly. "I meant it."

He felt the weight of her gaze. "Why?"

The shirt button he'd left loose at his neck wasn't enough and he yanked another one free. "What d'ya mean *why?* I liked you. We had great—"

"Sex," she finished.

"*Chemistry* is what I was going to say."

"The end result is the same."

"Where are you going with this, Amelia?"

"I don't know." She sighed. "I've just been trying to figure out how much I imagined about that night and what was actually real."

He didn't need light. He closed one arm around her waist and pressed his other hand against her flat abdomen, feeling as much as hearing the sudden breath she inhaled. "That is real."

"Yes." The one word sounded shaky. "But sex is not love. Having a baby doesn't mean love, either."

"Sometimes it does." He wanted to get out the words. But they felt stopped in his chest by a lifetime of disappointments. "Jess and Mac are having another baby. Trying again for a girl. So maybe she really had been in that hardware store to buy pink paint."

"I'm happy for them." Her voice was low. She gently patted his chest once. Then once more. "Think about it before you fire Tanya," she murmured. And then she stepped out of his arm and started up the street, disappearing into the dark.

Chapter Fifteen

Amelia's eyes glazed as she stumbled up the street.

"Amelia!"

Quinn was not going to come around. He wouldn't let himself, and she couldn't bear it.

"Don't walk away from me."

Her chest ached. She'd never understood that a heart breaking was a physical breaking, too. She could barely force herself to move when all she wanted to do was curl into a ball. She swiped her cheek and forced her feet to move faster. "What are you going to do? Throw me over your shoulder?"

"Please." Just one word. Rough. And raw.

Her feet dragged to a stop.

A block away, she could see the lights of the Cantina. Could hear the music playing on the night.

She didn't have to look back to see Quinn coming up

behind her. She didn't even need to hear his footfalls on the pavement. She could feel him.

"Toby and Angie's adoption was approved this afternoon. Did you know that?"

"Yeah. I saw him and your uncle James together. D'you think he's the one who gave him that money?"

"Aunt Jeanne wouldn't take the money he wanted to give her, so why not? He can afford it." She clasped her arms around her waist, trying to keep the pieces of herself from splintering on the road and nodded toward the festivities. "Everyone in there is celebrating," she said painfully. "Everyone in there is happy. Julia and Liam can walk into a room and light it up simply by looking at each other. Colton and Stacey are like two halves of a whole. I think Jude would lay down his life for Gabi and Christopher and Kinsley—" Her voice broke. "They're all happy. They're all in love. Is it so wrong to want that, too?"

"No."

She turned on her heel and looked up at him. "I could marry you, Quinn," she whispered. "Justice of the peace or a minister. It wouldn't matter. I could stand up in front of either and promise to love you for the rest of my days. And I wouldn't be lying." She sniffed but the tears kept coming. "But the marriage *would* be a lie, because I know you don't love me. And I can't live like that." She turned again, desperate to go somewhere, anywhere, for a little peace.

"And I can't live without you."

Had she gone so far over the edge that she was hearing things now, too?

"Don't leave me."

She sucked in a shuddering breath.

"Amelia." He closed his hands over her shoulders and turned her toward him. "Please." His low voice cracked. "Don't leave me." His fingers tightened, almost painfully.

"Quinn—"

He closed his mouth over hers, his hands moving to cradle her face. "Don't," he said hoarsely, brushing his thumbs over her cheeks. "I can take anything but that."

She could no more stop her hands from grasping his shoulders than she could stop loving him.

He kissed her again, lightly. Tenderly. The way he had that very first time. "If you leave me, I won't be able to take it. I love you," he whispered. "More than I've ever loved anything or anyone. And I am terrified. Okay?"

She wound her arms behind his neck, her heart cracking wide. "Nothing terrifies you."

"Not being good enough for you does." He dragged her arms away, holding them captive between them. "Not being a good enough father." He shook her gently, as if trying to convince her. "Not being a good enough husband. If I failed you or the baby—"

"You won't," she cried. "You can't fail me if you'd just love me. You think I'm not afraid? I don't even know how to make a baby's bottle. Infants can't eat peanut butter sandwiches!"

He folded her against him, tucking her head into his shoulder. "I know how to make a bottle," he said roughly. "Jess made me learn years ago. That's the easy stuff, Amelia. I'm talking about a life. What do I have to offer you?"

"Your heart," she said thickly. "Offer your heart! It's the only thing that matters. If you're afraid, be afraid with me. I can't bear it if you shut me out."

"Oh, my God," a voice said from nearby, startling them both. "Get a room or get on with it."

Amelia stared into the darkness, appalled when Ophelia Malone strolled closer. All of her pain, her uncertainty where Quinn was concerned, coalesced into a ball of hatred toward the paparazzo. *"You."* She started to launch herself at the dreadful woman, but Quinn held her back. "Haven't you done enough?"

"Evidently not." Ophelia sighed slightly. She held out her hands to her sides and Amelia spotted the camera she was holding.

She pulled against Quinn, but again he held fast. "She's not worth it." His voice was cutting.

"Why do you do this?" Amelia demanded of the woman. "Why do you go around making peoples' lives a misery? Is the money that good? Is it just that you enjoy tearing people's lives to shreds? What is it?"

"Oh, the money was good. Very, very good. But it didn't work anyway." Ophelia circled around them, giving Amelia's clawed fingers a wide berth. "Even knowing what sort of person you really are, Lord Banning *still* isn't giving my sister a chance."

Amelia shook her head, suddenly lost. "What?"

Ophelia sighed again. "You really are as dumb as a post," she mocked. "Your rancher there has more smarts than you do. At least he built that successful little ranch of his out of nothing but ashes. What have you ever done but smile pretty for the cameras while your mummy does all that charitable work that has people thinking she's such a saint?"

Quinn set Amelia to one side of him and snatched Ophelia's wrist with his free hand, making the other woman drop the camera. "Keep it up," he spat, "and I'll let her at you."

"Who's your sister?"

Ophelia shook off Quinn's hold and crouched down to pick up the two pieces of the camera. She held up the lens to the light from the Cantina, then tossed it off to the side of the road. "So much for that pricey little thing." She pushed to her feet. "Astrid," she clipped. She circled around Quinn until she was near Amelia again. "Astrid is my sister and if it weren't for *you* and your eminently suitable pedigree, Lord Banning would have chosen *her*. He would have gone against that decrepit father of his and married my sister whether she was a common shop girl or not!"

"You're insane," Amelia whispered, shocked to her very core.

Ophelia held out her arms. "Guilty as charged, no doubt." She suddenly tossed the camera at them and Quinn caught it midair before it could hit Amelia. "I don't have the stomach for this anymore. I'd like to say I hope you'll be happy together, but we all know I'd be lying." She turned on her heel and started walking down the street. "Taa taa, darlings."

Amelia pulled against Quinn's hold.

"Let her go," he muttered.

"She's…she's *vile!* I can't believe that woman is Astrid's sister."

He dropped the camera on the ground and turned her back into his arms, his hands sweeping down her back. "You know her?"

"Astrid? She sells coffee in James's building. And he's crazy about her. But he's had years to go against his family and marry her. Now that he's the Earl of Estingwood, he could do whatever he wants. But he won't."

"Why?"

"Because she's a commoner," Amelia said simply. "She's divorced. She has a child. Take your pick."

"I thought that stuff didn't matter anymore."

"It matters to the Bannings. And above all things, James is loyal to his family."

He pressed his lips against her temple. "I don't want to talk about James."

"Neither do I." From the corner of her eye, though, she kept watch of Ophelia, long enough to see the woman climb into an SUV and roar off down the street in the opposite direction.

Quinn suddenly pushed her away from him. "Where were we?"

Her throat tightened. "I don't know," she whispered.

"I do." Holding her hands, he abruptly went down on one knee, right there in the middle of the street. "I think this is the way it's supposed to go. Never did it before."

She inhaled sharply. "Quinn—"

"My heart is yours, Amelia Fortune Chesterfield. It has been from the second you agreed to a dance with a simple cowboy."

Tears flooded her eyes. "So is mine. Yours, I mean. My heart." She laughed brokenly. "I'm making a mishmash. And there's nothing simple about you."

"Will you marry me?"

She nodded and pulled on his hands. "Yes. I don't want you on your knees, I just want you by my side."

He rose and caught her close. "Preacher or a JP?"

She dragged his head to hers. "As long as it's soon, I don't care," she said thickly, and pressed her mouth to his. Joy was bubbling through her, making her feel dizzy with it. "Take me home?"

He cradled her tightly, lifting her right off her feet. "Kissing me like that is how getting you pregnant started off," he warned. And then he laughed a little and swore. "I can't. I don't have my truck. I rode here with Jess."

She groaned. "I want to be alone with you." She sank her fingers through his hair, reveling in the realization that she *could*. "I don't care how shameless that sounds. I need to be alone with you."

"You're killing me," he said gruffly, and kissed her so softly, so sweetly, that she would have fallen in love with him all over again if she hadn't already done so.

Then he gently set her back on her feet. Kissed her forehead. Her cheeks. "We'll go back and borrow some keys from someone."

"And then you'll take me home?"

He lifted her hand and kissed her fingers. "And then I'll take you home." They started back toward the Cantina, but Amelia suddenly ducked under his arm and ran back to retrieve Ophelia's camera.

"What do you want that thing for?"

She pulled his arm over her shoulder once more and fiddled with the camera as they continued walking back to the Cantina. "There's got to be a memory card in here somewhere." She held up the camera, squinting in the light from the strands hanging in the trees. "Ah." She spotted the storage compartment and freed the tiny square inside before handing the camera to Quinn. "Don't toss that aside either," she warned. "There might be internal memory or something that will need to be erased."

"Ophelia's gone." He brushed his hand down her hair. "Nobody else is going to care about that thing."

"Probably," she agreed, "But I'm not taking any chances." She went over to one of the umbrella-covered tables and reached for one of the candles burning inside short jars. "Mind if I borrow this for a moment?" she asked the people sitting there, and when there were no objections, carried it back to him.

Holding the jar between them, she dropped the memory disk onto the flame. "No more Ophelia Malone," she murmured, watching the thing begin to sizzle and melt, and feeling like the last load was lifting from her shoulders.

When the memory card was no longer recognizable as anything but a misshapen blob of plastic, she blew out the candle and carefully plucked it out of the wax.

Then she dropped it on the road and ground it fervently beneath her heel.

Quinn lifted the candle out of her hand and set it back on the table. "Remind me never to make you really mad," he said when she finally stopped grinding.

"I know how to fox hunt, too," she told him, looping her arm through his. She couldn't seem to get the smile off her face, but then she couldn't imagine a reason why she needed to.

Quinn Drummond loved her.

What she'd feared was only a dream was real. And she was going to treasure that for the rest of their days.

"Fox hunt," he repeated warily. But he was smiling, too, and he absently hooked the camera strap over his shoulder.

"My father taught us." She looked up at the balcony above the umbrellas and saw her mother there, talking with Orlando Mendoza and looking unusually animated.

"Once upon a time my father was a pilot," she murmured, nodding toward the balcony. "The Royal Air Force."

Quinn pulled her close against his side once more, as if he couldn't stand even a few inches separating them. He tilted his head looking upward, his gaze sharpening slightly. "They look—"

"Cozy," Amelia finished.

"Interesting." He steered her toward the entrance of the Cantina that was no less crowded than it had been earlier. "Maybe Horseback Hollow will end up appealing to more of the Fortune Chesterfields."

As much as the idea delighted her, she was presently more interested in Quinn. "You promised something about keys?"

"Yes, ma'am," Quinn said softly and kissed her right there in front of the Hollows Cantina for all the world to see. Then he tugged her after him through the crowds. Jess and Mac were sitting all cozied up together at their small table, clearly unworried whether he ever returned or not. The stairs were still crowded and he exhaled impatiently. But Amelia dragged him through the swinging doors to the kitchen where there was another staircase.

Not grand. Not the center of attention. But entirely welcome. At the top, he threaded his way around the tables there.

Lady Josephine was sitting once more next to Jeanne Marie and Deke and her smile deepened when she saw them. "Have you figured out where your fortune is, then, Quinn?"

"Yes, ma'am," he said and lifted his hand linked with Amelia's. "I surely have." His eyes met Amelia's. "Love's the fortune."

Her smile trembled and she leaned into him. "Keys," she whispered.

He threw back his head and laughed. "Keys." He spotted Liam. "Lend me your truck for the night and I'll *consider* selling Rocky."

Liam reached into his pocket and tossed the keys over several heads. Quinn caught them handily.

Amelia giggled, squeezing his hand.

And they raced for the stairs.

Epilogue

Quinn parked his truck near the tree house tree and went around to open Amelia's door. "Come on."

She tilted her head up toward his, a smile on her face below the bandanna he'd tied around her eyes before they'd left the ranch house.

It had been a week since the Cantina's grand opening. A week during which they'd barely left one another's side. A week in which it was finally sinking in that Amelia was his.

She loved him. She wasn't going anywhere. She was filling the empty parts of him, and together they'd fill the empty rooms of their home.

"What are we doing?" Her voice was full of laughter.

"You'll see." He took her hands and helped her out of the truck.

"Not exactly." Her lips tilted. "Since you've blindfolded me." She turned her head from side to side as he drew her closer to the tree, obviously trying to get a sense of where they were. "Do I hear the creek?"

He moved behind her and slid his hands around her waist and kissed her neck below her ear, right where he knew it would make her shiver. "Good instincts."

She sighed a little, shimmied a little with that shiver, and covered his hands with hers, pressing them against her belly. She rubbed her head against his chest. "On occasion. I picked you, didn't I?"

"That you did." He kissed her earlobe. "Okay, you can look."

She tugged the bandanna off her head.

"I knew it," she said, laughing in her triumph. She peered up into the tree branches. "You've finished the floor! When did you have time to do that?"

He'd finished a lot more than that. "When you're lazing around in bed, snoring."

"I don't snore."

"You do." He kissed her nose. "Daintily. Like the lady that you are."

She rolled her eyes. "Oh, that makes it all right then."

He laughed softly. "It's safe for us to go up."

Her dark eyes roved over his face while a smile played around her soft lips. "*Us?* As in now you're going to let me climb a tree?"

His hands slid down her hips. "Only because I'm here with you. So do you want to go up or not?"

Her eyes sparkled. "What do you think?" She quickly yanked off the sandals she'd been wearing and tossed them onto the grass, then set her bare toes on the first foothold and deftly began climbing.

"Just go slow, okay? Be careful."

She looked over her shoulder at him, grinning and looking more like a teenaged girl than a pregnant woman. "Fine warning from the man who puts temptation in my path."

She continued up with Quinn standing below her, and between his distraction over the view of her bare legs beneath her summery pink dress as she went, even he had to admit that she seemed to know exactly what she was doing. "How often did you say you used to climb trees?"

She laughed. She'd reached the base of the tree house and pushed open the door in the floor. "Every day that I could get away with it." In seconds, she'd clambered through the hatch, and then there was only silence.

He imagined her up there, seeing the preparations he'd made early that morning while she'd been sleeping in his bed.

Their bed.

A moment later, she leaned over the high side boards that formed the walls of the tree house, her long hair hanging down past her shoulders. Her youthful grin was gone, replaced by a soft expression. "Are you going to stand around down there, or join me?"

He kicked off his own shoes and climbed up.

It didn't take him any longer than it had her, but in that brief time she'd still managed to slip out of her dress, and was laying on the thick blankets he'd spread out on one side of the structure.

He let out a breath.

She propped her head on her hand and smiled slightly, holding one of the daisies he'd stuck in a jar to her nose. She was wearing sheer panties and a bra the same pale blue color as the Texas sky. "This *is* what you had in mind, isn't it?"

He crawled through the door and dropped it back in place. "Yeah." He shucked his own clothes, pitching them in the corner.

Her lashes swept down and pink color touched her cheeks. "I'm wondering if Peter Pan ever got up to such mischief."

He knelt down beside her, and she rolled onto her back, her hair pooling out around her head. "Peter Pan was a boy," he murmured, sliding one strap off her shoulder and kissing the creamy skin there.

She ran her thigh against his as she bent her knee and dropped the flower in favor of closing her hand boldly around him. "And you're *no* boy."

He exhaled on a rough laugh and caught her hand in his, pulling it away. "Not so fast, Lady Fortune Chesterfield." He stretched out next to her and slid off the other bra strap, then unsnapped the tiny silver clasp between her breasts holding it together. "I have plans for you."

"That'll be Mrs. Drummond—" her voice hitched when he caught one of those rosy crests between his lips "—to you."

He smiled against her warm flesh. Already he could sense small changes in her body because of the baby inside her. Her breasts were fuller. Her nipples a deeper pink. "Soon as you finally say whether you want a minister or a justice of the peace, that's who you'll be." He kissed his way down her flat belly, anchoring her hips gently when she shivered and twisted against him.

"Minister," she whispered. Her fingers slid through his hair, clutching. "And soon."

He nuzzled his way beneath the sexy little panties that matched the bra. "Impatient to make this all legal?"

"Yes." She suddenly twisted, reversing their positions

and pinned him on the blankets. "And I want to say yes before I'm big as a house. But I want my brothers and sister here, too. And you'll need a suit since you lost your jacket at the Cantina the other night." She kicked off her panties and sank down on him, letting out a shuddering moan.

He clamped his hands over her hips. "You're not always gonna get your way like this, princess." He sucked in a sharp breath as she rocked her hips against him. "I'm only indulging this need for constant speed you've got 'cause—"

"You love me." She leaned over, rubbing her tight nipples against his chest, and kissed him.

"—you're pregnant and at the mercy of your hormones," he finished.

Then, wrapping his arm around her waist, he flipped her onto her back. Loving the color in her cheeks and the way her eyes went an even darker brown, soft as down and feeling like home.

"And because I love you," he said the words quietly. They were coming easier, but even when he didn't say them he wanted her to know he would never stop feeling them.

Her eyes turned shiny and wet. She laid her palm along his jaw and brushed her thumb over his lip. "If I'm a princess, you know that makes you my prince."

"I don't care what you call me, Amelia—" he sank into her "—as long as it means *husband*."

She gasped, and twined her legs around his hips, arching against him. "This…tree house is off-limits the second our son—"

"Daughter—"

"—hits puberty," she managed breathlessly.

He laughed and thumbed away the tears leaking from her big brown eyes. "Damn straight it is," he agreed. And then he kissed her and together, they flew.

* * * * *

YOU HAVE JUST READ A HARLEQUIN® SPECIAL EDITION BOOK.

Discover more heartfelt tales of **family, friendship** and **love** from the Harlequin Special Edition series. Be sure to look for all six Harlequin® Special Edition books every month.

♦ HARLEQUIN®
SPECIAL EDITION

*When small-town cop Ali Templeton finds the uncle
of an abandoned infant, she wasn't expecting a
famous author—or an undeniable attraction!*

*Read on for a sneak preview of
the next book in the AMERICAN HEROES miniseries,
SHOW ME A HERO,
by New York Times bestselling author Allison Leigh.*

"Are you going to ask when you can meet your niece?"

Grant grimaced. "You don't know that she's my niece.
You only think she is."

"It's a pretty good hunch," Ali continued. "If you're
willing to provide a DNA sample, we could know for
sure."

His DNA wouldn't prove squat, though he had no
intention of telling her that. Particularly now that they'd
become the focus of everyone inside the bar. The town
had a whopping population of 5,000. Maybe. It was
small, but that didn't mean there wasn't a chance he'd be
recognized. And the last thing he wanted was a rabid fan
showing up on his doorstep.

He'd had too much of that already. It was one of the
reasons he'd taken refuge at the ranch that his biological
grandparents had once owned. He'd picked it up for a
song when it was auctioned off years ago, but he hadn't
seriously entertained doing much of anything with it—
especially living there himself.

At the time, he'd just taken perverse pleasure in being able to buy up the place where he'd never been welcomed while they'd been alive.

Now it was in such bad disrepair that to stay there even temporarily, he'd been forced to make it habitable.

He wondered if Karen had stayed there, unbeknownst to him. If she was responsible for any of the graffiti or the holes in the walls.

He pushed away the thought and focused on the officer. "Ali. What's it short for?"

She hesitated, obviously caught off guard. "Alicia, but nobody ever calls me that." He'd been edging closer to the door, but she'd edged right along with him. "So, about that—"

Her first name hadn't been on the business card she'd left for him. "Ali fits you better than Alicia."

She gave him a look from beneath her just-from-bed sexy bangs. "Stop changing the subject, Mr. Cooper."

"Start talking about something else, then. Better yet—" he gestured toward the bar and Marty "—start doing the job you've gotta be getting paid for since I can't imagine you slinging drinks just for the hell of it."

Her eyes narrowed and her lips thinned. "Mr. Cooper—"

"G'night, Officer Ali." He pushed open the door and headed out into the night.

Don't miss
SHOW ME A HERO by Allison Leigh,
available August 2018 wherever
Harlequin® Special Edition books and ebooks are sold.

www.Harlequin.com

HARLEQUIN®

SPECIAL EDITION

Life, Love and Family

Save **$1.00**

on the purchase of **ANY**
Harlequin® Special Edition book.

Available whever books are sold,
including most bookstores, supermarkets,
drugstores and discount stores.

Save **$1.00**

on the purchase of any Harlequin® Special Edition book.

Coupon valid until September 30, 2018.
Redeemable at participating outlets in the U.S. and Canada only.
Limit one coupon per customer.

52615825

Canadian Retailers: Harlequin Enterprises Limited will pay the face value of this coupon plus 10.25¢ if submitted by customer for this product only. Any other use constitutes fraud. Coupon is nonassignable. Void if taxed, prohibited or restricted by law. Consumer must pay any government taxes. Void if copied. Inmar Promotional Services ("IPS") customers submit coupons and proof of sales to Harlequin Enterprises Limited, P.O. Box 31000, Scarborough, ON M1R 0E7, Canada. Non-IPS retailer—for reimbursement submit coupons and proof of sales directly to Harlequin Enterprises Limited, Retail Marketing Department, 22 Adelaide St. West, 40th Floor, Toronto, Ontario M5H 4E3, Canada.

U.S. Retailers: Harlequin Enterprises Limited will pay the face value of this coupon plus 8¢ if submitted by customer for this product only. Any other use constitutes fraud. Coupon is nonassignable. Void if taxed, prohibited or restricted by law. Consumer must pay any government taxes. Void if copied. For reimbursement submit coupons and proof of sales directly to Harlequin Enterprises, Ltd 482, NCH Marketing Services, P.O. Box 880001, El Paso, TX 88588-0001, U.S.A. Cash value 1/100 cents.

5 65373 00076 2 (8100)0 12373

® and ™ are trademarks owned and used by the trademark owner and/or its licensee.

© 2018 Harlequin Enterprises Limited

HSEHOTRCOUP0718